Dr. Orgasm

WOL-VRIEY

Burning Bulb
PUBLISHING

Dr. Orgasm

WOL-VRIEY

Burning Bulb
PUBLISHING

Dr. Orgasm
By **Wol-vriey**

Burning Bulb Publishing
P.O. Box 4721
Bridgeport, WV 26330-4721
United States of America
www.BurningBulbPublishing.com

Cover designed by Wol-vriey with the following licensed image from Shutterstock: Sexy passion couple (image # 136329590) © Vita Khorzhevska
Author Photo: Lolade Akinsowon © 2014.

First Edition.

Paperback Edition ISBN: 978-0692514566

Printed in the United States of America

DEDICATION

This book is dedicated to the female orgasm.

THANKS/ACKNOWLEDGEMENTS

The Usual Suspects + Teresa Pollack.

ODE

There was a cool doctor who flew a pink shoe,
Though the commies disliked her,
There was little they could do.

PART 1: METAPHOR

CHAPTER 1

The sky was melting. As though the Divine Artist had tired of His initial composition on the World Canvas, its solidity dissolved in chunks, the colors of overhead segueing into each other without rhyme or reason.

From her bedroom window, Courtney Taylor watched the aerial acid trip in bemusement. Given the circumstances, given her pain, the liquid sky seemed oddly appropriate. She felt like melting away too, flowing down into a puddle of herself, dissolving into a mix of crushed emotions . . . and then rebuilding herself into something more than what she now was.

But it wasn't all chaos up there in the melting heavens. She gasped as a large pink shoe—a lady's ankle boot—floated across the sky. Behind the pink shoeplane streamed a purple smoke banner:

A Woman's Right to Come is Sacrosanct! Her Orgasm is Her Human Right!

Courtney smiled for a moment. *Thank God for Dr. Orgasm. Someone has to carry the standard for these things. I'm rather weak now, but . . .* Her smile collapsed.

Like it was walking one-footed across the sky, the pink shoeplane flew out of view. Its purple proclamation hung in its wake for a few moments, then the smoke letters were sucked into the background of chaos, becoming part of the warped kaleidoscope of Courtney's vision.

She was saddened by the shoeplane's departure; it seemed a lost part of herself. She had the horrible premonition now, that, no matter how hard she tried, she'd never climax again. All that was left to her now was the wildly fermenting sky; reflected in her fermenting loins, bubbling passion that gave birth to frustration . . .

She stood watching the swirling colors, letting them hypnotize her, letting them fill her with their emptiness: blue, green, red, yellow, white and purple smoke; black and still more black; all mingling into a limbo transparence of nothing. The feeling was eerily appropriate, like apathy was harvesting her brain. She stood in that mental wasteland, that sexual landscape without hope of deliverance, wondering where all the good feelings had vanished to, where all the sexual ecstasy her raging hormones had promised her in her teenage years had evaporated to like water.

Then, just as suddenly as it had vanished, Dr. Orgasm's pink shoeplane was back again. Only now, it wasn't alone: it was being pursued by a horde of creatures. Dark indistinct horrors that could only have one source.

Courtney's heart instantly fell. The communists!

God, god, god!!! Please help her, help her, help her! Courtney thought desperately as the airborne pink shoe—she imagined it worn by a distraught woman who was fleeing with all her might across the dissolved heavens—was slowly caught by the dark creatures with their teeth of smoke and fire, sucked into their collective maw, and bit and torn apart. She saw their fog-like ethereal hands break the tall heel off the straining metal fuselage, watched teeth bite off the transparent toe-cockpit and swallow it. Yet other fog-fingers peeled off the aircraft's pink skin like it was a candy wrapper, then yanked out the shoe's innards like they were chocolate; raised shiny metal and plastic and sparking wires to mouths that were tunnels of smoke with tornado teeth.

Noooo! Courtney mentally moaned.

The pink shoe began bleeding. She realized—understood—now that it was a living thing. And it was dying . . . everywoman's last hope was dying. Dr. Orgasm—the ORGASM—was dying.

The shoeplane began screaming . . .

It howled like a woman giving birth, like a hungry infant, like a castrated man, like a wolf with its foot caught in a bear trap, like a gunshot lion, like a sailor fallen amongst sharks . . .

And its blood flowed red, and the red solidified and mingled with the colors of the melting background till Courtney couldn't separate them. And the black creatures laughed and cackled and fed on the screaming shoe-shaped aircraft, and their teeth biting into its shrieking metal had a strange ringing sound to them . . .

*****

Courtney Taylor—slim, beautiful, blue-eyed, blonde—woke up, her heart racing. The bedside phone was ringing, loud strident buzzes.

Despite its compelling summons, however, she first looked out of the bedroom window.

To her relief, the sky wasn't melting.

Dr. Orgasm's shoeplane wasn't out there either. Once a defiant fixture of the skies over the city of Metaphor (and indeed all of Innuendo), no one had seen Dr. Orgasm's pink footwear-aircraft for six months now.

Courtney remembered her dream and shuddered. *Have the communists really gotten to the doctor? (She IS number one on their shit list.) That would be an absolute disaster for everyone. And for me in particular.*

There was nothing outside the sixth-floor window but blue morning sky and bright white clouds. Down in the distant streets, antigravity traffic moved at a placid pace.

The bedside phone had meanwhile stopped ringing. Looking around, Courtney now realized she was alone in bed. Her boyfriend Radio must have gone to the living room to surf the airwaves.

The phone rang again. She picked it up, winced once at the 'Mother' on its screen, then accepted the call. Her parents lived on the other side of town.

"Morning, mom," she yawned into the mouthpiece while stealing a glance at the wall clock opposite the foot of the bed, her unclothed body slowly beginning to feel like hers. "How come you're calling me so early? It's barely six a.m."

"I'm worried about you, dear." Mother was fifty-five and worried a lot, goodmeaningly, and largely about Courtney.

"Oh, mom, I really wish you wouldn't. The doctors have told you bothering yourself over everything is bad for your health. I'm fine. You know I'll call you if there's any trouble."

"I just can't help it, dear. I sometimes—"

"Take your anxiety pills, mom—that's what they're for," Courtney interrupted, afterwards yawing again. Then, before her mother could reenter the conversation, she added: "How's dad?" Her father was a calm man who never seemed worried about her. At least she assumed that to be the case, and paradoxically found that perception almost as annoying as she found her mother's ceaseless concern over her wellbeing. Didn't her dad care about her? Worrying about someone meant you cared, didn't it?

"Oh, he's well. You know your father—even if he's feeling poorly he won't tell me. Maybe you can talk some sense into him, dear. You know, get him to go in for a checkup. He hasn't been to the doctor for two years. Keeps saying he feels fine, but I'm worried that . . ."

"Alright, mom. I'll call him later."

"And, sweetie . . . ?"

"Yes, mom?" *Sweetie? Ah* . . . Courtney sensed this was the real reason her mother had called her this early in the morning.

"I know you say it's not my business, sweetie, but . . . well, are you still dating that boy? I mean Radio?"

Courtney rolled her eyes. "Please, mom, let it go. We've been over this times without number."

"I *can't* let it go, darling. I just can't stop worrying about it. I keep imagining if the two of you get married: your children . . . it's bad enough that some kids have imaginary friends, but yours might—"

"Be able to hear them in their heads? Mom, I've told you over and over. All he picks up are radio signals, not voices."

"What's the difference? I was talking to Dr. Mitchells yesterday. You remember him don't you—Tia's father, you and she both went to elementary school? Well, he said . . . he said hearing voices in one's head is the classic definition of schizophrenia. And that's a medical condition. So that's why I'm concerned, dear."

"Mother, Radio is not a schizo! Please! I've told you, he picks up wireless signals in his head, that's all!"

"And he can tune himself to them too; like he's a machine. You told me so yourself. And do stop shouting at me, Courtney."

"Okay, I'm sorry I raised my voice. But what do you expect, mom, when you wake me up at six in the morning to advise me to break up with my boyfriend?"

"It's for your own good."

"Mom, you keep forgetting that I'm damaged goods too—have been ever since the communists caught me."

Her mother was silent a moment before replying (they'd discussed this also several times before): "Damaged goods? That's extremely harsh, darling. I really wish you'd not refer to yourself that way."

Wiping the remnant of sleep from her eyes, Courtney sat on the edge of the bed. "There's no other way—no nice, politically correct way—to put it. I am damaged goods, mom. I've not come once—been completely unable to have an orgasm—since the commies got through with me."

"But the doctors all say it's likely just temporary; you're still getting over the trauma of the horrible experience."

"They're lying. It's *permanent*; can't be fixed. The bastards told me back in Vaginismus that I'd never climax again in my life. I assure you they weren't joking."

Her mother attempted a joke: "Not even with toys, dear? Remember how I always used to caution 'toys before boys' when you were a teen?"

"Mom . . ." and all of Courtney's frustration was loaded into her words, "I'm a complete, total mess. The communists screwed me up big time. It's in my brain, not in my groin. Everything works fine down there—I want it, I get wet, it feels nice . . . but there's just . . . there's absolutely no release. No orgasm, period. No matter what Radio and I try . . . toys, pills, creams, positions, it just doesn't happen. There's the buildup to climax, but no release . . . ever . . ."

"But that's not your fault, dear. Maybe Dr. Orgasm can help."

"She's missing, mom. And even if she wasn't, the communists are still after her."

"In any case, you're blameless in this. A victim. That's completely different from Radio—"

"Mom, it's not Radio's fault either that he's the way he is! He was born like that. Just leave us be. I love him!"

Courtney expected her mother to ask her to lower her voice again. It didn't happen. She thought she heard her mother catch her breath, figured she was thinking up an appropriate retort to that most ultimate of responses (to Courtney's mind there was very little valid argument one could put up against a simple 'I love him'), and continued speaking:

"Mom, I understand your worries. I appreciate your concerns, too. I honestly do, but please, I'm no longer you and dad's 'little girl.' I'm old enough to make my own decisions, and I have. I love Radio and he loves me, and he accepts me how I am, and we're happy in our own fashion, and (her mother's silence now sounded ominous) . . . Mom? Hey, mom, are you still there?"

The silence from the phone continued. Courtney gave a start as she heard a crashing sound from the little speaker; not the sound of the phone being dropped, but distant, like someone was slamming a door . . . or breaking through it. Then came a similarly far-off yelp of horror and surprise. Next, a loud bloodcurdling scream.

Then her mother began shrieking.

Now Courtney was frightened. "Mom, are you and dad okay over there?"

Her mother's voice finally gasped from the phone: "Y-y-your f-f-father…"

"Mom, what's happened to dad?"

"A giant bee just broke into the house and stung him. H-h-he's been turned to stone."

"St-stone?" Courtney felt like she'd been drenched with cold water. A giant bee? That meant the communists. "Mom, get out of there!" she yelled.

"No! Stay away from me!" her mother shrieked at someone, then there was the muffled sound of her running and slamming a door behind her.

"Mom, mom . . . say something!"

Her mother's breathless voice replied: "It's the communists! They're attacking the city!" I've locked myself in the kitchen and they're everywhere outside. The sky is almost black with giant bees and aircraft!" She paused to catch her breath. Courtney heard banging on the kitchen door and what sounded like a muffled voice demanding that her mother 'open up.'

Courtney looked out of her bedroom window again. The morning sky was clear as usual. Over the phone, however, the banging on the kitchen door continued.

"Mom . . . mom?"

Her mother's voice returned; sad and broken: "There's loads of them outside the door, and they're peeping in through the window at me. They killed your father, Courtney; turned my darling Harold to stone." She began crying loudly. "You know, sweetie, I always wanted to see you get married. Just be happy with Radio."

"Mom, what are you talking about?" In the background, beneath her mother's words, Courtney heard a loud explosion of breaking wood. Then loud buzzing filled the speaker. Beneath the buzzing, occasionally surfacing into indistinct words, swam a male voice. Courtney sat limp and horrified, phone in hand, waiting.

"No, stay back!" her mother shrieked. "Keep away from—!"

Her trembling voice turned to a liquid burbling like her throat was suddenly full of water. Courtney's ear filled with the splattering sound of rainfall on rooftop, only she knew it wasn't rain she was hearing.

Her mother's phone clanged loudly as it hit the floor.

Receiver pressed to her ear, Courtney remained sitting on the edge of her bed, disbelieving what had just happened. Both her parents? *Mom and dad gone just like that? Like inconsequential mistakes on paper someone just erased?*

Then the dropped phone at the other end creaked as if someone had just picked it up. Courtney waited, expectant, though dreading what she'd hear.

"We're coming to get you too, you little slut," a dark communist voice said. "Run all you want; we'll get you back."

The line went dead.

Courtney leapt to her feet, flung down the phone, and ran to find Radio.

CHAPTER 2

Courtney ran into Radio as he was exiting their living room.

He smiled at her. "Morning, baby, I was just coming to talk to you. I've both good and bad news. I just picked up a trans—"

"The commies just killed mom and dad!" Courtney wailed, flinging herself into his arms. She sobbed loudly against his chest, her free-flowing tears soaking his shirt.

Brian 'Radio' Lewis was tall, sandy-haired, and thin. Courtney found him quite dashing, with his calm brown eyes and easy smile. Now, as her panic subsided—panic caused as much by the cold voice on the phone as by her parent's passing—she was relieved that she wasn't alone here and now. *My parents are dead, and I heard them die! Heard my mother liquefied* . . . The terror threatened to overwhelm her again. She was vaguely aware of her boyfriend's hands holding her close and stroking her naked back, of his asking—"Your parents? How?"—but his caresses and words seemed far off, way-out-of-focus impressions.

Radio's strange mental makeup meant he felt little emotion. In times of crisis, he wasn't so much a rock as a mountain. Imperturbably immovable.

Perplexed now, he held on to Courtney as she worked through the load of her grief. Then he gently led her back to their bedroom.

He sat her down on the bed. Sat beside her. She was still crying. He held her again. She looked at him now, finally able to get a hold on herself.

"Your parents . . .?" he prompted again gently.

"The commies are attacking Metaphor." She pointed to the dropped phone on the bed. "I heard them kill both my mom and dad." Her voice was cold, brittle like ancient paper. And just like old brittle paper, it gave off an air of flammability, of a burning rage just waiting to erupt. Now that Courtney's initial shock was past, anger was finding its place in her soul. The communists had taken too much from her—

way too much. Powerless against the oppressor or not, it was getting to time for some payback.

She leapt up off the bed, grabbed her bra off the back of a chair and slipped it on. She pulled on panties, opened the closet and extracted jeans and T-shirt. Boots. Large gun.

"I was coming to tell you I'd just made contact with Dr. Orgasm," Radio said. He too was getting dressed, trading pajamas for jacket and jeans.

"She's alive?" Hope rang bright in the question. Then her voice turned cold again. "Dr. O can wait. From what mom said, the eastern sky is full of Bees. They'll be arriving here any minute now."

"Yeah, she's alive," Radio said, walking to stand beside Courtney and pulling open a closet drawer. "She's discovered Vaginismus' plans to invade the city, and wants me to warn Mayor Healy."

"Too late for that now. Time to fight." She cocked her weapon. "I just hope these damn bugshot guns work like they're supposed to."

Then the room visibly darkened. Alarmed, Courtney looked out the window. A black and yellow mass was spreading fast across the sky, obscuring the clouds from view. The black/yellow expanse began breaking into smaller chunks. Then smaller and smaller ones.

Damn, she thought in horror, *the commies really mean business.*

Then the bedroom window shattered and a horse-sized bee flew in at them.

Trapped in the moment, Courtney stood entranced as the huge mutated insect landed on their bed. Its wings blew up a storm in the room, scattering her cosmetics and jewelry everywhere. Her favorite orange wig flew out the window as if vacuumed. Books, magazines and CDs were instantly dislodged and displaced.

Still she stared at the Bee. At the huge body wrapped in yellow and black rings with its six thick bristly legs; and behind the thing, the red sting, thick and flexible as a gator tail. The sting dripped snot-like yellow venom. (The massive insect smelt of honey and paradoxically, of death, as if death was a fragrance.) She watched the insect's vibrating transparent wings, the right wing sporting a yellow death's head rendered almost invisible by its rapid motion. She watched its black twitching mouthparts, and its eyes . . . faceted black diamonds the size of baseballs.

The moment lost its inertia. The Bee launched itself off the bed at Courtney, its sting swinging forward between its legs to impale her.

Radio yanked her out of harm's way. They both crashed to the floor.

The Bee smashed into the dresser opposite the bed. Its body destroyed the vanity mirror. Its sting shattered the wood, dug deep into the wall. A moment later, both dresser and wall dissolved into transparent bluish jelly that heaped on the floor.

Wings beating like it was angry, the Bee jerked its sting back again and reared back to dart at Courtney and Radio, both of whom were still down on the floor.

Courtney swung her gun up and shot the Bee in the underbelly. The insect made an almost human noise of pain, then exploded.

They covered their eyes as chunks of it splattered them.

The part rain ended. They got up, brushed the muck off.

The room was full of dead stinking insect. No misleading honey odor now. White gore—intestines and lungs and a heart—covered all the walls. Fragments of insect leg and brain (and one coal-black eye) studded the blue jelly the wall and closet had previously transformed into.

"The weapons work alright," Courtney said grimly. "But the results are smelly as poop."

Radio pointed out of their bedroom window at the insect-filled heavens. "Let's go, baby. There's like a million more where this one came from. We need to link up with one of the city defense units, try to find my sister and Matt and Teresa."

Courtney nodded. She shot another Bee that was climbing into their bedroom window. This one dropped back out into the morning sky. As it fell it blew apart into a black, gold, and white shower of separate organs.

Courtney and Radio ran out of the apartment.

***

The corridor to the elevator was a route of confusion full of yelling people: men and women alone or ferrying/carrying kids, hobbling old folk, several pets barking at their owners. There were some Bees in the corridor, but most of the pandemonium was pure panic, more the sum of the peoples' own fears than the result of the actual danger they were in.

"Damn," Courtney said as they stepped out into the madding crowd. "It's fucking insane out here."

"Yes," Radio agreed. "They can escape down the stairs to the shelters, but they're too scared to think straight. For ages, we've all known this day was coming; and it never came—and now it's here…"

He stopped talking. A Bee was zooming towards them. They weren't its target, however, but a little girl who seemed to have lost her parents.

Radio shot the Bee just as it reached the girl. It blew to bits, coating the walls with bug mess.

"Fuck," Courtney said in disgust. "Too late." The little girl was a statue now, a stone gnome in the middle of the corridor.

A man ran out of the press and grabbed the statue. "Oh, Lucy, Lucy, Lucy!" He knelt over his petrified daughter and bathed her body with his tears.

Watching him, Courtney felt like her own heart was breaking. She felt tears coming; the loss of her parents threatened to rip her emotions open like a psychic knife. She tugged Radio's sleeve. "Let's get the hell out of here."

He nodded. "Wait a moment. He strode off towards the melee of people fighting to enter the elevator, their very numbers having blocked its mechanism. It wasn't their fault either: two Bees stood at the rear of the terrified press, picking off people at random. Already, the floor around them was covered with blue jelly embedded with stone fragments. In the cramped passageway, the Bees' range of motion was limited, but it was a mere matter of time before they killed—petrified or dissolved—everyone in the corridor.

Radio shot both Bees.

"Hey, everyone, listen!" he shouted above the confused babble. "Calm down! The elevator isn't the only way out; some of you take the stairs!"

The noise calmed. The people turned and allowed Radio and Courtney to shepherd them out of the corridor and downstairs towards safety.

CHAPTER 3

"The Bees are everywhere," Teresa Pollack growled, pointing her gun at the yellow/black cloud hanging over the city. The insect mass writhed and throbbed as she watched it, the Bees circling restlessly around each other.

"There's too many of them," her husband Matt replied. He was driving, Teresa riding shotgun. Their transport was a Metaphor City Defense AG—an antigravity jeep—with a bugshot cannon mounted on a platform between its front and rear seats. Matt swerved the vehicle around several petrified people, then around a street corner.

Once past the street angle, a Bee immediately got in their faces. The monster insect buzzed toward the transport, aiming for Teresa.

She ducked. Matt rode the wheelless vehicle out of the Bee's path, its red sting almost slicing his head in two.

Teresa gasped. "Fuckin' left-winger!"

The Bee zipped past them then returned to attack again, stinking of honey and death. It flew in hard, again aiming for Teresa. Before it reached her, though, one of the transport's other two occupants, the blue-haired amazon Heather Bowen, let off a burst of shells from the jeep's mounted anti-bug cannon that splattered the huge insect against the wall behind them. The Bee remained there like it was glued in place, then slowly, cracks of fire appeared through its skin and its body fell apart in little chunks like it had been butchered.

Teresa looked back at Heather. "Thanks."

Heather gave her wife Miki Bowen (who was down in the back seat) a high five. "Six for me, two for you."

Miki—a Japanese beauty with hair (and eyebrows and eyelashes) as blue as Heather's—smirked back. "I'll catch up, you'll see. Shit! Look out!"

Another Bee was swooping down at them, dropping toward Heather at an incline along the wall. Heather flung herself flat. Miki fired over her head. The Bee exploded in midair.

Miki helped Heather up. "Six–three now, baby; *I am* catching up to you."

(Heather and Miki both had blue hair, not as a result of either genetic inheritance or a dye wash, but instead, as a permanent mutation from being caught in the Weird Rain while out patrolling the Dreamfields. Both women were immensely grateful that only their hair—though *all* their body hair—had been infected/affected.)

Matt slowed the antigravity transport to a crawl; there was no thoroughfare here. All ahead of them the street was a mess of crashed and burning vehicles and a mob of terrified, panicking people attempting to dodge the insect assault from the sky. People were falling where they stood like insecticide-doused flies. The four defenders in the vehicle could only watch—the extent of the attack was well beyond the scope of their weapons.

(All four of them wore faded army camo—they'd been on routine City Defense dawn patrol when the trouble started.)

A Bee plunged its sting deep into a redhead's back. The next moment the woman turned blue-transparent—like water wrapped in cellophane. The Bee's red sting was visible inside her body spurting its yellow venom into her. Then her see-thru 'wrapper' burst and her new jelly content plopped to the floor. And that was all for her.

Dropped from high overhead, two turned-to-stone men crashed to the ground and blew up into pebbles and gray smoke.

And so it went on: people fled every which way. Some slipped in puddles that had recently been other people, maybe even their own loved ones.

A man fleeing a Bee ran towards them. He looked back to see if it was gaining on him. Seeing that the yellow/black mass of death almost had him, he made a sharp right turn, one that took his legs into a puddle of human-jelly. Two steps later, the inevitable happened: he lost his footing and fell, skidding sideways to knock himself unconscious against a petrified woman's stone buttocks.

The pursuing Bee hovered over the unconscious man. Teresa drew a bead on its backside and shot it. The rear part of the insect exploded. Its front half, however, dropped right on its intended victim. On the impact, blood spurted from beneath the Bee's remains. The red flow didn't slow.

Heather winced. "That guy's dead for sure now." She fired a cannon burst at some giant insects attacking people up ahead, saw two or three explode, then gave up in disgust. "This is just nonsense. We're completely outnumbered."

Matt Pollack parked the bulky vehicle under a storefront overhang. He and Teresa turned to face the blue-haired women seated in back.

Matt was a large, beefy man. Handsome with a cleft jaw and short military-cropped hair. Dark eyes that were now very bothered. "This isn't some routine punitive commie raid," he said. "It's almost like they're trying to take Metaphor over. Or to wipe it out."

Teresa Pollack—small and dark, well-tattooed and overly serious, large silver hoop earrings swinging from her ears—concurred. "Yeah. I've never seen this number of Bees anywhere before."

Heather nodded. "And without the commies themselves. Where are those assholes?"

"Thankfully, there's no gobblers around," Teresa added. "Not yet anyway."

Miki gestured across the street. Like with her wife, all the fun was now vanished from her face; she was all dead-serious business. "Hey— there's one of the commies now." She hefted her rifle. "Want me to off him?"

Matt shook his head. "Nah, there's sure to be more of them around. We'll just draw attention to ourselves. We watch."

Ducking down in the antigrav transport so only the tops of their heads showed, they all watched the communist, a tall spindly figure in a yellow latex catsuit. The man wore yellow boots and gloves too. His head was completely covered by a monstrous black gasmask. His only weapon was a long knife. Its blade reflected the sun across the street at them.

"He looks like a refugee from a S and M dungeon," Teresa said with a scowl.

"Or some kind of storm trooper asshole," Heather whispered back.

The communist didn't do anything unexpected. He strode through the carnage of fleeing people and pursuing insects, gesturing now and again like he was directing air traffic.

A woman fled towards him. He tripped her up so she fell face down in a heap of human-jelly, then knelt on her back and slit her throat.

Then he cut her head off.

Next thing, standing in the pool of blood pumping from her neck, the communist unzipped his bodysuit at the crotch and began to copulate with the woman's severed head. He held it up by its thick black hair while he slid his penis into her open, gaping mouth, pumping his yellow-clad hips back and forth in a steady rhythm. Around and above him the carnage continued.

Teresa had had enough. "Screw not giving our position away." She laid her gun over the edge of the transport door, sighted along its barrel. Beside her, Miki was puking into the rear foot well, heaving like she intended on losing yesterday's breakfast and lunch as well as dinner. Heather was holding Miki, her own face contorted with horror and rage.

"Don't," Matt cautioned his wife. "She's already dead."

"Fuck that. And why are we just sitting down here like scared rabbits anyway? We're supposed to be defending people."

"Just don't shoot the son-of-a-bitch."

She ignored him. Her gun cracked. The next moment the communist dropped the head he'd been screwing. The yellow-clad man stood shock still for a moment, then looked around. His penis was still hard, covered with the woman's blood and her last spittle. Even at this distance the organ seemed to be throbbing.

White liquid spurted from the gunshot wound in the communist's chest.

"You won't kill him like that," Heather said. "Always aim for the head."

Teresa adjusted her aim and fired again. The communist, who'd now noticed them, and who, without tucking his erection away, had just started their way, froze as his head exploded off his shoulders. White goo spurting from its neck, his body fell right on top of the woman he'd just killed. It looked like the two headless corpses were having sex.

Matt had been right though: there were other communists in the houses bordering the street. Now they rushed out—a platoon of yellow-clad male and female bodies all wearing the same grotesque gasmasks; masks that almost seemed modelled on the heads of their mutated insect charges.

The communists, knifes held ready, examined their man's headless body for a moment, then, noticing the City Defense transport, headed straight for it. Like they'd been summoned by telepathy, a squadron of Bees now detached themselves from among those attacking the street and buzzed in the AG's direction.

"Time to get the hell out of here," Matt said grimly, straightening out of concealment and flinging the antigravity jeep's controls into reverse. The vehicle flew backwards with increasing acceleration. It slammed into a series of petrified people, smashing their stone corpses to powder.

As they retreated, Teresa, Heather, and Miki (who still had puke on her lips), kept up a barrage of covering fire. Guns and mounted cannon filled the air with flying metal-and-chemical death. Bees exploded left and right of them. This time there was no good-natured spousal banter tallying number of kills; all three women's faces were masks of the most intense concentration.

Several communists were shot down. Those still having their heads intact all got up again. The commies now broke into a run to catch the retreating antigrav transport. They ran faster than normal humans, their yellow bodies streaking like upright cheetahs, while squirting streams of white liquid from wounds that didn't seem to hurt them no matter where the bullets had struck.

The retreat down the street—a mere fifty yards to the corner—seemed to last forever, time being measured now in racing heartbeats, each of which itself lasted an eternity. The communists grew ever closer. The Bees were unending in the sky—black and yellow the colors of oblivion, the metaphor of liquid or solid termination; no matter how many the three women killed there were seemingly a hundred more to take their place.

Then Matt banked the AG hard right out of the intersection, reversed the gears and floored the pedal. As the transport leapt forward, Teresa and Miki fell back down in their seats. Heather was flung sideways left; Miki grabbed her just before she flew out into the road. Teresa gave Miki a hand in pulling Heather back into the vehicle, which by now was halfway down the street, burning up distance, converting their pursuers into a fast-fading threat.

They slowed after a while.

Matt heaved a sigh of relief. "Damn, that was close." He gave Teresa a pointed gaze that screamed: *Next time you listen to me!*

Teresa said nothing, sat staring stonily ahead. Now the adrenalin rush of their escape was over, the horror was hitting her hard. A man fucking a severed head in the mouth wasn't something she saw everyday.

Heather said angrily, "Teresa, what the hell were you thinking? You could have gotten the four of us killed back there."

"Easy on her," Miki said, her eyes hard. "That communist pig just cut off a woman's head and had sex with it. He got what he deserved. At least she did something about it; not just lose her dinner all over the upholstery like I did."

Heather let it go; she stretched a hand forward and patted Teresa's shoulders. "Good job, girl. You made the right call."

They took stock of their surroundings. This far down the new street was mostly shops. There were few Bees in sight and apparently no communists either. The commies clearly *had* been here earlier though: several stone-frozen people decorated the sidewalks and through two or three shattered windows they saw piles of quivering blue jelly.

"I think Metaphor is royally screwed," Teresa said, surfacing from her blues. Her face was strained, like she was near crackup. "I know we planned for a communist attack . . . but this . . . it's . . ."

She ran out of words, simply gestured at the sky with her gun. Overhead, where Stygian clouds of Bees hung like morning nightfall, and the shimmering metal of a myriad communist aircraft glittered like stars in their firmament. The day was dark like it was holding its own funeral.

They drove on, past bust-up storefronts and jelly mounds that had recently been people, past crashed wheelers flaming like furnaces, past overturned AG cars that floated upside down, several of these last with stone people held in place by seatbelts, the weight of the corpses rooting the AGs to the spot like anchors. One overturned antigravity school bus sat in an obscenely massive hill of jelly dotted with satchels and schoolbooks. No one commented as they floated past the terrible sight; their faces were taut with anger and disgust at the implications of the carnage.

Matt began calling City Defense Central on his cellphone. "Can anyone hear me? The shit and the fan have collided out here. What's the goddam backup plan?"

No response, just a damning 'Network Unavailable' from the phone. He handed it to Teresa. "Keep trying; we need to get hold of Oldfield."

Up ahead, over the far end of the housetops, three explosions lit the black sky a vivid red. The sound made them all start. Another six or seven explosions rent the air. The red/yellow inferno outlined a fiercely burning high rise.

"There goes City Hall," Heather said glumly.

Matt parked the transport by the next intersection. He looked at the three women in turn, Teresa with his phone pressed to her ear. "We can't keep driving around in circles. We need a plan. I was heading for City Hall, but that's clearly a waste of time now, so—"

"Hold on a minute," Teresa said. "I'm through to Baxter. . . . Hey, Baxter, what the hell is going on? . . . What? . . . ." Her face turned pale as she listened, her lips compressing to thin lines; her horror seeped into her companions without words. "Oh, alright, will do—we'll meet you there."

She hung up, looked at the others. "Mayor Healy's dead. Apparently Deputy Mayor Ron Jackson was working for the commies. He'd rigged City Hall to blow; setting off the first bombs was the signal to start the attack."

Matt grimaced. "Any word from Oldfield?"

"Yeah, Baxter had just finished speaking to him when I got through. He says the city's lost, City Defense is too badly compromised now to offer any meaningful resistance to the communist invasion. He's had to shoot four guys already this morning—Andrews one of them—"

"Andrews was a commie plant?" Miki interjected. "Damn!"

The surprise on her face was reflected all around their group. They all knew and liked Marc Andrews, one of the most vehement anti-communists in Metaphor. If Andrews could be a commie, they really were in deep trouble.

"Oldfield didn't believe it himself," Teresa continued, "but a team sent to Andrews's house found a whole closetful of anti-orgasm propaganda. There was also a two-way radio built into a closet, one that only broadcasts and receives on commie spy frequencies. Oh, and his wife Nina is missing too."

"Communists among us," Heather spat. "Reeducate me on this, anyone: why the hell is female sexuality so threatening to the assholes?"

Teresa replied: "Duh? Girl, Florence Rigid, the communist leader, has never had an orgasm in her miserable life. So figure it out: the frigid bitch is jealous of us hot-blooded horny broads, doesn't want us having a good time in bed?"

"Bypass the sex-education class and go on, darling," Matt said. "What else did Oldfield say? Do we have a plan B?"

Teresa made a pissed-off face. "We evacuate the city. Commandeer as many buses, trucks, and vans as we can, save as many citizens as we can. Orders are to ship everyone out of town. Baxter says the safest route out is via that disused subway tunnel over on Norton and Fifth; our guys currently have it secured from the commies."

Matt pondered on that a moment, then said, "I get Oldfield's thinking: the Norton subway tunnel leads out of the city for a good distance. I'm not sure, but I think it connects with Route Zero somewhere in the Dreamfields. So if—"

"Get down!" Miki yelped, she and Heather swinging their guns up.

In a well-rehearsed maneuver, Matt and Teresa ducked flat in the front seats. Miki and her wife fired a salvo over their heads, blowing two oncoming Bees—bristly arthropod death approaching at high velocity—back down the street, where both exploded in midair, the monster insects' splattered remains coating opposing storefront walls like dirty whitewash.

"Metaphor is fallen," Teresa said when she and Matt were upright again. She looked at her husband. "Oldfield's right: Let's start rounding people up and getting them out of the city."

Matt gunned the AG's engine.

Before they moved off, however, his phone, which was still with Teresa, rang. She looked at the screen then passed it to Matt. "It's Radio."

Matt accepted the call. "Hey, dude, what's the news? . . . . Man, it's a total freaking mess over here too. . . . You're with Courtney? . . . Okay, where are you guys? . . . Applegate? . . . Okay, listen, man: we're heading south, to Norton, Oldfield's ordered a complete pullout . . . we'll be in your area in say, thirty minutes, with a refugee transport convoy. Where are you guys? . . . Thompson Avenue, the St. Laurence Street corner? . . . Yeah, just wait for us there, we'll pick you up."

He hung up and looked around. "Radio's just confirmed it—it's a complete mess all over."

"Metaphor is fallen," Teresa repeated quietly to no one in particular.

Matt flew the jeep down the street, looking for vehicles to convey people in. His female companions said nothing; their scared, angry eyes spoke volumes more than words would ever manage.

CHAPTER 4

Radio relayed Matt's message to Courtney.

The two of them were hiding inside the St. Laurence Street corner drugstore. The storekeeper's petrified body lay beside the counter behind them. The corpse had a massive hole in its chest where the Bee had struck it, and was cracked clean in two at the waist, its granite-textured intestines and kidneys on display.

(Scenes like this here in the shop had become familiar to them far too fast— everywhere they looked was a depressing more-of-the-same.)

Courtney grunted at the relayed info, then resumed her horrified staring up and down the street outside. The gory carnage that had formed the backdrop to their escape from their building had been scant preparation for the nightmare now facing them.

The air over the street was a throbbing egg-yolk-in-fry-pan carpet. Giant bees everywhere.

"It's like a mad waxworks exhibition," Radio observed.

Courtney couldn't agree more. Both road and sidewalks were covered with lines of frozen people, open-mouthed-screaming, their preserved terrified expressions replaying the harrying horrors of their abrupt deaths.

The blue person-jelly filled the streets in a veritable deluge. (There were two sub-species of Bees, distinguished by which of their wings bore a yellow 'death's head' decoration: The 'left wing' Bees, whose stings petrified their victims, and the 'right wing' swarm, whose venom contained a liquidizing agent.) People-statues stood in knee-high blue goop like stranded marble islands. And between the frozen dead waded the dreaded communists, grotesque as hell in their yellow catsuits and hideous black gas masks. Their long knives glittered like murder frozen into metal shape.

Courtney was finding it hard to wrap her mind around what she was seeing. Her basic impulse—to fight the attackers, to resist this invasion with every shred of strength she possessed—was nullified by both the apparent sheer scale of the communist offensive (at points the morning sky appeared to have vanished amidst the Bee and aircraft tapestry—how did one fight/repulse infinity?), and more immediate, by their both having run out of ammo during their initial fight/flight downstairs. Empty guns won no wars. So, hating the fact that she, a dogged fighter, was forced to cringe before the relentless communist onslaught, Courtney hid. Hopefully, Matt and Teresa Pollack would arrive soon. Hopefully too, the City Defense couple would be packing the heavy artillery along. And then . . .

Courtney itched and bitched mentally, dying to be able to take the fight to the damn commies. After all what they'd stolen from her, she was itching to jam a huge angry porcupine up communist leader Florence Rigid's anus. And that would be just the beginning of the evil bitch's suffering, the tip of the iceberg of her sorrows. She'd . . .

Courtney became aware that Radio was talking to her. "What?"

He tapped his forehead. "Highball just called. She and Jeff are coming over here. They were headed for our apartment, but . . ."

Courtney nodded. Highball was Radio's elder sister, Jeff her new boyfriend. Highball's nickname came from when she'd worked as bartender at a snazzy uptown joint. "Where are they now?" she asked.

"Two blocks away. Covington. Jeff's truck got rammed by another; they're chancing the rest of the way over on foot."

"They damn well need to hurry then. Matt and Teresa will be here any moment now."

"They'll make it. They're down the road from us. If City Defense arrives early, we'll keep a lookout for 'em."

"Hope you're right, baby. Oh no, Shit!"

"What?" But Radio had already seen what had Courtney horrified:

Almost directly across the street from them, somehow (by either blind luck or maternal intuition) a woman had secured herself and two little children (Courtney couldn't tell the kids' genders) in the space between a tripod of stone corpses. She'd ducked herself and the children into the hill of blue jelly between the bodies and all three had played dead.

How the ruse had been discovered, neither Courtney nor Radio could determine. They watched the communists lift the pathetically screaming trio from the muck.

The mother was stripped naked, her pale flesh jiggling. A communist woman stabbed her deep in the throat, the resulting red jets of blood splattering her own big latex-cocooned breasts. Then, while the victim bled out, another communist upended her in a wheelbarrow position and began sodomizing her.

Courtney almost shit herself with rage at the sight—the man's penis was enormous, ripping up further the expiring woman. Memories flooded Courtney like injections of pain. Of her being in Vaginismus, the communist capital, of . . .

Then one of the communists grabbed up one of the screaming children—a girl—then unzipped his crotch. Black pubic hair flashed, then penis-pink.

Hell, no! Before Radio could stop her, Courtney was out through the broken shop window and halfway across the street, yelling her lungs out. She had no idea what she intended doing—there were at least twenty communists ahead of her in addition to the living rug of Bees buzzing everywhere, and she was unarmed to boot—but some 'outrage overload' switch that had triggered in her mind screamed at her to stop this atrocity from happening. No one—not even damn fucking Satan himself—was raping a little kid while she was anywhere near. She was vaguely aware that Radio was shouting her name somewhere behind her, then all hell broke loose.

The communist about raping the little girl had paused in extracting his cock once Courtney began yelling. Now he and the other communists froze (almost as rigid as the dead statues all around) and watched the angry woman charging at them and the man running along behind her.

Skidding and slipping in her mad rush, barely keeping her footing across the jelly, Courtney reached the nearest communist. He swiped at her with his knife. She slid aside then kicked him the balls.

He dropped his knife and went down. She grabbed his knife out of the ooze, skidded around the commie still raping the kids' mother's corpse (Courtney couldn't resist a glance at the man's penis which resulted in her shuddering from how massive the implement was—like a rolling pin), then she'd reached the man about raping the girl.

She stabbed him in the chest (missing the oddity of how the knife slid through the yellow latex as easily as if it was butter, as if the man lacked sternum and ribs), left the knife stuck there, grabbed the dangling child from him (the little girl had stopped screaming, like she'd realized that compared to Courtney's infuriated howling, she needed years of practice to match decibels), looked around once for the other kid (a younger boy who'd also ceased shrieking and now just looked confused), yanked that one from commie hands, and then was gone like the wind, charging away down the street with both children tucked under her arms, headed for the next intersection, where Highball and Jeff should be arriving about now.

Behind her, she was aware of the noise of the commies emerging from their startled freeze. And giving pursuit.

Insistent overhead buzzing assured Courtney that the Bees had joined the chase.

Both her child burdens had meanwhile resumed crying. Courtney ignored their noise; it was inconsequential . . . What mattered was getting them somewhere safe. Then she and Radio could . . .

Oh, shit, I forgot Radio!

Boyfriend-worry cut through kid-worry. Courtney paused her breakneck flight a moment and looked around.

Radio was thirty yards behind her. He'd found a light machine gun somewhere and was firing at the communists. The bastards were still advancing, however (as though the bullet holes dotting their bodies were movie props), with, above them, a marquee of Bees—'Your Death Is At Hand' announced in hairy black and gold. Radio fired, the Bees exploded in parallel and series. It made little apparent difference in the grand scheme of sexual annihilation—the insects seemed literally endless in quantity.

Okay, kids, it was great while it lasted, Courtney thought angrily. *Sorry, but . . .*

Pounding feet behind her announced Highball and Jeff rounding the next street corner.

The pair reached Courtney. Without any exchange of pleasantries, she thrust the little girl at Highball. Little boy balanced on cocked hip, she jogged back the way she'd come to grab hold of Radio.

"Rescue's over, baby. Let's get the hell out of here."

"No need," he said, pointing ahead, up-street to where their pursuers had now turned back towards a commotion behind them. Overhead, fire mushroomed in the sky as if someone was setting of miniaturized nuclear explosions. Bees were dropping from the air like meteorites. Radio smiled grimly. "Matt and Teresa just arrived." He handed Courtney a jelly-smeared pistol. "Time to give the invaders an ass-kicking of our own."

***

A lone gray cat stood perched atop a statue's head—likely its owner's—mewling its abject confusion at the day. A lady communist walked over to the new statue and stretched up a hand to the cat. After a moment's hesitation, the animal went to her, leaping onto her yellow glove. She walked back to her squad members, petting the cat and murmuring, "There, there, now—everything's going to be just fine, girl," to it, her voice through her gas mask sounding like the echo of Death's passing.

CHAPTER 5

The doctrine of Communism—of the female orgasm (or 'coming') being an evil thing to be stamped out at all costs—was the brainchild of Florence Rigid.

The communists were ethical rapists. They raped, not because they were aroused, or power drunk, or because of cross-gender hatred, but because they wanted the victim to HATE sex forever thereafter. Communist men (and their women, via dildos and tissue-tearing fisting) worked to leave a legacy of pain in the flesh of their victims, an easily-recalled lifelong horror of all forms of erotic gratification. "Once the gnarled fingers of Vaginismus have caressed you, you'll never WANT to love another," was Florence Rigid's proud boast. And she meant every word of it.

CHAPTER 6

A burst of fire from Matt and Teresa's City Defense cannon erupted a quadrant of Bees into blazing airborne lamps.

"Gotcha!" Teresa yelled from the AG's gun platform. She swiveled the cannon around towards a fresh sector of the sky, then fired again. More Bees met the same fate.

Below her, in the transport's driver's seat, Matt grunted approval then ran down a trio of fleeing communists. Yellow-sheathed flesh warped into shattered shapes beneath the antigravity jeep.

Floating down Thompson Avenue with their tagalong convoy of fugitives (the rescued citizens were behind them, huddling in two armored antigrav trucks driven by Heather and Miki) towards their rendezvous with Courtney and Radio, the couple now had backup. Major backup. They'd hooked up with Shaniqua Banks, a dreadlocked black Major in charge of two AG 'greenhouses.' Greenhouses were mobile defense farms, thirty-meter-long glass boxes—like transparent train carriages—powered by the gas and bioenergy emissions of their vegetable contents. Greenhouses were hard to break, their surface glass tempered to steel consistency. More important, they were designed for work out in the Dreamfields and carried heavy artillery—flamethrowers, lark torpedoes, and neutron cannons, weapons the communist's aircraft and Bees couldn't handle.

One greenhouse rode beside Teresa and Matt, the other watched the convoy's rear. Their trip south through the burning city had so far consisted of Shaniqua's unit incinerating whatever lay in their path and overhead. So far, both aircraft and Bees had given them a wide berth.

"It's a crying shame we've so few greenhouses," Teresa called down to her husband between bursts of fire. "We'd clear the dickspits out of the city."

He grunted as a clump of frozen people crunched to dust against the transport's front, then jerked his thumb left at the glass train floating beside them, live trees its odd passengers. "Yeah, but they're not designed for this kind of sustained shooting!" he yelled up at her. "Their weapons are just to knock out big Dreamfield critters. Let's just hope we're not using up their power faster than the plants can make it. We've got to make that rendezvous!"

Teresa didn't reply. His pragmatic negativity infected her. *No need to remind me of that!* He was right: greenhouses had limited capacity; they had no way of knowing how drained both vehicles' fuel stores were by now. Shaniqua had confirmed they'd been full earlier, but with this kind of mess to carve a way through . . . Thankfully, they'd so far not seen any gobblers. Remembering those obscene horrors, Matt's words now had a chilling ring to them.

Teresa looked left, through the greenhouse's cockpit walls. Shaniqua Banks was standing by the vehicle's driver, the pair framed by hanging greenery. The major was holding her thick dreadlocks in one hand, gesturing ahead with the other while yelling into an earpiece microphone. A moment later, a roof-mounted neutron gun pulsed out a white energy beam. Next instant, several approaching shop fronts on their right exploded, filling the air with flying brickwork and yellow-clad people—a communist ambush. Through the accompanying flashes of fire, Teresa made out four human forms running towards them, legs pumping desperately as they dashed around crashed burning Bees. Two women carrying kids and two men.

"It's Courtney and Radio!" she yelled down at her husband.

"Seen 'em!" He swerved the transport to the sidewalk so they could get in.

While the four runners piled into the vehicle—Radio and Jeff in front, the women and kids in back—Teresa kept up a barrage of covering fire at several Bees which, seeing the stopped vehicle, had grown bold and flown down to pick them off.

One of the attacking Bees was right over their vehicle when it blew apart, raining chunks of itself down on them all. In the back seat, the little girl screamed as she was sploshed in the face with exploded-insect goop.

"Damn, this stuff stinks," Courtney groaned.

Shaniqua's greenhouse was pulling ahead of them. Matt put the defense transport in gear again and raced to catch up. Behind them, the passenger trucks, which had been forced to stop to maintain the convoy's shape, revved up again.

"What's the news, dude?" Matt asked Radio, their standard greeting since high school (considered normal enough when your best friend's head functioned like a wireless receiver). Now though, this slice of banter held an air of tragedy.

"Dr. Orgasm's still alive," Radio replied with his usual calm. "I tuned in to a broadcast of hers this morning. "She asked me to warn the mayor about . . ." he spread his hands at the carnage, "this.""

"Mayor's dead," Matt replied. "That punk Ronnie Jack—"

"Dr. Orgasm's alive?" Teresa interrupted as Courtney climbed up beside her on the gun platform. "That's hope of a sort."

"I don't see what she can do in this case," Jeff said.

"It means the commies haven't won yet, baby," Highball replied, her arms around the two kids. "As long as the doctor is still free, there's hope for sex."

"Hi, Ball," Matt said, another old joke greeting. This time from Metaphor University, where they'd dated for a year. (Teresa didn't know Matt and Highball had been lovers. There was an in-conspiracy between Matt, Radio, Courtney, and Highball to keep her in the dark on that fact. Else she'd insist that the pair were never alone together anywhere; which would be complicated, as, when not in City Defense camo, Matt and Highball worked in the same interior décor supplies office. It was actually Highball's office—she was Matt's boss. Or, with the city falling apart around them, they *had* once worked in the same office . . .)

They blew through town at speed. Their plan seemed to be working.

"I don't like how they're not attacking," Highball said, her scarlet hair whipping around in the breeze.

"They're afraid of us," Teresa retorted.

A black gull-winged helicopter flew up the street at them, its wing-mounted guns spurting death their way—liquefying venom extracted from the stings of right-wing Bees.

Outside the body, the yellow poison had to hit right to do harm. The chopper's first burst of death fell way short of their advance. Its semen-like smell reached them amidst the stink of jellied meat and burning. The chopper rose to bank for another attack. Two pulses of greenhouse fire turned it into charred wreckage that crashed through a building's glass front.

"Another com bites the dust," Courtney's cold voice floated down on the wind." Then: "What the fuck is that?"

'That' was an entire section of the right side of the street ahead exploding sky-high, a wall of demolition that made existence a blocked tunnel beneath the hanging Bee ceiling. It happened again, the obliteration of their escape route thickening as the street's left side also collapsed into rubble.

"Gobblers," Courtney said as the monsters destroying the street emerged aboveground. "Doesn't today's nightmare ever end?"

"Shit!" Matt exclaimed, screeching their AG to a halt. His eyes were hard as stones.

Beside them, the greenhouse stopped too.

CHAPTER 7

Gobblers. The very word held intense terror for them all.

Gobblers were monster brown worms. To Courtney they seemed negro penises that had overdosed on growth hormone—the fat head with its tunnel of teeth, the even fatter body that was all stomach. Gobblers lacked an anus; each simply incorporated whatever it ate into itself and grew bigger and bigger.

Gobblers were designed to feed, and feed they did; they ate the world without end. All mouth and no brain. "Resistance Is Vain!" their horrible wrinkled bulks silently shrieked at existence.

Now, as the walls to the street fell away ahead of them, Courtney prayed they'd make it through. *What the fuck?* Monsters overhead, monsters ahead. She looked back from the gun platform. In the cockpit of the following truck she made out Heather's stony face. The blue-haired woman's eyes were cold—Courtney thought she read fear in them.

The convoy froze now like it had been glued to the street.

"We're just two hundred yards from the Norton tunnel," Matt said below Courtney. "It's round the next corner, and now this bullshit has to happen."

The wall of dust ahead cleared. The road thronged with the massive worms, some larger than the houses they squirmed between. An impasse of gross, hideously mutated annelids.

No way we're making it though that lot, Courtney thought. *Time for plan C. And it had better be a fantastic one.*

She looked to her left, saw that in the greenhouse, Shaniqua Banks was trying to catch their attention.

"Hey, Radio," she said, "tune into the major."

Radio also looked left, saw Shaniqua gesticulating, then twisted his right ear. (No one understood how that worked, not even Radio himself, but it did—both his ears functioned as programming/tuning

34

dials. They didn't rotate, but moving them as if they did somehow 'tuned' him.)

"I've got her," he said after a moment, his eyes now flat and dead like he was staring inside of himself. "What do we do now, Major?" (Courtney knew her boyfriend was speaking aloud for the others' benefit; he could transmit telepathically.)

Through the glass walls of the greenhouse, Courtney watched Major Shaniqua Banks jerk up in shock as the question sounded in her earpiece. She gaped at the transport. Courtney stabbed a finger down at Radio. Still shocked, the major nodded, then replied into her mouthpiece.

"She says to retreat," Radio told the others a moment later. "The greenhouse's guns *can* take on the gobblers, but the vehicle's power store is down to a tenth-charge; any sustained firefight will knock out its engines, meaning we'll have no protection for the last two hundred meters to the tunnel."

"Shit. Okay. Retreat which way?" Matt asked.

Up ahead, the pile of gobblers squirmed like a god's living excrement. It bothered Courtney how the gobblers seemed to be waiting, not normal behavior for creatures that were ravenous feeders. In addition, several communist helicopters were landing in front of the humongous worms, clearly implying that the gobblers weren't about to start slithering towards them.

Well, you'll definitely have to come get us, she thought. *No way are we riding down there to you.* She looked around at their party of eight: the two shivering kids she'd rescued (the girl's name was Alicia; her little brother, who'd just pissed himself from fright on spotting the gobblers, was Vincent), herself and Radio, Matt and Teresa, Radio's flame-haired sister Highball and her latest macho paramour Jeff. *We're quite a group. Now we need to not get eaten.*

Courtney was also suddenly aware of an odd rumbling sound. And no, it didn't seem to be the Bees' omnipresent frustrated buzzing. She tried to get a fix on the sound's source, but it was impossible, the world was too distracting—in addition to the auditory cloud of insect and aircraft noise, the little boy had begun sniveling. The girl sat eyes wide. Both children were pressed tight against Highball's sides, snug in the loop of her arms around their little shoulders.

Courtney stood, hands tight on her gun, waiting for someone to figure a way out of this fresh layer of mess. At this point, she was certain it wouldn't be herself, not with her mind teetering on the edge, her thoughts floating somewhere between void-blank and raw static. But that buzzing below the buzzing . . . She glanced sideways at Teresa, to see if she'd heard it too. Teresa clearly hadn't, her gaze was riveted ahead on the gobblers.

Radio had meanwhile passed Matt's question on to Shaniqua and was relaying back the answer: "She says: we go back, then through that last right side street we passed. According to her greenhouse map, its only a short distance across before it connects to Martin Drive, which runs down to Lincoln Station. The major thinks it'll take a while for the commies to shift the gobblers over that way. We should have a clear run down to the station. Once everyone's safe inside we can—"

Two things happened simultaneously then. First Radio jerked upright like someone had shot him in the head, while on their left, the house wall erupted outward over the greenhouse. At the same moment, Courtney had a vision (it *was* happening but seemed like a vision) of a massive ripping in space—jaws like a framed black hole coming together over the front of the greenhouse. A screeching, ripping sound. The greenhouse cockpit was engulfed in a brown mass that seemed liquid.

Then the massive brown extrusion from the rubble was gone, withdrawn again through the demolished building frontage, and Courtney and her friends were left staring.

The gobbler had completely eaten the greenhouse's front third. Major Shaniqua Banks, the driver, and the front gunners, were gone. Gone for good. Vanished as nourishment into the giant worm's digestive system.

"Shit!" Teresa said. "Our protection's gone."

That was the rumbling sound I heard, Courtney realized. *The gobbler was tunneling through the foundations.*

A sudden burst of sixth sense made her look back past the destroyed greenhouse. Noise made the others turn also.

Shit! Courtney thought, seeing the massive gobbler crashing out of the wall opposite the rearguard greenhouse. *It's a trap! We're being ambushed!*

They all watched as the far-off worm withdrew, this time clearly with a mass of ripped-off metal and glass vehicle trapped inside its maw. The rain of electric sparks like fireworks flashing around its teeth clearly didn't bother the creature; maybe its huge bulk simply didn't register pain.

"That's the second greenhouse out of commission," Teresa said. "Also it's now blocking the way—our retreat's just been cut off. We're as close to royally fucked as possible now."

Courtney refused to let Teresa's statement get to her. It was obvious that they were done for; but why state the obvious? *And are we done for?* She looked down the road, at the blockage of vehicles and worms. Now, the communists were getting out of the helicopters, their yellow forms strutting with confidence like they knew the game was up for their quarry. *Yeah, maybe we are.*

Courtney didn't bother to look up. She knew that any moment now the Bee buzzing would intensify, signaling the final onslaught.

She knelt forward on the weapon platform, bent over Radio. "You okay, baby?"

He shook his head. "That disconnection was so abrupt, I . . . forget it, I'll survive." He looked forward once, then turned to Matt. "Dude, let's get out of here."

Matt frowned at Radio. "Plan C?" His eyes, however, were relieved; that was the great thing about having Radio around: his inability to actually panic meant that, once he was in Matt's crew, no matter how desperate a situation got, Matt always knew someone was calculating the angles.

"Yeah," Radio replied, talking faster than usual. "There's always a way out, even if it's suicide." He looked around at their expectant faces. "Okay, everyone, here's what we do: Jeff and Highball, you guys rush back to the passenger trucks. Tell everyone not to panic, but to get the side flaps open and be ready to make a rush for this hole . . ." he pointed opposite, past the ruined greenhouse, into the ruins the gobbler had left, "immediately we give a signal. Teresa and Courtney, just keep manning this cannon; watch for any sneak attack from the Bees overhead. I might be wrong, but the communists aren't about striking us down just yet. To them, we're bunnies in a sprung trap—no escape. But Matt and I might need covering fire, particularly if they work out what we're up to."

"What are you and I doing?" Matt asked Radio. "What *are* we up to?"

Radio pointed up at the roof of the destroyed greenhouse. "We're taking down that neutron cannon and blasting a way through the city's foundations into the sewers." He jerked a thumb back at the two passenger transports. "Hopefully, we should be able to sneak everyone down to the sewers before the commies catch on."

Matt nodded then looked around at the others. "Yeah, guys, let's do this."

Jeff and Highball picked up a child each, then along with Matt and Radio, they leapt out of the vehicle and dispersed, leaving Courtney and Teresa watching the sky.

A hundred meters away, the landed choppers abruptly rose skyward, the mountain of gobblers surged forward.

"Radio was dead wrong—the attack's started," Teresa said nervously. "They've got us outnumbered say like a million to one." She winced. "From what we know of the shits, I was expecting them to wait for the arrival of video crews to record the massacre and rape-fest."

"Shut up, Teresa!" Courtney snapped. "That ain't any kind of funny." She spat out over the front of the vehicle. Her heartbeat had ramped up a gear, doubled in pace; and now she could hear the sound of the Bees descending above them. Her friend's suggestion of their very possible fate wasn't what she needed to hear right now.

Teresa glanced sideways at Courtney. "Sorry. I forgot they had you in Vaginismus for a while."

"Forget it." She looked over at the greenhouse. The glass train still hovered on its gyros/stabilizers despite losing its cockpit. Matt and Radio could be seen running inside the greenhouse, view of them obscured in swathes by the vehicle's menagerie of flora. Overhead the Bee buzz grew steadily louder; the insects were realizing that the greenhouses were now harmless. One swooped down in an arc at the front transport. Courtney shot it without thinking. It crashed into the mouth of the gobbler-created tunnel in the building by the greenhouse. Blew apart.

"Time to live and die," Courtney said.

"Looks like dying," Teresa said.

"Dying's preferable to being taken alive by the communists, trust me." She scowled; there were more Bees everywhere now, the yellow/black monsters swirling figure-of-eights over the next intersection, where the gobblers had now stopped their advance. Two ground units of communists were charging at them, however.

Teresa said, "They're keeping the street blocked so we can't make a dash for it. Radio's plan had better work."

Tight-lipped, Courtney glared at her. (She really wished Teresa would shut up. It was bad enough being frightened; she didn't need constant reminders as to why she was scared.) Behind them, Heather was out of her truck's cab and shrugging herself into a huge gun harness with an ammunition backpack and helmet with attached laser sight. Several other people were out of the trucks too, loading up and sighting arms at the sky.

The charging communists, knives flashing like scalpels, ran in close enough to hear their echoic yells. Their airborne choppers started firing.

"Give the bastards hell!" a man shouted somewhere.

Courtney and Teresa ducked the first salvo of gunfire, then leapt up and returned it.

The battle erupted—a conjunction of rage on both sides, death-and-honey Bee-stink the spice of combat. Explosions shattered the heavens, blew up the world. The street was a mere frame, a too-weak stage to host such morbid theatre. It fell away in sheets like it sensed its inadequacy to contain the ambitions of both sets of performers.

For Courtney Taylor, Teresa Pollack, and the other Metaphor survivors, fear and courage (normally considered poles apart) now became one and the same emotion, melting into motivation—simply the desire to remain alive, or, if winning proved impossible now, to not fall alive into communist hands.

Hurry up, Radio! Courtney thought as incandescent lead and things much deadlier zipped left and right everywhere. *We need to get the hell out of here!*

CHAPTER 8

Being inside the greenhouse was like navigating a portable jungle. Matt and Radio stared for a moment down a central aisle webbed in by interlocked branches, then Radio pulled Matt sideways into a stairwell.

"We go up here; the mounting will be on the upper deck."

They climbed hastily, the greenhouse bobbing fiercely as it was struck by communist fire.

Upstairs in the greenhouse was more of the same. Like holidaying in the Amazon. Between the plants, the floor they ran over was transparent, its prior dark polarization turned off when the vehicle's engines were eaten.

Consideration of that fact raised a question in Matt's mind: "Dude, how're we going to power the cannon?"

"Each one has a backup battery under the gunner's chair. It's designed to hold enough charge for about a minute's defense if the engines die, so the crew can be evacuated to safety." A peek outside showed Radio his girl Courtney flinging herself down into their vehicle's rear seat as a mass of Bees zipped low over their AG transport. "We'd better hurry."

Pushing aside several branches, they stepped into the greenhouse's middle gun turret. The neutron cannon stood there, a deceptively slim tube mounted atop a vertical axle that rose out through a hatch in the glass roof. (Radio and Matt were struck by how much like being outside being inside here was: the see-thru ceiling seemed nonexistent, the real ceiling the Bees flying everywhere, the one difference the lack of the insects' annoying sound.)

The gunner, a fat middle-aged man, was slumped out cold in his chair, hammocked in by the seat's safety harness.

"Try to wake him up," Radio told Matt. "I'll search for a toolkit."

He ran off toward a clearing in the vegetation where he'd sighted a bank of closets.

Matt began shaking the gunner. He was conscious that they had no time, conscious of his wife and Radio's girlfriend outside, conscious of the pair's trust in them. The greenhouse shook as it took a barrage of hits. One air-to-surface missile streaked in through the vehicle's severed front and exploded, filling the air with wood and water. Those trees by the entrance caught fire. The smoke spread inward fast. Matt, still shaking the unconscious gunner, began sputtering.

"Hey, Radio, hurry up!" he yelled.

The gunner began coughing then. The man stared at Matt in confusion for a moment, then smelt the fire and remembered where he was.

He jerked upright, began hurriedly unbuckling himself from the seat. "Where's Major Banks?" he asked Matt.

"Dead." Matt tapped the cannon's vertical support. "Sir, we need to dismantle this gun fast or we're all going to be—"

"I only found this," Radio said, emerging then from the trees and holding out a plastic box. "No electric screwdrivers or laser knives anywhere." He saw the gunner had revived. "How do we disconnect this cannon?"

Before replying, the man glanced out of the greenhouse's wall. His face turned pale; rows of stone people—transformed while fleeing—lined the truck sides. A woman dissolved to jelly as he watched, the blue mess plopping down in the street like ejaculate from an invisible monster penis.

Radio and Matt stared too, largely because their point transport now swarmed with communists slashing at Courtney and Teresa.

The three of them simultaneously tore their eyes from the scene. The smoke on the upper deck was thick now, black fog cancelling view of the outside through the front of the vehicle.

"We *can't* disconnect this cannon," the gunner said, his forehead beading with sweat, "but there's a portable one we carry for emergencies. Hold on, I'll get it out."

He dashed off for the rear of the vehicle before they could question him further. Radio and Matt spent the intervening seconds before the man's return—each one felt like an eternity—watching Courtney and Teresa single-handedly repulse a unit of communists. (It was frustrating to be unable to help—the cannon turret had no openable side panels.) Teresa's face was white with panic as she fought, her already big eyes now staring larger-than-life. Courtney's expression, on

41

the other hand, was grim. She was clearly scared too, maybe even more so than Teresa, but more than that, as she ceaselessly shot, kicked, pummeled and slashed at the attackers (she'd somehow gotten a communist's knife off him or her), her face bore a cold determination to not be recaptured by the commies. Radio found that like Matt beside him, his hands were clenched with worry and he was making involuntary jerks and twitches with each of Courtney's close shaves. (He found this unusual emotion flow odd.)

The men's shared agony ended. Spinning around at a noise, they discovered the gunner had returned, lugging along with him not one, but two silver 'shotguns' attached by black cables to bulky battery packs.

The gunner kept one portable cannon, handed Radio the other.

Radio slung the battery's carrying strap over his shoulder, and next aimed the shotgun at the greenhouse wall. A trigger pull, a blast of white light, and the bulletproof glass melted away in a circle, leaving a huge hole.

He nodded to Matt, "we're good to go."

He paused a moment, then poking the cannon through the newly created hole, he fired again, this time swinging the cannon's pulse in a tight beam, carefully frying to a crisp the communists massed around Courtney and Teresa. The commies' gas-masked heads exploded off their necks like their bodies were yellow soft drink cans under too much internal pressure.

Surprised at the sudden assistance, both women turned to see their helpers.

Matt gave them a grim thumbs-up. Then he, Radio, and the gunner ran the gauntlet of flaming trees through the greenhouse and down out to the street.

CHAPTER 9

Crouched by a blue heap of jelly between the front truck and the right side of the street, Highball watched the fighting. She still carried the little boy; with the planned evacuation of the trucks, there was no one to hand him to.

Little Vincent gaped over her shoulder, his expression a mixture of fear and wonder. The bright explosions, thunderous noises, and strange transformations happening before his very eyes made him feel like he was watching a TV animation come to life.

Highball was wondering how today could have gone so wrong after starting out so right. One moment she'd been luxuriating in bed in her Causeway Flats penthouse apartment, having doggy-style sex with Jeff, panting hard toward her sweet orgasm, buttocks high in the air, breasts crushed into sweat-damp sheets, fingers clutching at nothing, mouth groaning delicious obscenities, red hair scattered all over like the residue of a crashed airplane, her windowed expression that of a dazed slut having the fuck of her life, and the next moment . . . a swarm of Bees had floated into view outside.

Jeff had instantly gone limp inside her, his prick deflating like a pricked balloon. Despite her own shock, she'd taken over, rubbed out her orgasm. Highball wasn't about to be deprived of her climax. Screw the commies.

The morning sped downhill from there. They'd begun calling people, discovered the world had gone to shit.

And now they were all fighting for their lives.

She turned, her gaze flicking down from the burning sky to settle on Jeff. Little girl secure in the bend of his left arm, gun in right hand, he was shouting a conversation with blue-haired Miki Bowen between bursts of gunfire. Both were squatting by Miki's rear truck, along with a few other defenders. (The pair were watching away from her, out between the rear gap.) Their position was a good one: Here on the right side of the street, the space between the trucks and buildings was too narrow for the Bees to descend through; the best the insects could manage was fluttering overhead to be blown apart by those below. Everyone on this side was temporarily safe. (She had no idea of the situation on the other side of the street. The truck's side flaps were unbolted, ready for the evacuation, but still kept up to keep the Bees out.) Of course, if another gobbler crashed through a house . . .

Jeff popped a large blue pill into his mouth. Highball pondered that; this made the second this morning: he'd earlier taken one before they'd had sex. Some kind of vitamin-extract-energy medication was all she'd gathered from his mumbled explanation after the bottle had come in the mail yesterday. These energy pills had to be extra-special for sure: after realizing he'd left them in her penthouse, Jeff had insisted on their going back for them. It didn't matter how many Bees were buzzing around the high-rise, Jeff wasn't leaving the building without that pill bottle.

She returned her attention forward, regarded their raging battle against the horrible odds they faced, watched her friends kick commie ass. *Wow—I had no idea Courtney and Teresa were this badass! Go girls!*

Little Vincent stiffened on her neck and pissed himself again. Highball sighed as the urine wet her top, soaked through her bra to her breasts. She patted his back, forced surrogate-maternal instinct through her own terror. "Calm down, kid. We'll be out of here soon."

The boy didn't reply, his attention fully taken up by a woman—one of the truck defenders—moaning and dissolving to a jelly puddle behind Highball.

She turned to see what had him so entranced. The boy spun in her grip to keep watching till he was actually sitting on her breasts.

Jeff had turned too at the dissolving woman's tortured noise. (A Bee had somehow dangled its sting through a gap in a roof-front and stabbed her in the back of the neck.) The other defenders seemed paralyzed by the sight. Jeff put down the little girl, stood up, and popped the Bee in the belly. It blew up, its guts plopping into the fresh puddle of woman.

Admiration tingled through Highball as she watched Jeff.

"Goddamn asshole insects," he growled, returning to crouch by Miki again. (His little female charge looked about to faint from horror.)

Highball knew Miki and her wife Heather quite well. On Matt's invitation, she'd attended the blue-haired couple's wedding in company of Frankie, her previous boyfriend.

Remembering Frankie, she licked her lips. Frankie had been a bodybuilder.

Highball (her real name was Sheila Lewis) liked macho men: Hairy guys. Muscles out to everywhere. No faggy-looking over-groomed metrosexual guys for her. Hell no!

Here and now, Jeff Bellbrook perfectly fit Highball's boyfriend profile. He was tall and dark and handsome. More important, though, he was muscular as hell. One of those guys who worked out all the time like they were scared of being picked on if they were too small. Sculptured pecs and deltoids, abs that looked chiseled from rock (slapping his buttocks actually hurt her hand). His cock was small, but she honestly didn't mind that; he was very good with his tongue and fingers and besides, his member had an upward curve to it that always rubbed her G-spot just right. She was honestly thinking of marrying him, if they could work out the pre-nup details of course. Jeff was a trucker; didn't have a lot in the bank. Highball had worked hard for ages, was worth a lot of money now . . . it seemed wrong to gamble half of that on . . .

"Highball!"

She snapped out of her reverie. Jeff was waving to her. "Hey, wake up! Let's go! Matt and Radio got the cannon loose!"

She leapt up, rushed across to him. She saw that they were the only two left on this side of the street; the other defenders had vanished around the trucks' ends.

Clutching Vincent tight, she proceeded through the space between both vehicles. Jeff followed behind her, Vincent's sister Alicia a limp burden across his shoulder. The child *had* fainted from fright.

Out in front was a melee of confused and scared people.

People were pouring from the left sides of both trucks, surging forward en-masse in a stream of terrified humanity towards the hole in the building.

Jeff shoved her into the river of bobbing heads. "Go, go—I'll meet you inside."

Angry at his violence, she looked sharply at him. His eyes weren't on her, but focused overhead, alert for low-flying Bees. His mouth was a thin bloodless line, his fingers stiff on the trigger of his gun. He fired up, then looked down, was surprised to see she was still beside him.

"Go, go," he repeated, shoving her even harder this time.

Beyond them, Courtney and Teresa were firing non-stop at the insect ceiling. Beyond both women, the street boiled with brown worms surging forward at everyone.

This is utter madness, Highball thought, *like the world is contracting around us to swallow us up.*

She quickly kissed Jeff's cheek, then went, was fast borne off in the people-current towards safety. The mob pressed around her stank of sweat and fear, stank of urine and dirt. She was certain she smelt just as bad.

"Look, Bee!" Vincent yelled suddenly over her shoulder. "It's coming fast!"

Highball didn't bother looking back. Carrying the child was like having eyes in the back of her head. She instantly ducked down between the press of people.

Looking up again a second later, she saw the insect's red sting puncture back-to-front through a man's head, jerking him up off his feet into the air. It was a right-wing Bee: the dangling corpse dissolved in midair; his liquid remains splattered those fleeing ahead of her.

Watching that transformation—solid meat turning transparent blue like reality was being drained from it—ran Highball close to mad. She could feel herself starting to lose her mind; her one chance at keeping her sanity was reaching the hole in the wall, where, now they were around the side of the greenhouse, she saw Matt directing traffic, gesturing people in.

Hefting little Vincent higher, Highball began forcing a path through those in front of her, a pummeling, kicking, screaming route through the solid mass of equally terrified human flesh ahead. Her single misguided glance right showed the gobblers now speeding towards them. It was clear that not everyone would make it to safety.

Hell no! The casualties will not fucking include me!

She clawed, kicked, punched, bit a hand that grabbed her face . . . ran over several prone bodies, at least two of which jerked beneath her feet like they were still alive . . .

And then she was aware of Matt pulling her in through the opening, of him separating her from the breathless crush of people. She collapsed against him, numb with relief, shocked that she'd survived.

He secured her up behind him, up on a platform of wall that had collapsed through a living room into a bedroom. She put Vincent down; crouched with the kid between her legs, picked white bug-bits from her red hair.

Matt returned his attention to shepherding people in through the hole. She watched him pull out his phone, place it to his ear:

"Chief? . . . Yeah, Baxter reported right: It's a total rain of piss down here; the fucking commies have blocked us off. It's wormageddon out here. We're coming under them . . . Radio's down in the sewers with another guy burning thru the walls. . . . We've ladders set up for people; problem is them not being in such a damned hurry they break their necks getting down there. . . . About two hundred initially, but we've lost about a third so far. As long as the worm that bit out this hole in the wall doesn't come back for dessert. If it does, we're screwed good."

An intense commotion outside the hole roused Highball to her feet. Holding the kid's hand, she peered out through the bedroom window at a mad inrush of jam-packed people. She shuddered: Down in the street, the gobblers were eating away at the edge of the refugees, huge vacuum-tubes of meat scooping up those on the outskirts of safety. The only thing delaying the feeding worms from mopping up everyone was the crush caused by their own frenzied impatience to reach their prey. They thrashed around and bit at each other in anger; some gobblers were even snapping Bees out of the air for food.

She at first couldn't see Jeff, then she made him out. He was with Heather and Miki. Miki was now carrying Vincent's still-fainted sister Alicia; Jeff was helping Heather hastily unbuckle her bulky backpack.

And also, dangerously close to the feeding monsters, Courtney and Matt's wife Teresa were still in the City Defense AG transport. The pair weren't shooting anymore, but were now both down in the front seats, with Teresa in the driver's seat. Then Heather flung her detached backpack into the rear of the transport. She shouted something to the two women; Courtney shouted back.

As everyone else rushed to get out of the gobblers' way, Teresa started easing the vehicle forward towards the worms.

Puzzled, Highball looked down at Matt. He'd pocketed his cellphone, was now fighting to get through the crush of people and out of the building, while yelling, "Teresa! Courtney! Get out of the damn jeep! What the hell are you both doing?"

Then next, Highball saw Jeff leap into the cab of the foremost of the two trucks, the one Heather had been driving. A sick feeling in her heart, she watched him put it in motion after Teresa and Courtney.

Vincent shivered beside her. "The big worms are going to eat them all," the little boy said with deep feeling.

CHAPTER 10

Thirty-six seconds.

Courtney's heart beat extra-hard as the AG slid towards the line of gobblers.

Her mind shrieked at her as the black wall of holes—the worms' compressed mouths—grew larger, caves of human extinguishment into which hapless victims were steadily vanishing.

She glanced into the rear of the vehicle, at Heather's large backpack. Heather's last shouted words after throwing it into the rear seat crashed around in her skull like cymbals: "It's a forty-five second fuse! Try to get the fuck out by forty!"

Behind their vehicle, Jeff drove the truck after them. She squinted, read in his expression do-or-die determination.

She looked front again. They were much nearer to the huge brown worms now, way, way too close in Courtney's estimation. This near to the gobblers, the creatures were like brownstone residences of death, chunks of displaced rubble falling from their sides. Their progress hampered by their sheer number, they inched forward by slapping the seal-like flippers that grew from their sides against the ground. (Some people said gobblers were the larval stage of *holes*, those abyss-like scourges of the Dreamfields. Watching the advancing wall of black teeth, Courtney could well believe it.) The communists were nowhere to be seen now; they'd left their hellish pets to mop up the victims.

On Courtney's left, running in abject terror, people streamed past like constructs of liquid fear being flushed into the hole in the wall.

She made out Jeff fighting against the tide of people, pushing towards herself and Teresa while yelling at them in horror. She understood Jeff's fear; it looked like she and Teresa were about committing suicide. *Sorry, man, but we've got to do this!*

Beside Courtney, Teresa's face was steely as she inched the AG as close as she dared to the packed mass. Light flashed off her hoop earrings, off her meticulously manicured black fingernails.

They were driving a bomb at the worms. Heather's ammo backpack, rigged to explode. "Park it and run!" was Heather's instruction. "Once it detonates, it'll blow the transport's engines sky-high!"

Twenty seconds.

"I think this is close enough," Teresa said in a thin, scared voice.

Courtney agreed. They were super-near the gobblers now, in a temporary street clearing formed between the massed worms and the rearguard of terrified people; mostly the elderly, who simply didn't have the legs to run. The clearing was covered with blood and human bones.

One more thing, still. Courtney looked back. The following truck was sliding across the street, blocking off the space between their transport (and the gobblers) and everyone. *Smart thing letting Jeff handle this bit,* Courtney thought, *but it has to be done nice and easy, parked with a luxury of time we don't have.*

Jeff clearly realized that too; he wasn't parking nice and easy. The truck front slammed into the house next to their exit point, its rear smashed into the opposite storefronts. All its side panels were already back up in place to prevent the explosion reaching the refugees on its other side.

Twelve seconds.

The gobblers were close enough to touch now; the foremost of them inches from biting into the AG's hood.

"Okay, let's get the fuck out like Heather said!" Teresa yelled. Both women leapt out of the transport and dashed back (Courtney glancing one last time at the bomb in the backseat). They slid/rolled under the truck, and then were out on its other side and racing to join the rearguard of escaping people. On their right, Jeff was running just as hard away from the truck.

Matt was running towards them; they gestured him back. With relief, he backpedaled, not taking his eyes off them.

No time to catch their breath:

Three seconds. Two . . . one . . .

BOOM!!!!

Everyone who hadn't made it inside the hole yet was flung flat by the explosion's shockwave.

Courtney's head went numb for a moment, like time had stopped. Then she was aware of a ringing deafness in her ears. She rolled over to look back the way they'd come.

The wedged truck had done its job—it still blocked the road. It was on fire, however.

More important, though, were the burning gobblers on the truck's farther side. Some of the worms had outright exploded: flaming chunks of their bodies lay across this nearer part of the street. Most of the gobblers, however, flamed fiercely now, their massive bodies standing straight upright towards heaven like pillars of fire, then crashing down over houses. Some were so high up, their tops were invisible in the Bee cloud. And their noise! Like an array of off-key demonic tubas.

Shit! Courtney thought, suddenly aware of the possibility of a flaming gobbler crashing down their way, over the truck and onto their escape route. Around her, she now realized, lay ranks of corpses, not those frozen by the Bees, but hapless unfortunates trampled to death in the human stampede. Squashed faces, burst eyeballs, bodies twisted into obscene contortions, limbs now curved in shape from repeatedly fragmented bones . . .

A far-up gobbler exploded, setting ablaze a communist helicopter. The aircraft fought against gravity a moment, then blew up and plummeted out of sight.

It rained hot stinky meat.

Thankfully, the Bees remained way up overhead. (The insects had initially fled the street to avoid the advancing gobblers; they remained up there now from their instinctive fear of fire.)

Courtney felt relieved. They'd got the job done. The street was clear now, everyone who wasn't dead seemed to be safe inside the building. But, damn, they'd lost a hell of a lot of people.

Her ears cleared up in stages. Sounds returned—the crackle of fire, sizzling worm meat . . . insistent feet approaching . . .

A shadow fell over her. It was Matt. He was smiling, holding down a cellphone at her.

"It's your boyfriend," he said. "Mind-hacking my phone again."

She sat up, took the phone from him. "Radio? . . . Hi, baby. . . . my phone must be busted. . . . Yeah, I'm fine (She kept a fixed gaze on the burning truck and worms, the flaming annelids swaying in their incineration.) . . . What's it like down there? . . . You've reached

Oldfield? Great!" She looked around. "Yeah, just about everyone's safely through here too now. We took a huge pounding though. . . . The commies? Why ask? Fuck the commies. . . . Okay, love you too, baby; see you soonest."

That was that then. She handed Matt's phone back to him, then he and Teresa pulled her to her feet. Teresa was bleeding through the white dust coating the left side of her face.

"Time to be well away from here," Teresa said. Her voice was hollow, lacking acknowledgement of their triumph.

Courtney understood: Teresa's eyes kept flicking to the dead—to the trampled corpses, the petrified people (whole and shattered) and the sickening piles of blue jelly everywhere.

They stepped inside. The hole was now empty again. Ahead of them, the heads of the last wave of descending refugees were just vanishing below ground. Off to one side, Radio's sister Highball was patting the little boy Vincent on the head.

Courtney pointed back outside. "Some of us should still stay and keep guard. If the Bees and commies come down after us—"

"Not me and you anyway," Teresa cut her off. "We're both out on our feet."

"Don't worry," Miki said, walking towards them from the makeshift stairs. "We've got that covered." Miki's blue hair was a dusty mess. Vincent's dozing sister Alicia was draped over her left shoulder. She pointed outside the building, at gray metal motion beyond the destroyed greenhouse. "Jeff's gonna ram the second truck up into the opening. With all the confusion outside that the burning gobblers are making, it'll be a while yet before the commies work out where we are."

"And then," Heather added, joining them, "they're likely to think we're all hiding out in the building, and try to send the Bees in through the upper windows."

Courtney nodded. Her mind felt jellied. While totaling the numbers of surviving friends and acquaintances, she let the others lead her forward to the ladders down to the sewers. *Me and Radio, Teresa and Matt, Jeff and Highball, Heather and Miki—everyone's accounted for. We've all made it for the moment. Looks like our entire gang's gonna make it alive out of Metaphor too. And then we'll look for Dr. Orgasm. After this blowup, we definitely have to find her. The future depends on it.*

PART 2:
FRAGMENTS OF A
NIGHTMARE

CHAPTER 11

Donald Oldfield, head of Metaphor Civil Defense, was a stocky Syrian War veteran. 'The Chief' had graying brown hair and eyebrows, hassled gray eyes, a flattish nose, and thin lips. He had a large usually stubbly chin.

Originally a Boston, Massachusetts native, Oldfield had (after one fine morning dropping his daughter Ashleigh off at kindergarten) made a wrong turn onto Milk Street on his way back home, accidentally driven through an OD—an otherworld door—and found himself here in the land of Innuendo with no way to get back home.

He'd been stuck here for the past eighteen years.

Shortly after his arrival in Innuendo, Oldfield had heard stories of the large numbers of space-time portals up in the eastern Moral Mountains. The Puritans who dwelled on the mountain slopes, however, didn't welcome visitors to their cities. Even for a battle-tempered veteran like Oldfield, attempting to leave Innuendo that way would have be a suicidal quest to undertake. So he'd acquiesced to making the best of his situation. He'd be sorely missed back in Boston, and he missed his family badly, but his daughter had her mother Dawn to look after her, and he'd left them both a goodly chunk of cash in the bank, so . . .

Thankfully, most residents of this place were human, and those demon-folk one routinely came into contact with were friendly enough.

Not so the damned commies.

With experience of both realms, Don Oldfield drew a clear parallel between Innuendo communists and the Arab terrorists of his own realm. He saw no distinction between the two: both were out to impose their own limited worldview on others, and were willing to stoop to the most despicable depths—wholesale murder—to get what they wanted.

One committed murder in the name of religion; the other committed murder to . . . Oldfield quailed, it seemed ridiculous that anyone would be so hell-bent on abolishing womankind's highest physical pleasure. *But there you have it,* he thought grimly. *The bastards are all crazies. When the hell did any of these madfolk ever do anything sane? If they did, we wouldn't be fighting them, would we?*

Oldfield found it odd too that the troublemakers here were called *communists.* The name made sense in a sense—the commies were against women *coming*—but he hoped it wasn't a universal trend, like if he tomorrow stepped out of Innuendo into another realm and encountered other communists, they'd be shitheads too.

*** *

There were seven of them at the ad-hoc conference Oldfield called aboard the third of the eight greenhouses now ferrying survivors out of Metaphor: he and his assistant Angel Weiner (a thin middle-aged lady with short black hair), Matt and Teresa Pollack, Courtney and Radio, and Jeff. (Highball, Heather, and Miki were currently back in the fourth greenhouse, helping settle down the sixty or so children that had been rescued. Courtney would have been with them too, but Radio had insisted she stay for the confab.)

It was an hour now since they'd blown up three buildings to seal the Norton Tunnel entrance before setting out for safety. A fusillade of lark torpedoes had done the job of a hundred wrecking balls in twenty seconds, each metal bomb-bird screeching insanely as it streaked towards its target. The fury of the buildings' collapse still echoed in everyone's ears.

Their expressions a mixture of horror and relief, the seven of them sat circling a table on the greenhouse's upper deck. (They were all smudged and dirty, wearing bloody uniforms and clothes now more like rags, stinking of sweat and survived fear.) They were in turn surrounded by a grove of lemon trees. Looking up or sideways between the trees showed a monotony of slow-passing gray rock broken by the occasional glimpse of decorative mosaic from an old subway station. Their progress was slow, as the foremost greenhouse was having to expand the subway tunnel in places to accommodate the convoy.

Oldfield heaved an angry sigh, scratched his unshaven chin. "Ladies and gents, I'll cut right to the chase: For the moment at least, we've lost Metaphor. That is a fact. The damn commies own the city now. We're on the run; we need a place to hide out and plan resistance; to maybe even take on Vaginismus itself." He frowned. "I was constantly telling Mayor Healy we needed to take the fight to the commies with a preemptive strike and he—"

"The mayor is dead, Chief," Angel Weiner interrupted. "He paid the price for his diplomacy in the face of clear aggression. Those of us left alive can't afford to be soft like he was."

"Just another dumb liberal if you ask me," Oldfield growled.

"How many units made it out?" Matt asked. "How many survivors are we altogether?"

Angel replied, "Concerning *everyone*, we don't know. The City Defense communications network is dead—the communists have clearly disabled it to forestall us regrouping. For all we know, though, we may be the only survivors."

"But we don't know that for sure, right?" Teresa asked. "There may be others, only we can't contact them."

"Yes, yes," Oldfield agreed impatiently. "Let Angel finish." He looked at his assistant. "Go on."

"Okay. So for all intents and purposes, we must assume we're completely on our own. Any plans we make or decisions taken here can't take our having any external help into account." She tapped the table for emphasis, looked around from face to face. "Dig?"

"Go on, Angel."

She glanced down at a tablet PC in front of her. "There are two hundred and forty-six of us aboard the eight greenhouses. On average, thirty in each. The breakdown? Eighty-six men, sixty-nine women, and ninety-one teens and children. The kids are all in vehicles four and five. All rescued pets are in Greenhouse Two."

She stopped speaking. Outside, the gray swept past them like flushing dishwater. The soothing smell of lemon was all around, a calming counter to their worries.

"How much armament do we have," Matt asked. "What I mean is: how charged are the greenhouses?"

Oldfield replied, "They're all full, though with all the blasting our point vehicle's doing to widen the tunnel we'll likely have to ditch it once we're aboveground again. Either that, or wait a bit for its batteries to recharge." He got to his feet, paced around the grove, his boots muffled on the grass carpet. "The main reason I brought you all up here is, we need to decide where to head for. Angel, the map please."

Angel tapped her tablet. A nine-feet-square section of the greenhouse's left side instantly converted from a transparent window into a digital monitor screen. "Thankfully, WEB still works, though we're connecting to it from Chastity and Prudence." She ran slim fingers over the tablet touchscreen—a large colored map of Innuendo flared up on the wall monitor, the depicted country being almost exactly square in shape.

Oldfield picked a rubber-tipped cane off the table, strode over to the monitor, and began pointing out landmarks.

"We're currently here," he said, tapping the middle of the screen. "Metaphor, the center of Innuendo. We're headed slightly south-east."

"That's dangerous," Courtney instantly objected. "We're heading right into communist territory."

Oldfield nodded grimly. "It's this tunnel. Unfortunately, we've no choice for the moment but to follow it."

"How's that? Can't we burn our way out?"

Angel replied, "We're currently five stories underground." She smiled at Courtney's next forming question. "*Yes*, the greenhouses' cannons *can* excavate a path to the surface, but cutting a shaft directly overhead isn't any use to anyone, is it? So we'd have to go up at an incline, which would at the very least triple the amount of rock needing to be dissolved—"

"Which would run down the batteries and render our weapons useless," Radio finished for her.

Angel smiled sweetly at him, which Courtney definitely didn't like. She nodded though. "Makes sense."

Oldfield grunted and went on: "So with that understood, we follow this damn tunnel down to *here*." He tapped an 'X' on the map. "Phantasm."

"There's nothing there."

"No, not anymore since the city went missing. Its underground stations are all still intact though." He tapped a thick road-line further up the map, about ten miles left of the X. "And now, here's our actual destination—Route Zero." He gave a cold grin at their confusion. "Yes, Route Zero, rumored to be part of the legendary Endless Street at its ends. Then we head north into the Dreamfields."

"Route Zero is fucking dangerous," Jeff said, popping a blue pill. "Just about every single town along that highway is a version of Freakville. Trust me, I'm a trucker, I know."

Oldfield nodded. "Yes, I agree it's dangerous, Jeff. At the moment, however, it's our best option. Maybe our only real option."

"Fuck danger," Teresa said. "We live and die. But just how do we connect from this damn subway to the surface? I don't see any connection."

"Easy enough. Angel, the detail map."

Angel slid her slim fingers over her tablet again. The wall-screen image altered to show a linked network of surface roads and underground tunnels.

(Outside their plant-filled glass antigrav train, rock walls flowed past in an inexorable fluid gray.)

Oldfield resumed his narration: "What you're viewing now are road construction maps. After the town of Phantasm vanished into thin air four years ago, Healy and Jackson—maybe the one thing that pair of incompetent seat-warmers did right—sent two crews—one military, one metaphysical—out here to investigate why the town went missing. They wanted to ensure the same didn't happen to Metaphor— everyone was scared Phantasm had been swallowed up by a city-sized OD, and that it might still floating around out here.

"The town was gone; the road system, which we're looking at, wasn't." He traced a short line on the map. "But still, they built this connection up to Route Zero, just in case they needed to make a fast break out."

"A long story this is," Matt said. "C'mon, Chief, fast-forward to the point."

Oldfield looked around those gathered at table. "The point is, ladies and gents: when they were done, the crews both bricked-up and concealed the tunnel again. Meaning, the commies don't know it's there."

"So we're home free?" Teresa asked. "We just reach Phantasm and drive off surface, ride into the sunset? Like a happy ending to a bad dream?"

"Something like that," Matt said. "I get the chief's point: since the commies don't know about this new side exit; they'll be expecting us to travel farther down from Phantasm—another hundred miles—and emerge at Depravia. There's certain to be a big ambush building up there now."

"That's if they even bother coming after us at all," Angel said. "The invaders might think we got buried in the rubble, or even be so overjoyed with their conquest that they don't bother with what has to be simply one motley crew of terrified refugees." She snapped her fingers for emphasis. "We're simply considering scenarios here. Either way, the chief thinks we'll have at least two days before there's any chase on, if there is one."

Oldfield nodded. "The question, ladies and gents, is: *where* do we vanish to in the next two days?" He pointed to the map. "At our current speed, we'll be arriving at Phantasm in forty minutes. We need to have made up our minds before then."

"I suggest that we search for Dr. Orgasm," Courtney said instantly. "I think it's imperative that we find her."

All eyes at table locked on her.

"Is that so?" Chief Don Oldfield asked with barely concealed irritation. "Please explain why you think so."

CHAPTER 12

The fourth greenhouse; lower deck.

Scared, upset, angry children were everywhere about Highball. Their screams, moans, and complaints were like needles sticking into her mind and body.

The children were spread out through the glass carriage. Some leaned against the greenhouse trees. Others stood dejected and wept, carrying teddy bears and books. Two kindergarteners Highball passed still had their school satchels on their backs. The pair stared at her as if unsure whether or not they were on a school trip.

This greenhouse carried the twelve-year-olds and under. All the teens were back in the fifth greenhouse.

"I want my mommy!" a little boy was yelling just ahead of Highball. "I want my mommy!!!" She grimaced. The kid was dirty like he'd been buried in a mudslide, caked with brown, with just his blue eyes and the pink of his yelling mouth visible; even his hair looked like chocolate cake frosting. Thankfully, though, the child didn't seem hurt anywhere; he was just scared, uncomfortable, and maybe hungry. Let him cry then; let off steam.

Next to the boy was an older blonde girl with blood-caked hair and dazed eyes. She sat in one place, half-covered by leaves, staring at the opposite wall. Seated by her were two sandy-haired toddlers, both chewing stolidly on blue pacifiers and staring out through the vehicle's glass walls like they were hypnotized by the passing rock surface.

Highball spotted Vincent, the child she'd helped rescue. He and his older sister Alicia sat with their backs to a tree in a trampled cabbage patch. The pair were holding hands and eating sandwiches while watching the gray exterior pass. Both seemed calm enough, which Highball, remembering Courtney's explanation of how their mother had died, found worrisome.

Looking like some white plant trapped between two dwarf palm trees, a little girl was rubbing bunched fists in her eyes and bawling her eyes out, the dirt on her cheeks streaked with tears.

Highball stifled sobs at the sight. These were the uninjured children, the lucky ones. Most were just in shock, their weeping sobs of confusion.

The rear of the greenhouse had been converted into a surgery/hospital for the less fortunate kids. Back there was where most of the moaning and screaming was coming from as doctors and nurses fought to save young lives and limbs. (There was another surgery, for adults, in Greenhouse Six.) Heather and Miki were back there now in the children's surgery, helping out. Highball had also initially been assigned to the hospital, but she'd promptly quit after witnessing the amputation of a ten-year-old boy's irreversibly mangled leg, using just local anesthetic.

She was on a collection errand for her new station. She hurried past the children towards the middle staircase, carrying two loaded armfuls of the table napkins now being used as baby diapers.

She rushed up the stairs, to be met by a cadence of angry infant howls and a swirl of baby-poop smell. "Here they are, here they are."

A nurse grabbed an armful of napkins from Highball and got to work changing diapers.

The front part of the upper deck had been turned into a nursery, every available plant that could be ditched had been thrown out of the greenhouse. Every flat surface that didn't have wires attached to it now bore a child under a year old, with grass and leaves used as swaddling.

There were twenty-seven babies in all to take care of, not counting the six with their mothers in the other carriages. The start of the escape tunnel from Metaphor had been right by an orphanage. The infant's six nurses from the orphanage were the ones looking after them, the women moving from makeshift bed to makeshift bed, tucking in, petting the angry, gurgling with those smiling, wiping shitty asses.

Highball admired the nurses' commitment to their little charges. Up here, she was just the gofer.

Lucky for the kids, she thought, dropping her other armful of napkins into a wicker basket. "Do you need anything else from below?"

A nurse picked up a child and rocked it gently. She was short and had a pleasant face, wore a blue uniform with a pinned-on cloth cap. "Is the water for their food okay yet?" she asked Highball.

"It's boiled, but way too hot. Still needs to cool. You've more than enough formula though."

The nurse beamed though her eyes were tired. "So Chief Oldfield *did* load everything for us." The child she was carrying yawned. She turned it so its chest pressed against hers, patted it. "Have a seat, dear," she told Highball. "We're fine for now."

Fine for now. The words sat in Highball's head, haunted her after she'd walked through the upper deck's trees to a bench by the wall. She sat there, first staring at her harried reflection in the glass—*Damn, I look like horse shit!*—then no longer seeing herself, but trying to come to terms with the destruction that had occurred.

Fine for now. No, she wasn't fine for now. Highball felt completely desolated. *In two hours (or is it three?) I've lost everything I've worked to achieve in my thirty-two years of life. And . . . this is the worst part of it: I can't even get angry about it. My business, my bank account, my penthouse—everything's destroyed. I reached the top rung of the ladder of success, looked around, enjoyed the view, and now? Bam!—it's all been yanked out from under me. I've nothing at the moment, and . . . but . . .* She peered back through the veil of leaves at the six orphanage nurses working so calmly in their blue uniforms, taking care of the babies, then remembered all the other distraught children downstairs, and that harrowing amputation she'd watched . . . *Shit, they've all lost way more than I have. Most of those kids don't even know where there parents are, or they watched the commies murder them!* Then another horrible thought struck: *Thank heavens mom and dad died back when they did!—I couldn't take it!*

It seemed wrong to Highball to not be able to bemoan her loss. Even a short episode of self-pity would have helped her cope better, she was certain, but such emotional wallowing now seemed not just selfish, but borderline narcissistic.

She looked back outside at the gray flow, at the solid dead river of tunnel, her green-eyed gaze dragging in slipstream. Yes, she felt now like this tunnel, like she was racing to a nonexistent future.

A stiff drink would have helped too now, but there was no chance of that at the moment—at least not here in the children's transport.

She just managed to keep from falling into the abyss of intense depression by remembering the one thing she still had: her boyfriend. Jeff's escaping too was a major plus. She wasn't actually alone at this trying time, like so many others were . . .

She caught her reflection in the mirror-wall again. 'Pissed-off redhead' best described her expression: pretty face pruned up by tumultuous emotions impossible to express—relief at surviving, anger at being rendered broke, tempered joy at Jeff's escape too.

Another great thing? Her brother Radio had also survived. But then, Radio escaping Metaphor alive was so expected by Highball as to be overlooked; his overly calm manner had always made her feel the world couldn't hurt him. (Highball didn't dislike her younger brother; her seeming indifference to him at times resulted from Radio's own lack of emotion. She saw no point expressing sib feelings he was clearly unable to reciprocate.)

And just then, a fond memory made her grin. She remembered back when they'd been students at West Metaphor High and she and Matt had discovered that if Radio tuned his head to a music station, then held onto bare loudspeaker wires, the music in his brain would play out of the speakers. They'd had great fun testing this and pranking friends of theirs who had no idea what was going on. Radio's loudspeaker projection worked with any kind of signal: talk shows, the news, whatever. The only requirement was that he held the bare ends of the speaker wires in separate hands: positive in his left hand, negative in his right. (Playing music out through speakers also made him thirsty as hell for sodas, like the electrolytes in his body needed recycling.)

Occasionally when drunk or stoned, they'd have Radio 'play' just static or white noise.

She exhaled a wind of pent-up breath, laughed softly, caught a faint scent of mint from the leaves over her bench. It was nice to remember those times of being young and carefree. Now, while not exactly old, she felt stifled. Which she guessed was an expected emotion given the circumstances.

Another memory returned: while searching the upper deck's drawers for napkins earlier, she'd discovered a handbag full of vibrators and other sex toys. Definitely not something she planned on mentioning to the nurses. Normally, Highball never left home without a vibrator in her purse—one never knew when the mood would hit and the boyfriend not be available to help scratch one's genital itch— but today, seeing the sex toys had made her shudder. *Who on earth remembers to pack stuff like that at a time like this? Or were they already stashed here in the greenhouse before today?*

"Sheila? Sheila?"

It took a moment for Highball to realize the voice was calling *her*—no one called her 'Sheila' anymore. She looked away from the glass; the nurse who'd been rocking the baby was parting leaves and peering in at her.

She got up and went to her. "I'm sorry, I got carried away in thought. What do you need me for?"

The woman indicated a table arranged with baskets full of empty feeding bottles. "It's time we go mix the little darlings' formula. The water must be cool enough by now." The baby noise in the nursery was now much less, as dry diapers had calmed the infants.

Highball nodded. "Sure."

Carrying three of the baskets, she followed two nurses downstairs.

She stepped off the lowest step into the subdued dread of the older children. A loud scream from the hospital section announced what she was certain was another unavoidable amputation. She looked right; Heather Bowen appeared in the surgery door for a moment, puked over a rose bush, then vanished back inside. Even ignoring her bloodstained clothes, the look on Heather's face told Highball more than she wanted to know—something was going badly wrong back there. The screams continued, then they abruptly dulled to a wet moaning even more unnerving than the child's yells had been. The horror was infectious—a number of previously calm younger children now began bawling again.

Highball walked quickly after the pair of nurses. No, she couldn't cope with the children's pain. Deep abhorrence of the communists surged up in her, utter outrage that the sex-hating bastards could cause this kind of agony to little innocents.

To keep her mind off the horror back in the surgery, Highball wondered about her friends currently at the conference with City Defense chief Oldfield. Like a knife stabbing a victim, she desperately forced her mind into this tread of thought.

It was complicated, she knew. The best plan their convoy had now was to go in search of Dr. Orgasm, the genius scientist the communists were desperately trying to locate and kill. Radio had confirmed that she was alive. Highball and all their other friends believed him. The problem was, Oldfield wouldn't. The City Defense chief thought Radio was simply a schizophrenic (and a dangerously delusional one at that), not any kind of gifted mutant. As far as Highball could see, no way in hell would Oldfield agree to setting their course to some coordinates her brother gave him. So Highball had cautioned Matt, Radio, and Courtney to not mention Dr. Orgasm at their discussion. But Courtney, with normal expected deep-in-love girlfriend zeal, had disagreed with the suggestion. She'd insisted she'd mention Doctor Sex.

Okay, Highball could understand why Courtney would do that. Courtney definitely needed fixing. But still, she could—

"Sheila, Sheila, are you okay?"

With a start, Highball realized they'd already reached the greenhouse kitchen. *Damn, I was sleepwalking while awake!* She came out of her introspection, saw the nurses looking at her worriedly. "Yes, I'm fine. Sorry, I keep getting distracted."

"It's hard not to be," one nurse agreed simply. "This is an utterly horrible day. It's a wonder were not all running about mad."

Highball nodded. She put down her emotional baggage. On the nurses' instructions, she picked up two large cans of baby food formula from a carton on the floor and began opening them.

CHAPTER 13

Courtney was visibly simmering. Oldfield had bluntly rejected her suggestion that they search for Dr. Orgasm.

"Yes, we'll head north," he'd said. "But for the City of Tropes, not some random destination."

The meeting had just ended. Chief Oldfield got to his feet; bone-slim Angel Weiner followed suit.

"Matt and Teresa, you two come with me," Oldfield said, his face lined with stress like the responsibility for the convoy was weighing him down. "We'll shortly be arriving at Phantasm Station. Let's go brief the drivers as to our new course."

Making a furtive gesture to Courtney to calm down, Matt and his wife followed Oldfield forward and downstairs.

Courtney glared furiously after the departing quartet.

Radio shrugged at her. "Sis already told you it was a bad idea to mention it at all."

Courtney looked at Jeff. He nodded agreement.

She didn't immediately reply the two men. Instead, she took some time to get a grip on her anger, breathing in and out deeply, holding each breath till she imagined she felt it inflating her breasts.

Finally she said, "Oldfield just doesn't like you, Radio. I could read it in his eyes. He was thinking: 'Who the hell let this crank out of the loony bin?'"

Radio shrugged back. "He does have one point though—the communications I've been getting could be fakes."

"They're *not* fakes," Courtney said flatly. "We all know that—Dr. Orgasm *is* alive. And she's out there waiting for us to find her. She's our only hope." She pointed down the aisle between the trees. "And that meathead Oldfield is too obtuse to see it."

"You know," Jeff said, "I've got to agree with the chief on one point. "How *can* Dr. Orgasm be our hope? She didn't help stop Metaphor's destruction, did she? Maybe she simply couldn't . . . maybe she can't help us. She's on the run herself, right?" He shook palms at Courtney's cold glare, then grinned. "I'm not saying Oldfield isn't a meathead, just that Dr. Orgasm herself hasn't done us much good so far. Or done her own reputation any good for that matter. If anything, she's done more harm than good to both—for all we know the communists might have blown up Metaphor just to ensure she wasn't still in it." He looked left at Radio. "What's your take on this, man?"

Radio frowned, his brow wrinkling. "It's complicated: Oldfield's right to be skeptical, I guess; at least until we get a communication from Dr. O telling us her exact location." He stroked Courtney's arm. "Good thing is, baby, we're headed north anyway. I'm certain the last transmission came from that direction, so we'll still be getting closer to her. We'd be in a very difficult situation if, for instance, the chief had insisted on heading west."

Courtney bit her lower lip hard. As always, Radio made perfect sense. And as much as she hated to admit it, so did Oldfield's decision. (Considering things rationally now, she realized that she was incensed with the City Defense chief's decision largely from her own frustrations, even though Oldfield's so-called 'logical' conclusion was definitely clouded by his skepticism of her boyfriend's abilities.) He was right: In their current straits, they couldn't set out on an indefinite course; the northern City of Tropes was a good place to head for.

And, inconceivable to Courtney as it was (if it were true it would be akin to pulling her very foundations out from under her), the transmissions Radio had intercepted *could* have been fakes.

But no, Courtney didn't think Dr. Orgasm was dead. Courtney didn't dare think that. Dr. O couldn't be dead. Courtney needed her to be alive and kicking!

(Dr. Orgasm had reputedly developed the O-pill—a tablet that made a woman almost automatically reach a sexual climax. Orgasm on demand. Finding the doctor and getting her hands of some of those O-pills was Courtney's only possible hope of having a normal sex life again. And she damn well knew it. No—Dr. O couldn't be dead!)

Jeff said, "Courtney, like Angel pointed out, if the transmission Radio picked up was from the real Dr. Orgasm, why the hell did she only broadcast when the attack was already underway? Why not before? Even to me that smacks of a communist ploy to confuse us. To feed us hope where there's none."

"She could have broadcast before and we missed it," Courtney said, her voice tight as ropes binding her hopes around her body.

Jeff raised a skeptic's eyebrow.

She ignored it. "Radio listens for her every morning. It takes a lot of mental effort to search distant airwaves, so he normally only does it when he's fresh out of bed. So that's no proof it wasn't her."

Jeff looked a question at Radio. He nodded back, eyes calm though full of queries of his own. "I'd swear it was her, man—I know her voice. But let's leave it be for the moment."

Jeff shrugged his broad shoulders then fished about in his left trouser pocket for a moment. Courtney watched him shake a large blue lozenge out of a bottle of them then pop it in his mouth.

He noticed her staring and grinned. "Vitamins to boost my immune system. Have to keep taking 'em for the next week."

She forced a smile. Jeff seemed a nice guy, not an asshole like some macho-looking men she'd met, men who were all cockiness and bullshit. Highball was lucky to have him. She knew Highball drooled over muscular men, the more hunky the better—they'd often joked about that, how when some of those bodybuilders hugged her with their huge biceps it felt like being in the grip of a python. An incredible feeling, Highball claimed it was, feeling all that muscle wrapped around you. Watching Jeff now, each of his biceps almost the size of her thighs, Courtney could well believe it. And the guy was really handsome too.

"We're at Phantasm Station," Radio said as they felt the subtle side pressures of a change of direction.

Courtney looked out of the glass wall. Gray stone was giving way to metal and plastic and a wide space with lights, with overhead, large girders curved over a cavernous space clearly designed for big transports.

They flowed forward between concrete platforms.

Courtney grimaced at the piled skeletons by the platform doors. Some seemed human, some animal; some were simply linkages of oversized bones for which she lacked a reference point.

Then they were past, through that morbid space and making a left turn which continued up at a relaxed incline.

Courtney saw Matt and Teresa walking back towards them. Both looked angry. Husband and wife sat down at the conference table.

"What's the matter?" Courtney asked.

"We've been assigned to the last greenhouse."

"We?"

Teresa rolled her eyes. "All of us—Matt and I, you and Radio, Jeff and Highball. Even Heather and Miki."

"Why on Earth would Oldfield do that?"

"He says the eight of us are to keep rearguard watch for the commies—we're the only ones he trusts to do the job right."

"That makes sense, I guess," Jeff began, then looked confused. "But . . . the girls are more useful helping with the kids. They're short-staffed back there, aren't they?"

Matt winced. "Dude, it's not what you think. Oldfield's *exiling us* to the last vehicle. He wants us out of his way."

Jeff went wide-eyed.

Courtney asked, "Why in the world would he do that?"

Teresa gave a cold laugh. "Because he thinks we're dangerous. He's scared we might stage a revolt and take over the convoy."

Courtney gaped at Teresa. "*What?* But that's crazy. How could he think that?"

Teresa smirked. "Girlfriend, you completely freaked him out with your insistence on our going hunting for Dr. O. So now we watch the skies for ET instead."

"Except," Matt added with a sardonic smile, "maybe we attempt to prove his fears right and take over command?"

"I'm all for taking over," Jeff said. "The way the chief's thinking, he'll get us all killed sooner or later."

"He's scared *we'll* get *him* killed," Radio said. "Hard to fault that."

"It's that Angel Weiner he's got with him," Teresa said, pulling a disgusted face. "The skinny twit keeps assuring him that he's right. The kind of hold she's got on the chief, I'm sure she's fucking him."

Courtney followed the conversation with only half her mind. *How dare Oldfield banish us—kick us to the curb?* This really pissed her off. Her previous grudging acceptance of the rightness of the chief's refusal to start searching for Dr. O fell by the wayside. *He's begun power-tripping now, eh?*

She looked past Teresa, out of the greenhouse. They'd more or less leveled out again now, their vehicle floating past rows of metal pillars in what seemed an underground car lot. The empty space looked like it'd make a great residence for ghosts. Feeling a sudden chill, she returned her attention to her companions.

Teresa was saying, "I'm with Jeff for giving Oldfield the boot. In fact give me that honor—I'd personally love to stick my boot up his hairy old ass, relocate his fucking hemorrhoids for him." Having contributed that, she got out a nail file from her soiled camo uniform and began repairing her manicure.

Courtney watched her with amusement; it was welcome comic relief amidst this overwhelming tension—a nail file in this dire situation? She wondered if Teresa also had nail paint/hardener in her pockets. Teresa was obsessed with keeping her fingernails and toenails in perfect condition. Courtney couldn't even start to recall how many times she'd listened to her bemoaning a cracked nail like it was her whole world cracking up.

Her grin widened. Highball was worse—she almost always had a vibrator on her. As she'd more than once explained: "So what's wrong if I do? It's just backup for when my boyfriend ain't available. What's most important is that I'm faithful, see? I don't ever screw around. Not ever." Courtney couldn't argue with that. She grimaced. *So Teresa has her manicure/pedicure fixation and Radio's sister has her dildos. And me? What do I have? Do I have anything other than the enduring sense of how mucked up I am?*

More immediate, though, she needed to take a shower. She looked around at her companions' dirty faces. *We all do. We damn well stink.*

Matt was staring at Radio. "What's the news, dude? You think we should kick the Big Kahuna out of power, or what?"

"No," Radio replied flatly. "We do as Oldfield says. Everyone's already demoralized enough without any infighting. We stir things up now, we'll just get loads of people killed. And we'll be setting the stage for further rebellion." He waved a cautionary finger. "And remember, in addition to being possibly the only survivors from Metaphor, we're on the run—we need all the fighters we've got . . . alive, and on the same page" He laughed. "And . . . here's the ironic thing: this discussion we're having simply proves the chief's right to be wary of the lot of us."

Courtney was angry that she agreed with Radio. Fighting would defeat their purpose—they could get killed, and then she'd never find Dr. Orgasm and her fantastic and very necessary O-pill.

She looked at the others' faces, gauged responses. Jeff seemed to be brooding. He looked unsatisfied, like he'd have liked a fight if only to burn off some unspoken frustration. Matt looked perplexed. For all her stated belligerence, Teresa was clearly indifferent to the outcome. She was examining her right hand fingernails, holding them up to the light, a slight smile on her lips like she'd just glued her world back together again.

That was that then. Courtney yawned at Matt. "So when do we effect the transfer to the last greenhouse?"

"Tonight. Stopping will be less dangerous then. Apparently, excavating the tunnel used up less battery power than expected— Greenhouse One still has enough juice to run on for a while."

She nodded. "Fair enough." Then she looked around at the nearest upper deck trees. "Guys, I'm hungry, anyone care for an apple?"

Radio and Jeff raised hands.

Teresa looked up from her manicure, her dark eyes now calmly amused. "Pluck a couple for me too, darling. I can't wait to see how all this plays out."

She looked at Matt. He nodded. "Yeah sure, some for me too."

Jeff popped another blue pill into his mouth. Courtney began wondering what-the-hell kind of vitamins it was that you never stopped eating. And *big ones* as that?

She found a basket and began plucking fruit for their makeshift lunch. Apples, oranges, bananas, pears . . . a few grapes.

Around them, their greenhouse transport sped on towards Route Zero.

CHAPTER 14

Night had fallen. Viewed through the glass greenhouse roof, the gray clouds seemed puffs of factory exhaust polluting the ebon sky.

The convoy had stopped for a while. Courtney was in the kids' greenhouse to tell Highball, Heather, and Miki about the chief's orders moving them all to the last vehicle.

Downstairs was calm; lots of kids everywhere. The younger kids and toddlers were mostly asleep on makeshift beds or patches of grass. The older children ate sandwiches and sipped drinks. Courtney was relieved: though they still looked harried, most of the children seemed past their initial shock. Of course, the following days would be hardest for them, as they came to realize that they were alone in the world now.

She looked around some more, saw Vincent and Alicia, the kids she'd rescued, sitting peacefully on a bench. Both were eating donuts and in turn gesturing out of the window at the nightscape revealed by the greenhouse's interior lights. Watching them made her smile.

Heather poked her blue head out of a door at the far end of the greenhouse. She didn't notice Courtney, just dry-heaved into a clump of flowers and disappeared again.

Courtney headed for that rear door to see Heather, then, at the middle stairs, she met a descending blue-uniformed nurse carrying a basketful of empty feeding bottles. The nurse informed her that Highball was upstairs with the babies. She thanked the woman and climbed, emerging in the midst of an animated gaggle of teenage girls coopted from the fifth greenhouse to help with the infants' feeding time.

"Highball!" she gestured as her friend sauntered past carrying a baby girl and a feeding bottle.

Highball turned and saw her. Before Courtney could utter a word, however, Highball handed her both the gurgling infant and bottle and steered her to a bench. "Have a seat, I'll join you in a moment."

Courtney sat. She put the teat the baby's mouth; the baby grabbed the bottle with her little hands and took over feeding herself. Courtney relaxed; the child was warm against her rising and falling breasts, an affirmation that the future still existed.

All around Courtney, cradling lustily sucking babies in their arms, teen girls chatted, some standing, leaning on trees, some, like herself sitting on benches watching the landscape beyond the road. One thing the girls had in common was how they all looked confused. Courtney completely empathized with them. She understood that their emotions were in turmoil. Most of the girls' talk was to reassure themselves that they weren't mad, that they'd not simply imagined the day's events of giant insects and gas-masked murderers razing their hometown.

The world goes on, she thought. *Yes, we're soaked in pain, but life damn well goes on.*

Highball arrived and sat down opposite her, carrying a plump little Asian boy who'd also already commandeered his feeding bottle. She looked at Courtney expectantly. "What's going on? You're not just here to help, I can tell." Her eyes widened in sudden alarm. "Nothing's happened to Jeff has it? Or Radio? Oldfield and Matt haven't gotten into a shouting match, have they?"

Courtney explained why she'd come.

Highball listened in silence. "Shit, girl, I warned you not to tell the chief about us going to find Dr. Orgasm."

Courtney bristled. "You're saying this is my fault?"

"In one word—yes." She stood up, stared down at Courtney. "Look, I'm not blaming you, okay—I'd have done the same if it was Jeff, and I know you love my brother, but . . ." She frowned. "Hey, tell me: there's other people in that last greenhouse too, right? Or is it just us?"

"Nope. No one else. It's just us. Everyone else is being moved forward in case there's a firefight. That's Angel's excuse anyway. But that's clear B.S.—we're essentially being placed under house arrest. Or 'bus arrest' as Teresa calls it."

Both babies had now drained their feeding bottles. The plump Asian baby Highball carried was gurgling happily, then he made a long watery fart that made both women wince.

"Time to change his diaper," Highball said.

Courtney grinned back. "Without disposables available? I'm sooooo glad that's happening to you, not me." Her own little blonde burden had now let go of her bottle and was yawning. Courtney stood up, began rocking the child to sleep.

Highball was frowning. Courtney was unsure if this was due to their summary relocation and 'bus arrest,' or the diaper-changing task at hand, which would likely be problematic using just table napkins.

Then, abruptly, Highball's dour expression burst into a broad smile. Shifting the baby into the crook of her left arm, she dragged Courtney after her through the mob of helping teens towards a pair of momentarily free nurses. Courtney followed bemused.

"Is everything okay, Sheila?" one of the blue-uniformed women enquired of Highball.

She nodded back. "I've just been reassigned to convoy security. Chief Oldfield's orders. I have to leave right now."

The other nurse frowned. "You? But . . . but you're a natural with the babies." She gestured around at their teenaged helpers. "And we're *still* short-handed."

"Oh, I'm sure the chief will send someone else up to help," Courtney said. "He'll have to. I was told to fetch Heather and Miki too."

Both nurses rolled their eyes. Highball handed one the Asian baby. "I think he's pooped himself."

Courtney gave the other nurse the now snoozing baby girl. Highball then yanked her away from the pair of visibly displeased women. Not down the stairs as she'd expected, but along the aisle leading to the rear of the greenhouse.

"Are we headed for the rear stairway?" Courtney asked, as, now out of sight of the nursery section, they pushed apart the branches and ferns growing across their path.

"Sssh," Highball replied, then pulled Courtney aside into a storage room filled with metal cabinets. Once inside, she hit the light switch, crossed briskly to a desk by the right wall and slid open its main drawer.

"What are you looking for?"

Highball turned back to Courtney and handed her a large blue handbag. "Look inside," she said.

Courtney unzipped the bag, then gasped at its contents. "Whose vibrators are these?" Her eyes roved over the shiny plastic rods. It was an extensive collection too—two purple and gel-green 'lipsticks,' a blue two-pronged 'rabbit' vibro, several 'multispeed' silver phalluses, and, nestling in pride of place amongst a bed of anal beads and plugs, a seemingly brand-new cordless white Magic Wand, the rechargeable vibrator's fat silicon head a promise of the most deliciously creamy female pleasure imaginable.

Just looking at the selection of sex toys made Courtney tingle.

Highball leered. "There's some really kinky ladies working in greenhouses for sure."

And then, Courtney remembered that she could no longer reach orgasm. She stared dully at the bagged vibrators. "Put 'em back, Highball; let's just go."

Highball smirked. "And leave all these pretty joysticks behind? Are you kidding? They're coming with us."

"What do you need them for? You've got Jeff."

"'Toy's before boys,' mama always said. Nah, I don't mean it like that. They're not for Jeff and *moi*. I'm thinking more of you and Radio using them."

Courtney's eyes widened; she suddenly felt completely mortified. *"What?"*

"They might work; you never know. If you guys find a place where the mood is right . . ."

Courtney felt close to tears, like she was being ripped open and exposed. It was an irrational feeling she knew; she and Highball had talked about her sexual block many times, with Radio's redhead sister offering lots of caring advice . . . but here the embarrassed feeling was just the same. "Shit, Highball . . . C'mon, just put them back and let's just go. They must belong to someone. And we're running late; we need to go tell Heather—" But her eyes had fallen on a corner of white paper peeking between two strings of black-and-red anal beads. She reached into the bag and retrieved it.

It was a business card. Suddenly she burst out laughing.

"What so funny?"

Courtney handed the card to Highball, who read its lettering out aloud:

Ms. Angel Weiner.
Executive Assistant to Metaphor City's Head of Defense.

Highball burst out laughing too. "Ha ha ha! I don't frigging believe this: they're *Angel's* dildos?"

"Damn," Courtney gasped. "And all the while, here I was thinking Oldfield was filling her gap."

Highball had problems controlling her mirth. Finally she got her laughter down to tiny giggles. "Maybe he is. Maybe Angel's simply a nympho." She grinned at Courtney. "What do you say now? You still think we should leave her stuff here for her?"

Courtney smirked. "Screw Angel—let's pilfer them. Serves her right for helping get us exiled. Ha ha ha! Teresa is gonna love this."

And Courtney realized then that this was probably the first time she'd laughed all day. Draping Angel's bag of sex toys over her shoulder, she decided the theft was worth it if only for comic reasons.

***

They walked through the aisle of trees to the rear stairs. Once downstairs, Courtney pointed Highball to the surgery door, which had several bloody finger-smears on it. "You go tell Heather and Miki—I don't want to see what's behind there."

Highball's face tightened. "I don't want to—"

The surgery door opened. Miki peered out, looking sick. (Courtney now saw that the rose bushes to the left of the surgery door were spattered with vomit.)

Miki's blue hair was covered with muck and she had blood on her face like it had been sprayed on her. She stared at Courtney and Highball confusedly for a moment before realizing who they were.

"Get Heather," Highball said. "We're out of here—Chief's orders."

A look of intense relief and gratitude entered Miki's eyes. She retreated back through the door again and shut it, but not before Courtney had caught a good glimpse of a dead legless kid stretched out on a table.

That did it for Courtney: all the good humor that had built in her from finding Angel Weiner's sex toy stash drained from her. She nodded to Highball (who herself really looked like she'd rather be someplace else)—"Shit, I just remembered I've something to do at the front of the greenhouse!"—and walked off briskly before the other could protest.

Courtney found distraction a short distance later.

"Hey, Vince, look! It's Aunt Courtney!" a young female voice yelped.

"Auntie Courtney! Auntie Courtney!!"

Startled, she turned. It was little Vincent and his sister Alicia. The pair were dashing towards her with beaming faces.

She squatted to hug them both, unable to restrain joyous tears from spilling down her cheeks. Seeing both children alive and happy made her feel great.

"So how are you both?"

"We're fine, Auntie." Alicia drew her towards their wallside bench. "Come, come, Auntie Courtney. Come and see."

She looked back once towards the surgery. Outside the door, Highball was explaining things to Heather, who seemed even more relieved than her wife previously had. Miki had her arm around Heather's waist and was looking rather dazed.

Courtney forgot the trio, let the happy children drag her through the trees to their bench. The three of them sat together, a child on either side of her, staring out at the shadowy countryside. Around them, other kids either slept peacefully or watched the countryside too.

"We saw a frog out there," Vincent said.

Courtney feigned surprise. "You did?"

"Yes," Alicia confirmed. "It was a big one, big as a car. And very green."

Courtney was intrigued. "So what did the big green frog do?"

"Oh, it was hopping along through the flowers," Alicia continued with gusto, "but when it saw our greenhouse it crashed into a tall, tall flower and fell over."

Vincent laughed. "It was kicking on its back."

Alicia laughed.

Courtney laughed too. It felt really nice to be happy.

After a while, Highball, Heather, and Miki joined her and it was time to go. She kissed both kids goodnight, said she'd try to see them tomorrow, and then they were outside again.

"Well, girls," Highball said as they strode through the night toward the last greenhouse, waving to the children through the walls. "At least we've done some good today."

"Yes we have, haven't we?" Courtney replied in a pleased voice, waving to Alicia and Vincent one last time. Then a thought struck her. "Hey, Highball, what's with all those blue pills your guy keeps taking?"

"Jeff? Oh, the lozenges. You noticed?"

"He doesn't seem to stop. What are they? Steroids?"

"They'd better not be steroids. If they are, I'll fucking murder him—I've warned him to stay away from steroids. But I doubt they are. He says they're vitamins."

"Vitamins?" But they're so big. And . . . what sort of vitamins do you eat all day long?"

"You know, that's rather a good question."

CHAPTER 15

The convoy resumed moving. Seated now in the cockpit of the rearmost greenhouse, one hand on the steering wheel, Jeff swallowed another of the blue lozenges.

Highball looked at him oddly, then shrugging, she got up and went to fetch them drinks.

Jeff patted her buttocks as she left; Highball was a nice, solid package. He was glad she was his, and that he'd soon be able to satisfy her in bed like she really deserved.

Jeff Bellbrook was overly conscious of the size of his penis. His circumcised manhood was four inches long when erect, and not particularly thick by way of compensation either—way, way too small in his estimation.

Now too, he regretted getting into the bodybuilding scene. On a small nerdy guy (or a dwarf, even) a four-inch member wouldn't look too bad. Jeff, however, was six feet tall and rippling with muscle. Whenever he looked at himself in a mirror, his penis seemed an afterthought stuck on him by the Almighty simply because he was a man and all men had one.

And then, he imagined people would think he'd taken up bodybuilding from feelings of sexual inadequacy.

And it was too late now to stop pumping iron. If he did, he'd go flabby, pile fat over the redundant muscle, and soon his cock would be invisible beneath his belly.

Tortured by worry over his size as it affected his sexual performance, Jeff did all he could to compensate in bed—he studied books on how to eat pussy and give women mind-blowing orgasms, how to use his fingers right, the right way to suck on a woman's nipples, lick her anus . . . but he felt it wasn't enough.

No matter how much his girlfriends gasped and moaned in pleasure at his expert ministrations, no matter how much their bodies trembled or thrashed with orgasm, no matter how much they professed their immense satisfaction afterward, Jeff thought they were all lying to him out of pity.

For instance, Jeff just *knew* Highball was faking her orgasms. No way was he satisfying a totally hot red-blooded redhead like that. It mortified him whenever she pressed up against him after sex whispering how wonderful it had been. Lies! Fake passion! He loved Highball, but it was clearly one-sided; Highball was obviously only staying with him till a better-endowed man came along.

This was Jeff's cross, and he bore it badly, too blinded by feelings of sexual inadequacy to realize that the women he slept with really appreciated the pleasure he gave them, didn't care about how big or small his penis was, and most important—here and now—that Highball was devoted to him, fast falling in love with him, was actually thinking of marrying him.

***

The long blue pills? Jeff had gotten the lozenges through an ex-girlfriend, Brie Blue, who now worked in the porno industry. A chance meeting in the gym the previous weekend had led to them leaving for drinks together.

In the bar, Brie had winced on sitting down. Jeff's concerned enquiry led to her embarrassed confession that her vagina was smarting badly, result of a major hardcore session the previous day. "If the pain keeps up like this, I'll have to see the goddam doctor. Fuck, people don't realize how hard making money with your ass gets." Brie polished off her drink and snapped fingers at the waiter for another. Then she began angrily telling Jeff the new tricks her male co-stars were using to keep ahead of the competition nowadays.

A name surfaced and kept repeating: Dr. Brentwood.

Dr. Lou Brentwood was the maverick scientist both male and female porn stars frequented for body-enhancing surgeries and other procedures. He was also one of those 'jack of all trades' scientists always coming up with new gadgets and pills.

"He used to be Dr. Orgasm's assistant, till either he quit or she fired him—versions vary. I heard their split was over porn—she hated our 'faked' orgasms."

Brentwood's latest invention was a 'STRETCH' cream which temporarily increased the size of a man's erection, which was what

Brie's last co-star Rod Rodstein had used, and the reason she was hurting badly now.

She grimaced with remembered pain. "His cock looked like your arm. It felt like I was being fisted. And the mongoloid son-of-a-bitch kept pounding away like my cervix was the Great Wall of China and he wanted to bust through it and overthrow the Emperor."

Then she saw the 'interested' look on Jeff's face. "Oh shit, don't tell me you want some too. What is it? You're one of those Misogyny bastards? You hate your girlfriend and need a legal way to kill her?"

"No, no, it's nothing like that at all." Desperate for her help, Jeff whispered out his size problem to Brie.

To his chagrin, she burst out laughing. "But we fucked lots of times and I never noticed." She stopped laughing when she saw how worried he was. "Jeff, for God's sake, you were great in bed—way better in fact than lots of guys I've slept with. You've a confidence problem, not a size problem."

"More size would help my confidence."

Brie mused on that, then nodded. "That's true I guess, but Brentwood's 'STRETCH' cream won't help you." She shifted on her chair and winced. "Take my word for it—no woman will ever call you back again after the first date."

"It's worth a tryout."

She shook her head. "Not for we ladies, it ain't—no one wants a guy with a cock like a Pringles can." She fiddled about inside her handbag for a few moments, then handed a card to Jeff. "Here's Brentwood's phone number and email."

Jeff received it gladly. "Thanks." Then he realized that Brie hadn't let go of the card yet. He tugged on it. She shook her head.

"What's the problem?" Jeff asked. "You're changing your mind? Brie, I need help. I'm in love with the most beautiful girl in the world, and... and..."

Brie still didn't loosen her grip on the card. She sighed. "And you're scared she's gonna dump you 'cos your dick's too small?"

Jeff nodded.

"How long have you been dating?"

"Three months."

"You've been sleeping together, right?"

Jeff nodded again.

"And, does she push you away when you kiss her?"

"No. She pulls me closer."

Brie let go of the card. "I'm telling you—it's all in your head. She likely loves you even more than I did."

"Thanks, I re—" Then he jerked up in shock. "You *loved* me? But... but . . . we broke up."

"Oh no. *You* broke up with *me*. I wept, I pleaded, I tried to stop you leaving, but . . ." She rolled her eyes, flung her hands wide in exasperation. Then her eyes widened in shock. "Wait . . . oh, no. You mean to tell me it was because of . . . this?" She sat back as if defeated. "You broke up with me because of the size of your penis?"

Jeff couldn't reply. His shamefaced look was all the confirmation she needed.

Brie got up, gathered her handbag.

"Wait, I'm sorry. Don't leave. Where are you going?"

"I'm off to have a good long cry." She leaned over the table, tears already streaming down her cheeks and ruining her makeup. "Look, Jeff, please don't make the same mistake twice. If this lady loves you as much as I did, don't blow her off just because you don't feel man enough for her."

"I'm honestly sorry. I had no idea that—"

"Shut up! Let me finish." Her tears were pouring now, splattering the table. She tapped the card. "Call Brentwood if you must. But don't ask for that damn cream that messed me up yesterday. Ask him for some enlargement pills with a permanent effect. He's sure to have some." She peered intently at Jeff, her gaze cold like it was trying to freeze her tears. "Can I count on you to do that and not be an asshole again? Please, do it for that woman you're dating now, who I'm certain loves you, even if you're too egocentric to see it."

Jeff looked down at Brentwood's card, then back up at Brie's cold face. He nodded. "Yes. I'll do it."

Brie bent forward and kissed him on the cheek, her tears falling on his face.

Then she turned and walked hastily out of the bar. Jeff watched her go, more confused than he'd ever been in his life. Brie's confession floored him: *She was in love with me? In love with me?*

***

Jeff called Dr. Brentwood once he got home. Hearing that Dr. Brentwood had been Dr. Orgasm's co-researcher reinforced his faith and expectation of a solution to his problem.

And staying true to his promise to Brie Blue, he asked the doctor for penis enlargement pills.

The doctor had a warm soothing voice. "Yes, I do have some, Jeff, but they're experimental, so I must warn you about possible side effects. The pills are new and I haven't field-tested them yet."

"I'll be your guinea pig, Doc," Jeff hurriedly offered.

"Will you now? It could be rather risky." Dr. Brentwood sounded cautious, but Jeff heard a clear undertone of delight in his words.

"Doc, what kind of side effects can I expect?"

"They differ from person to person, that's the only certain thing about them." His voice turned a little oily, like a salesman worried the potential buyer might change his mind. "But, Jeff, I guarantee you an appreciable increase in the size your member. Both in its length and thickness. That's a stone cold assurance." A slight pause, then the added caution: "But you've no idea—*I've* no idea—what else will happen."

Jeff mused on that for a few seconds. "What's in the pills?"

"Nothing poisonous. Just a hodge-podge of nutritious chemicals."

"Okay, I'll do it. Your lab address is on the card Brie gave me. Should I drive over and collect them?"

"No, I'll be out most of today. I'll put them in the post to you. What's your address?"

Jeff told him, then asked, "What's the dosage?"

"One say every two or three hours. The pills have a cumulative effect, so the more you take the faster you'll see results. But not more than twelve a day. There's fifty in the bottle and you should begin to notice a difference by the next morning. Then keep taking them till your organ is the size you desire it to be." He paused speaking for a moment—Jeff heard him moving something on the other end of the line—then resumed: "I was checking that I've enough pills to send you. I do; no need to make more up quickly. Now remember: call me once you notice anything odd. No, that might be too late: ensure you call me every three hours. Let the phone ring into voicemail and leave a message stating how you feel. If there's any trouble I'll call you back."

Jeff nodded into the phone. "No problem, Doc. I'll do that. Is that all?"

Dr. Brentwood replied that it was. Jeff thanked him profusely and hung up.

Jeff waited impatiently for the pills to arrive. A two-day wait, but they'd finally come yesterday afternoon. Staring at the blue pills in their plastic bottle, he'd felt like one on the verge of being reborn.

Jeff hadn't immediately taken any of the penis enhancement tablets, deciding to start the course the next morning so as to keep proper count of how many he'd swallowed for both his and Dr. Brentwood's records.

'Next morning' was today, and so he'd been taking them ever since. The results so far? He felt good, energized even, as he drove the greenhouse, but whether this was an effect of the medicine or just from his anticipation of its results, he couldn't tell. From time to time, his penis tingled, but so far he could detect no changes. But, no hurry, this was still just the first day of the course, and he'd so far taken only eight tablets.

Still forty-two left to use.

He did realize he had no way to call Dr. Brentwood now though to report back the results or any bad side effects. But this didn't really bother him. He felt just fine.

Above all, he was impatient to see the doctor's promised results. Jeff wanted his penis to be IMMENSE, so could REALLY satisfy Highball in bed.

He didn't believe any of that 'penis size doesn't matter/women prefer love' nonsense Brie Blue had told him. Oh, no, Jeff knew she'd just been lying to make him feel better. She was a porn star, wasn't she? Surrounded by BIG DICKS all day long?

CHAPTER 16

Night settled like an increasingly heavy weight on those in the last greenhouse. Six of those who weren't driving sat relaxing around a lower floor table, recently-emptied dinner plates heaped in its middle.

Matt was watching the wilderness through the trees. Beside him, Radio's eyes were unfocused, like he was looking somewhere outside this world.

Heather and Miki were slumped in their chairs, looking completely out of it. Heather caressed Miki's hand in her lap. Both their eyes were less horrified than before.

Seated opposite the men, Courtney was watching her boyfriend.

Beside her, Teresa giggled over the contents of Angel Weiner's purloined handbag: "Damn. Bitch or not, the woman definitely likes her pleasure."

Matt looked her way. "What's in the bag, honey?"

"Just a girl's best friends."

He made a funny face. "Diamonds?"

Teresa and Courtney laughed loudly. Matt tried to snatch the handbag from them, the pair held it away. They laughed louder.

Highball strode out of the cockpit then to sit with them. "Okay, Jeff's still taking those damn pills." She shrugged, seemed to forget about it, grinned at Courtney. "One benefit of having this greenhouse all to ourselves . . . is the privacy." She gestured right and left down aisles hemmed in by gorgeous fragrant blossoms. "I can't believe how much space we've got. It's ludicrous: we've twelve bedrooms to choose from."

Courtney nodded. "Yeah, like we're in a mobile hotel."

"We're in a fucking mobile prison," Teresa spat. "Don't sugarcoat the facts."

"Lighten up wilya," Courtney growled back. Then she looked concernedly at Heather and Miki. Miki was now leaned forward, cheek resting on her forearms which were crossed on the tabletop. "You guys okay?"

Heather shook her head. "Not by a long shot. We've both seen too much horror today."

Highball nodded sympathetically. (They'd found no beer, spirits, or wine in the greenhouse, which might have helped relax them all now.) "I honestly don't know how you two could stand it."

Miki yawned; it sounded to Courtney like she was in pain. "Someone had to. If we'd all run off . . ." She scowled at the dark look that came over Highball's face at her words. "No, I'm not pointing fingers; you might have noticed us puking every ten minutes or so. We wanted out of there as much as you did. But then, the kids needed us."

"Yeah, the kids," Highball agreed.

"A fucked-up scene for all," Heather said angrily. "Fuck the damned communists."

"Fuck their leader even more," Courtney added. "Power-drunk insane bitch."

"You know what I'd love to do to Florence Rigid?" Heather asked. "I'd love to personally shove a stick of dynamite up her vagina and light the fuse, splatter her all over Innuendo." She leapt to her feet, pulled Miki up after her, blew a tired kiss at the men. "'Night, guys; my baby and me are off to bed."

"'Night, guys," Miki seconded. "Ah so, we get first pick of the bedrooms."

Arms around each other, the blue-haired couple trudged off, both dragging their feet like their minds were already asleep and dreaming.

(For a moment, Courtney considered asking Teresa what she and Miki had been discussing earlier: At one point, when Heather had gone to pee, Miki had dragged Teresa off aside and the two had begun giggling secretively. *Shit, Teresa, not here,* Courtney had groaned. She recalled that Miki and Teresa had been college roommates once and there'd been rumors back then about the pair being more than just friends.)

The others watched them go, then Matt tapped Teresa on the shoulders. "Time we retired too, princess. I need to kip so I'm fresh to relieve Jeff when he gets tired. Oldfield would just love having us crash the greenhouse to prove his theory of our unreliability."

Teresa nodded and got up. Courtney took the blue handbag from her, then walked around the table to tap Radio out of his daze. "Hey, baby, time for bed. I've a big surprise for you."

Watching her brother's eyes slowly refocus, Highball smiled. It was amusing, how possessively Courtney was holding the bag of sex toys. Then, remembering something, she frowned and pointed to their dining table "Hey, if everyone's leaving, who's gonna help me do the dishes?"

Courtney shrugged. "Girl, just pile 'em in the sink and go keep Jeff company. We'll all wash up in the morning."

Highball rolled her eyes. "Okay then, I'll do that. She pointed out through the transparent wall at the black night. "But . . . if we all go to bed, who's gonna be watching the skies like Oldfield ordered?"

"Fuck Oldfield," Teresa yawned back at her. "Not me anyway. I'm too tired to care if his ass gets melted to jelly."

Highball glared at Courtney. Courtney tapped the blue bag. "Me neither, boyfriend's big sister; I got business to take care of."

"I'll stay, sis," Radio volunteered.

"Oh, no, you won't," Courtney instantly countered, dragging him off after Matt and Teresa who were already twenty feet away and ascending the middle stairway.

"But I'm not sleepy," Radio protested.

Courtney shook the blue handbag at him. "Trust me, darlin'—we ain't gonna sleep."

Highball stared after her departed friends, then she sat fuming. *I can't believe it. They all abandoned their posts? Everyone? I'm just as dog-tired as them all and . . . Shit—looks like I'M watching the skies tonight!*

She cleared the table like Courtney had suggested, checked on her darling Jeff for five minutes, then climbed to the top deck herself and made herself comfortable in a chair. She leaned back, stared out through the transparent roof to watch for Bees and communists.

It was a waste of time. Highball was much too tired to play sentinel. An afternoon of looking after babies had completely worn her out.

She was asleep and snoring loudly in five minutes flat.

CHAPTER 17

In standard greenhouse design, Courtney and Radio's bedroom looked more like a garden than anything else. Gorgeous flowers stood in pots in the corners and around walls draped with pungent aromatic vines. Yellow gourds dangled like chandeliers from the ceiling, with the night visible between the lattices that suspended them. The overall effect was of a scene from a romance about ancient Asian princesses.

The bed was large and soft, and perfumed by the lovely big blooms everywhere.

Courtney began taking her clothes off. "Let's shower," she told Radio while dropping her pants, "Then I want to try it again here."

"Try what?"

She tapped the big blue handbag. "Try to have an orgasm." Panties followed pants onto the floor; filthy T-shirt and bra topped the pile.

He undressed too, followed her into the attached shower.

In the falling water, they soaped each other up. Courtney took her time with washing Radio's buttocks and penis, enjoying the heavy feel of his testicles cupped in her hand.

He kissed her forehead, rubbed the bar of soap over each of her nipples in turn, making tingles of fire shoot through her body, flaring up from her groin to her throat.

In response, she grabbed his penis, squeezed it. She loved how different he was from her, his hairiness contrasting her smooth skin, loved how his masculinity complemented her femininity, how his hardness matched her softness, how his other hardness—now erect and throbbing desperately in her small hand—felt just right: thick enough to pleasure her immensely, long enough to fill her. Still holding him hard as the warm water washed the soap off them both, she pressed against him, her arousal rising as his hands cupped her buttocks and squeezed.

Courtney was uncertain why she was suddenly so aroused after such a horrible day. Was it the fallout of all the day's fighting and their subsequent flight? Her body's desperate need to release tension? Or had the desire simply been building in her for a while and had now peaked at an inconvenient time? Or was she ovulating, her body demanding she inject it with semen?

Whichever it was, she was impossibly horny.

They toweled off. Impatient to get started, she dragged Radio back into the bedroom, pulled him down into her soft embrace on the soft, soft bed. Began kissing him passionately. He responded in kind, his hands roving over her body, arousing her even more, stoking up the fire in her flesh. Flesh against flesh, his hard penis stabbing into her belly.

She pulled her lips off his. "Make love to me."

He looked at her, desire and worry in his eyes. "I don't want to leave you unsatisfied again."

She winced at that; then pushed away the memory of all their—of all *her*—previous failures in bed. "The handbag's full of vibrators. I want us to try them; maybe they'll break the curse. Here, outside of Metaphor, sex may work again."

He looked at her intently, concerned with shielding her from another disappointment. She nodded. "Let's do it, baby. I've got to come soon or I'll die."

He spread the bag open, spread its contents out on the bed. Courtney picked out two vibrators, the white cordless Magic Wand and a shiny silver phallus. Almost as if Angel Weiner kept her sex toys ready for every contingency, both vibrators had fully charged batteries.

Radio kissed her ear. "How d'you want us to try it?"

"Suck my breasts while I masturbate," she said. The floral perfume was heavy in the room, thick and aphrodisiac. Courtney really felt she might make it here and now.

He laughed. "A vibrator is truly a guy's best friend."

He lay beside her, caressing her body. Courtney masturbated with the toys. Despite his own clearly visible passion, Radio made no attempt to penetrate her.

She slipped the smaller vibrator into her sex, let the Magic Wand buzz against her clitoris. It throbbed in her crotch like a second heart, one that pumped electricity, not blood. Like heating water, she simmered then almost boiled, her crotch seemed to be melting around the sex toy. Radio knelt over her, dropping his lips onto her stiff nipples and sucking at first gently, then slowly harder. She felt his mouth on her breasts like it was far away, a disjointed sensation that had her floating over herself. He licked and sucked on, squeezing her breasts while she pleasured herself, moving his lips to suck at her throat as her pleasure built.

She could feel her orgasm near, almost see it even, hovering like a watching ghost. A bound unhappy ghost stretching gaseous fingers toward her. Despite the intensity of the pleasure ravaging her body, like her every nerve was on fire, she couldn't reach its hands, those hands that longed to grasp her and smother her in climactic cooling waters.

She floated on a plateau of flawed eroticism. She was a queen ruling over a realm of unsatisfactory sensation.

Courtney's pleasure now altered into frustration. There was no gradual change; abruptly her physical joy inverted into its own dark sister. Her fall from grace to grass, from ecstasy to agony, began.

After a while she rolled onto her left side. Radio gripped her from behind, spooning, his body warm and complimentary to hers. She felt his penis throbbing between her buttocks. Its location filled her with a momentary rush of fear; her anus had suffered terrible abuse at the hands of the communists. She corked the bottle of her fear: she wasn't in Vaginismus any longer, she was here with Radio, who she knew loved her, why then fear? She concentrated again on her feelings, imagined the throbbing cock was the gearshift to a car, moved one hand back to grab it, fantasized she was driving Radio—driving him out of his mind with pleasure . . .

It was no good—his hands on her sweaty skin, his mouth kissing her neck and back, the vibrators pleasuring her sex, the sensuous romantic aroma of the flowers . . . everything failed. In her mind's eyes, her climax turned from a ghost of ecstasy trying to touch her into a terrified fugitive fleeing from her clutches, a phantasm of satisfaction she'd clearly never catch. The more her body reached for that peak of crowning physical glory, the further away it got from her, the farther down she fell. Her body felt like it was running on one G-spot, the point of no return, the nerves of her vagina overloading into a black hole that sucked away the anticipated honey, leaving her with nothing, just an agonized hellish burning in her flesh.

And finally, it was gone for good. She was left bereft, a once-grassy plain scorched and barren of life, her erotic delight become disgust, her previous promise of joy now nothing but the most horrible disappointment and pain of desolation.

She slumped defeated; let go of her sex toys and burst out crying, weeping fiercely out her anger, her fists first pressed tight to her face, then beating hard on the bed sheets. The tears ran cold and long down her cheeks.

"Shit," she groaned through her tears. "This is way worse than female circumcision. The better it gets, the worse it gets."

Radio frowned. This had been a bad idea from the get-go, particularly after the horrible day they'd all had. But just like she, he'd *hoped*, hoped that Courtney might experience a breakthrough, might finally be able to make it again.

He tried to turn her towards him. She first resisted, then gave in grudgingly and let him hold her close, his now limp penis pressed against her pubic hair. She felt horrible now, utterly horrible; worse than ever before even. At first it had seemed like tonight, here in this greenhouse, she'd achieve sexual release. But now, feeling her sexual neurons firing insanely, her clitoris inflamed, her vagina dripping like it was bleeding desire that would never be satisfied, it was too much. She felt practically suicidal.

"We'll find Dr. Orgasm," Radio said gently. "Once you take an O-pill, you'll be fine."

Courtney kept crying against him, drenching his chest with her sorrow. "Will we? Will we? And even if we do, will her damn miracle pill do me any good?" The way she felt now, she doubted anything could save her.

And she really needed saving: Now, just as after every other time she'd had sex since being held captive in Vaginismus she felt so used up, so desolate. Utterly incomplete without her orgasm, once something she'd so blithely taken entirely for granted.

CHAPTER 18

Highball jerked awake suddenly. Had she heard a sound?

She leaned out of her chair to look around. "Jeff, is it you?"

No reply. No one was top deck with her. She realized she'd dropped asleep while watching the heavens for attackers. She squinted up through the greenhouse roof. "Some great sentinel I am."

The glass train was still in motion, the throb of its silent engines like the heartbeat of the night.

Highball yawned, realized she was utterly, ridiculously even, tired out. She got up and walked rearward between flanking trees. A momentary thought brought a grin: *I wonder how Courtney and Radio made out with the toys.* Then: *I need a bedroom myself—my body feels like lead!*

Pausing with one hand on the railing of the middle stairway, she considered descending to the cockpit to go check on Jeff. Another deep yawn convinced her otherwise; she needed to sleep. A glance at a clock hanging from the dwarf cherry tree near the stairs confirmed to her that finding a bed was currently her smartest course of action: it was two a.m. Besides which . . . the stairs were shifting in and out of focus as she stared at them. No point breaking her neck.

She staggered her way further back.

The first door was unlocked. She pushed it open, caught a glimpse of outlined white skin on the bed amidst the plants. Heard voices. Courtney and Radio, or was it Teresa and Matt? Then she heard agonized weeping—that meant it was Courtney. *Shit, the vibes didn't work?*

She silently shut the door and moved to the next. This bedroom was empty. Not bothering to undress, Highball got into the soft bed and lay on her back staring up at the night sky through a web of hanging multicolored orchids. The flowers' scent was heady perfume, she felt it caress her emotions, fading the past day's memories.

To her surprise, Highball didn't instantly fall asleep again. Watching the night pass her by in the minutes before the bliss of unconsciousness reclaimed her, her mind filled with groggy thoughts, dreamy recollections triggered by the floating gray shapes of Innuendo's nighttime clouds:

One evening about a year ago, she and Radio had visited Matt and Teresa at home and had met Chief Oldfield and Angel Weiner there.

From their initial City Defense discussion of new ways of detecting and combating Florence Rigid's communists and Bee swarm, the conversation had turned to one about the nature of Innuendo and the universe.

"Innuendo is part of Bizarro," Oldfield had said, "that strange wonderful realm where everything is possible; where everything impossible elsewhere exists in some form or other." He'd smiled sadly: "My world was nothing like this. Life there made logical sense. Well, it used to before OD's—space-time portals—began opening up everywhere."

The others present had listened, then agreed and disagreed. Most of the disagreement centered around the definition of 'logical sense,' with everyone else present other than the chief being adamant that Innuendo was a completely 'logical' realm to live in.

But now, as Highball finally slipped away into sleep, she found herself wondering. *Is Innuendo really just a part of Bizarro, one just currently going through a bad patch? I mean we all went through hell yesterday, murder and destruction, our lives destroyed before our very eyes.* She shivered a little as her eyes slowly lost focus on the sky. *Maybe there are different sorts of Hells,* she postulated. *Maybe Hell is as much a concept of existence as it's a place of eternal suffering. Determined by that definition, Innuendo, simply by being residence of the sort of horrors the communists perpetuate, is definitely Hell, whether or not Lucifer lives next door.*

CHAPTER 19

Teresa Pollack sat musing on the toilet. For all intents and purposes, she could just as well have been taking a dump out in the bushes: sweet-smelling shrubs hemmed in the porcelain bowl, while flowering vines hung overhead like Christmas decorations.

Black lace panties down around her ankles, Teresa regarded her tattooed feet a moment. She loved tattoos: In addition to stars on both feet, a heart on her inner right ankle, and a cute cat on her inner left ankle, and lines and squiggles . . . she currently had the first six digits of Pi inked on her right foot. She intended to keep on with the incompletable sequence, adding on a few more numbers at a time in a rising spiral that reached all the way up her right leg. She giggled. Maybe she'd stop it at her anus—fundament to fundament, circle to circle.

She reached for the toilet roll, her eyes rising to consider her other ink art as she did so. *Wow!* She admired those she could see. She had a trio of stars on her left wrist, pretty black birds over both breasts, an intricate butterfly/city motif on her sternum, another much larger sinister butterfly/skull meld between her shoulder blades, a sacred heart on her left shoulder blade, a Zelda Tri-Force marking on her right shoulder blade, and inked all the way down her right side, her favorite—a large spooky skeletal girl in black lingerie sitting in a graveyard by a tombstone engraved with the inscription 'RIP JINX.' Her lower back piece was a large lily wrapped in laurel leaves between two Blood-for-Blood skulls.

She paused a while to wipe clean, then laughed depreciatively at herself. *Yeah, I'm a rock chick alright; got the look down pat.* Her gaze shifted to her pierced nipples with their stainless steel rings—those felt truly great when Matt suckled on them during sex. (No sex tonight though: Matt was fagged out; and he shortly had to take over driving from Jeff.)

Her eyes lingered a moment on the green inkings on her lower belly (her only colored tattoos, all the others were done in black ink): Two woven cords of clover stems . . . thirteen on each side, trailing down to a four leaf clover over her Brazilian-waxed vagina. She giggled at the pink slit. *Pussy got the name 'cos it's usually hairy right? Thanks, Brazil.*

She dumped the browned toilet roll, got up, flushed, pulled up her panties again. (Teresa found it amazing—no, ri-cock-ulous—the sort of shit the human body came up with, always brown and stinky, no matter how diversified and aromatic the meals that originally comprised it had been, as though the flesh really was the factory of corruption churches claimed it was.)

She opened the toilet door and stepped out into the street. It was a warm summer midmorning, so it didn't matter that she had just underwear and a tank top on. Her AG, a maroon red Jeep Cherokee, was parked by the roadside.

After a moments reflection on how she'd forgotten her handbag and credit cards again, she decided she didn't need them anyway today, and got into the car and started it up.

Before driving off, she checked herself out in the sun visor mirror: The familiar face stared back. Pointy nose, gauged ears (two tattoos behind those—exclamation point behind her right ear, three stars behind the left; she *loved* stars!). Yeah and that skin dark as a Nepalese princess's. *I'm an exotic blend of feminity*, she thought. Her heritage was Eastern European: half Czech and half . . . the other fifty percent of her gene pool was equally split between Lebanese and mongrel ancestry.

Her hair was black. Not the Asian/Native American kind of black that had a nearly blue sheen to it, but rather the Negro/Arab/Latino type of black hair; and it was damn long as well.

Her eyes were dark too, almost black themselves, but after staring awhile, maybe for too long, you'd conclude they were simply the darkest brown imaginable. She also had Polycoria—two pupils—in her left eye, normally a rare condition in dark-eyed people. (She could only actually see out of one of the pupils, but there were most definitely two holes in her iris. Neither pupil was dead in the center, either; the extra one was very little and to the lower left of the large, functional one.) She shrugged. She'd gotten used to it. The doctors had told her she was lucky, the condition sometimes caused blindness.

A sudden sense of urgency possessed her. Wondering why she was spending so much time admiring herself, she flipped the sun visor back up. *I've gotta be somewhere now, right? Before the fucking day burns through, right?*

What was her rush? Something about a phone call? No way to be sure though—she'd left her cellphone back in the bedroom with Matt. And that's if she'd even get a signal anyway, what with the fucking communists bombing Metaphor today. Fuck!

Driving off from there, her gaze shifted from the road up ahead to her left forearm. To the faint grouping of dots on her milk-chocolate skin, now being erased by time. Vestiges of the bad smack habit she'd had for a year or so.

She shuddered from the memory of that time of dark cravings, when heroin addiction had squeezed her soul and body like she was a tube of paste. Dark streets, shady dealers, shooting up 'cos if you didn't set that liquid horse free to gallop through your veins, your anxiety and depression would ride roughshod over you in its place. It was six of one or half a dozen of the other. Either way, for Teresa, being hooked on smack had been a lose-lose deal.

Her fingers lifted to her neck, the unconscious action freeing her from those grim recollections. Feeling the faint bruises on her throat made her grin a bit from memories of fucking Matt. She stroked the faint rednesses like they were lovers, and of course in a way they were. Even just the memory—oops she was getting wet . . . She giggled— Ha ha ha!—recalling the look on Matt's handsome face the first time she'd asked him to choke her during sex . . .

But she was getting distracted again; any more of this and she'd start masturbating right here in the car. And she had to be somewhere else, didn't she? It was fucking important that she saw something . . . or was it someone? Saw someone . . . or was that *become* someone?

She drove, smoothly navigating her AG between houses, then past the large open spaces between those. Faithville here was just a little place down in southern Innuendo, lying right in the shadow of the Moral Mountains.

Fingers tapping the steering wheel, other thoughts flittered through her brain: Her procession of violent boyfriends, lots of them while she was doing smack. Nah, that wasn't much of an excuse, the guys were just violent shitheads . . . Being beaten bloody for smart-mouthing someone or for not saying anything at all. It seemed violent men simply needed an outlet, and she'd provided a convenient focus for their rage, rage that was sometimes simply their inability to communicate their hatred to a universe that didn't give a rat's ass about them.

Teresa shuddered. Thankfully, that stage of her life was long past, her demons—both narcotic and male—successfully exorcised. She'd done it: She'd kicked the drugs out of her life and Matt had come back into it. She was married to Matt now, and he loved her. She'd even gotten him 'hooked' on choking her during lovemaking.

Laughing, she drove between two huge blue rabbits, the one on her left munching a carrot bigger than herself. The rabbit that didn't have a carrot started hopping towards her Jeep. She floored the pedal; no point in waiting around to find out how strong its teeth were, or if it thought human flesh was a good substitute for vegetables.

There weren't too many people or cars on the road, and soon she was there: Gran Pollack's house.

Now it got confusing in her head. She couldn't stop—she had to drive on farther down the road to Granddad's shop, needed to inform him a guy had been stabbed. Who? Oh yeah, that was Gran's next door neighbor Richie Kisner, wasn't it? Yeah, Richie. Either his girlfriend was cheating on him, or was he cheating with someone else's girl? Cause didn't matter, only the effect did: Richie had been stabbed thirty-eight times by the other guy. Teresa winced. Yeah, that pissed-off motherfucker ripped his chest open with the fucking knife, then stabbed him in the genitals too several times for good measure, likely to ensure he'd never fuck anyone again. Even without a penis of her own, Teresa winced in sympathy: Shit, that was just plain nasty—you've already killed the guy for sure, why damage his dick too? It's not like he'd be using in the afterlife.

She was just passing the house now, could already see Richie stabbed to bits and bleeding away his life on Gran's front porch, and little Teresa Pollack was there too; looked like the girl was holding Richie's hand. And Teresa's dad Chuck was running up the drive towards them.

Okay, I'll just turn in here, maybe this time we'll get Richie to hospital before he dies on us . . .

But her damn car wouldn't stop . . . it just kept speeding on.

(Up ahead, where the road wended through a meadow, were a flock of blue rabbits . . . over and behind those, Dr. Orgasm's pink shoeplane puffed out vagina-shaped exhaust clouds and the slogan 'Fuck and Come, Girls; Never Settle for Less than the Best!')

But Teresa just had to see what was happening on that porch. Only one way to do that . . . *Fuck, I gotta be younger again? This age-regression thing's cramping my style.*

But . . . a moment later, there she was: Eleven years old again and back kneeling on the porch, and Richie was holding her hand and bleeding from chest and crotch. His chest looked like a red pincushion. He was gurgling blood everywhere. She was confused, her young mind expecting 911 to get here quicker. Behind her, the screen door was soaked with blood. Inside the house, Grandma Ann was still having hysterics.

Looking up from Richie's tortured face, she was relieved to see Dad climbing the sixteen porch steps. (Richie had already bled all over them on his way up). Beyond Dad, Teresa saw her older self driving along the road, looking in towards the porch where Richie lay dying. It was odd; she knew the red Jeep wouldn't . . . no, couldn't . . . stop here— something about it being impossible for two versions of her to be in the same place at the same time—so her older version would keep driving past the murder, always wanting to stop and help the past, but unable to; but still, holding it in mind...

"Pleeeeeaaaasssse!" Richie gurgled, forcing Teresa to forget the future and gaze back down at him. She had no idea what he wanted, so she just wiped his forehead and said, "You'll be okay, everything will be fine. Just hold on, help is coming . . ."

Then Dad was up on the porch. She could smell the drink on him, but his usually sad eyes were real worried now. Seeing how punctured Richie was, Daddy's military training kicked in and he ripped Richie's shirt off and literally dug his hands into Richie's chest trying to prevent him from choking to death on his own blood. (She knew stuff like this was one reason Dad drank so much—in the army he'd seen more gore than he cared to remember. She was also glad he didn't beat her and her brothers when he drank; not like several of her friends at school who got regular alcohol-inspired ass-whippings.)

Meanwhile, inside the house, Grandma Ann was still freaking out. Her voice rose and fell in cadence like a church organ.

Watching Dad with his hands inside Richie's chest, all red now as he tried to drain Richie's lungs, Teresa was puzzled, wondering why the EMTs hadn't yet shown up like they always did on TV, though she figured part of the reason everyone on TV was always punctual was because each program aired at fixed hours and if you weren't on time, the audience wouldn't get to see you. So for instance, the ambulance couldn't afford to be late then 'cos the drivers wanted their face-time, right?

"Teresa," Dad said.

"Yes, Daddy?"

He looked at her hard, his face saying this wasn't the kind of shit he wanted his eleven-year-old kid involved in. "Go wash your hands at the spigot and get inside with Gran, okay? I'll handle it from here."

She nodded, stared once more at Richie (whose eyes were dull and out of focus now) and left them. Heading over the grass to the spigot, she saw in the far distance a monster blue rabbit eating a red Cherokee Jeep. Teresa winced. *Oops, the Big Bad Blue Bunnies caught Future Me again?*

Still wincing, she turned the tap and washed her hands.

Then suddenly she felt a painful cramp in her belly. She shut off the water again and dashed into the house, racing for the toilet.

Grandma Ann still looked traumatized. She was standing in the center of the living room, liver-spotted hands clasped over her breasts in an attitude of prayer, her tearful gaze cast ceiling-ward, mouthing silently to God.

Teresa dashed past the old woman. *Oops, it's happening again. Gotta run, gotta run . . . !*

She made it to the toilet just in time. Slipped down her shorts, sat. As her bum touched the warm plastic seat, the even warmer poop slipped out into the water.

No, she knew, I'm not scared shitless. *It's just . . .*

She grew up rapidly on the toilet. Each turd she ejected felt like two years dropping away from her—like she was shitting out the past. Soon she was older, much older, and also had to take out a tampon first; then she was older still and worriedly peeing over a home pregnancy test strip; and then . . .

And all the while she was emptying her bowels, trees and vines were growing around her in the toilet like they were using her feces as fertilizer, and the day was getting way darker.

Finally, it was tonight again, and she was here in the greenhouse, with the stars overhead and herbal scent everywhere.

The past hadn't exactly been fun to visit again. Teresa wiped, got off the can, and made her way back into the bedroom where Matt was still fast asleep.

As she climbed back in beside her husband, one last memory played in her head:

After the cops had taken Richie's corpse away, she'd had to mop all the blood off the porch (and while doing so, prevent her dog Tug from helping her out with its tongue.) At eleven years old, she'd found that real odd: she'd always assumed the cops took care of cleaning up when someone died. Like the spilled blood belonged to the county now, just like the corpse did.

CHAPTER 20

Morning visited and entered.

Jeff woke up, sat up in bed. After dusting the first cobwebs from his mind, he turned to his left and grinned down at Highball, who was still fast asleep. With her red hair spread out over the pillow like a starfish turning to silk threads, and her mouth partly open, she looked touchingly beautiful in her slumber. Like himself, she'd fallen asleep fully dressed.

He turned from staring at her. Yawning softly, he peered out through the hanging leaves that served for drapes in this transparent vehicle. It was fully light already, the sun risen in the distance. The landscape rolled past smoothly, mostly building-sized mushrooms, with the occasional (and even larger) rabbit or frog or kangaroo hopping along in the distance.

Seeing the huge animals, Jeff felt a tinge of fright at the convoy's vulnerability while traversing Route Zero. It wasn't that the greenhouses didn't carry enough artillery to level a city . . . it was that . . . being a trucker meant Jeff had seen all sorts of weird things as he ferried stuff between Innuendo's cities. No shit. The danger of places like this (he reckoned they must be deep in the Dreamfields by now) wasn't so much that you couldn't fight off danger; it was more that you simply didn't expect what form the danger would take. A frontal attack was easy to defend against—here, surprise was the enemy.

He gazed out once at a distant two-headed six-legged giraffe that had to be at least sixty feet high, then his attention was caught by something else beyond the giraffe, high over the building-like mushrooms: A momentary rent in the clouds through which seeped— it honestly looked to Jeff like an asshole voiding shit—long brown clouds.

Bizarro, he realized. *The corrupting influence of the world.*

The rent sealed up. The excrement-like clouds remained, expanding brazenly into the placid morning. They broke apart into chunks which floated off in different directions, some to fall as the Weird Rain, some to simply corrupt other clouds into versions of themselves.

And, if the scientists are to be believed, also corrupting the very air we're all breathing, Jeff thought, carefully swinging his legs out of bed so as not to wake Highball. His feet hit the floor. He got up, shrugged at the view. *Nothing any of us can do about that. This is Bizarro . . . so . . .*

He needed to pee, he headed for the toilet.

Inside, he examined himself in the mirror while unzipping his pants. Jeff knew he was handsome. *Yeah, man, you're good-looking; at least enough chicks think so. It's just this tiny dick of yours which—*

Jeff suddenly realized that the penis he'd just pulled out his pants felt odd. Startled, he looked down at it. Then he forgot about pissing.

There was no doubt about it. His penis was noticeably bigger. Jeff kept gaping at the organ. *Dr. Brentwood's enlargement pills worked? They fucking worked. THEY WORKED! THEY WORKED!!!*

Almost going out of his mind with delight, Jeff attempted to measure the increase in his member. He pulled the organ out to its full length, then, when that proved unsatisfactory, quickly stroked himself to erection.

That done, he grinned broadly. Yes, he'd grown at least two-and-a-half inches overnight—he had to be about six-and-a-half inches in length now. And his cock was also noticeably thicker, not overly so, but he could see it.

The only side effect he noticed was that he now had more pubic hair than before. Both thicker, and with a wider spread. His scrotum was also hairier.

A happy warmth suffused him. Oh yes, *Highball is going to utterly LOVE me now. Hmmm, I could stop here, what with me having no way to contact the doc if anything goes wrong.* Then he sobered: *But . . . but is six inches enough to satisfy a beautiful hot-blooded woman? Definitely not. I need a lot more cock to tame that thoroughbred filly of mine. I mean, just imagine the shock in her eyes when I actually FILL her.*

Jeff's bladder interrupted his thoughts then. He peed while dancing on the spot, rapturous in his delight.

"Hey, baby, you okay?"

Jeff froze, looked over his shoulder. Highball stood in the doorway, wiping bleary eyes.

"Morning water, baby." Jeff quickly shook his member dry and packed it away. *No need for her to see it just yet,* he figured. He zipped up, then pointed to the bowl. "You want to pee too before I flush?"

She shook her head. "I just woke and you weren't by my side. So I came . . ." She looked at him curiously. "You sure you're okay, baby? The way you were dancing just now . . . ?"

Jeff reddened, walked over to take her in his arms. "My butt was itching." He pushed a red veil of hair away off her lips and kissed her. She yielded like chocolate melting on his tongue.

Oh, Highball, Jeff thought, *I really, really love you. More than you'd ever believe if I told you. And I know you'll soon love me too as much as I love you.*

They broke apart. "I love you baby."

"I love you too."

She pulled him towards the bed. "I've still got cotton wool between my ears, and my bones all ache." She winced. "Yesterday was an utter nightmare." She sat on the edge of the bed. "When did Matt relieve you?"

Jeff remembered he was tired. "About three." Opposite the foot of the bed, a clock dangled like a mechanical fruit from a tree branch. Jeff stared at it. "It's just six now. I'm relieving him again at nine—we're doing six-hour shifts. Radio too. I'm not sure if either Heather or Miki can drive this beast, but if they can we'll reduce the shifts to maybe four hours each."

"How interesting," Highball said in a completely disinterested tone of voice. Still fully clothed, she lay back in bed and stretched out her arms to him.

He licked his lips, pumped his crotch at her.

She shook her head. "Oh no. Not now, stud. Later, next time you're off-shift. Jeff, please just get into bed and hold me. Kiss and pet me. But absolutely no sex; I'm so not in the mood this morning."

Jeff grinned. "Okay." He pulled out his bottle of penis-enhancement pills, shook two of the blue lozenges into his palm, then popped them into his mouth and swallowed.

Highball watched him narrowly; he waved off her questioning gaze. "Just vitamins, baby. You've absolutely no idea how well these ones work."

She nodded. "Oh, goody. I need a pick-me-up. Can I have one?"

He shook his head regretfully. "Men only; unless you want to grow a beard."

"Ugh!" Then her expression turned even more suspicious. "Baby, you're not treating an STD, are you? Because if you've been screwing around on me, I'll fucking kill you. I mean it."

Jeff laughed and lay down beside Highball. "Darling, I assure you on my honor that my penis feels better than ever." He kissed her soft yielding lips again, stroked her clothed nipples. "And later today, you'll feel it too, harder than ever before."

She tingled under his caresses. "Oh, whatever. Let's cuddle," then she shook a warning finger at him, "But remember—no sticking it in me."

Jeff grinned and pulled her close, wrapped her up in his muscular arms. "Oh, I'm in no hurry now, baby. No hurry at all."

CHAPTER 21

Heather Bowen woke up to the sensation of something warm worming its way into her vagina. Next, a soft pleasant feeling enveloped her groin. The warmth increased till she was squirming.

She opened her eyes. Miki was between her legs, performing cunnilingus on her.

She didn't speak, she was still fagged and the scenario had the elements of a dream to it—Miki's shiny blue hair swirling back and forth across her waist as her delicious tongue labored in Heather's crotch. Then Miki's fingers went to work in her sex too, the feeling pure pleasure. Heather lay there, her legs spread and bent at the knees, staring up, out through the vine-latticed glass ceiling at the blue morning sky.

Without realizing it, she began groaning as the pleasure lifted her up on bird-like wings. She soared.

Miki looked up at the sounds and saw Heather was awake. She paused the motion of her penetrating fingers in the wet vagina for a moment and grinned.

"Happy birthday, darling."

Heather stared down between her breasts in shock. (From her viewpoint, Miki's face looked like a blue-haloed sun rising over brown-tipped hills of white flesh.) It *was* her birthday! Today she was twenty-six.

She groaned. "Shit! In all yesterday's activity I plumb forgot!"

"Good thing I didn't." Miki dropped her mouth back down between Heather's thighs and the pleasure resumed. Her tongue flicked the clitoris; her fingers resumed their languid in/out movements into the roseate vagina.

Heather relaxed and went with the flow. She felt so, so tired; the sensation coming from her sex was practically anesthetic. She spread her thighs wider and pushed up her hips to meet Miki's tongue. Her hands traced contours on the sheets, circling back and forth, then they slid down and grabbed bunches of Miki's hair. She yanked on its thready blue silk, let it slip through her fingers like water.

Miki increased the speed of her fingering, stabbing the spread cunt fiercely while her mouth sucked lustily on Heather's swollen sex bud.

"Oh fuck!" Heather gasped. A rush of heat consumed her. Fire streamed from her vagina down her legs to her toes; rushed up through her belly and filled her breasts; squirted from her nipples like invisible milk. Yesterday's tension and today's feeling merged into sensation overload. Feeling like she was melting into the bed, she came. She jerked, she flailed, she surged through herself in torrents.

Once Heather began her climax, Miki stopped fingering her and rubbed Heather's clitoris fiercely, sliding her fingers back and forth over the wet knob. Heather quivered on the bed like a cut worm. Still rubbing her sex, Miki slid up her body and began sucking her nipples, left-right-left-right-left-right . . .

"You're fucking killing me!" Heather screamed, then went limp.

Miki kept rubbing her clitoris. Heather stared at the sky through orgasm-blurred eyes. Her body felt liquid now, scattered everywhere like droplets of dew.

Miki kissed her. She smelt her vagina sweet on her wife's lips, the odor reversing up through her mouth into her nose, up further into her brain. It was an intoxicating stink. She raised weak arms and clutched Miki, hugged her like she'd never let her go. Soft lips pressed against other soft lips. Her crotch tingled in afterglow as the raging rapids of her lust again became a calm brook, one lit by sunbeams of pleasure.

Their mouths parted.

"Happy twenty-sixth birthday, darling."

"Holy shit!" Heather gasped back. "That was too, too fucking much."

Miki grinned. "It's too bad, though—the stripper I hired couldn't make it."

Heather laughed. "I didn't miss him. Besides, there's always next year." She pulled Miki close again and they kissed, their indistinguishable blue hair tangling, till they seemed a beast with a single head.

***

Once, while out on City Defense patrol, Heather and Miki Bowen had gotten caught in the Weird Rain.

It had been noon of a lovely sunny day. Driving through fields of fragrant blossoms had gotten both Miki and Heather aroused, and once certain there were no monsters close by, they'd parked their AG transport under the crown of a giant blue toadstool, stripped naked, and begun making passionate love on the vehicle's rear seat.

(Back then, Heather Bowen had been a brunette, while Miki Shimada, being Japanese, had glossy black hair that hung halfway down her back.)

They'd fucked each other good and long, their bodies synchronized that day into sapphic engines of pleasure. Both girlfriends had had several orgasms, then they'd just lain there, Miki (who weighed less than the big-boned Heather) on top.

(Metaphor was visible in the distance, an architect's outline of a city.)

Between kisses, they'd planned their upcoming wedding, trying to work out how to not invite Courtney Taylor (who, for some reason Heather didn't understand, Miki loathed), while inviting her boyfriend Radio (who they both adored). Radio would be coming for certain anyway, as he was their coordinator Matt's bestie.

"So, tell me: *why don't* you like her?" Heather probed while enjoying Miki's weight on her body, like her girlfriend was a shield from the world's pain, one keeping her in love's cool shadow, just like the toadstool crown overhead blocked out the sun's rays.

"She's creepy-like . . . well, you know. I can't put my finger on it, but she's so *ugh*!"

Heather kissed her. Miki's lips were small, but perfect. Along with her almost triangular face and almond Asian eyes they gave her an exotic beauty.

Their tongues twined awhile, then separated. Heather said, "Baby, you sound like you had the college hots for the chick and she rebuffed you." Then her eyes widened. "Hey! Or were you in love with Radio and you're pissed that he chose her over you?"

Miki grimaced. "Radio hardly feels any emotion. That's why Courtney likes him—he can't *see* how creepy she is."

"You know you just dodged answering me, right? Are you jealous of Courtney?"

"Fuck her." Miki was tight-faced.

Heather slipped a hand between their pressed groins, stroked Miki's clitoris. "How about *you* just fuck *me* instead, baby. Your gorgeously hot body turns me on no end. I can't wait till you're officially legally mine 24/7."

"I'm already yours 24/7."

"Nah, you could run off tomorrow—maybe if Radio dumps Creepy Girl for you." She winced as Miki bit her on the shoulder. "Stop it— I'm just joking." Her eyes turned sober. "It's odd though, deny it all you like, there's just something about being married that beats the girlfriend–girlfriend game. Like wet cement setting hard."

Miki laughed. "Like wet cement setting? That's how you view it? Darling, marriage is an asylum; who the hell wants to be in an asylum?"

Heather kissed her again. "Both of us do. We're human; creatures of society. Two weeks from now we both intend locking each other in ball-and-chain and—"

"Damn, you're scaring me now. You make it sound so morbid. I'm not even sure I want to get—"

"Shut up," Heather said tartly, digging two fingers deep up into Miki's cunt, and jerking them in and out to ensure Miki did indeed keep quiet.

(Heather Bowen wasn't interested in Miki Shimada going on any pseudo-feminist anti-nuptial rant here. She didn't believe that crap anyway. Her reasoning was simple: if marriage between men and women was enslavement of women, the same logic had to apply to marriages between just women, or just men: it meant one of the pair was enslaving the other, or both were enslaving themselves . . . which made no sense . . . or maybe each spouse enslaving the other *was* the whole point of wedlock. Wed . . . *lock*? Duh? That meant you were either being locked in/up with the other person, or you were locking them up, or they were locking you up! Heather LOVED the concept of marriage, the idea of its sanctity, the concept of having each other as one another's personal property [something she never voiced out], loved the idea of that flimsy bond of a paper contract and a gold ring that it would nonetheless take a judge's oxyacetylene torch to melt through. She wanted Miki to herself. Period. Eschewing all other horny little tight-asses who'd like to snatch her snatch away from her. Heather Bowen would have happily married a guy; she'd just not met any she liked as much as she liked her pretty little Japanese fiancée.)

She forgot the argument and just made love to her girlfriend again in the sixty-nine position, enjoyed the sweet feeling of fingers and mouth and tongue on her gaping wet cunt (enjoying also the salty tang of Miki's equally wet cunt), while slobbering sensation devoured her like a pack of hungry leopards.

It was while gasping loudly through her fifth or sixth orgasm (she'd quickly lost count) that she'd noticed the distant sky split and the shit-like clouds spurt through.

Feeling like she was dissolving as Miki expertly stroked her, she enjoyed her orgasm to the fullest. There was no danger, the Bizarro clouds were far off. Even broken apart, they were blowing away from she and Miki, and if they did float over this way, the toadstool's crown would prevent any cloudfall hitting them.

She been wrong in this last. As she and Miki later worked out, there'd been not one, but *two* 'sky-rips,' the second of these close-by and obscured by the toadstool's bulk. A freak wind must have blown one of the Bizarro clouds down low, and smashed it into the side of the fungus's stalk. The cloud split in two, with some of its fragments being whipped by wind right around the toadstool's side towards the lovers.

Heather's head had been wagging between Miki's thighs when the brown fragments covered them. Realizing what had happened, they'd both leapt up in the back seat, horrified. By then, though, the brown fluff had been absorbed into their skins. They sat down, holding hands, watching the two halves of the shattered Bizarro cloud blow away across the flower fields.

"We're fucked," Miki said, not looking at Heather. "The Weird Rain fell on us!" She began weeping. "I don't want to turn into a monster! You won't love me then!"

Heather was more pragmatic. "I don't feel any different," she said, reaching out to comfort Miki. "It might not be as—"

Miki was now looking at her. "What? Why'd you stop talking?" Panic leapt into the Japanese girl's eyes. "What's wrong with me!"

"Your hair! It's turned all blue!"

"Shit! Yours has too!"

"Damn, our pussy hair's blue too, and our armpits."

"And our eyebrows. But were not monsters, are we? I don't have extra eyes or noses anywhere, do I?"

"No, no, darling. Do I? Do I? Tell me—am I fucking okay too?"

"Yes, yes, yes, yes! Yippee!!!"

Impossibly relieved by their unexpected let-off, the pair clasped tight and began kissing again.

Finally they separated and dressed hastily. Then both newly blue-haired women drove back to Metaphor as fast as they could.

***

Now, Heather slowly came to her senses again, feeling her body solidify back from seeming liquidity. She had scant respite however:

Grinning, Miki pinched her left nipple. "Roll over; get on your hands and knees."

"Uh, uh," Heather protested. "I'm good for now." She made to sit up. "It's your turn."

Miki pushed her back down. "Be selfish this morning, darling. It's your birthday. Your total satisfaction is all I can give you as a present."

"Don't be silly, baby; just having you mine is the only present I'll ever need. Being married to you is like having Christmas Day every day."

Miki kissed Heather, then tapped her on her shoulder. "Get on your hands and knees anyway."

Heather assumed the position. "You sure you don't want us to do it sixty-nine?"

"No, darling. Just lean your head down on the pillow, close your eyes, and relax while I get you off again." She giggled. "I know I'm gonna get off just from eating you, girl, you're sweeter than honey."

Heather did as she was told. Facing out of the bedroom, towards the greenhouse wall, she lowered her head between her arms. Shut her eyes. Waited, her every sexual neuron tingling with anticipation.

She felt Miki's fingers spread her buttocks, then wet fingers slipping over them into her sex. Then Miki's tongue touched her anus and stars exploded in her brain. *Oh, oh, oh, oh!* The room's floral fragrances sat in her mind like alcohol.

Miki's fingers glided in and out of her, stroking her deep. Her body quivered, her legs trembled. She felt weak but exalted. All her energy was concentrated in her anus like she'd shit it out; Miki's mouth on her anus felt like a leech sucking it out of her. The fingers sliding in and out of her vagina moved faster, jabbed her deeper. And Miki's other thumb was rubbing her clitoris.

Miki licked her buttocks one after the other. Heather's thigh muscles clenched tight as fists. She grabbed handfuls of pillow and groaned. Her groaning grew higher in pitch and volume, ending as a loud sequence of senseless noises, a frog hymn in praise of the joys of the flesh.

Miki's tongue moved back to her anus, then down to suck at the soaking vagina. Heather's eyes jerked open as she was penetrated by first tongue, then three fingers at once, the digits sliding back and forth like transports to nirvana. The other hand kept working over her clitoris. Miki shook her mouth back and forth between Heather buttocks; faster and faster.

"Oh, holy fuck, I love you!" Heather groaned as her orgasm hit her. She was trembling now like she'd shatter; her limbs almost giving out beneath her.

Miki raised wet lips from between Heather's buttocks and beamed. "Happy birthday, darling. This one's all for you." Then she submerged herself between the white globes of flesh again and resumed licking the bared wet ass hole, her tongue swiping it up and down.

Heather's limbs gave out. Panting hard, she collapsed; lay flat like a human pancake. Panting equally hard, Miki collapsed on top of her. They lay like two starfish staring out of the vine-draped glass at the passing day.

"Happy birthday once again, darling," Miki said, kissing Heather's left ear, grinding her sopping crotch over her wife's buttocks. "Many happy returns of the day."

"This was the best birthday gift ever," Heather gasped when she'd got some breath back. "Literally the best ever."

Miki grinned. "And it'll be even better in the years to come."

They lay like that, happy and loving each other, till they felt it was time to go join the others for breakfast.

CHAPTER 22
10:30 a.m.

On Miki's request, Teresa was baking a surprise birthday cake for Heather. She was alone in the kitchen. Except for Jeff who was now back at the wheel, all the others were outside, seated around the downstairs dining table (which had since yesterday become their informal communal center).

The kitchen door was shut because the others didn't want Heather smelling the cake. It helped that the door sealed almost airlock-tight. The kitchen's ventilation was via grilles and air expellers in its walls and ceiling.

Teresa opened the oven door. The sweet baking smell flooded the room.

She tested the cake with a fork. Almost done, ten minutes more should be enough. She reset the timer to that amount, then sat back to wait.

Sitting, she watched her reflection in the wall glass, watched also the landscape through her mirrored body like her image was a ghost. She appraised her dark gypsy-like face, with its drawn-back hair and silver hoop earrings. Her face was lined, her expression tired despite the long night's sleep and some sweet wakeup cunnilingus from Matt this morning when he'd gotten off driving. She knew her tiredness stemmed from that damn dream she'd had while sitting on the toilet, about being young again and watching Richie Kisner bleed to death after getting stabbed.

Now why the hell would I dream that after all these years, and it was utterly realistic as well . . . Dad . . . Gran . . . even the old house . . .

She concentrated on herself, her gaze locking on her reflected eyes. Teresa Pollack had big eyes and knew it. They heightened her attractiveness, but also, such large eyes made her look like she was staring when she wasn't. Particularly since she was rather thin: a hundred and ten pounds on a 5'6" frame. Her mouth was small, her nose pointy (almost triangular), but the combined effect of her features was pleasant and pretty.

And her hair, that LONG black hair now wrapped up in an untidy bun. She had a weird phobia about having short hair, hadn't been to a salon in fifteen years, had no intention of visiting one anytime soon. She would NEVER cut her hair, no matter how unhealthy it got! And even if she did cut it, she wasn't growing it shorter than the bottom of her ribcage! But her hair was so long now that if she didn't keep it up, it hung into everything, dishwashers, toilet water, just everything. So it had to be wrapped up behind her head.

(Like with the rest of their group, her clothes were clean again, courtesy of using the greenhouse's express laundromat.)

She stopped checking out her reflection, checked out her nails instead. Oh no! Another one needed filing! And their black paint was so chipped! A kind of nervousness settled on her: *Where the heck am I supposed to find nail paint out here?*

"Oh, how I fucking hate the fucking commies," Teresa groaned aloud in exasperation.

The oven timer sounded then. The birthday cake was done.

***

Like Courtney had suspected yesterday, Miki and Teresa *had* once been lovers. It had been a brief tango—during the one university semester they'd been roommates, they'd gotten drunk together one night and ended up in each other's arms. They'd eaten each other out and fallen asleep.

They'd continued having sex nightly for a week, before Teresa realized she honestly wasn't enjoying the sexual relationship; that, while she liked Miki as a friend, she didn't want her, or any other woman, as a lover. Teresa realized that she was neither bisexual nor homosexual, but had accidentally been beersexual for one night. (She'd only ever reached orgasm once with Miki, and that was on the first night when they were both bombed. After that, though she had experienced pleasure when they fucked, it never again amounted to a climax. And by the end, the feel of Miki's tongue in her vagina had made her skin crawl.)

Miki had wanted more, Teresa had wanted less. After several sessions of intense female drama and recriminations, Teresa had moved out and gone to room with Courtney. Thinking Teresa had simply left her for another girlfriend, Miki had detested Courtney from that day forth.

Then Courtney and Teresa had met Radio and his best friend Matt, with Teresa instantly falling for Matt (which Miki could forgive) and Courtney being equally swept off her feet by Radio (which only made Miki hate her more, since Miki worshipped the very ground Radio walked on).

But, Miki and Teresa had since repaired their fences. (The main residue of their one-time relationship was that Miki always stood too close to Teresa now while talking to her, like she wanted to kiss her, or maybe, just wanted to torment her with memory.) Despite all Teresa's protests to the contrary, however, Miki still believed that she and Courtney *had* been lovers, and so that feud still continued. It had subsided now though (now that Miki and Heather were married) to a simmering dislike that couldn't be bothered to blow up into outright animosity.

Now Miki and Courtney were always painfully polite and nice to each other, even though they actually couldn't stand one another's guts.

CHAPTER 23

Up front in the cockpit, Jeff popped a blue pill as he drove the greenhouse. That made three so far today. Now he knew they worked, he'd decided to use the full complement of twelve pills a day.

He grinned. His only dilemma now was resolving how big he wanted his penis to grow. Eight or nine inches seemed about okay. Then he shook his head. Nah, what if nine inches wasn't enough to keep Highball happy? He'd heard some women were 'depth queens': you had to practically puncture their wombs with your meat for them to get off. He rubbed a hand over his chin—this was the main drawback of the pills, the accompanying hairiness—maybe twelve or thirteen inches ought to do the trick. He laughed aloud—"Yeah, just imagine me with a one-foot dick!! A ruler-cock!"—then looked around nervously, hoping none of the others had heard his outburst. Particularly the guys, who might want to share the pills with him.

Okay, Jeff did have one worry: his penis had widened as well as lengthened. *Highball has a small tight pussy, I don't want to rip her all up, just because . . . that's what Brie warned against! Hey!—what do I do if my penis ends up as thick as my forearm?* He scrunched up his face in thought. *Okay, I really need to keep a good watch here. As thick as Highball's forearm is fine—I can still ease little johnson into her nice and slow—but once it gets bigger than that, I'm stopping the pills. No point killing my darling . . .*

Grinning, he squeezed his crotch—*Shit, it already feels bigger again, oh, thank you, thank you, thank you, God!*—then returned his attention to the road ahead.

He sped up slightly till there were only forty yards or so between Greenhouse Eight and the one ahead.

Greenhouses were easy to drive. There was a steering wheel, gas and brake pedals, then eight touchscreens that regulated everything from gear changes to cabin air pressure.

The windshield was a single glass sheet, the top center portion of which functioned as rearview and also let the driver see what was happening on both of the vehicle's floors. Like now: he touched the 'Cameras' screen, then grinned at the images of the others seated around their table, particularly the serious look on his darling Highball's face. Ooh, she looked good enough to eat! Eat her pussy that was.

Radio was talking. Jeff turned up the sound: ". . . until she opens up a frequency she's sure the communists aren't monitoring, there's no way to know for certain where Dr. Orgasm is, but—"

"But she's up north, right?" Highball enquired of her brother. "You're at least certain of that?"

"Yes, she's definitely up north. The only worry is—if the communists traced her call to me, and she's had to flee her hideout."

"Shit! Highball gasped, "If that's happened, she could be literally anywhere."

"I really hope not," Courtney said. "We need . . . no, we *have* to—"

Jeff cut off the transmission, switched the rearview from 'internal' to 'default,' once again showing the road behind. *Courtney seems obsessed with finding Dr. O, like she imagines the woman's the savior of the world or something. Hey, wake up, girl! It's not like she did Metaphor any good.*

He'd rejoin the conversation shortly. Now, however, the convoy was approaching a large hill. The road didn't look like it was curving, they seemed headed right for the hill. (Over the hill, for a moment he imagined he saw a pink shoe zipping between fluffy clouds, the high heel vanishing into marshmallow white pillows. Then the vision resolved itself into a figment of his imagination. He laughed. *Oh, Courtney would just love that: us unexpectedly encountering Dr. Orgasm.*)

After peeking ahead a bit, Jeff began searching the 'Cameras' screen for the control that radio-linked video transmissions between the vehicles. In one sense, the entire convoy was a single unit. By wireless hook-up to the vehicles in front, this vehicle's rearview screen would let Jeff view the road ahead of the convoy as seen through the front greenhouse's cameras.

(Like in the rest of the mobile terrarium, the cockpit was draped with vines. A shelf of bonsai trees ran below the ceiling above the co-driver's door. Here it was possible to see the bioenergy wires that fed power from the plants into the greenhouse's batteries. An apple tree grew right behind the driver's seat, its branches shooting out over Jeff's head to provide shade. Pairs of the tree's thicker branches had also been teased forward [both across the cockpit's side glass and between the seats] to make armrests for the driver.)

Outside the greenhouse, the landscape hadn't so far changed much, which Jeff was relieved about. The flora was largely still the building-sized mushrooms, some of which now had equally huge crickets sitting on their crowns. The space between the giant fungi was predominantly orange sand with a dotting of large blue flowers.

With this being Route Zero, part of Endless Street, things could have been way, way odder. Even so, this portion of the road had no fixed consistency. In places it was black like spilled paint, in others it was red like spilled blood, in others it seemed granite, in other parts white marble veined with red and blue . . . The landscape itself warped, the inconsistent route itself becoming the only constant thing. Route Zero would exist no matter what; what lay about it could be debated. Sometimes (like had happened with Phantasm) whole cities up and shifted to wherever. Jeff and the other truckers had one main rule: 'keep your eyes on the road, mo'fo, and not the world around it you imagine you know . . .'

Jeff finally worked out the video hookup controls; the rearview screen turned static then was replaced with the view as seen from Greenhouse One. Now the approaching hill loomed huge in video. Jeff saw that he'd been right: Route Zero now became a tunnel through the hill. Onscreen, the start of the tunnel loomed as a jagged arc, and then the light dimmed as the greenhouse sped into the darkness beyond.

For a moment Jeff was worried: this could be dangerous, maybe he'd better alert the others in case there were gobblers in there. And he now found it rather weird that the damned commies hadn't attacked them since they'd fled Metaphor.

Almost unconsciously, he got out his bottle of penis enlargement pills and popped one. That made him feel better. *Ooh, yee-hah, baby. There ain't nothing like a big dick to give a guy confidence in the face of danger.* He laughed. *Hey, monsters—I'se got's me a monster of my own to take y'all on! Hey, commie boys and girls—this Jeffrey's here gun shoots come too!*

On the screen, the first greenhouse was rolling on into the gloom. Jeff realized he'd been worried about nothing. (The whole convoy had slowed now, which made sense—in the vehicle's headlights the tunnel floors and walls looked uneven; no point crashing into a rogue rock outcropping.)

The vegetation in the cockpit suddenly smelt intensely exhilarating to Jeff, he sensed them in a way he never had before. He removed his left hand from the wheel, ran his fingers through the leafy arm-rest. The apple tree's leaves smelt delicious to him. That was odd; had they been specially treated for such an effect?

The smell filled his brain. Without thinking, Jeff plucked off a handful of leaves, put them in his mouth, and chewed.

He was surprised: the leaves had none of the bitterness one normally associated with them. They tasted great. He swallowed, plucked some more leaves off the branch, ate those too. Damn, these leaves tasted really good. He plucked off some more . . .

While chewing the apple leaves, he switched the rearview video from the front greenhouse's display back to his friends, gave it sound.

"No shit, guys," Heather was saying. "So there we were out in the Dreamfields and this huge monster attacks us."

"Yeah," Miki seconded. "My gun jammed. I thought we were goners. Done for."

"So what happened?" Courtney asked.

Jeff smiled. Courtney was cute, with that silky white-blonde hair and those sweet blue eyes and snub nose. Pretty hot bod too. Okay, nowhere near Highball's class, but she still rated highly in his opinion. She looked very upset this morning though . . . sexually frustrated. That was it: the lady was clearly hard up. Like she needed a good fuck to cheer her up. Jeff remembered Highball telling him how Courtney had trouble coming. She'd been interrupted before he got the whole story from her, but Jeff figured he knew what Courtney's problem was: Radio had to have a small penis also—it was a common enough problem with these geeks: huge brain, little dick.

Jeff gave his crotch a good squeeze. *Yeah, I can feel it, it's growing like a baby.* He let his mind wander in fantasy. *Okay, Radio baby, I like you. Maybe if I've few of these blue tablets left, you can have them, you know. They'll turn you into a real man. Enable you give your honey a proper good time.*

He laughed. *Or if you're unfortunate and I've used all the tablets up, you can hire me to show Courtney a real good time for you.* He laughed. *Nah, Highball'll kill me if I try that cheating nonsense on with her. Still, Courtney looks like she does need a good roll in the hay. Like she needs five or sex rolls, even.*

He focused ahead again. The hill—a dull-brown mass of earth patched with green vegetation—loomed closer now. The sixth greenhouse had just entered it.

Shortly our turn, he thought. He had no idea how far the hill went on for, but it would be good to be out of the open for a bit. *This hill is momentary protection from any watching commie eyes. Then we're out the other side and scared of our own damn shadows again.*

Then he reached up, ripped off the end of a climbing vine—creeper, leaves, and flowers—and stuck it in his mouth.

Hell yeah! he thought while chewing. *These damn plants sure do taste good!*

He returned his wandering attention to the screen. Courtney was saying: "I think Dr. O is just laying low. It's—"

Miki shushed her. Then the wallscreen to the left of their table flickered to life, showing Chief Oldfield.

On seeing the chief's grizzled face, Jeff winced with displeasure, then he shrugged: yesterday was over; one really couldn't argue with City Hall.

They were almost at the tunnel entrance now. The end of the greenhouse ahead of Jeff was vanishing into the dark cave like it was being swallowed. The tunnel entrance was asymmetrical, with several rock projections dipping from overhead, like the hill had begun growing down over it again after it had been hollowed out, or like someone with a giant blowtorch had attempted melting the opening shut.

The hill itself rose up huge and solid and brown; an utterly impressive, landmark.

Jeff grimaced, then switched the screen back to default rearview mode again. He didn't need the distraction—this looked like some hardcore rocky terrain they were about travelling over. *Yeah, the front drivers were right to slow down. If the rest of the tunnel interior's anything like this preview, I'll need all my concentration. Gotta be real careful here; don't wanna crash the greenhouse. For all we know, given the slightest opportunity or excuse, Oldfield might just abandon us.*

Absentmindedly, he plucked a handful of leaves and chewed on them.

CHAPTER 24

Breakfast was long over.

Since last night's profound disappointment in bed, Courtney was barely holding it together. Just marginally. Her mind felt frazzled, like her brain was about exploding out of her head. Her sex still buzzed angrily, her body felt like it was mad at her for taking it so close to heaven, and then, *yet again*, dropping it off a precipice into the raging flames of unsatisfaction . . .

She looked around their table amidst the trees. After eating, Matt had gone upstairs to man the greenhouse's central neutron cannon and watch the skies for Bees. ("Guys, enough slacking already," he'd joked while heading for the stairs.) Teresa was still baking. (Courtney felt somewhat sheepish now her last night's suspicions that Teresa and Miki were planning a lover's tryst had proved baseless. Okay, yes, so the pair *had* acted suspiciously that semester at university, suspicions made even odder by Teresa's staunch refusal to explain [both then and now] why'd she'd quit rooming with Miki—her story that Miki both wet her bed and farted stinkily every night sounded too farfetched for Courtney to really lend credence to—but, hey, that meant nothing now, right?)

With Jeff driving, that left Highball, Heather and Miki, and Radio and Courtney gathered here at their 'command table.'

Courtney had been holding court for a while now. Talking took her mind off her depression. In the light of day, and with no communist attack on the convoy so far, their being banished back here didn't seem so bad after all. Except that they might soon start getting on each other's' nerves from sheer boredom and proximity. Thankfully, the greenhouse was big enough that they didn't have to see each other unless they really wanted to.

Most of Courtney's monologue had so far been about the 'extreme necessity' of their finding Dr. Orgasm. Preaching to the converted, as Radio called it.

"I hope everyone not clearing away their dishes isn't about becoming a trend here," Highball suddenly interrupted her. "If you guys for one minute imagine I'm going to keep picking up after you all, you've another think coming."

Courtney looked down. The breakfast table was covered with oily plates and trays, bacon rind, halves of bread, toast crumbs, knives and butter, drained teacups, apple cores and pips, squeezed lemons . . .

"I'll give you a hand now," Heather said, starting to rise. "You're right, *this is* a mess; you'd think kindergarteners just ate here."

"No!" Highball said sharply.

Heather looked at her in surprise. "But you just said . . ."

"We're clear up later, darling," Miki interjected, making angry eyes at Highball that yelled: *Hey, don't you dare screw this birthday surprise up!*

Highball snuck a wink at Courtney. Courtney managed a smile back. All the women were in on the surprise; they just had to keep Heather away from the kitchen. But what the hell was keeping Teresa in there anyway? How long did baking one cake take? (Things were complicated because none of them could open the kitchen door to enquire without releasing the baking aroma into the vehicle.)

A diversion was needed.

Courtney thought of one: "Guys, I hate sounding like a scratched record, but—"

"You are, you are, but we like the song," Highball interrupted with a grin.

"—but Dr. Orgasm . . ."

Heather took the bait. She frowned, ran fingers through her blue hair. "You want something from her, don't you, girl? This isn't just about us recapturing . . . freeing Metaphor. What's in it for you?"

Starting from Heather, Courtney let her eyes range around the table. "Dr. Orgasm has developed the O-pill. It's a drug that makes you come, pure and simple."

Miki giggled. "You're shitting us, right? How can *a pill* make you come?"

Courtney shrugged. "I don't know either, but from what Radio gathered..."

All the women looked at Radio who'd been sitting there, staring perplexedly at an empty teacup.

He shook his palms at them. "According to what I picked up over the airwaves, the pill contains an agent that relaxes specialized sexual receptors in the brain as well as making both the clitoris and vagina extra-sensitive. The female anus and nipples too. Once a woman uses the pill, even the lightest touch of a feather is supposed to be enough to make her climax."

"Wow! Imagine coming from having your nipples sucked," Miki said.

"That's actually not an unknown happening," Radio said seriously. "Some women do have breast orgasms. It happens a lot to women breastfeeding their babies—to about eight percent of them I think—but they generally deny it."

Heather made a face. "Can you guys prove any of this? I mean about the O-Pill, not the breast orgasms. Or is it just more Metaphor anti-commie propaganda?"

Courtney was about replying, but Highball spoke first. "This news is on the level. See, it was a commie broadcast my brother picked up. About seven months ago. That's the reason the commies went so hard after Dr. O—they wanted that fucking pill at whatever cost. I hear she only got her shoeplane aloft by the tips of its see-thru toes."

"I think the commies have shot her magic shoe down," Heather said. "No one's seen it since Dr. O vanished."

"No," Courtney countered, "I think Dr. Orgasm is just laying low. It's—"

"Shush, guys! It's the chief!"

They shushed. Miki was pointing to the wallscreen, which had just flickered into life and was showing Chief Oldfield's craggy face. The chief seemed happier this morning.

"Morning, Chief," Heather said dutifully, with more than a hint of resentment in her voice. "How're we doing today?"

"Fine, fine, y'all. We'll soon be out of this tunnel and in daylight again." He frowned, gestured behind him through a clump of trees, at the black rock floating past the transparent walls. "We're having to go slow, though—the walls are irregular . . . we don't want to use the cannons lest we bring the ceiling down on our heads . . . you guys'll see what I mean once you're inside."

Then Oldfield clapped his hands and laughed. "Happy birthday, Heather."

Heather's eyes widened in shock. She giggled and covered her mouth with fingers. "Chief, you remembered?" She looked around the table in mock anger. "Unlike this lot here."

Courtney and Highball gasped. "It's your *birthday?*" They looked at Miki in pretend shock. "Hey, Japanese wifey," Highball growled, "why you not tell us spouse get older?"

"I forget," Miki giggled, doing her best to keep a straight face. "Too much morning sex scramble Japanese memory like eggs."

Oldfield grinned. "Miki was planning you a party." Beside him, Angel Weiner stepped into view, wearing a party hat and funny nose and glasses. She and Oldfield began singing, "Happy birthday to you! Happy birthday to you!" Other surviving City Defense personnel stepped into the viewscreen's camera range and joined in the singing. "Happy birthday to you! Happy birthday to you!"

Courtney and the others joined in too. *Yes, this is just perfect,* Courtney thought. *Okay, Teresa Pollack, where are you? That cake must be done now. Don't you dare spoil this beautiful moment with bad timing!*

On cue, the kitchen door opened and a beaming Teresa emerged bearing a massive birthday cake. Courtney now understood what had taken Teresa so long in the kitchen: she'd somehow managed to both ice the cake a lovely pink and inscribe 'Happy Birthday, Heather!' on it in blue words that perfectly matched the birthday girl's hair.

On seeing the cake, Heather broke down in tears. "Oh! You guys didn't forget! Oh, oh, oh! This is just fantastic! Fantastic! Fantastic!!!" She grabbed Miki and kissed her hard, while the others cheered. Then while everyone resumed singing 'Happy Birthday' again, she hugged and kissed everyone at the table, tears streaming down her cheeks.

The sound of singing had brought Matt down from the top deck. He beamed at Heather. "Happy Birthday, girl!"

They hugged.

"Oh, I just love you guys!" Heather turned to the screen, "Thanks, Chief! I'll never forget this in a million years!" She gaped at the pretty pink cake again.

Oldfield grinned. "Okay, Heather, one more thing: Once we're out—"

"Hold on a minute, boss," Angel interrupted him, pulling off her funny face. "Hey, did any of you see my bag yesterday?"

The other City Defense staff now melted from the picture and returned to their posts.

Courtney barely concealed her mirth. "Your *bag?* What'd it look like?"

"Blue leather Gucci handbag. Distressingly expensive. It has a number of my personal items in it, and some documents too." She peered hard at them. "It was in one of the upstairs offices in Greenhouse Four."

Angel's thin face was caught in a mix of anger and embarrassment. Courtney didn't trust herself to reply; she looked pointedly at Highball. "You were up there yesterday minding babies, did you see anyone with it?"

"Nah," Highball said, then shook her head wearily. "Has to be one of the teens took it; you know what kids are like sometimes. There wasn't anything *really sensitive* in it, was there?"

Courtney could just hear the laughter in Highball's reply. Angel's face turned dark onscreen. *Oh, my God—she looks so, so embarrassed. She knows she left her business cards in the bag and if those teenagers have her vibrators they'll know exactly whose they are.* Courtney was well aware that Radio was staring at her in amazement, but she avoided his eyes.

"Oh, those blasted teens," Angel spat angrily, then looked at Oldfield. "Sorry for interrupting you, boss, I just didn't want to forget. You were going to say?" She calmed a bit. "Is it about what we discussed?"

Oldfield nodded. He cleared his throat, smiled through the screen. "Yes, I've been thinking. Ladies, the teens *are* getting out of hand in Greenhouse Four. The nurses keep having to settle arguments over which baby belongs to who now—the teenage girls have started adopting them for themselves. How would you ladies like to give us a hand with keeping them in line?" He gestured around at the trees flanking him. "The guys should be able to watch the skies alone. Can you, Matt?"

"Yeah, Chief, we'll be fine. All the guns are powered up okay."

Teresa was meanwhile cutting up the birthday cake. Their greenhouse was just nosing into the tunnel, its dark rock walls cutting off view of the flowery flanking fields.

Highball nodded at the screen. "Sure, Chief, count me in."

Miki and Heather (who was still wiping joyous tears from her face) both nodded too. "Just maternally-precocious teens, right?" Miki asked cautiously. "We don't have to go into the surgery again?"

"No, no. Thankfully there's less demand for that now." He nodded. "Okay, that's settled then. Once we're out of this damned tunnel, we'll call a halt so you girls can cross . . ." Then his face turned white with fear. "Oh my God, what the hell is this!?"

Angel Weiner was also staring horrified at something off-screen.

Then, the next moment, that off-screen something was onscreen and all those at the table in the last greenhouse were watching with utter disbelief in their eyes.

Courtney was unsure how she didn't pee herself from fear now. Several things—they looked like saw-toothed iron tentacles covered with hair—had suddenly jerked into view and speared both Chief Oldfield and Angel Weiner through and through.

Both the chief and Angel hung jerking in midair, metal stuck through their bodies, gushing blood from many holes. Then something else—Courtney couldn't tell what it was—smashed into Don Oldfield from both sides at once, pulping him between its folds.

Courtney's last view of the chief was of his gray eyes popping from their sockets, then of his brains—that creamy white mess had to be his brains—squirting like toothpaste from both his empty eye sockets and from cracks in his crushed skull. Beside him, Angel Weiner was simultaneously being shredded into a bloody unrecognizable mess.

And then the screen went dead.

They were still all gaping at the dead screen, wondering 'What the fuck?' when Jeff came charging down the aisle towards them, his face white with panic.

"RUN!" RUN!!" he was screaming. "The tunnel is alive! It's eating the convoy!"

It was a single, frantic warning.

Jeff reached them, paused for a split-second to grab Highball up into his arms, and then was past them, running hard for the rear of the vehicle.

Courtney imagined she froze, but she wasn't sure. She was suddenly aware of herself running like mad with Radio behind her as the tunnel walls slowly closed in on the greenhouse and fat metal tentacles punctured through the vehicle's almost unbreakable glass questing for them.

CHAPTER 25

"This is literally the worst day in history to get older," Heather wept. She stood clasping Miki tight. Miki was stroking her hair, trying to console her. She was wet-eyed herself.

All eight of them—Courtney and Radio, Jeff and Highball, Matt and Teresa, Heather and Miki—had escaped unharmed.

However, not one of them believed what had just happened.

The entire convoy was gone. The tunnel had slammed shut on the first seven greenhouses and the front half of the eighth—everything that had so far entered into it.

Then, while they'd watched in confusion (and with violently beating hearts) from the rear half of the greenhouse, the entire hill that had housed the tunnel had sank underground, leaving a normal road in its place.

The unbelievable, the unthinkable, the unspeakable, had happened.

The eight of them stood between the trees in the end of the sheared (and still floating) vehicle and gaped.

"There were twenty-seven babies in the fourth greenhouse," Highball said finally. "Babies, kids, teenagers . . ." She too began crying, then turned and buried her face in Jeff's chest.

Jeff held her and looked perplexed, like he still didn't believe he'd saved everyone by slamming on the brakes when he did.

Teresa was weeping too. As was Matt.

Courtney didn't cry. Not because she didn't want to, but because the tears felt frozen in her eyes, like her eyes had seen more than eyes were meant to, and had no possible response to such outrage. She remembered the two kids she'd risked her life to rescue yesterday. *Shit! Shit! Shit! Little Vincent and his sister Alicia were in there! They just got eaten too!*

"Everything's fucking gone?" she asked in a horrified whisper. "Everyone's dead except us? Just like that?"

From behind, Radio laid comforting hands on her shoulders. "Yes," he replied calmly, his the only other voice amidst the sound of weeping.

***

Once they'd gotten some control over their emotions again, the eight survivors walked in single file down the gauntlet of in-house trees to the point where the greenhouse met open air. At the shearing point, they spread out into the foliage either side of the aisle, then stood there staring.

The rim of cut glass that framed them was cracked like shards not yet fallen from a shattered mirror.

Ahead of them Route Zero was its normal smooth self, the country either side of it showing no sign of disturbance. On their left a field of giant flowers grew right up to the seamless blacktop.

"Shit!" Highball exclaimed. "Two hundred and forty—was it?—people gone like they'd never existed. Shee-it!"

"Calm down, baby," Jeff said soothingly. None of them, not even himself, noticed next when he plucked some leaves from a maple tree and began chewing them.

"It was a gobbler," Radio said. "Possibly the largest gobbler in existence."

"A monster that size shouldn't exist," Courtney said, like she blamed him that it did. She stood pressed against him, their fingers touching but not locked.

"Everything exists somewhere. We just had the horrible luck of running into it."

Heather, Miki, and Teresa sat huddled together on a bench. All three women were still crying.

"You're sure this wasn't a commie trap, Radio?" Matt asked. "The shitheads could have known we were headed this way. I mean, up to now we've seen absolutely no sign of them."

Radio shook his head. "Most unlikely; a creature this big must be impossible for them to control, else they'd have used them during their assault on Metaphor."

"I feel empty, like something just sucked my soul out," Courtney said, hating herself that the tears wouldn't come. "I want to crawl into a hole and sleep forever, then wake up to find that none of this ever happened."

"Me too," Highball said. "What the fuck do we do now?"

Matt and Jeff instinctively looked at Radio. "What's the news, dude?"

He shrugged. "We keep following Route Zero north. The loss of the convoy leaves us absolutely no choice now but to hunt for Dr. Orgasm." He gestured back into the vehicle. "We take what food and weapons we can find; it looks to be a long hike." He pointed up at the top deck. "We're kinda lucky the storerooms and offices didn't get eaten up too."

"The kitchen did though," Courtney said. "We're gonna be plucking a lot of fruit."

Heather spoke up from her bench. "Not so. There's a pantry upstairs near our bedroom. There's boxes of cereal and candy and other stuff in there. A fridge too."

"We'd better get a move on then," Jeff said. "And not just 'cos of the commies. There's several towns along this road that we don't want to camp close to come nightfall."

With Radio leading the way, they tramped back into the halved greenhouse and began packing what they could.

CHAPTER 26

Working mostly in silence, they salvaged what they could from the greenhouse. The women bagged up food and spare underwear, the men looked around for tools and weapons.

Everyone was initially upstairs and downstairs and in all the rooms at the same time, until the girls had found all they wanted and retreated downstairs, leaving the guys top deck.

"Where the hell did they stash the portable cannons?" Matt growled after Radio reported not finding any. "There should be at least one of them aboard."

Jeff, who was standing almost in the glass archway formed by the vehicle's missing front half, scowled back. "I think the chief had them removed before letting us aboard. Easiest way to prevent us staging a hostile takeover. It's either that or . . ." he jerked a thumb back at the emptiness over his shoulder, "they were kept in the front area." (The shearing had completely excised the middle neutron cannon as well.) He pointed up through the tangle of vines crisscrossing the glass ceiling, at the greenhouse's rear cannon. "And we've no tools to take that one down."

"We can forget dismantling it anyway," Radio said. "It'd be a total waste of time. The batteries are too heavy to carry any useful distance."

"And . . ." Jeff said musingly, "Oldfield might have run their charges down anyway to ensure we couldn't turn them on him."

Matt flinched at the suggestion. "I doubt he'd do that."

Jeff shrugged, his broad shoulders lifting like wings. "I'm just saying, that's all. It's what *I'd* do if I didn't trust me. Disconnect the power so . . ."

"Shit. You mean he left us as sitting ducks all night long?"

"Too late to find out now. I'll just say we're lucky the communists didn't attack last night."

Radio said, "Actually, guys, if it wasn't for the chief kicking us back here we'd all be down in the belly of the beast now. Look, there's no

130

way to know if he set us up to be killed or not, so let's just forget it. May his soul rest in peace."

Jeff's suspicious expression sobered. He and Radio both respectfully crossed themselves.

Matt made a face. "So all we've got then are *small* firearms?"

Radio nodded. "Yup. Pray we only meet small critters."

Courtney poked her blonde head between the dwarf palms framing the top of the stairs. "Hey, Radio, you guys ready yet? Everything's packed and ready to go."

"Yeah, babe, we'll be down in a sec," Radio replied.

Courtney vanished back downstairs.

The three men headed for the stairs, then, just before they started down them, Matt turned back towards the rear-mounted neutron cannon.

"Where are you going?" Radio enquired.

Matt frowned at him and Jeff. "Guys, I need to know that Chief Oldfield didn't screw us over—didn't set us up to be Bee food."

Jeff made a face. "Look, the man's dead, what does it matter?"

"I worked with him in City Defense for ten years. He was my friend. I need to know that that kept on until the end, that our friendship meant something after all."

"Hey, hey," Jeff said, "I'm sorry I ever suggested treachery to begin with. But . . . are you *sure* you want to fire that cannon? What if it doesn't fire?

"Yeah," Radio added quickly. "Let sleeping dogs lie, dude. I think it's enough that he'd clearly reconsidered things by this morning."

Matt shook his head at them. "No. I need to know this." Before the others could hold him back, he walked quickly to the neutron cannon, flicked off its safety and pulled the trigger.

Nothing happened. The only sound was the thumping of their own hearts.

Matt stared up at the silver needle of the cannon's barrel, then slowly, his eyes wide with horror, his gaze fell again onto his friends.

Then his face flushed with rage. "That bastard! That slimy son-of-a-bitch! He did set us up! Left us completely defenseless back here! Fuck! You mean I sat up here this morning nursing an uncharged weapon!?" His eyes turned confused. "But . . . but . . . but all the gauges . . . the power gauge still reads 'full.'"

Radio said, "Easy to fake. You just need to disconnect the . . . hey, look, man, we did tell you not to."

"I can't believe it, that's all. I just can't believe it. We were *friends*, goddammit! That should count for something."

Jeff had no reply to that. He pulled out his bottle of blue pills and ate one.

Radio said, "I think he simply weighed the lives of everyone in the convoy against ours. Balancing the safety of two hundred and forty innocent people against eight potentially dangerous ones isn't much of a contest; the scale tips squarely towards the multitude. Man, forget it: In his shoes you'd have made the same call."

Matt nodded, though his eyes were broody. "Okay. Maybe I would have reached the same decision if the roles were reversed; maybe I'd have done the same thing." He frowned. "Okay, I'll forget it, but don't let Teresa hear about this. Agreed? One word in her ear and she's certain to freak out."

Radio and Jeff nodded.

"Let's go, man," Radio said. "The girls must be curious by now as to what we're still doing up here."

They turned back towards the stairs to see Teresa facing them. "What is it I'm not supposed to hear about?"

"Er . . . nothing, darling," Matt sputtered.

"Whaaatt is it?"

"Honest, darling, nothing," he repeated even more unconvincingly.

"Matt!" Her already strained-looking face began looking even more strained.

"Look . . . maybe we'd better tell her," Radio said.

She placed hands on hips. "I'm listening, Radio."

"We're really low on ammo. After what's already happened this morning, Matt was scared you and the girls would freak out if we told you."

Teresa rolled her eyes. "Is that all? We found two shotguns downstairs and several boxes of shells."

"You did?"

She nodded. "Look, guys, if that's all that's been keeping you up here, come down now and let's get the hell away from here. This place is already giving me the creeps and I think both Courtney and Heather are about having nervous breakdowns."

She walked over to Matt, linked her hand in his. They walked back together.

Jeff and Radio followed the couple.

"You know," Radio whispered to Jeff as they descended the steps. "We should really be thankful to Chief Oldfield for disabling the guns."

"Huh . . . how's that?"

"Shh! Neutron cannons run on the principle of Unity Fusion—which means if their discharge doesn't hit anything, it'll keep on going for a distance, then explode anyway. If that cannon had fired when Matt pulled the trigger, he'd have unwittingly sent out a sky signal to every communist outpost in the area that we're here. They'd have homed in on us like sharks on blood."

CHAPTER 27

Packs on backs, bags and weapons in hand, the eight of them walked the north road.

They kept on the right side of Route Zero, keeping close to the highway.

They went long stretches without speaking. When thirsty or hungry, they opened a bottle, or unwrapped something, then discarded the empties into the fields they passed.

They'd automatically separated into couples: Matt and Teresa in front, Courtney and Radio bringing up the rear. Between those pairs, Heather and Miki, and Highball and Jeff walked side by side (on left and right respectively), with Miki and Jeff on the outsides of the rough diamond their procession formed.

It was late afternoon. The sun, though still hot overhead, had started its fall from power into dusk.

Since setting out from where the convoy had been eaten, they'd seen no one else. Just the odd bird or flying beast. Twice, they'd noticed the sky rip and squirt through Bizarro sludge, like toothpaste made from shit, but the brown clouds had stayed far off to the east and there'd been no need to take cover under the massive mushrooms that still dominated the landscape, though now from farther in from the road.

No towns yet though.

To their left and right, everywhere was sunflowers. Yellow, yellow, yellow with their honey-brown centers. A pleasant visual carpet, but one that one quickly tired of seeing.

The monotonous trudge over the distance had had one positive effect: The farther they'd gotten from the site of the morning's disastrous incident, the easier it was for all of them to imagine it had never happened. The dreamlike atmosphere engendered by the floral roadside carpet helped in this, and maybe the flowers' calming smell had a soporific effect too. Whatever/whichever it was, by this point, their spirits, while not exactly 'up,' were far from still languishing in the doldrums. Even Heather and Highball, who'd been the hardest hit by the children's deaths, smiled occasionally now. Their smiles were sad, but not brittle, were indicative of bruised but not broken spirits.

Courtney's frame of mind was largely representative of that of the rest of their party. She was aware that they'd *survived*. Had survived, not by any special intelligence or abilities any of them possessed (except maybe for Jeff's quick reflexes), but because a set of freak circumstances had placed them right on the fringe of the danger zone.

She was aware also that no one else in the convoy of greenhouses had stood an ant's chance of saving themselves. Even with the neutron cannons—how do you melt through a living mountain? (Lark torpedoes, which *were* designed for mass destruction, would also have proved useless here, and they'd already used up the convoy's entire stock of rocket-birds blocking off their exit from Metaphor.) She was certain that that last sight she'd had—of Chief Oldfield's brains spurting out through his eye sockets—would haunt her forever; *Shit! His eyes were hanging down on his cheeks on their nerves!*

And yet . . . they'd survived. They had. Somehow. But . . . the danger was far from over. Every step they took out here was into the unknown. They were looking for Dr. Orgasm, but where the hell was she?

She was holding hands with Radio, her boyfriend, her soul mate, her lover. (She was really glad he was here beside her now, just like she was certain all the other women were that they had their partners with them.) She turned, looked at him, wondered what he was thinking.

The vacant look in Radio eyes told her he was currently only 'half-here' with the rest of them. His mind must right now be scanning the airwaves, sifting through media broadcasts from all over Innuendo, seeking that elusive burst of transmission from the great doctor of sexual liberty.

Like Courtney, all the others knew they had to find Dr. Orgasm now, no matter what. That was a resolved issue, no longer a topic for debate. From its genesis in possible fanatical whimsy, this quest had now evolved into a matter of survival, of mounting firm resistance against Florence Rigid's doctrine of Communism before it crushed the entire land of Innuendo in its repressive climaxless iron grip.

***

A horse neighed somewhere close by. Courtney stiffened at the animal's earthy sound. She imagined she could see the handsome stallion or mare's muscular piebald frame, its proud head and flaring nostrils and powerful flanks, imagined herself stroking its white mane, holding it still while slipping a foot into the stirrups . . .

Quickly, before they became a flood, she dammed the seeping memories that the horse's neighing brought back. Dwelling on the good would certainly segue into the bad. (Before the communists caught her, Courtney Taylor had loved riding; had often prowled the weird woods outside Metaphor on horseback. But since then . . .) She caught herself before she began crying, tightened her grip on Radio's hand.

***

They'd gone thirty minutes without talking when Teresa said. "Hey, what's with this damn road anyway? It just keeps going, going, going and going on, seemingly towards oblivion." She gestured left and right beside them. "I mean, we've been walking between these damn sunflower fields for hours now."

"Well, Route Zero is also called Endless Street for a good reason," Jeff replied. "I've been out here before driving my truck for actual days on end and not seeing another vehicle. And then, other times, this same route seemed way shorter, like I slipped into a 'long cut' that other time and never noticed."

"A long cut?" Courtney asked from behind them. "What's that?"

"It's the opposite of the normal 'short cut,'" Highball replied for Jeff, flicking a white butterfly off her red hair. "You accidentally sideslip into an OD route that makes your journey take longer than it should, even though the odometer reports the exact same distance as before."

"It's maddening as hell," Jeff continued. "And what makes it way odder still is . . . every single time it's happened, my ETA at my destination has been correct, practically to the hour and minute." He shrugged. "Like no extra time passed in the interim."

Courtney winced. "I really hope we're not stuck in one of those here. I'm already tired of carrying these bags."

"Nah, we're good there," Matt called back to her. "Look! Right up ahead. There's some buildings coming up. We should shortly have shelter."

"Yeah, I see them," Highball agreed.

"Where?" Teresa asked.

"I don't see anything either," Courtney said.

Highball pointed. "Look inside from the road a bit, here on our side, near where the trees start again. Looks like a small settlement."

Courtney nodded. "Yeah, I see the houses now. There aren't many of them either. It shouldn't be too dangerous to stop awhile." Nonetheless, she tightened her grip on her pistol.

"Okay, now I see them too," Teresa said. "It'll be great to sit down; damn, my legs feel pulverized."

They walked closer to the group of buildings, which soon turned out to be old ruins. Empty holes in blackened walls. Most of the roofs had caved in.

They approached through thickening forest. By the time they'd reached the ruins, the nearby trees were tall green slats blocking off view of the interior on both sides of the road.

They moved into the living room of a bombed-out house with a good view of the road. Rusted furniture springs lay about. Thick grass on the floor showed it had been ages since anyone had lived here.

No windows meant the room had a lot of possible exits in case of ambush.

"Okay, everyone," Jeff said when they were all inside. "I've good news and bad news."

"Good news first," Heather said, dumping her knapsack by a wall then flinging herself to the grassy ground. Miki followed her down; both women then used their bags for pillows. The blue-haired pair lay side-by-side staring at the sky.

Courtney and Radio (who was still practically sleepwalking) sat in another corner. Courtney began massaging her legs fiercely. Highball sat on a windowsill rocking back and forth, her eyes tracking Jeff curiously. (He'd just gotten out his bottle of blue 'vitamins' out again. She was wondering how many he'd eaten so far today.)

Matt too looked at Jeff. "What's the problem, man? Is this a bad place?"

Jeff popped a blue pill then nodded. "Yeah, this is a really bad place to be." He frowned. "But okay, good news first like the lady requested:

We're lucky. This clump of buildings proves we didn't get stuck in a long cut. I know this place well, I've driven past it countless times in the past."

"And the bad news?" Teresa asked in a nervous voice. "What's that?" She'd been pacing restlessly since they got here, her eyes darting from door to window and back again. She'd not yet dropped her gun and looked like she wanted to shoot someone.

Jeff sighed. "We're right on the outskirts of the twin towns of Misandry and Misogyny." He nodded at their instantly alarmed faces, then pointed through an empty window at some other buildings. "Yes, yes, believe me, it's true. Where we are now used to be the old town of Misandry; then they had an argument with Florence Rigid and the commies bombed it. So, after they'd patched up their differences, they rebuilt Misandry further in from the road."

"Misandry. That's where they cut guy's scrotums off and wear their penises and testicles on necklaces, isn't it?" Miki asked sleepily from the floor.

Jeff gulped. "Yes, castration central. And on principle too, not 'cos you did anything to earn such a fate."

Miki made a gesture. "And across the road, that's where they, you know?"

Jeff nodded impatiently. "Where they stick barbed wire up inside women's vaginas and fuck them with it, or run it between their legs and buttocks and jerk it back and forth like dental floss—and on principle too. I saw a dead girl they'd 'flossed' once; the mess left between her legs looked like a ravine. Yes, yes; they're each as bad as the other—two halves of the same gender-hatred coin."

"Ouch!" Highball yelped from her window perch. "Barbed wire inside my pussy? You've gotta be shitting me!" She leapt down, began collecting her bags. "You know what, guys? I think . . . no, *I know for sure* that I've rested enough already. Let's all just get the F out of here." She scowled at her boyfriend. "Hey, Jeff, let's go—if you lose your balls, I won't love you no more."

The other women also began quickly gathering up their stuff; Heather and Miki were up off the floor in the proverbial flash. Courtney followed them up.

Jeff raised his hand. "No hurry."

Teresa poked him in the chest. "No hurry? Are you fucking nuts? Man, if you've got spare testicles, my husband certainly hasn't." She looked hard at Matt. "Right? Right?"

Matt rolled his eyes.

"Hey, girls," Highball said, already halfway to the outside, "I'm outa here! Catch up with my ass by the road. Barbed wire in *my* vagina? You must be out of your damn mind."

Heather and Miki started after her, with Miki calling back, "Hey, Teresa, Courtney, what the hell are you guys dallying for? You wanna get pussy-flossed?"

"Hey, let Jeff finish!" Radio said loudly over the commotion, his first words for over two hours.

His voice held a tone of command. Everyone simmered down. "Okay, talk," Teresa told Jeff. "Why shouldn't we bolt from here now?"

"Because," Jeff replied, "I think we can steal a ride from one of the two towns." He looked around. "We're all tired of walking, aren't we?"

Everyone mused on that.

"Steal a fucking car from Misogyny?" Teresa asked after a bit. "Uh, uh. Not on this one, man; you can count me out. *My vagina?*"

"And that goes for the rest of us as well, baby," Highball said. Courtney, Heather and Miki nodded intense deep-felt agreement.

"There's *two* towns nearby, right?" Highball continued. "It's either us girls go to Misandry for a car or you guys head for Misogyny? You guys go."

"Ladies, Misandry's just a mile off through the forest. Misogyny is ten miles across the road."

"So? We're tired, we need our beauty sleep." And like they'd rehearsed it, All five women simultaneously lay down on the grass and tucked their hands behind their heads.

"Girls, there's no danger; the Misandrans hate *men* and you're all women."

None of the five on the floor replied him. All stared up at the evening sky, with Miki whistling a pentatonic melody.

"It looks like they've made up our minds for us," Radio said, getting up and walking over to Jeff and Matt. "Let's do it."

Jeff nodded, then checked his watch. "Ten miles you say? If we're fast about it we'll be there and back before sunset."

Matt looked confused for a moment, then got it: "Yeah, we'll be riding back, won't we?" He grinned down at his wife. "Hey, sweetie, remember where you are, okay? Don't catch the fever and castrate someone before we get back."

Teresa gave him the finger. "Go to hell, darling." Then she blew him a kiss. "Just make sure you come back from there alive."

The men set out. The women remained lying on their backs. After a while, Highball said, "Were they really expecting *us* to go find a vehicle?"

Teresa said, "With our luck today, it's practically guaranteed we'd have discovered Jeff got the directions mixed up and Misogyny's on this side of the road." Her face creased up with worry. "Shit. That had better not be the case; if Misandry's over there and the guys get caught—"

"Calm down," Highball persuaded, "Jeff's a trucker; he knows this route. There's utterly no chance of him getting the directions wrong."

"But what if . . . ?"

Courtney yawned. "Keep quiet, please, I'm trying to relax. It's nice and soothing down here."

"Yes it is," Miki agreed. "Almost like lying on the slopes of Mount Fuji in the spring."

Teresa kept quiet. She was fidgety, however, her eyes jerking across the heavens as if the fluffy clouds hid communist warplanes.

***

Down on the soft cushiony grass, Courtney watched the clouds float past.

At first, she felt nice and relaxed. Her mind emptied of her troubles. Like she was herself a cloud, she floated off from yesterday's and today's horrors. But staring at the white clouds acted almost like counting sheep: inch by inch she drifted into a trance-like state, and before she knew it she'd gotten trapped in the prison of her memories.

Just like during the several times she'd been hypnotized to attempt a cure for her trauma, she could neither wake up nor fall asleep. All she could do was remember:

PART 3:
THE BRUTAL DISGUSTING RAPE OF COURTNEY TAYLOR
OR
WHY COURTNEY CAN'T COME ANYMORE

[CONTENT WARNING: You DON'T have to read this part of this novel. This part of the book contains extreme sexual violence and is not recommended for ANYONE. Remember, you won't be able to unread any of this stuff later. So, if you're either squeamish or get offended by gross content, please jump forward to PART 4 on page 209. You'll still be able to follow the story. Thanks!]

CHAPTER 28

It began on a pleasant, late-August morning.

The horse, Sultan, was extremely frisky, which she liked. The chestnut Arabian stallion surged like an ocean of muscle beneath her as they crossed the fields.

Up in Sultan's saddle, Courtney Taylor laughed. Though she'd never tell anyone, one reason she loved riding was because it felt great having something so big and muscular between her legs. Something she could control. It felt immensely empowering in a non-sexual sense. The sensation she got while riding was weird: the only sex in it was how she sometimes got aroused when her crotch ground against the front of the saddle. Other than that, everything was just a rush of raw power, like she believed men got in racecars. She'd driven an F-1 racecar herself once but had felt nothing. Maybe women weren't built right for *that* thrill, the clitoris too high up in the groin, maybe you needed low-hanging testicles so you felt the buzz, the rumble of the engine and all those horsepowers deep in your balls.

Whatever the reason, racecar driving hadn't worked for her. This did. Once up in the saddle and out of the stables (and outside Metaphor) she felt semi-divine, with the world at her feet. So she rode as often as she could; which wasn't as often as she would have liked; work—she managed a flower store—many times spilled over onto the weekends, which was her only real riding period. Holidays too, but Radio didn't really like the outdoors, and Courtney was smart: she knew one didn't think only of one's own pleasure if one wanted to build a relationship with a guy. Particularly one who loved you.

She slowed the horse to a brisk canter. They were just reaching the edge of the Safe Zone that ringed Metaphor. Safe, because up to the row of pines marking it out, the city's presence negated all effects of the Weird Rain. Ride beyond those trees, and whatever you got into was no one's certainty and anyone's guess.

She drew in the reins, stopped the horse twenty meters from the tree line. She felt the beast's clear resistance to her controlling it—it wanted to go forward into the trees.

She patted its mane. "Oh no we don't, Sultan. No point tempting fate, we get too close and . . ."

The stallion stood trembling. She felt its impatience to run in its stiff muscles; in its frustrated breathing as below her its lungs swelled its sides. Its behavior today was unusual: though naturally frisky, most days Sultan calmed easily.

Or was the horse nervous? Did it sense a communist presence nearby?

Courtney scanned the row of trees but saw nothing. She didn't expect to see anything: the communists would be fools to advance this close to Metaphor, what with Chief Oldfield's City Defense on red alert at the moment. Reportedly, Dr. Orgasm had also picked up several communist propaganda broadcasts stating that their army was currently fighting in the south of Innuendo, trying to overthrow the homophile governments of Sapphia and Gaye.

Radio had also confirmed this last to Courtney.

She was armed, however—a pistol holstered at her right hip—just in case. Any communists that tried on any nonsense with her out here would have themselves to blame.

Sultan still moved uneasily behind her. Courtney kept a firm hold of its reins; worked to steady it. Her mount's unease began to affect her; she began thinking it was best to return Sultan to the stables. She'd come back tomorrow Sunday; likely pick another horse.

But for now, time to go make love to Radio! At the thought, Courtney's body tingled, her vagina clenched sweetly with ghosts of the morning's climaxes when she and Radio had done it sixty-nine style.

Yes, yes, it's time to go home. She turned the horse back toward Metaphor.

Then, about to spur Sultan into a gallop across the wide plain separating them from the city, she paused, yanking back hard on the horse's reins to halt its motion.

The City. Metaphor's buildings looked strangely grimy in this pre-afternoon light. Though she'd seen her home from a distance many times before, Courtney felt a peculiar disappointment today: Metaphor seemed nothing like the bastion of sanity it was. Its concrete and glass structures were there, its outlines familiar in their solidity; but . . . something missing from the city.

Or had been added to it.

"It looks like the communists have stained it," she groaned aloud. "Like their anti-sexual filth is slowly corroding our walls, eroding away our lives." In a parody of defeat, she slumped in the saddle. *Sure, we keep resisting them, but is this a prophecy in vision? How long will it be before their sexually repressive ideas seep into our brains in our sleep, and we all wake up one morning wearing yellow spandex and black gasmasks too? Damn!*

Over the city, bright sun shone though white clouds. To Courtney's mind, the sunlight only heightened the spread of commie rot—now her eyes made out clear gray patches on white walls, patches that crawled like spiders over the buildings, trapping the citizens in its nebulous web.

Courtney was suddenly in no mood to ride home just yet. She spun Sultan forward again to face the trees. Any sight was better than that behind her.

A movement jerked her eyes up overhead. In the distance, well away over the trees, the air was ripping open and lumps of Bizarro squirting through.

She grimaced. *Where does Bizarro come from anyway? And how is it even possible for the sky to split open like it's nothing more than a sheet of pale blue cloth?*

Then with alarm, Courtney realized she had a bigger worry. Without a command from her, her horse Sultan had suddenly burst into motion, and was galloping toward the edge of the Safe Zone.

"Whoa! Whoa!" she yelled as the ring of trees drew closer and closer, yanking hard on the reins, while her horse, clearly insistent on reaching some target outside the Safe Zone, completely ignored her commands and galloped faster.

***

They crashed through the barrier of trees, with Courtney now holding on for dear life. The horse seemed to have gone mad under her. Leaves and branches whipped her face and she had to drop her head almost into Sultan's brown mane to not be blinded by pine needles.

Then, just as abruptly as they'd begun, the trees ended and she and the horse were charging over a plain studded with tall brown rocks and even taller violet flowers that hung down like church bells.

With the leaves and branches gone, Courtney dared look up again. Sultan was slowing now, as if whatever insane instinct had cast it through the protecting pines had waned.

Oops, Courtney thought, *I'm way out in the Dreamfields here. I'd better turn this damn fool animal around right now.*

She hauled long and hard on Sultan's reins till it finally shuddered to a halt. She sat in the saddle there in the middle of the Dreamfields, as winded as if she and not the horse had done all the running. The smell of the purple flowers was everywhere, their fragrance lulling her.

She turned in her seat. Metaphor's towers were distant now, as if (she couldn't resist the simile) . . . as if the floral perfume were a lens that made things seem farther off.

Turning around again, Courtney's gaze was caught by sudden motion to her left, a short distance ahead and behind the closest dangling flower. Sensing it too, her horse neighed in fear.

She patted the animal, pulled her gun. "This is more your fault than mine, Sultan, so let's at least see what it is. Hopefully, it's not something dangerous to Metaphor."

(Courtney didn't actually like the fact that she had to investigate whatever it was that lay behind the flower, but, with the commies getting desperate nowadays—Radio had told her they were scared that Dr. Orgasm was developing a new sexual super-pill for women—she felt they were liable to try anything. Such a pill, if it existed, would completely put Florence Rigid out of the sex-repression business.)

She spurred the brown stallion forward, around a border of robust purple petals, each one larger than her entire body. The flower's interior was a glossy vermiculated indigo that faded suddenly to white in the bell's heights (seeing as the humongous bloom hung upside-down).

Once they'd turned the corner, she pulled up sharp. A brown smoky mass lay on the grass.

It's a chunk of Bizarro, Courtney realized in horror. She instantly looked up, checking if she'd missed the ripping of sky that usually preceded such arrivals. (The distant Bizarro ingress from earlier was sealed up now; the brown clumps it had left behind floated across the far off sky like turds bobbing in a swimming pool.) But no, the air overhead here was clear; this chunk of insanity must have blown in from someplace else. Either that, or the rip that had brought it to Innuendo had happened in midair.

Sultan sensed her alarm; the horse stepped back several paces, grinding its flank (and Courtney's left leg) painfully against the flower.

The brown chunk on the floor twitched with life. Slowly, it fragmented into a pile of black insects, bugs like big beetles but blind, eyeless, and without any antennae. Some of the insects quickly burrowed into the earth, others milled about restlessly.

Are these things morph bugs? (Courtney had heard creepy tales of the insects Bizarro sometimes brought—amongst other things—but had never seen them.)

One insect ran into a chunk of rock. The insect vanished into the rock substance; the rock instantly grew several furry legs.

She winced. *Yes, they're definitely morph bugs! Those look like cat legs!*

Then Sultan neighed sharply, like it was in distress. Then it reared, almost bucking Courtney off its back. When the horse had settled again, she looked down to see what had startled it.

Damn, there's human hands growing from its leg!

Sultan's left foreleg was coated with hands of all sizes, shapes and colorations; one hand was green with long orange fingernails.

Sultan neighed and neighed in fear but now seemed rooted to the spot. All Courtney's spurring and yanking on its reins to make it turn had no effect whatsoever. She pulled her gun, fired thrice into the mass of insects then gave up; the bullets had no effect on them. There were too many of the bugs to hurt and the noise didn't scatter them like she'd hoped it would. She quickly reholstered her gun; after almost being flung off the horse once, she realized she needed both hands on its reins now.

Like bats homing in on a tree by radar, more of the big blind black bugs now swarmed the horse's feet. They vanished into Sultan's legs, clambered up to reach its flanks, were dissolved into its sides also. Other morph bugs were grabbed by the hands growing from Sultan's legs, where they kicked and slimed to be free.

Though alarmed, Courtney was also perplexed—the ebon insects seemed transparent in places. They also appeared to have gears inside them, like they were actually little machines.

Then Courtney realized that her horse was melting. First its hooves then its lower legs were slowly dissolving to black jelly, while Sultan itself let off a series of humanlike screams of horror and pain.

Her own precarious situation now made itself overtly clear to her. *If I either fall into those things . . . or if they climb up here to me!*

Quickly, as the horse melted away under her, Courtney jerked her feet up out of the stirrups and climbed up on its back.

She'd almost timed it too late: the black beetles—the morph bugs— were already streaming fast up Sultan's flank to reach her when she ran down the stallion's back and leaped over its tail onto a clear patch of grass.

Then she was off; running hard back towards Metaphor.

***

Once certain she'd escaped the morph bugs, Courtney checked herself to make certain none of the insects had latched onto her clothes.

Relieved to find that they hadn't, she now looked back.

At the end of an aisle of humongous purple bells, Sultan's tail flailed once, then slumped in defeat. Simultaneously came a neigh that even at this distance sounded thunderous. Then all was silent, except for her thudding heartbeat, and a soft humming she first imagined was the sound of her frazzled emotions.

Courtney wept for Sultan. The stallion's passing seemed so pointless. Damn, the morph bugs hadn't even killed it for food, they'd just . . .

The humming grew louder and nearer. Suddenly understanding that the sound was external, she spun towards it.

Oh, shit!

Ten yards to her right, a huge metal saucer hovered in midair.

Oh no, she thought in horror, *it's the commies!*

Moving like a flash, Courtney swept her hand down to draw her gun again. As her fingers grabbed its grip, however, something hit her in the back of the head—it felt like a hammer breaking through her skull—and next thing, the grass was rising to meet her like a bed.

Oops, I'm in so much trouble, was her last thought before the darkness fell on her like night.

CHAPTER 29

Courtney awoke in a warm, cream-colored room. It had no windows or furniture other than for several tall plastic cabinets lined along the wall to her right.

She was naked, gagged, and strapped tightly down, able to move only her head. Her legs felt both raised and widely separated.

By straining her neck upward, Courtney made out that she lay on a Y-shaped metal table (the split in the 'Y' occurring at her crotch) and with her legs secured to the table's two arms. And yes, her legs *were* both widely separated and raised, almost like she was about to deliver a baby. Both the Y-table's lower divisions were hinged in two places, clearly allowing for adjusting her legs in a multiple of directions.

One final detail leapt in through her eyes, surged up her optic nerves: her vagina had been shaved completely bald.

So much better to rape you, honey. The horrible thought budded in her head like mental cancer. She couldn't imagine any other explanation as to why she was so arranged. The Y-table granted anyone free access to her crotch. And that *anyone* was obviously the communists.

I don't feel wet down there, so nobody's violated me yet. But they might just have cleaned me up afterwards . . . but I don't feel sore, so . . .

Breathing hard from the effort of keeping her neck raised for so long, she let her head fall back down to the table.

How long have I been out for? There was no clock in the room, none she could see anyway; no ticking either indicating one's presence.

The door on her right marked out an ominous negative time to her: Soon, very soon, footsteps would walk up to this very same door, and it would open and disgorge her nightmares into the room.

And then . . . She raised her head again, stared down between her breasts at her shaved sex, at her separated legs. And then . . .

A feeling of panic now suffused her. Biting down hard on the gag in her mouth, she fought against her terror, tried to swallow it like saliva; digest it away. But . . . how did you resist the inevitable? If the communists were the irresistible force, she was far from being an immovable object. And she knew it. At the moment she was most definitely a prisoner in Vaginismus, the communist stronghold. *And no how am I leaving here unhurt, if I ever leave here at all.*

(Many were the women and men the commies had abducted. Few ever returned home, and those that did were all horribly mutilated, most of them almost out of their minds as well from the horrors they'd experienced. Indeed, it was believed that these returnees hadn't really escaped Vaginismus, but had rather been dropped off in the countryside; communist signposts intended to strike the fear of Florence Rigid into any naïve fools who still imagined such a thing as sexual security existed in Innuendo.)

Courtney finally got a grip on herself. At that moment, however, the door clicked open and the communists entered.

Courtney's fear instantly returned. And now, she had no buffer of displaced time to pad its effect.

***

There were four communists, two male, two female, all wearing their yellow one-piece catsuits and black 'spaceman' gasmasks. Both men were tall and muscular and had exceedingly broad shoulders. The foremost woman was slim with small pert breasts; the other woman short and muscular, but with an expansive bosom. All four communists seemed to be naked under their yellow uniforms: Courtney clearly made out both women's nipples and the outlines of the men's penises in their crotches.

"Welcome to Vaginismus, Courtney Taylor," the lead woman saluted her in a histrionic cartoonish voice. "I'm Meghyn. Now remember: Once you've come our way, you never come anyway again."

How do you know my name!? her eyes screamed at them. But then she realized she had other, bigger things to worry about. One of the male communists was already unzipping his crotch.

If the gag hadn't been in place, Courtney would have screamed on seeing the size of the man's penis. Bound as she was, all she could do was clench her fists in impotent horror. The communist's member looked like a white python unfurling from his crotch. He stroked it to erection. Courtney's eyes bugged out in her face from sheer apprehension as the penis got bigger and bigger. Finally it was as thick as a beer can and over twice as long.

"Hurry up, soldier," Meghyn said in her fluty voice, "Put it in, put it in! Courtney is clearly as impatient as I am to get started with this."

Courtney shook her head violently, the tendons in her neck standing out like ropes. *I'm not! No, I'm not!*

Holding his fat erection like it was a spear, the communist strode between the Y-table's wings. Once in position, he roughly parted the lips of Courtney's vagina and inserted the massive penis. She gasped as the organ's head spread her sex wide, then gasped again in shocked pain when he thrust forward into her, hard and violent, like a battering ram breaching a castle wall. Courtney was aware of her body ripping down there, of herself bleeding.

The communist slammed away into her, gripping her thighs to steady himself.

Behind her gag, Courtney screamed and screamed and screamed. Her eyes filled with tears that streamed down both sides of her face.

"Very good," Meghyn commented. "Very good. But slow down; our glorious leader Miss Rigid wants this horny little bitch to really feel it."

The communist raping Courtney slowed the pace of his thrusts.

"That's much better," Meghyn said. She tapped the second male communist on the shoulder. "Now, you, fill her mouth."

Courtney's gag was summarily removed by the short and muscular female communist.

"Stop!" she shrieked as the man unzipped himself. "Please! Sto—"

Her sudden painful cessation of words was both from the man in her loins giving a particularly hard thrust into her bleeding sex and also from the new man plugging her mouth with his member. His penis tasted unwashed and stank like it hadn't ever been cleaned—stank of smegma, sweat, dirt, bacteria . . .

Her eyes widened further in her disgust. Finding sudden reserves of resolve, she spread her mouth wide, readying to bite down hard on the cock and sever it from its owner.

"If you dare bite," Meghyn said just as she was about to do so, "I'll have all your teeth pulled with pliers."

Courtney let her jaw slacken again, let the communist's smelly penis (which was almost as huge as the first man's) down deep into her throat. The erection instantly blocked off her air supply and made her gag. It was held in place in her throat till she was choking and clawing the table in her desperation to get some air in, then was slid back up again. Then back down deep, throttling off her urge to vomit. Finally, the penis slid out of her throat to the stretched ring of her lips, permitting her to hack in a few breaths, then it was shoved deep into her neck again.

The rape went on. Courtney's body swam between twin agonies of suffocation and pain as she was violently violated. Around her mind floated a cold mist of terror. *I'm going to die! I'm going to die!* Her fear was greater than her pain, almost anesthetic, and it allowed her a sort of detached perspective on her situation. It also distorted her perception of events: In their yellow catsuits and massive gasmasks—it was impossible, for instance, to tell what color of hair either woman had, or if both were bald—her rapists looked like sci-fi aliens.

The communist using her mouth grunted, gripped her hair, and began coming.

"Don't you dare spit it out," Meghyn warned, "Or else . . ."

The threat hanging, Courtney swallowed the salty ejaculate. The man had seemingly buckets of it for her to drink. He came on and on and on. Her defeated mind raged with the impossibility of what she was experiencing. *Communists are called that because they're supposedly made of semen, right? Evil-sperm-filled cretins symbolically clothed in yellow because at heart, they're nothing but cowardly woman-abusers; and their gasmasks are because they don't really have personalities other than the rapist one . . .*

She'd taken her mind off of her swallowing task. The commie's semen backed up into her nose, completely clogging her breathing. Meghyn laughed while she snorted the white liquid everywhere.

The man finished filling her mouth with sperm and stepped back. Simultaneously, the man between her legs gave a massive thrust that felt like it had dislodged her cervix and began coming too. She screamed from fresh pain—his semen felt like boiling water cooking the cuts in her vagina.

She ran out of pain for the moment, looked right to beg Meghyn for mercy.

"Please!" she gasped. "Please—"

Her eyes widened in horror. Meghyn too had unzipped the crotch of her catsuit and was fondling a large stiffening penis.

"There is no mercy here," the transsexual communist informed Courtney. "Only agony. Pure delicious agony. That is the golden rule of Vaginismus. Miss Rigid wants you to have your fill of pain before she returns." She snapped her fingers at the stocky female communist. "When he's done, get between her legs. I'll take her mouth."

The stocky woman had been partially hidden from view by Meghyn's body. She stepped forward; Courtney saw she had strapped on a large spiky dildo.

Meghyn stepped up to Courtney's mouth and stuffed her hard penis between the slack unresponsive lips.

"Ah, just the way I like it: nice and wet—I love sloppy seconds."

Meghyn left her penis lying in Courtney's mouth, bobbing on her tongue like she expected her to do something with it.

I'm not sucking you, bitch, Courtney thought defiantly.

The other woman had meanwhile replaced the man between Courtney's legs. She prepared herself for another painful intrusion, then was horrified when Meghyn said: "Not her vagina—her anus. Do it hard, without lube."

"No!" Courtney screamed as she was invaded through her rear, the thick dildo stinging like salt rubbed into a wound. (Now, she really wished she'd agreed to try anal sex all those times Radio had suggested it.) Her anus felt like it was tearing; then she sensed it had indeed torn: at the same moment the penetration became both easier and more painful, like her blood was lubricating the dildo.

The communist woman leaned over Courtney and squeezed her breasts. She laughed. "She's real tight down there—a virgin." Bent over like that, she seemed a sprawled yellow bug, her face an opaque blur in the gasmask's glass oval. She removed her hands from Courtney's breasts, gripped her thighs again and slid the dildo deep inside the wetly protesting anus. Then out again, making a thick stink of excrement assault Courtney's nose. "She's packed full of crap too."

"We'll widen her up." Meghyn slapped her erection hard on Courtney's tongue. "Resistance is futile, you slut; like it or not, *you will* suck me." She laughed, and before Courtney even realized she had, produced a shiny switchblade from somewhere. She clicked it open, pressed the blade against Courtney's nose. "Now, except you want to start breathing air directly into your brain, I suggest you put your mouth to its God-given use."

She dug the knife into Courtney's left nostril, cutting her slightly. Blood trickling down her cheeks, Courtney tightened her lips around Meghyn's penis and sucked while the trans-commie leaned back and squeezed her latex-wrapped breasts.

Meghyn's crotch was perfumed, but the pain of the rending assault on Courtney's rectum threatened to make her vomit from nausea. *Oh, God, fucking please make it stop!* It was hellishly painful. Also, each thrust felt like the commie woman's dildo was forcing the excrement back up Courtney's guts, up to her mouth.

(The two male communists meanwhile sat on short cabinets by the wall, watching the rape and masturbating their huge members. Occasionally—when Courtney jerked in pain or yelped loudly—they laughed and gave themselves high-fives and thumbs-ups.)

Still, knowing she'd be noseless if she didn't, Courtney managed to suck Meghyn to orgasm. Slapping Courtney's breasts violently, printing red fingermarks on her white skin, Meghyn ejaculated another bowl-load of semen into her mouth. While wishing she was courageous enough to let herself choke to death on the ghastly smelly liquid, Courtney swallowed it all.

Finally, Meghyn gave a loud contented sigh and stepped back from the table. The next moment, the dildo between Courtney's buttocks was sharply removed. She gasped as air rushed up her torn, bleeding backside.

"Okay, boys, are you ready?" Meghyn asked.

"Yes, Madam," echoed their husky replies.

Dull-eyed and slack-jawed from mingled pain and emotional trauma, Courtney could only gape at the two men as they walked towards her again. *Oh no, please, God, not again!*

She wasn't raped again, however. Instead, her head was tilted back upright, and both communists spurted their viscid white slime into her mouth, with Meghyn waving her knife over Courtney's right eye to ensure she swallowed every drop of their flood-like ejaculations. (Courtney now realized that her belly was full—full of rapist semen.)

When this was over, Meghyn and the two men packed their soft penises back into their latex clothes. The second woman stripped off her dildo, now stained (like her crotch) with shit and blood.

Meghyn walked over and stroked Courtney's face tenderly. "Okay, darling, you've had breakfast and lunch. We'll be back in eight hours to feed you dinner. And once again: welcome to Vaginismus, Courtney."

Courtney stared at her speechless.

All the communists laughed. Then they left.

CHAPTER 30

Time ran out of meaning for Courtney. The lights never went off in the room where she was held captive. Her only way of measuring time's passage was when Meghyn and her goons came to rape her. This happened with clockwork regularity, seemingly every morning and evening. At first, she counted the communists' visits to her cream-colored prison, but after a while, with no way to keep records, the incidences blurred into the carriages of a single train of abuse that appeared to have been occurring forever, and which would continue forever.

Soon, she had no idea how long she'd been held captive, it could have been a month, it could have been a year. She shat and pissed where she was and the communists didn't reprimand her for doing so. (She quickly realized her excrement never piled up under her ass.)

In periods of thought, she found her situation cruelly ironic: Except for the endless torrent of pain and suffering, these communist men had the sort of bodies Radio's sister Highball pined after—big and muscular like they'd been pumping iron from the womb, using their mothers' fallopian tubes for barbells. No shit. The sexy redhead would cream herself silly—have visual orgasms—just seeing these guys' abs and pecs. *So why couldn't Highball have been the one to get captured by the commies? Why'd it have to be me? Huh?* She didn't wish her current terrible experiences on anyone, least of all her potential sister-in-law, but . . . *Goddamit! Life's just so unfair . . .*

Occasionally, she was released from the Y-table, but only when Meghyn and the others wanted to triple-team her. Even at these brief vertical periods, however, she was kept chained hand and foot; she had zero chance of either resistance or escape.

She was bent over the table, spread eagled and brutally penetrated, usually by three assailants at once. Or held up in midair between both men, one of them in each of her front and back holes, their transsexual commander up on the table grabbing her head and ramming it down on her fat erection, so that as usual, Courtney was choking.

They used her like she was a doll, bending her this way and that at will, at times almost breaking her in half in some horrendous contortion. Fucked her like she as a bitch, one who didn't know she was in heat.

The transgender Meghyn always visited Courtney in the company of three other rapists—their horrible ubiquitous gasmasks making it impossible for her to tell if they were the same three, or other abusers—two men hung like horses, and a short woman wearing a thick bristly strap-on. Their masks muffled their voices, so those were no giveaway to their identities either.

Their brutality was always the same, though.

(On the first of her occasions of 'freedom' she discovered the Y-table was designed with both a scooped slide and hanging pail under her buttock area to collect her excrement and a wide runoff gutter between the table's wings to collect her urine. To clean her off after sex, the communists simply hosed her down with warm water ("Don't expect to die of flu, darling," Meghyn mocked once. "Not a chance.")

And Courtney? She suffered it mostly in silence, after discovering insults and blows (in those rare fleeting moments when her hands were unshackled) brought her only additional degradation.

The relentless sexual humiliation took its toll. By the end of the first six 'rape sessions,' Courtney had adjusted to the complete feeling of worthlessness such ill-use automatically created in a woman. Her resignation wasn't cowardice, but apathy: *She who's hit rock-bottom can't really fall further, can she?*

But the pain continued, and if anything heightened, till she dreaded the door to the right of the table opening and disgorging the yellow-clad men and women.

Her mind became more and more frayed. Soon her sanity was close to collapse, her personality dangling from mere shreds of memory; the memory that she was human, more than this 'nothing' the communists had made of her. And in the dark hours between one savage sexual assault and another she wondered why she bothered to remain sane. But she always had a ready reply to her own question: *I want to look Florence Rigid in the face and spit on her!*

And her anger was strength. Her anger kept her alive and vibrant, where otherwise she'd have mentally imploded (as unknown to her, most women and men Meghyn brought into this same room had).

But mental alertness, even that propping up an increasingly diseased and collapsing mind, had its drawbacks. Courtney *felt* . . . oh, she felt every horror of this seemingly endless incarceration. Every penetration, every beating, felt like a new death she was dying, her femininity being interred, used as fertilizer in which the commies were growing a version of herself purged of free will and human rights.

Pain and violence; violence and pain. All evil.

(She spent long hours thinking of her boyfriend Radio. She knew he had to be going nuts by now, trying to find her. Or had he given up hope too? She imagined Radio sitting frozen in a chair, twirling his ears madly, tuning his mind in hope of catching news of her somewhere amidst Innuendo's airwaves.)

All this time, she was fed nothing. Her only nutrition was her daily intake of communist semen. Occasionally, before ejaculating in Courtney's mouth, Meghyn would drop a handful of pills onto her tongue. "Antibiotics," she'd explain before flooding the protesting oral cavity with come again. "We can't be too careful with your health here. Our glorious leader Miss Rigid wants you in prime condition, so no infections from ass-to-mouth."

She grew skinny from the malnourishment, with her belly protruding like that of a child with kwashiorkor from each new semen influx.

Semen for breakfast and dinner till her shit dribbled like water from her ass.

And yet the communists continued to abuse her, to painfully fuck her morning and night, till confused, Courtney wondered if Vaginismus was actually Hell, with Florence Rigid simply another name for the Devil, and there was never going to be any end to her torment.

CHAPTER 31

The daily rapes continued.

"Where is Florence Rigid?" Courtney gasped in agony once. "Does she even exist?"

Meghyn laughed. "Of course she does. Our glorious leader is currently away pacifying the town of Misandry. Those uppity bitches think they call the shots in Innuendo. Miss Rigid says no orgasms, period; but the Misandrans want concessions, claim that for a woman to hate men is enough . . ." She grabbed a painful handful of Courtney's hair in a yellow-gloved fist. "But that is not what communism is about! We say: no orgasms, period."

"But that's just double standards. You commies all come," Courtney protested, wondering why she insisted on speaking when she knew the dangers of expressing her opinion to these psychopaths. "You come over and over again."

In response, she could practically feel Meghyn smirking behind her gleaming metal mask.

"We're *communists*, you stupid vagina. We're packed full of *come*. It has to come out somehow."

"Even the women?"

"*Of course*—don't be sexist now." Meghyn crocked a finger at the female communist. "Come here, soldier."

The stocky woman, who'd been masturbating by the door, gloved fingers deep in her sex, walked over. "Yes, Madam Meghyn?"

Meghyn handed her a knife. "Cut off your nipple; the right one."

The woman took the knife from Meghyn. She pinched her right nipple tight in its covering of yellow latex, pulled it out from her breast, and slowly sliced it off. Courtney winced as the knife cut through fabric and flesh. Despite what she'd heard/knew about the commies, watching this woman mutilate herself like this horrified her. Worse still, the woman in the gasmask showed no signs of discomfort—she didn't flinch or squeal as she hurt herself. Which made Courtney wonder: *Is she even hurting herself?* No blood flowed from the wound, just a white liquid dribble.

Done, the woman placed her severed nipple beside Courtney's head.

"Now, milk yourself into her mouth—let her taste you."

The woman in the gasmask did that too. She bent over Courtney's head and squeezed her wounded breast hard. White liquid squirted into Courtney's mouth. Its pungency filled her nose. Yes, it was semen alright! And the quantity! With each bout of applied pressure, the come pumped out from the woman's breast. Soon Courtney's mouth was slopping with breast-come which she didn't dare spit out. She swallowed, then when the stinky gush didn't let up, swallowed again and again.

"Okay, that's enough, soldier," Meghyn said finally. "Repair yourself. I'm sure uppity Miss Taylor here believes me now."

The other woman picked up her nipple and replaced it back on her breast. The wounds—both flesh and fabric—healed instantly, leaving the breast as new. She wiped her wet fingers clean on Courtney's hair.

Meghyn laughed. "How do you like our taste?" Her voice turned serious. "I hope you understand this now: we communists come because *we are* come—it's our nature to ejaculate. You humans, however, are animals, beasts propelled by base instinct—"

Courtney said, "And your exalted Florence Rigid? Is she an animal too?"

One of the men slapped her, filling her mouth with blood. "Shut up, you dumb hole! Don't you dare insult the glorious leader!" Courtney wished she was free and had a knife. She'd cut off his huge penis and stuff his anus with it. That'd teach the rapist son-of-a-bitch. (She realized she was talking too much today, but didn't care. This might even turn out for the best for her—maybe they'd kill her by accident if she angered them enough.)

She glared at Meghyn, seeing her own reflection on the woman's metal 'face.' "I asked you a question, you stupid tranny cunt: Florence Rigid. She's as human as me, ain't she? So what makes her in any way better, you bastards? Why not just rape *her* instead?"

The man made to slap her again; Meghyn stopped him with a gesture. There was a pregnant pause, when Courtney imagined she'd definitely overstepped her bounds and was dead as dogshit, but then Meghyn giggled.

"You're a right feisty little bitch, Courtney," she said. "So tonight we'll try something a little different to cure your bad attitude."

Courtney was summarily flipped over on the table and arranged with her buttocks in the air. Her ankles were bound to the table's wings, her wrists secured above her head.

"Get on top, in her ass," Meghyn next instructed her female counterpart. The woman instantly complied, lying on Courtney so her stiff aroused nipples poked Courtney's back, then slipping her dildo into Courtney's already aching ass hole.

Meghyn snapped her fingers at one of the male communists. "You too, get inside her."

The man obediently strode between Courtney's legs.

Courtney tensed, expecting the dreaded painful intrusion into her vagina, but what she got was way worse. The man began forcing his penis into her anus alongside the dildo. *Hiroshima!* her mind screamed, almost snapping from the pain like her anal sphincter appeared to be doing.

Meghyn masturbated along with the abuse, sliding a fist back and forth over her bone-white penis. The stiff nipples topping her bobbing breasts were testament to her excitement.

Courtney fainted from the pain.

When she awoke, the communist woman still lay on top of her and she was still being raped hard up the tail by both of them. In her universe of unbelievable agonies, this was the most unbelievable she'd yet experienced. She screamed and tried to shit the rapists out—she knew she'd been destroyed down there. Her crotch felt horrendously wet; whether from blood or semen or her own watery excrement, she couldn't tell.

The man came in her. Then the pair pulled out of her behind.

Immediately Courtney's ass was empty, she felt like she needed to take an immense shit. By now, she had no shame left—the communists had seen all of her there was to see, had robbed her of all sense of self-worth and dignity—so she just did it there on the table with them watching. Only it felt like she was squeezing a baby out of her anus. One with a really large head. And it hurt like childbirth too.

She finally got done with her painful shit, then wondered why the communists were laughing.

"Oh what a pretty pink sock you have!" Meghyn yelped.

"Pink . . . what?"

"It's a porn expression," one of the men replied. "Your rectum just fell out of your anus, honey."

"What a lovely pink donut," the other added.

"And I'm going to fuck it," Meghyn said.

"Please, no!" Courtney pleaded. "Don't!"

"Yes!" Meghyn quickly walked into the gap in the table and inserted her penis into the extruded portion of Courtney's rectum. She fucked it long and hard, squeezing the displaced pink tissue violently around her erection, making it bleed from fresh tears. Meghyn's fat erection invaded Courtney like an army, tearing up into her bowels via the exposed tissue. The communists all laughed, while Courtney screamed and screamed blue murder then passed out again.

This time when she came around, the communists had all left. She was instantly aware of horrific pain between her legs like someone had emptied concentrated sulfuric acid into her anus. She felt the bloody, semen-soiled solidity of her prolapsed rectum between her buttocks, compressing them like a malformed stillborn child . . .

And so it went on for Courtney Taylor day after day after day. Rape, rape, and more rape. More degradation than she'd ever imagined possible. Soon she was living right next door to crazy, teetering right on the brink of losing it. Really, really close to the edge.

CHAPTER 32

And then, just like that, one day it was all over.

The door to Courtney's cream-colored cell swung open and Meghyn entered.

The transsexual woman's body language showed she was clearly displeased about something. Behind Meghyn, three other communists, all male, entered.

"Free her and bring her down to the lab," Meghyn said in a pissed-off voice.

"Lab . . . lab . . . lab . . ." Courtney stuttered inanely. By now she was practically mad from her ordeal, more out of her head than in it. On seeing the four enter, she'd been preparing to be *really* raped. That was her only function in life wasn't it—to be a communist comebucket, a worthless piece of female plumbing to be used at will?

But today was different.

"Lab . . . lab . . ." she stuttered again as her starvation-shriveled arms and legs were freed. "Lab . . . lab . . . rape . . . fuck . . . fuck . . ."

"Shut her up, for fuck's sake!"

The next moment something touched Courtney's forehead and she fell unconscious.

***

She dreamt.

She lay in a soft and luxurious bed, having sex with an utterly gorgeous man. He was a total hunk, just perfect and incredibly well-hung, and she was so wet and willing, her labia spreading like sun-warmed petals to accommodate his supreme girth.

Outside ornate bowed windows, large peacocks flocked in a garden tapestried with giant golden and purple flowers, the monster blooms filling the room with a decadent scent of the Orient that wrapped itself about both she and her lover like aerial silk.

And he was fantastic in bed, understood her body better than anyone else ever had before, his tongue stroking her clitoris, feather-soft fingers caressing her breasts; and his organ too—so huge, the penetration so deep, filling her to her utter brim, trilling all her nerves to sensory overload.

Their bodies moved together in delicious synchronicity amidst the room's perfumed ambience, flowed into one another till she felt nothing else but herself.

And then she was coming, coming, coming. It was incredible: She gasped, she grimaced; she burnt out of herself, melted through the walls, ceiling, and floor; blew out like glass exploding from windows. Each orgasm was joyous balm that soothed her, both body and soul.

The sex was fantastic, as good as it could ever be. Absolute utter perfection.

CHAPTER 33

When Courtney awoke she was in another room. A blue room with a lot of medical equipment to which she was hooked up. Her emaciated form lay tucked in a soft bed with blue sheets and a floral duvet. This room had a window opposite the foot of her bed, with at the moment, its white drapes closed.

Suddenly realizing she wasn't chained anymore, Courtney sat up in bed, causing the duvet to fall off her body.

She grimaced on seeing herself. *I look like a concentration camp victim.* Her breasts hung down, empty bags of skin. Her belly stuck out like there was a baby in it. Above its taut protrusion, she could clearly count her ribs. Her hands and legs were more bone than flesh.

There was one difference, however, from the past months (Weeks? Years?) of her sexual ordeal. Her vagina and anus didn't hurt. Indeed, her entire crotch felt wonderful, like nothing bad had ever happened down there.

And, thinking hard, she suddenly realized that she couldn't actually remember too much about the past. She recalled being raped, but by who? And even the sexual violation itself was fuzzy.

She remembered her sweet sex dream, then scowled it off. *That was just my subconscious compensating me for all the crap I've been through!*

She persevered with thinking. Slowly, it all came back: Being chained to the Y-table, Meghyn and three other commies, huge penises and dildos, her orifices tearing, blood and semen everywhere, no food . . . But while the memory existed, it didn't hurt. It seemed somehow natural that she'd been raped, like she'd deserved it. It had been good too . . . really good.

She giggled at the pleasant memory of how she'd been anally double-teamed till her rectum prolapsed, then, suddenly realizing how out of place her happy reaction to such a horrible recollection was, fear gripped her and she shuddered to the depths of her soul.

"Oh hell!" she gasped aloud as the full horror of her thoughts struck her. "I'm *happy* I was gang-raped? My mind's broken!"

"That isn't the case," a soft female voice said to her right.

Courtney spun towards the speaker, wondering both how she'd been in the room without being noticed, and how long she'd been there.

"I'm Florence Rigid," the woman said, stepping out from behind a screen. "How do you feel, Courtney?"

In response, Courtney just gaped at her first-ever sight of the communist leader.

Florence Rigid was, like Courtney, a slim blonde. She was very good-looking, with calm gray eyes and full lips. Alter her hair color to red and she'd look a lot like Radiohead's sister Highball. She wore a light-blue dress that stopped just above the knee and flat-soled white shoes.

Despite Courtney's hatred of the woman, an overpowering awe now filled her like she was in the presence of a goddess.

Florence Rigid pulled a chair up to Courtney's bedside and sat. Her lilac perfume infused the air between them. "I asked how you feel?" Her soft voice demanded a no-bullshit reply.

"I feel better," Courtney replied, then added: "*Why* do I feel better? I've just been through the worst experience that any woman's ever had." She gestured at her body. "I mean, fucking look at me!"

The communist leader smiled coldly. "You feel good because I had you fixed. I can't have you losing your mind on me." She frowned. "Meghyn shaved it horribly close this time: a day or two more and you'd have been utterly useless. I still have need of you."

Courtney had no idea what she meant. "How long have I been here?"

"You've been in Vaginismus for six weeks."

Six . . . ? Normally a dogged fighter, Courtney didn't understand why she wasn't even now leaping for Florence's neck and strangling her. Or better still, biting out her throat like a lioness would and playing in the woman's blood? Either way, rid Innuendo of this murdering bitch for good.

Florence Rigid read the angry emotions in her eyes. She laughed. "Oh, I had that fixed too. No matter how much you'd like to, you can't harm me. Your mind won't let you, so just forget it, okay? Besides, even if you could hurt me, if you did so, my forces would instantly kill you and feed you to the Bees. And since you're not going to be abused any more, and . . . since you're no longer angry about the rape you did suffer . . ." she shrugged, "why do something so stupid?"

Courtney was stumped by Florence's logic. "I won't be raped anymore?"

"No. There's no more need for it."

"Need for it? Was there a need for it before? Is there ever such a need?"

"Yes, in your case there was. The demands of scientific research at all times override the selfish rights of the individual."

"You sound like Dr. Orgasm, just way crazier."

Florence's lips thinned in anger. "Control your tongue, Courtney. True, I've no further use for you as a rape guinea pig, but I can still cause you a world of pain."

Courtney gulped and nodded.

Florence got to her feet. She pushed Courtney down flat on the bed, then sat on its edge looking down at her. Courtney made to rise again, Florence pushed her back down.

"Relax, you're not strong enough yet." She grimaced. "And you're all bones and belly now."

"That's hardly my fault. You'd be too if you'd been on a diet of nothing but semen for a month-and-a-half."

"Stop whining. I'll soon fatten you up again."

Courtney's gaze narrowed. Despite her awe of Florence Rigid, she was still pissed-off. But no, she wasn't pissed-off. That was the problem: it was impossible to be irate with someone while hampered in feeling the required level of outrage because effective memory of the outrage was being dampened by good feelings. And by good feelings that reached down to her vagina, of all places.

"So what kind of research required you to have me bound and sexually assaulted by your goons for six weeks?" she asked acidly. "And," her mind quailed as she remembered another of the woman's earlier statement's, "did you said you've *further* use for me? This bloody experiment isn't over yet?"

"I was about telling you that." Florence Rigid patted her knees, then pursed her lips. While talking, she smoothed crinkles in her blue dress. "It was Meghyn's idea really—she's my research assistant." She raised a hand to forestall Courtney's comments. "Uh uh—no questions till I'm done talking."

Courtney nodded.

Florence got off the bed, walked to the window and parted the drapes. It was about noon; light flooded the room. They also seemed to be upstairs.

Balancing her buttocks against the windowsill, looking more like a pretty blonde trainee nurse than the most powerful woman in Innuendo, Florence Rigid explained:

"Though she's undeniably brainy, Meghyn and I disagree on the best way to destroy a woman's orgasmic response. I believe psychology and medicine are best. She, possibly because of her nature, argues that an overload of physical abuse on a woman will in turn overload that woman's psyche to the extent that the very thought of sex becomes painful to her. We've been researching both approaches, the psychological and the physical, for ages." She stroked the drapes, frowned. "Unfortunately, we've never been able to either conclusively prove or disprove Meghyn's theory until you came along."

"Me?" Courtney gasped. "What's so special about me?"

"You're simply the perfect test subject for our experiment; exactly what we've been waiting for. Why? You've no sexual hang-ups. Okay, you don't like anal, but I don't count that as prudery; I mean, what do men always want up inside a woman's anus anyway? The vagina should be more than sufficient for them, right? I mean, provided by God or nature—pick one—accommodating penises is what it's there for in the first place, isn't it?" She frowned. "But so, okay, overlooking the anal thing, you're not a prude, you're not a nympho either, and you attain orgasm practically on demand. You're neither religious nor atheistic, you're mentally sound, you've no diseases . . ."

"I get it, I get it." (She did get one thing at least: The communists had some kind of equipment that could read her mind. The existence of such a machine would explain how Meghyn had known her name without being told. It also explained how they'd known her sexual peculiarities. And also, how Florence had 'fixed' her afterward. She shuddered as the 'pleasant' memories of her confinement caressed her again.)

Florence Rigid laughed like trickling water. "Actually, you *don't* get it, Courtney, but let's let that pass for now; all will be revealed in good time." She spread her hands demonstratively. "So, where were we? Oh yes; so once you fell into our hands . . . Oh, I will say this: you'd be surprised at how many women we catch have the strangest reasons not to have an orgasm. One woman was scared the mice would be watching . . . yes, *mice*." She laughed louder. "But enough of me rambling. Okay, we caught you, and I handed you over to Meghyn and her team."

"And they fucked me mercilessly for six weeks, fed me semen and—"

Florence Rigid grinned ghoulishly. "And we proved Meghyn's theory wrong!"

"Huh?"

Florence's grin was a white hole in her pretty face. "Yes, Courtney. Despite your ordeal at her hands, your sexual response wasn't damaged. You can still climax, will still come in fact, with ease. You took a physical battering, true, and yes, your mind almost broke, but you were still fixable. I fixed you."

The woman's gleeful smile never left her face. It was now that Courtney saw the sociopath in Florence Rigid. A bright gloss of fear coated the awe she already felt for the woman.

Florence strode back over to the bed. Behind her, a swarm of Bees—yellow and black insect death—floated low across the afternoon sky. The room was warm; the communist leader's incandescent grin had Courtney feeling like she was burning.

"What are you so happy about?" Courtney asked. "You've just proved that rape and torture don't work."

Florence's smile remained like it was painted on her face. "Rape and torture were only ever a means to an end." She clenched her fist before Courtney's face. "Though upset that she's been proven wrong, Meghyn understands that now. And so now we move on to my cure." She smiled at Courtney. "And I assure you, Miss Perfect Sexual Response, I do have a working cure for your vaginal ailment."

"Female circumcision?" Courtney asked in dread, already imagining a scalpel excising her clitoris.

"No, I'm not a savage. Besides, even circumcised, many women still reach orgasm. Vaginal ones, cervical ones, Breasts ones . . . anal ones even. The sensitivity just leapfrogs somewhere else in their bodies. Damn, it's such a bloody curse! But I'll cure women everywhere of it." Her gray eyes gaped wide. "Starting with you, Courtney. Starting with you."

"Please, Florence, don't fuck me up!" Courtney pleaded. "Please let me go!"

Florence Rigid laughed. "I would if I could, but this isn't personal, no, not at all . . . it's for the good of all women everywhere. Once they can't come anymore . . . they'll quickly evolve to a higher level, one where the weaker sex no longer dominates them . . ." Florence checked her watch. "Now go to sleep. It's been great meeting you but I've work to do."

Shit, she's completely nuts! Courtney thought. *I really wish I could kill her!*

Florence laughed at her. "Don't even *think* it."

Before Courtney could retort, Florence Rigid had pressed a short metal rod to her forehead and Courtney blacked out again.

CHAPTER 34

The next week passed Courtney by in a blur. She was fed, bathed, practically pampered by the communists. (An early examination in the bathroom revealed that all the damage to her sex and her ass had been perfectly surgically repaired.)

As Florence Rigid explained during the single additional five-minute visit she made to the blue room during this time, "I need you hale and hearty for the next stage of my work."

She refused to elaborate any further.

So the latex-clad and gas-masked men and women tended to Courtney. When questioned, they replied her courteously but curtly. Nothing was divulged of what was to come. Her dread anticipation grew by the hour.

She put on weight rapidly. In three days, she looked almost normal again, her grossly swollen belly now deflated. Except for the lines on her face from her ordeal, that ordeal had become a pleasant fantasy.

When she was alone, she stood at her window, watching the outside world. (Her room was on the fourth floor.) The view was of a large parade ground fenced in on three sides by buildings, with a honeycombed hill directly opposite. Bees came and went from the monster hive in their droves, throughout the day, their distant buzzing the soundtrack to life in Vaginismus.

Courtney wondered how the communists controlled the giant insects.

Behind the enclosing buildings and the Beehive, the city of Vaginismus itself rose like Metaphor's dark clone.

The commies were almost always carrying out marches and parades on the ground below. She watched them maneuver in their perfect ranks, their yellow bodies and black heads . . . like insects themselves. At any rate they weren't human, but mutants filled with semen . . . Monsters.

Did they even have faces under those masks? True, they seemed to, but she'd never been able to tell for certain.

This really breaks down to male versus female, she determined on close reflection: *Semen—testosterone; let's call a shovel a damn shovel, okay?—versus the female sexual response, that's all this is. The ages-old con in modern clothes. And, no, I'm not fooled by half the commies being women either; this is all just a testicular-fueled ploy to keep the female of the species in subjection to the damn patriarchy.*

During this period of her captivity, Courtney determined to fight this enemy—if she ever escaped this terrible place—with every ounce of her strength.

But how? she once wondered after reaffirming this vow. *Do I volunteer to work in Dr. Orgasm's research lab?* Then she'd smirked in irony; *No, I really don't think that'd be a good idea: with my current bad luck, she'll likely use me for a guinea pig as well.*

CHAPTER 35

The week ended. The morning came when Meghyn—Courtney could always tell it was her by her cartoonish voice—arrived and escorted Courtney down a network of corridors to Florence Rigid's office.

They reached a light brown door. Meghyn knocked; they entered.

'F. Rigid' the desk plaque read. The head communist sat behind it, chewing reflectively on a pencil.

Florence rose on their entrance. "Thank you, Meghyn." She looked Courtney over carefully, finally nodding her approval. "Yes, you look so much better now. We can finally begin."

A thrill of fear shot through Courtney at her words. "What do you want with me?"

"We're going on a little tour of the facilities," Florence replied. "You're certain to find it very enlightening." She stepped to the door. "Come, come, come!"

They left the office. Florence and Courtney walked in front, Meghyn behind. They proceeded briskly down yet more interlinked gray corridors, like this entire building was a research maze, one that measured human, not rodent, puzzle-solving aptitude.

Finally, they turned a corner into a corridor flanked by floor-to-ceiling observation windows. At its far end stood a closed metal door.

"Yes," Florence Rigid said with an ice-cold smile. "Here we are."

They paused by the first window on their left. "It's okay," Meghyn said, pushing Courtney forward towards the glass divide with soft hands on her shoulders that felt oddly comforting. "The glass is one-way: they can't see or hear us."

Courtney looked in. In a cream room, a bound and gagged woman lay on a Y-shaped table being violently raped by three men with huge penises.

Courtney gasped, then turned to stare coldly at Florence Rigid. Her words came out chilly like her mouth was a freezer: "This is the same

173

room *I* was kept in. You must have been watching me all that time."
She scowled. "You never went to war with Misandry like Meghyn
claimed, did you?"

"I did, actually. I just got back early. The bitches were pussies; one
hard boot to the ass and they began meowing for mercy." Her gray
gaze hardened on Courtney's face. "This is one of the Misandran
captives. I suggest you be grateful to me that your fate isn't hers."

"My *fate* was hers."

"Oh no, it wasn't," Meghyn added in her funny voice, now standing
so close to Courtney that she felt the woman's penis stiff against her
buttocks, her breath as excited echoes inside her mask. "You survived,
didn't you? And all in one chunk?"

Courtney tapped the glass. "What's her crime? The revolt?"

"No. She's ordinary, that's all; chick-full to the brim with
insecurities. Despite their stance on men, the Misandrans are just
another—"

"Hold on. Aren't you both after the same thing?"

"No. They hate men. I don't hate men—I just hate women enjoying
sex with them so much."

"And the lesbians then? They're your perfect women, right?"

"The lezzies?" She laughed mockingly. "Half the little shits think
they're men in disguise, the other half think they're *queer*—whatever
that means. No. In their own retarded way the lesbians are the worst
sort of woman."

"How's that?"

"They claim independence from men by giving themselves
orgasms." She smiled. "They miss the point: true independence is
being able to make do without having an orgasm, ever. A slave to
female instead of male flesh is still a slave."

Courtney nodded sagely. She already knew Florence Rigid was mad;
this dialogue just hammered the final nail into the coffin of her lunacy.

As if in conclusion, Florence waved a hand at the woman behind
the glass wall: "She's an emotional mess of gender hang-ups. No real
use to us, so . . ."

Courtney didn't hear the rest. Her eyes were glued to the scene
inside the room. One of the gas-masked men had just sliced off both
of the bound woman's breasts. Holding the two bleeding chunks of
fatty flesh together like burger buns, he proceeded to masturbate with
them, sliding his huge erection between them.

While the communist fucked her severed breasts, the mutilated woman thrashed high and low on the table. She was a horrifying sight, her eyes bugging down in egg-white disbelief at the two bare bloody patches on her chest. Her blood bubbled and spurted everywhere. Between her legs another man humped away violently, his huge penis forcing spurts of blood from the victim's anus with each thrust. The third man stood by, cock erect as a white spear, slapping his thighs in amusement at the sights.

The man masturbating with the severed breasts came, spurting long and plentifully onto the woman's bloody chest. Then he slapped his penis hard on the red wounds, making her flap up and down like a landed fish.

The woman's eyes showed the blazing torments of hell. Her mouth twitched around her gag and dribbled spittle.

The man who'd been watching walked over to the one sodomizing the victim, and tapped his shoulder. The rapist pulled out of the torn anus, releasing a flood of blood. The woman's legs were then unbound from the arms of the 'Y,' and folded up over her body, then chained in place so her thighs were on her savaged chest. This left the bloody vista of her buttocks and ruined anus on display. The man who'd fucked her breasts shoved one of them halfway into her anus, leaving the rest of it dangling out like a red hanky from a suit pocket. The other breast he threw away against the wall, where it splattered yellow and red.

One communist brandished a huge serrated knife.

All three men still had stiff erections. Courtney attempted to look away. She wasn't permitted to; Meghyn's soft hands moved up from her shoulders to her head and kept her facing the glass.

"Look," Florence Rigid said in a breathless voice. "It's utterly important that you see this."

She watched, gasping as the communist sawed off one of the woman's buttocks. It was messy, blood splashing everywhere while the victim just thumped helplessly up and down in place. Then the butcher handed the severed buttock to one of his companions, who wrapped the bloody ass-meat around his penis and began using it a masturbation sleeve. It looked like an obscene hotdog, red meat enclosed in white skin, the fat cockhead appearing and disappearing from its end like a pale piston.

The man with the knife began sawing off the woman's other buttock. (His previous target was now a jutting white island of pelvic bone in a lake of blood.)

Courtney puked against the glass, her revulsion streaming up out of her mouth in an endless bitter gush. She hoped the abused woman was dead, dead, dead. But somehow, she knew the woman wasn't, that the victim still had more horrors to suffer.

In a cool voice, Florence said, "She's seen enough of this. Bring her."

Courtney felt Meghyn pulling her away from the glass and numbly followed. They didn't exit the corridor, however; simply moved on to another window.

"Look!" Florence Rigid commanded. "Watch and learn about men!"

***

Inside this room three nude men stood blindfolded and shackled against the right wall. (This room looked exactly like the first, making Courtney suspect that all the rooms along the corridor were similar in design, and that she could have been imprisoned in any of them.)

All three naked men had stiff erections jutting from their groins. There were three women in the room with them: two female communists sat by the opposite wall watching a third—a human woman in a tattered dress—performing fellatio on the naked men.

Courtney felt immediate unease at the scenario. The floor was splattered with blood.

The fellatrix was currently sucking the man closest to the glass wall. On her knees on the wet red floor. Her pink lips moved back and forth over the man's stiff organ, revealing its wet length to the observers then swallowing it again. Her hands fondled the hairy scrotum. The man shivered, his mouth whispered gentle obscenities.

"She looks stoned," Courtney commented of the woman's glazed eyes.

"She is, or she'd get bored," Meghyn replied.

"Fellatio's the only job we've got for her," Florence added. "It's really all the little tramp is any good for."

One of the communists snapped her fingers. The kneeling woman stopped sucking that man's penis and moved to the next man, then after a short while, to the third in line.

Then it happened. Like she'd heard her name called, the fellatrix got to her feet and stepped back into a shadowed corner. Both communist women got up as well, only Courtney saw they'd both now picked up tools: one held a pair of gardening shears, the other a reddened set of bolt cutters.

"Shit!" Courtney gasped. "No! They're coming for—"

"Please be quiet," Florence Rigid said. "You already know these cells are soundproof. Spare your sympathy for those who deserve it."

"W-w-what did they do?"

A humorless laugh. "Too much. These three men are terrorists—though I know you consider them freedom fighters. Either way, they deserve what they get."

The communist woman with the bolt cutters reached the farthest of the blindfolded men. While Courtney fought against Meghyn's velvet-iron grip on her head to look away (for some reason, just as at the first window it never occurred to her to simply close her eyes), the woman placed the jaws of the tool tight around the man's erection at its root. With a sudden violent jerk, she clamped the bolt cutters tight, instantly severing the penis. Blood squirted from the man's groin like the wound was a tap. Squirted up and down, splattering the commie woman's yellow catsuit. The castrated man began twitching and screaming. Squirming, feeling his pain between her own legs, Courtney tried to read his lips.

The other two blindfolded men were now clearly aware of their danger. They fought against their chains. The communist ladies let them sweat it out a bit. Both men thrashed and yelled and pleaded for mercy, while the women playfully stroked their still stiff organs.

Florence Rigid laughed. "One of my favorite things about sildenafil citrate is how it lets the male body betray the mind. Just see how utterly tumescent their penises are, even though they're both now utterly terrified."

Indeed, despite his violent thrashing protest, the bound man nearest them ejaculated as a communist woman stroked him, his thick white emission covering her yellow fist. But next, while the semen still pumped from him, she quickly arranged the blades of the shears around his penis (and behind his testicles) and snipped both off.

A moment later, the woman with the bolt cutters castrated the middle man also. On losing his penis, the man's mouth gaped so wide in his pain that Courtney imagined his teeth would fly out of it.

The first man to lose his manhood already hung limp in death, the lake of his blood all over the floor. The other two jerked and screamed while they too pumped out red liquid from their crotches. Amidst the mess of their dying, the communist women bent and picked up the three severed penises, now limp again from blood expulsion. An impatient gesture summoned the fellatrix from her shadowed corner. She carried a transparent bucket—half-full of severed cocks—into which the three new additions were dropped.

"Just pet food," Florence Rigid said. "My dogs love dick."

Next, the female communists dropped their bloody tools on a table and began wiping themselves clean with towels.

Watching the scene, Courtney imagined the only reason she wasn't puking her guts out again was because of her resentment towards the men who'd raped her.

A door opened inside the room. Three muscular male communists entered and began freeing the corpses from their restraints.

Watching how easily the communists worked, stepping in the sea of blood like it was an everyday rain-drenched sidewalk, Courtney felt the world spinning. Her eyes were closing . . .

"She's fainting," Meghyn said, holding Courtney up.

Florence Rigid hissed. "We can't have that happening. You know there's more to see."

***

After a dose of smelling salts to revive her, and a shot to ensure she didn't faint again ("It'll also ensure you don't puke anymore."), Courtney Taylor was led towards another window, this time on the opposite side of the corridor.

"Why are you doing this to me?" Courtney pleaded, looking down the passageway to the metal door at its far end. At the moment that shiny, mirrorlike surface seemed to hold the end to her mental pain. She dreaded viewing whatever outrage she'd witness next. "I don't need to see all this shit. You've made your point."

Florence Rigid laughed. "Which is?"

"That you're ruthless."

"No. See? Once again, you're getting me all wrong. I'm not *ruthless*—I'm a *ruthless* scientist. Never forget what this is all about. Ruthlessness itself is worthless. Ruthlessness in the pursuit of a scientific objective is priceless. Do you understand it now?"

They'd just reached the window they'd headed for. Florence cocked her head to the left and smiled, tugging on the ends of her blonde hair. Her pretty face looked incredibly intense. "I think of you as a sister, Courtney. I want you . . . no . . . I *need* you to understand me. Maybe even love me in time; and no, to clarify, I don't mean that in a gay way. Understand too, that there is more to life than rape. Sorry, I meant to say *sex.*"

"Why do you hate sex so much?"

"Does it matter?"

"Hell yes, it does!" (Courtney was glad for this conversation. It meant she didn't yet have to look through the glass.)

"I *don't* hate sex. I hate men using sex to dominate women. Orgasm make a woman weak, makes her a slave to men. If women never came they'd rule over men."

"If women never came, they'd *murder* all men. Orgasm makes a woman strong, able to be herself."

"Lies, you little fool—LIES! Orgasm makes you vulnerable!"

Violently, Courtney was turned again to face the looking glass. "Watch, you silly little thing!"

***

Another horrible scene.

It makes no sense why anyone would do this, Courtney thought, while her mind struggled to accept the images facing her.

Another rape scene; one of unbelievable brutality.

A woman lay naked on one of the Y-tables. All of her limbs—both arms and legs—had been cut off, fleshy stumps left in their place. She was still alive—a respirator tube stuck in her mouth—and worse yet, awake and alert, her gaze flickering everywhere. But worst of all, she still seemed sane.

Courtney had no idea how the amputee had remained sane while watching what was going on:

Four male communists were using the woman's severed limbs as masturbation sleeves. They'd removed the bones from her cut-off arms and thighs and stuck their huge penises into the holes instead. (Her four stumps seemed deboned too, as if the bones in her limbs had been extracted whole.)

While humping the severed body parts, the men stood a short distance from the Y-table. Amidst squirting blood and meat juices, their penises slid to and fro into the arms and legs they held to their groins. Back and forth, back and forth, while their bodies tensed as if they were experiencing the most intense pleasure imaginable. Then, while Courtney watched, one of the men pulled his cock out of the woman's severed right arm, walked quickly forward to the table, and ejaculated copiously all over her face, making her squeeze her eyes tightly shut. Then, while he resumed humping the arm again (making its forearm swing back-and-forth like an unlatched screen door in a storm), another man pulled out of the left leg he was having sex with and also squirted semen over her face. Then the third and fourth did so too.

After each facial come-bath the amputee woman opened her eyes again, and Courtney saw clearly that she was completely conscious of all that was going on. The respirator in her mouth prevented her from screaming her pain, but it was inscribed there in her eyes for all to see.

"What did *she* do?" she asked Florence Rigid in a trembling voice. "Another terrorist? Or was she just sexually insecure too—a wasteful specimen?" Courtney was shocked to realize that she no longer really cared; she'd been violently shunted past her threshold of empathy. She imagined that it happened while watching the men being castrated . . . or was it now, seeing how the four mutant abominations in this room were fucking a woman's severed limbs . . . Then: *Oh, no,* she cringed inside, *I hope it's not the shot I was just given that's dulled my reaction!*

"What did she do?" she asked again. "Answer me."

"Dumb bitch talked too much," Meghyn replied. "Kept spouting out idiotic propaganda."

That confused Courtney. "What kind of propaganda?"

No reply was forthcoming. Meghyn, her nipples stiff with excitement and poking large as fingertips through her latex top, just breathed deep and fast inside her gasmask.

Now Courtney, looking down, saw that Meghyn also had her penis out, the organ throbbing hard, and she was masturbating to the scene in the room, where thankfully, the four men had finished fucking the woman's removed body parts. (The seeping punctured limbs lay discarded at random about the floor.)

"Can we go?" she asked, with a faked yawn. She hated the fact that her mind utterly refused to let her strangle Florence Rigid. "This is getting really boring."

"Really? Oh, they're not done yet."

Oh shit. "Not done? What the hell else can you possibly do—"

The question shut off in her throat. The four communists had now taken positions beside the bound, limbless, woman. While Courtney gaped in utter disbelief, each inserted his penis into one of the woman's four stumps and began to fuck the holes left by the previous removal of her bones.

No! No, NO!!

The four humped the amputee's stumps hard. Erect penises slammed in viciously, plunged deep to shoulder and hip joint in the remainder of arms and legs. Pink liquid like pus squirted out around their cocks. The woman flapped up and down on the table, unable to contain her agony.

(Meghyn was stroking herself firm and fast now, moaning like she was also in the room and raping the amputee. Florence Rigid stood by, as stiff as her surname, licking her lips, her gray eyes gleaming.)

Between the obstructions of the communists' moving bodies, Courtney finally made out the raped woman's face. She was flinging her head about and weeping copiously, her black hair plastered wet to her cheeks by both semen and tears. *Oh, my fucking God! Her eyes look like she's in Hell burning!*

The man raping the woman's right thigh ejaculated into the stump. Courtney watched his body freeze in mid-stroke, watched his buttocks stiffen up, then saw them relax again as a stream of semen began dripping out of the stump between its raw meat and his penis to splatter the floor.

Antiemetic shot regardless, Courtney began puking again. She bent over and let it rip.

Beside her, Meghyn let out a long gasp, then began ejaculating on the see-through glass, her come dripping like white worms to the corridor floor.

After a while, when she began dry-heaving, Courtney became aware that Florence Rigid and Meghyn were laughing boisterously.

Courtney looked up again. Inside the room, the obscene sexual assault was now mercifully over, the four men were high-fiving themselves. Their thick white semen poured from the amputee's stumps. Stump creampies. The raped woman was staring with a fixed gaze at the ceiling, her rising and falling breasts clear sign that she was still alive to suffer more of the same agony.

"Somehow I doubt the silly fool will still insist on claiming orgasm is a woman's human right," Meghyn's fluty voice giggled.

"I doubt it too," Florence Rigid agreed. "And the knowledge has cost her an arm and a leg."

"No; both arms and legs."

Louder laugher ensued. Then, like they'd suddenly remembered she was there, both women forcibly dragged Courtney off to another window.

CHAPTER 36

"Our glorious leader is a *strong* woman," Meghyn said. "Unlike you orgasmic sluts, she doesn't take nonsense from men."

They were peering into the corridor's last room, the one right next to its metal end door. (Claiming urgent business required her attention, Florence Rigid had left Meghyn and Courtney there and entered the shiny door. Meghyn's penis was still out, the pale rod still hard, still dripping semen on the floor. Courtney wished she had a knife so she could sever the organ from its amoral owner.)

Inside the room, a naked man lay bound on a low Y-table. He was arranged on his belly, his buttocks in the air, his face towards them. Once again, this room too was floored with blood; the ground shone wet and sticky. There were, however, no gas-masked women-in-yellow inside.

Courtney suspected they'd be along any moment soon.

"Men are full of shit," Meghyn said in an excited voice. "So, the wonderful Miss Rigid—"

The door at the room's far end opened and Florence Rigid strode in.

Courtney gasped. Florence was naked except for a long silver strap-on dildo at her crotch. Barefoot too. Like one performing a burlesque routine, she swayed forward with seductive steps timed as if music played in the room. Occasionally she stroked the dildo and said something to the man on the Y-table. Though she was still out of his field of vision, he could clearly hear her, because his eyes now turned scared-as-hell and he was clearly pleading with her.

After just a few steps, Florence's feet were red with blood up to her ankles.

Despite her hatred of Florence Rigid, Courtney was impressed by the woman's body. The communist leader looked hot, sleek and shapely, with no excess fat. Her nipples were stiff pink points on her breasts, hard with the arousal reflected on her face. Florence Rigid was about Courtney's size and shape, but looked better. Courtney couldn't help but feel envious: *Just plastic surgery, that's all, and now she's going to peg someone to show—*

She fell silent and stiffened at the same moment. She'd just realized what the shiny dildo harnessed at Florence's crotch was: It was a knife. A foot-long knife.

Oh no! She's not going to . . . !

Florence began dancing around the man on the Y-table, shaking her hips so the knife-dildo caught the light and flashed. Slow and sexy she gyrated, unhurried as a snake sure of its prey.

At the middle of her circuit around the table, Florence turned to face the glass and did a pelvic grind, rotating her buttocks in the bound man's face while making thrusting motions forward with the knife.

Courtney felt faint again. Seen up-close, it was an evil-looking knife, both edges of its upward-curved blade clearly honed to razor-sharpness.

She felt Meghyn's soft hands on her shoulders. "Our glorious leader will literally 'fuck the shit out of him.'"

Meghyn's stiff penis was now pressed hard against Courtney's buttocks. Courtney felt a deep dread at the organ's position—her longtime dislike of anal sex now heavily reinforced by the painful lesson of her six-week ordeal in one of these same rooms. All it needed was the slightest of motions—a raising of her dress and a shift of angles—and, like she'd done in the past, Meghyn would be sliding inside Courtney's anus again.

But Meghyn made no attempt to penetrate the ass in front of her; she appeared content to fill Courtney with terror instead. And she was succeeding.

Florence Rigid was now almost all the way around the table, currently dancing by the man's right knee. Her hands were over her head and she was fucking the air hard, looking away from the watchers. The man, however, was screaming, yelling for all he was worth. The silent words, "Please!" "No!" and the phrases, "Help me, somebody!" and "Oh, God!" were easy to make out.

Florence reached the end of her circuit, stood posed in the wide mouth of the 'V' formed by the man's split legs. She danced there for ages, tapping on his feet like they were bongos, while he kept screaming and pleading, his expression growing ever more frantic.

"Why doesn't she just get it over with?" Courtney gasped. It was a horrid statement, she knew, knowing what was coming to the man, but to her, making him beg and beg for a release that would never come was even more horrible.

"The glorious leader is a very patient woman," Meghyn said. "She never rushes things, not even sex." She giggled. "Most definitely not sex."

"Sex? Are you serious? This is murder."

"She hasn't done it yet. She's still teasing him."

Florence was still dancing between the man's feet. A faint hope that this might not happen formed in Courtney. "She won't?"

Meghyn wrapped her arms tight around Courtney from behind, ground her erection against the other woman's ass. "Of course she will. Why wouldn't she? But she likes foreplay."

"Foreplay? She's frigid."

"And that makes her the perfect woman." Meghyn ground harder against Courtney's buttocks, pressed her against the glass. She leaned forward, her metal headgear cold as death against Courtney's cheek and neck. "It's a foreplay of terror, baby. Anticipation. I love it."

Inside the room, Florence was now dancing forward between the man's legs. Her eyes were closed and she seemed to be humming to herself.

"Is there any music in there? Or is it all in her head?"

"What difference does it make?" She pinched Courtney's left nipple. "Her lover's in the mood for sure now."

The man on the table was crying now, blubbering like a spoilt infant. Florence Rigid had reached his spread buttocks and was dancing between them, rolling the foot-long gleaming knife at her crotch between their top curves as tears streamed down his face. His legs and buttocks were clenched hard against the dreaded intrusion.

Courtney, remembering with 'pleasure' her own ordeal, felt his pain.

Florence's eyes were open and dreamy now; she raised hands to her breasts, stroked and squeezed them, pulled on her nipples. Then she dropped her hands to the crying man's ass, spread his buttocks wider still, and pushed the knife down into the split, aimed for the asshole. Smiling, she leaned back...

"Don't either close your eyes or look away," Meghyn warned. "If you do..."

Courtney watched.

Florence Rigid bent forward to grab the man's waist, then she rammed her hips forward, burying the knife to its end in his anus.

At the terrible penetration, the man's eyes popped wide open. He screamed and didn't stop.

Florence Rigid's face now twisted up into a rictus of concentration. Digging her fingernails deep into the man's back, she began to fuck his ass hard with the knife-dildo, rocking her hips violently back and forth, slamming her pelvis into him. The man jerked forward with each thrust, each time almost lifting off the table then collapsing again as the long knife in his anus ripped him apart.

Florence's crotch and belly were soon splattered with blood; some blood from the man's ass had even squirted up to the underside of her breasts, just below her nipples. Her eyes were grim; this was serious fucking business. Sweat poured down her face and neck onto her breasts as she humped him harder and harder and harder, ripping him up more and more and more, and he screamed and screamed and screamed unheard.

Meghyn pulled Courtney down to a squat, so they were looking under the table. Between Florence's legs, blood streamed down to the floor like she was pissing it. They watched her knees first bend, then her feet heave off the floor as she impaled her victim on her knife-cock over and over.

Blood-red lumps of shit plopped down as well.

"See? He shits for her glory."

Courtney vomited again.

Meghyn pulled her up and away from her puke and once more pressed her against the glass. Standing gasmask-to-cheek, she whispered to her like they were lovers:

"In case you're wondering what his crime was; he did nothing. Zilch. He's completely innocent. Florence Rigid is Innuendo's great equalizer. She believes in the time-honored principle of 'an ass for an ass.'"

"I don't get it." Courtney felt about to pass out again. Inside the room, the man was now dead, his life all bled out through his shredded guts and rectum. Florence, meanwhile, continued to fuck his corpse, now humping away between his buttocks with her metal penis like she wanted to cut him in half. Florence herself was covered in blood. She stopped fucking the dead man for a moment to rub the red flow from his ass all over her breasts. (There were brown streaks in it.) Then she resumed fucking the corpse again, the silver knife thudding so hard into it that the table shook with her thrusts. The knife's tip burst suddenly from the corpse's back, then ripped a long line down alongside his spine to the top of his right buttock.

"I don't get it," Courtney repeated. "An ass for an ass?"

Meghyn giggled. "It's simple enough. Florence Rigid says that as long as men continue raping innocent women, she'll keep raping innocent men in return." She stepped away from behind Courtney to ejaculate against the glass, her fingers flying fast and furious over her penis. "Miss Rigid does this every day, sometimes three times a day. She also films these sexual encounters—soon we'll start broadcasting the recordings to everyone in Innuendo." Her mirth blew up into full-scale laughter; she tapped a finger on the glass. "He got off lightly. Sometimes Miss Rigid castrates a man first, then fucks the resulting hole in his crotch, just like he's a woman."

Courtney nodded weakly. Inside the room, Florence stopped fucking the corpse's backside. The blood-splattered communist leader (her legs were soaked crimson, her blonde bush looked like a redhead's; her breasts were taut red bubbles daubed with feces and grooved by runnels of sweat) walked briskly around the table to the dead man's head. There, after a wave to those behind the glass wall, she spread the corpse's jaws wide, inserted her knife-penis between his lips and began to fuck his mouth hard, making the knife puncture out of his neck.

Her pumping hips settled into a smooth rhythm.

Meghyn shook the last drops of come from her penis, then tucked it away. She moved behind Courtney again, running semen-stinky wet fingers through her hair. "She's a powerful liberated woman. All women should be this strong. If you were, then men could do nothing to you. And it's all because she never comes. That's the gift she has for you. To make you like herself; the first of her new race of viragoes."

Courtney was speechless. All she could do was watch Florence Rigid continue to maniacally have sex with a dead man's head, the knife-cock having now ripped out his entire throat.

CHAPTER 37

Too weakened by outrage to resist or protest, Courtney was dragged through the shiny metal door at the corridor's end and strapped down in a chair. Something like a salon hair dryer—a white steel-and-plastic helmet with ear grilles and a glass face shield—was dropped over her head. A noise buzzed in her ears then shut off.

She finally looked up and around. The same cream walls as elsewhere stared back. A few shut glass cabinets lined the walls. Directly opposite her stood an instrument console, all meters and knobs. Meghyn sat in front of it on a three-legged stool, looking like a massive yellow bug turning into a woman.

Time faded in and out. Meghyn said nothing, just occasionally played with her breasts. Courtney guessed they were waiting for Florence Rigid.

After what felt like an hour, the communist leader walked into the room. Florence was once again clothed and perfumed, the blood, gore, and stink of murder all seemingly magically cleansed from her. Gone too was her rage of the female avenging angel, her sexualist emotion; now she was once again cold efficiency.

Meghyn rose on her entry. "What kept you, madam? We've been waiting a long time." She pointed. "Courtney's all ready for you in the mind-chair."

Florence made a face. "It's that stupid bitch Carol Orgasm again. Oh, how I hate the slut!"

"Dr. O? What has she done this time?"

Florence Rigid leaned over Courtney and nodded at the satisfactorily stupefied look on her face, at the remnant traces of puke on her lips. "Some disgusting news just came in. Our spies in Metaphor report that Dr. Slut has just made an utterly unacceptable scientific breakthrough."

"Breakthrough?"

Still bent over Courtney, Florence turned her head to regard Meghyn. "Yes. She's apparently developed a pill—the O-pill she calls it—which grants women orgasms on demand. Just take one and you come again and again—can you believe that crap?"

"Shit!" Meghyn began pacing distractedly. Her huge headwear made her look like a confused plastic mouse. "If she's achieved that—"

"She's put us out of business? Not exactly, my little Meghyn." She straightened up from bending over Courtney. "Not exactly. But—"

"She's smarter than you," Courtney interrupted now Florence was out of her face. "You can't hack that, can you?" She was very worried. *Shit, Meghyn called this thing a 'mind-chair.' They aren't going to screw with my head some more are they?*

Florence Rigid rubbed her chin. "Carol? Smarter? Only if female intelligence is measured by how much one uses one's vagina. We went to the same schools, and . . . I graduated higher in class. Would you believe Carol slept her way through Metaphor Uni—was in every lecturer's bed? How's that for intelligence?" She giggled. "Though I guess some of the professors' smart DNA transferred to her through their semen. I mean, it must have—Carol guzzled literally gallons of it."

"You're lying!" Courtney erupted. "There's no records of either of you being alumni of Metaphor Uni."

Florence nodded. "You're right. It was a good joke, though. And I do honestly think that Carol Orgasm is a female opportunist slut. One who—"

"One who's just freed Innuendo's ladyfolk from your shackles."

Florence's face tightened in anger. "Shut her up, Meghyn. I need to think."

Meghyn stepped up to Courtney and stuck her gloved right hand into Courtney's crotch. She slipped four fingers up Courtney's vagina, then clamped down hard on the entrance with her thumb.

Courtney yelped with pain. Her eyes widened. Not just from the pain: she was shocked at how easily all four of Meghyn's fingers had slid up inside her. She'd felt nothing; there'd been no resistance whatsoever from her sex to the penetration.

Florence laughed at Courtney's surprise. "Ah, that's the one thing we didn't fix—your vagina is now as big as a cow's. Bigger, maybe." She snapped her fingers. "Show her, Meghyn."

Meghyn stopped clamping down on Courtney's sex and slid her entire right hand up inside it. Courtney's eyes widened more. She felt nothing, not even when Meghyn began fisting her hard. "What did you do to me!?"

"Just the toll of all the big-dick sex you had with me and the boys," Meghyn educated her. She turned her cyclopean eyespace towards Florence. "Two hands, madam?"

Florence nodded. The next moment, as easy as eating pie, Meghyn's left hand joined her right one inside Courtney's vagina. She slowly slid both hands in and out.

Courtney began crying; she felt nothing between her legs. "You . . . you evil bitch! You monster!"

"Now, now, don't be like that, Courtney," Florence Rigid mocked, "your disgusting clitoris still works perfectly. That's good enough, though it's also the problem—your entire sexual machine works too well. Oh, by the way, I didn't fix your anal expansion either—your rear passage is just as distended as your front now; haven't you noticed it's really easy to defecate? How the excrement drops out of you almost before you will it to? Sorry, but it would have wasted too much time to repair your holes beyond stitching up the tears, and now that Meghyn is satisfied that her theory of violent sex destroying female orgasmic capability is flawed, I was in a hurry to get you in here to prove to her that my fix works. But don't let that bother you—there's lots of monstrously hung men here in Vaginismus if you want filling. Several hung monsters too. And you won't be leaving here anyway, so . . ."

Courtney somehow made sense of Florence's abhorrent torrent of words. Fresh hatred for the woman filled her; fresh rage coursed through her like poisoned blood.

"Get your damn hands out of my pussy!" she growled down at Meghyn, who was still leisurely double-fisting her.

After maliciously punching Courtney's cervix hard, Meghyn complied. Her hands slurped loudly out of the distended vagina.

The cervix punch left Courtney winded, all the fight blown out of her in a rush of expelled air. Wide-eyed, wide-legged, and wide-sexed, she paid court to Florence who'd never stopped talking in the interim:

". . . So screw Carol Orgasm. I'll find her, and this time I'll kill her. And I'll get that damn O-Pill, I assure you I will. And I'll destroy the formula. And that will be that!" She grasped the air fiercely. "This close to victory, nothing will stop me—nothing." Eyes smoldering, she looked at Meghyn, who stood on Courtney's right, vagina-wet hands meekly clasped in front of her crotch. "Let's do this, and afterwards we start the hunt for Carol."

Meghyn nodded her bulky metal head, then she and Florence crossed the room and began fiddling with the knobs and switches on the instrument console opposite the mind-chair.

"Hey, wait!" Courtney called.

The pair looked back. "Yes?"

"Please, please, please don't do this to me." It was a melancholy wail.

Florence smiled coolly back. "But we *need to*, darling. I've already explained as much: this is all about research and salvation for Innuendo's women."

"Shit! But why fucking me?"

Florence laughed. "Don't be an oversexed airhead like your heroine Carol. Why we're choosing . . . using you? Oh, come on, Courtney darling. I already told you: Girl, as a test subject, you're perfect. A beautiful, sexually well-balanced woman with no hang-ups whatsoever. Girls like you are almost impossible to find in this promiscuous age of ours." She laughed. "Largely due to my crimes of course."

Courtney was dumbfounded. "You *know* you're committing crimes against women?"

"Of course not. I'm just being ironic, darling."

"So?"

"Reason it out with me—you in your perfect sexual liberation present me with my greatest challenge yet. If I can destroy *you* sexually, cancel out *your* tremendous ability to orgasm, then this new process I've developed will work on any woman in Innuendo."

Courtney gasped. "Fucking let me go!"

Florence's face hardened. "No, and if you don't behave yourself, I'll cut out your stupid vagina altogether and you'll end up urinating through a tube. Now be quiet, and take what's coming to you."

Florence and Meghyn returned to fiddling with the console for a few seconds more, then Florence waved back over her shoulder at Courtney. "Okay, girl, say goodbye for good to your big O."

Then she flicked one last switch.

Then, she and Meghyn turned to stare at Courtney.

***

At first Courtney felt nothing. She was still too outraged at how distended her vagina now was. Somehow that seemed even more horrible than her dread of never coming again. *Men like tight vaginas, men like tight vaginas, goddamit!*

Then the mind-chair's helmet buzzed . . .

Courtney became aware of a 'tightening' around her brain. Like a hand squeezing her head hard. Then, before she could yelp out her discomfort, the feeling had left her head and was falling through her body, down her spine. It surged forward to her nipples, from where it dropped lower still to her crotch. It floated around her sex, then clamped like lips on her clitoris. The tightness squeezed her clitoris for a long moment, then, in a rush like an internal wind, it swept back up through her body again, back into her brain, where it squeezed tighter and tighter till she fainted.

CHAPTER 38

Courtney dreamt.

She lay naked in a soft scented bed in an opulent bedroom. Through the windows she viewed a green sky with a yellow moon. Transparent dragons like living diamonds floated through the air, and below those, luscious orchards of fruit trees ran off into the distance like a green rug.

The bedroom door opened and a naked man entered. A tall, dark, and handsome man. Not her darling Radio; this man was way, way more attractive. But that was okay, somehow Courtney knew this was just a dream, an erotic fantasy built by her subconscious as compensation for all her horrible suffering in communist hands.

The man, the man. Oh, he was gorgeous. Broad-shouldered, deep-chested, with chiseled abs like a crossword puzzle and rippling biceps and thighs. Just sweet, sweet, sweet.

Her gaze dropped to his crotch. Her lips dropped open. Oooh, he was hung too!

"Damn, that's a big banana you've got," she said. "The biggest I've ever seen." Her heart beat faster and harder, she couldn't wait to get her hands on his penis. It had to be at least a foot long and it was wonderfully thick too.

He climbed into bed with her. She immediately grabbed his cock. It was hot in her grasp, and its upward-curving length throbbed hungrily for her. She milked it with her hands, then measured it against her arm. Oooh, he was exactly the length of her forearm. His balls were big too, like a hairy plum. She resumed stroking the penis, growing even more aroused as she worked it. A large pearl of pre-come formed in the slit in the penis glans. She closed her lips over the fat corona, sucked the liquid down. It tasted sugary, became sexual heat in her belly.

She kept fellating him. She made him kneel over her chest, so she could squeeze the shaft of his penis between her breasts while keeping its head in her mouth. He sexed her mouth, sliding his organ between the deep tunnel of her breasts. She loved that he was so long, so thick, so hard, so . . .

While she sucked him, he reached behind himself and stroked her sex, tilling it with his fingers. By now, her vagina felt like there was a fire in it. A fire about to consume her if she didn't get his fire hose down there soon. She was wet, dripping with her desire for him.

In a sudden desperation for him to quench the heat consuming her, she slipped her lips off his cock. "Fuck me," she gasped.

He took her instantly. She felt his huge penis spread her labia, then enter, a monster snake entering a tiny tunnel. A flood of sensation accompanied the penetration. After a moment's fear that she was too little to accommodate his massive girth, she expanded around him. And then it was perfect, him deep inside her, his glans stroking her cervix, his thickness stretching her so that each time he pulled out, it felt like he was taking her along with him. Then he slid in deep again and the pleasure repeated.

His lips dropped to her breasts and the feeling intensified even more. His right hand cupped and squeezed, stroked her cheeks and hair. And his cock—oh, that massive glorious cock, so deep, so right . . .

He made love to her perfectly. Way better than any man in her life ever had or ever would again.

Then slowly, this gorgeous pleasure she felt, this climb to ultimate sexual satisfaction—she knew this would be the orgasm of a lifetime, one that would transform her into a goddess—became a descent into the depths of frustration.

Courtney realized that she couldn't come.

They made love for hours. Her dream man was tireless—a sex machine. His hips pumped on and on and on, his body rising and lowering on hers, then against hers . . . under hers, in a multitude of sexual positions. His massive penis never softened for a moment, nor his hands and lips cease their kissing and caresses. She was wet too, never dried out in all the time they loved one another. She never slackened around him either; he was so big, it was all she could do to contain his monster.

But the climax, that explosion of sensation that would crown this most fantastic of fucks, never materialized. Orgasm for them both, or for her at least, hovered like a floating platform over her head. She could see it, but not touch it.

They made love for hours more, till the sky outside the window darkened to a night with a bloody moon and flying monsters, and the next morning rose. And still . . .

The pleasure became a bitter pill to swallow, the penis in her loins a heavy cross to bear. Her frustration grew and grew, till finally, after what must have been three or four days of non-stop sex, Courtney angrily pushed her dream man off her sweaty breasts and pointed to the door.

"Get out! Get out!!"

He looked at her in confusion. "I thought . . . I thought you were enjoying it, baby. Y-y-you said that you liked me." His prick was still hard, curved like a hot purple banana, still throbbing for her pussy.

She glared at it in utter disgust now. Her loins burnt with the fire he'd stoked in her.

"Get out! Get out!!!" she screamed at him in hatred.

He left, hurt, his head slumped.

Once he'd gone, she rolled up into a fetal ball on the bed and wept. Her vagina burnt now like it was being electrocuted. But there was no release, no release, no release for her. And she sensed there would never be. Not ever again.

Finally, wrapped in her horror, she screamed, "I can't come! I can't come! I can't—"

CHAPTER 39

Courtney jerked awake.

"—come! I can't come!" she screamed from her dream. "I can't come! I CAN'T COME!!!"

She calmed down, and took stock of her surroundings. She was still strapped down in the mind-chair, with Florence Rigid and Meghyn watching her.

The communist leader was beaming at her. "How was the dream, darling? Was the man everything you'd ever wished for?"

Courtney gaped at her. "I couldn't come." Then her expression turned to one of horror. "How'd you know I was dreaming about . . . ?"

Florence laughed, then pointed left at a wall-screen, where Courtney watched the dream she'd just had play out in real-time. She saw herself having sex with a man . . . and yes he did have an enormous penis. She grimaced with memory: *What is it with communists and massive dicks, anyway? It has to be compensation for insecurity of some kind. I mean, who the hell wants a guy with a rolling pin for a penis?*

"Of course we had to speed it up," Meghyn explained. "Or we'd have been here for four days. You had a similar dream after the rape experiment didn't you?"

Courtney remembered. Yes, she had had a sexual dream then too. And now she put her mind to it, it had featured the same man making love to her. But then there'd been no frustration, in fact she'd been orgasming like crazy. Her creamy climaxes had been endless.

She stared at the pair. "That was you too?"

Meghyn nodded, her metal head bobbing like a buoy amidst turbulent waves. "We were testing your orgasmic response after the rape experiment." The transsexual's shoulders slumped. "Unfortunately, there was almost no damage."

"But," Florence added, with a triumphant gesture at the screen (on which Courtney was just ordering the hung man from the bedroom), "we've now conclusively proved that *my* method works." She walked forward and bent over Courtney. "What you just dreamed is playback of the rest of your sexual life. Try as hard as you like, by every means available, you'll never have another orgasm again."

"No!" Courtney gasped, remembering the horrible frustration she'd felt in the dream. She looked at the screen (where she now lay blubbering in a fetal curl) then back at Florence. "No, please! Anything but that!"

Florence grinned back broadly. "I'm afraid that's *yes,* baby. But don't worry about it."

"Don't worry about it? Are you out of your damn mind?"

"*No,* I'm not, and *yes,* don't worry about it. You'll get used to it soon enough, and you'll become perfect, like me. I've never had a single orgasm in my life, and just look at me." Her brow crinkled reflectively. "Darling, pleasure makes you foolish; pain makes you wise."

"And sexual frustration?" Courtney spat acidly. "What good does that do?

It gives you a fresh perspective of yourself. A clear, untainted perspective. And it energizes you, makes you more aware of things. I, for instance, masturbate regularly to get my frustration levels . . . I mean *motivation levels* . . . up, but that's all."

"Being hard up just makes me bitch."

"That too, at first," Florence agreed, showing perfect teeth in a callous grin. "But then you're used to being a weakling. You'll get over it. Me? I rejoice in my power over my bodily desires. I've told you: if women never came they'd rule over men."

She patted Courtney gently on the cheek, then straightened out again. "Remember, I said I like you. So, once you're perfect, you'll join Meghyn and myself in perfecting my research and showing other women the way to total sexual emancipation." She laughed. "And together we'll find Carol Orgasm and kill her and destroy her research." She looked pointedly at Courtney. "Now, I can't be more generous than that, can I?"

Courtney had no words. She broke down in tears again.

CHAPTER 40

A week later, Courtney was working in the laboratory beside both Meghyn and Florence Rigid. (Her BSc. had been in botany, but she knew enough human biology to get by.)

It wasn't by choice; some psychological conditioning (and she clearly recognized it as such) had Courtney following the communist leader about like a sheep. Taking orders, doing whatever she was told. (Several times she helped feed Florence's dogs the severed penises— now diced-up and spiced—from the castration room. Florence had six dogs—two Chihuahuas, a Labrador, one Pekinese and two Dalmatians.)

But still, the nature of Florence's research chilled her, particularly that concerning children.

The sight of a row of baby girls (none of them over a year old) with metal prods stuck up their vaginas and being subjected to electronic shock treatment unnerved her.

"Catch them young I believe," Florence explained coolly. "Early religious conditioning has been clearly shown to prevent women from reaching orgasm, even after they've supposedly discarded such repressive doctrines." She sharply twisted the dial that regulated the shocks. The row of infant girls instantly began howling with pain. Most of the babies began pissing and pooping themselves.

"Stop it! Stop it!" Courtney yelled. The kid's noises were hammers pounding her conscience.

Smiling, Florence did so. The yowling subsided.

With tears in her eyes, Courtney gestured at the impaled babies. "Florence, what the hell does fanaticism have to do with *them?*"

"Women so conditioned by religion find it impossible to come because they believe it's wrong to do so. They believe God disapproves of their having any sexual pleasure, and they want to please Him." She smirked. "Him, eh? Why not HER? What I mean is, insert *me* in God's place for a moment. Imagine how great it would be if women everywhere didn't climax simply because they felt it would displease *me* . . ."

Wow, you really are a megalomaniac, Courtney thought.

". . . However, such religious conditioning definitely works. It's a great system, but . . ."

"Yes . . . ?"

"It just takes so damn long to install in the female mind. The girls have to go to schools . . ." She gestured at the baby girls. "Now imagine, if we could install that conditioning right from birth, from the womb even?"

Courtney winced. "Florence, you've already got a system that works. You used it on me; proved it with me."

"It only works on adults. You need to be well over puberty for it to take and hold." She gestured at the children again. So for them, they get shock treatment. Babies masturbate too, so we can measure each shock's effectiveness. If we can burn out their sexual response before they're a year old . . ." Smiling evilly, she twisted the dial again. The baby girls instantly began screaming and shitting themselves again.

"Excuse me a moment," Florence said.

One of the baby's vaginal prod had popped out. Courtney watched Florence pick the metal rod off the floor, lick it clean of dust, then reinsert it into the howling little girl's sex, afterwards taping the child's thighs together with duct tape to keep it firmly in place.

"Silly little slut," she grimaced, wiping baby poop off her fingers with a tissue.

Courtney fled the lab and puked herself silly. All the while she was spewing the contents of her guts she was wishing she could gut Florence Rigid.

CHAPTER 41

Outside of work, Courtney was given free rein to go wherever she wished. She wasn't guarded—it was understood that she couldn't escape.

So in the evenings and on weekends when she wasn't working with Florence, Courtney shed her lab clothes, and, warmly wrapped to defeat the chill of the ending year, walked about Vaginismus.

Unlike her first impressions gleaned from her room, when it had seemed almost a counterpart of her home city of Metaphor, viewed up close the communist stronghold was a grim place. Vaginismus was all gray concrete and steel, dirty glass and plastic, hard cold unwelcoming lines. Tall buildings and perfectly laid out streets, as if the city's blueprints had fallen to Earth from Florence Rigid's vagina.

Propaganda screens hung high and wide everywhere: 'F. Rigid is God,' was the one Courtney found most abhorrent. Others read: 'The Clitoris is an Aberration—Cut it Out!' 'Sex is Sinful; Orgasm is EVIL.' 'Stay Strong: Never Come.' 'An Orgasm a Day Keeps Empowerment Away.' 'Wanted: Pussy Freedom!!!'

There were many more slogans, some more inane than others; but the 'F. Rigid is God' one outraged Courtney the most.

That slogan was also the one the skywriting planes most regularly puffed out as they crisscrossed the sky above the city towers. Her heart pumping red anger, Courtney would pause by a lamppost and watch each yellow airplane spurt the cloud nonsense from its rear end in fluffy red letters: 'F. Rigid is God.'

More like she's the Devil, you assholes.

(Since her time in the mind-chair, Courtney had tried everything she could to have an orgasm, to prove Florence Rigid wrong. All to no avail. Her body heated up only for her fires to burn her out; there was no joyful explosion, just painful implosion.)

And then there were the Bees. The huge insects flew in thick swarms across Vaginismus, sometimes low in the streets, just over people's heads. At such times, while the communists applauded the passing Bees, Courtney (and most other humans she observed) always ducked through the nearest doorway to hide herself, her instinctive fear of the monster bugs too much to overcome. All it took was one prick of their massive red stings and flesh turned to stone or jelly.

Bees—the insect order Hymenoptera. *Hymen*optera? Courtney had no doubts at all in her mind that Florence Rigid using Bees to do her dirty work was her making some warped statement about human virginity: *I'm sure the crazy bitch thinks if women were never deflowered, they'd all be super-powered! Humph!*

The Bees were horror enough. She saw no gobblers, which she was grateful for. On her enquiry as to why this was, Meghyn blithely informed her that, "The monster worms are kept corralled well away from Vaginismus, out east towards the Moral Mountains, lest they run amok and eat our glorious city itself."

The communists were everywhere. Yellow catsuits and the ubiquitous gasmasks, with long knives sheathed hipside. The semen-filled metalhead species. Women, men, transsexuals; children of all three genders. That stumped Courtney. Not just that they had intergender children, but that the commies had kids at all. *They have kids?* The commie children were duplicates of their parents: yellow-sheathed bodies and faceless in their gas-masks too, like they popped out from the womb like that. Apparently they did: every pram she passed had a latex-clad, gas-masked infant in it.

There were many other humans in Vaginismus, most of them women. Like Courtney, all these women had strained faces with empty eyes. Empty eyes that no longer wished to see anything but couldn't stop because vision was automatic. They walked the streets like they were homeless. (Some of these hapless women [and men] would later be sent as commie spies into the other towns of Innuendo.)

Sometimes a communist flung one of the human women to the ground and raped her, sometimes even killed her, but for the most part they were left alone.

No one messed with Courtney though. It was clearly understood that she was the Glorious Leader's special one. The communists treated her with respect, with deference even.

Courtney discovered the communists regarded her now as their mascot. To them she represented the future; she was their model of the perfect non-orgasmic woman—the NOW.

CHAPTER 42

One morning, Courtney and Florence Rigid were out driving in a communist convoy headed west for the town of Gravid.

Florence was silent and fuming at the wheel of their antigrav jeep. Courtney knew why: Yesterday, in Metaphor, her spies had narrowly missed killing Dr. Orgasm. The doctor, however, had both escaped them and had now fled the city in her pink shoeplane. Florence had no idea where she'd gone.

It chilled Courtney that there was such deep communist infiltration in Metaphor—the assassins had masqueraded as members of City Defense, had apparently even carried valid ID.

The wind flowed cold around their faces, whipping their blonde hair to and fro. Staring at the passing countryside—large leafless trees being climbed by massive iridescent bugs, a mosaic of fallen foliage about the tree's bases, the breathtaking bareness and colors of autumn everywhere—Courtney didn't at first realize Florence was talking to her.

"Huh?"

Florence rolled her eyes. "I was asking—if *you* were Carol, where would you hide, knowing the glorious communist army was after you?"

Courtney tapped her fingernails on the glove compartment. "Hard to say. I mean, she's got a whole country to pick locations from."

"I know that. Where would *you* hide from me?"

"Hmm. Definitely not in Metaphor anyway; you've just proven—"

She shut up because a missile was streaking towards them. She had just enough time to make out its shark-like green shape and the tail of flame that powered it before the rocket slammed into the jeep directly ahead of theirs and blew it sky-high.

The world exploded into noise, smoke, and flame.

Then something hit Courtney like a punch to the head and her world went blacker than night.

CHAPTER 43

Courtney awoke to find Radio staring down worriedly at her. It was such an unfamiliar expression on his face (*What, Radio's actually worried about something?*) that she immediately burst out laughing.

"Hey, dude, what's the news?" she asked once she'd gotten her mirth under control.

He sighed with deep relief. "Don't move. I'll fetch the doctor."

He left. She looked around: She was in a hospital bed. She was also connected to a lot of tubes and gizmos. A drip in each arm. Her head ached. She reached up and touched it, felt the heavy gauze bandage.

"What happ . . . ?" Alarmed memory returned. *I was sitting beside Florence and a missile . . . an ambush . . .*

That was all she remembered.

Thankfully, Radio returned then, along with a tall balding man in a white coat—Dr. Olson.

Radio sat by her, holding her hand. Dr. Olson checked her vital signs, adjusted the flow on her drips, then smiled down at her. "How do you feel, Courtney?"

"I-I-I . . . how'd I get here?"

"Try to relax. Your boyfriend found you walking about just outside the Safe Zone tree line two days ago. You were covered in blood and mumbling nonsense. You didn't recognize him. You fainted in his arms and he brought you here."

"Two days ago? Doc, what date is this?"

"Friday, the sixteenth of November."

Courtney looked at him in shock. "The sixteenth? We left Vaginismus on the eight . . . the attack . . ." It was impossible: try hard as she might, she couldn't remember anything of the past week.

"You were in Vaginismus?" Radio asked.

She nodded. "I've been a commie prisoner for the last three months." She suddenly felt impossibly tired, like she carried Metaphor on her shoulders.

"That explains it then," Radio said. Beside him, Dr. Olson flipped papers on a clipboard.

"Explains what, baby?"

"We've searched everywhere for you. Me, Matt and Teresa . . . Highball too. I've been traveling the countryside hoping I'd find you. But I found absolutely no traces."

"Did you find the horse?"

"What horse?"

She yawned loudly. "Sultan, the one I was riding." Then she remembered that her horse was killed by the morph bugs. "No, you wouldn't have."

"So, the commies—"

She squeezed his hand—"Baby, I was with Florence Rigid"—then yawned wider and louder still. "Damn, I'm so tired."

Dr. Olson nodded to Radio. "We'll both leave you to rest now, Courtney. Being in Vaginismus can't have been at all easy."

"Doc, you don't know the half of it."

They left, she slept again.

***

Courtney remained in hospital for six weeks. She was well enough to leave by the end of the first week, but extensive vaginal and anal reconstruction surgery (the communists had really widened her up horribly) kept her there.

Radio visited her every day and was even allowed to sleep overnight in her room, which was great. After imagining she'd never see her love again, she was utterly delighted to have him back.

She never told Radio the full extent of what she'd been through; it seemed unfair to burden him with that. To Courtney, her inability to climax now would likely prove enough of a challenge for him. It really worried her: could their relationship even survive such a test?

She told him about the mind-chair, and what it had done to her. He listened as placidly as usual.

"We'll see," he said simply when she was done. "It might all be in your head."

"Baby, it's not in my head."

He leaned over her bed and kissed her lips. "We'll see. Good vaginal muscle tone helps a woman climax; and according to Dr. Olson, yours had been shot to bits, so that may have been the problem." He frowned. "Thank God it's fixed now."

She scowled. "Radio, this goes way deeper than simply tightening me up. I can feel it—something's wrong with me. I can just tell."

"Well, you'll be out of here soon, we'll know for sure then."

Courtney didn't reply. She hoped Radio was right, but . . . she'd been masturbating every day for the past week and . . . nothing. No orgasm. The only difference now was that, with all the vaginal distension undone, she got more pleasure from her fingers than she had when she'd tried the same in Vaginismus. But still, there was never any fruit to her labors. She'd lie there under the sheet, plowing the folds of her sex like it was a field, rubbing for all she was worth till she was sore and all covered in sweat . . . Sometimes she did it in the bathtub, her surgically-repaired sex filled with warm bubble bath—oh, such a delicious wet fullness—teasing herself up towards that sweet female ecstasy that finally spiraled down to anger and bitterness.

Each time she'd wind up crying tears of rage, liquid hatred towards Florence Rigid, that bitch who'd robbed her of this most basic of pleasures, of taking physical joy in her femaleness.

Oh, how Courtney hated Florence Rigid right now.

But maybe Radio was right; maybe in his arms, surrounded by his protecting love, she'd make it.

***

She also discovered now both how the communists had rendered her docile and how Radio had found her.

"This is a consciousness control chip," Radio said. "It was embedded in your skull, just over your left ear."

Courtney stared in horror at the gold pin lying in his open palm. It looked like something a man would stick in his tie. "This thing?"

Radio nodded. "It got damaged when you got hit in the head. It's still broadcasting though, runs on human body warmth. I picked up its frequencies in my mind while surfing the airwaves."

***

City Defense boss Donald Oldfield and his assistant Angel Weiner, with Matt and Teresa Pollack in tow, visited to debrief Courtney.

She told them everything she remembered about Vaginismus, about the city's design and population estimate, about the Bees, about the torture and murder rooms . . . and about Florence Rigid.

"She isn't just a passive threat," Courtney concluded vehemently. "She's not just pussy rhetoric, a female hot-air balloon. Oh no, she means every word she says. She's coming after us sooner or later."

Chief Oldfield nodded, scratched his stubbly chin. "And we'll be ready for her when she does."

Teresa made a face. "So *she* was responsible for that assassination attempt on Dr. Orgasm? We all thought it was the Misogynists."

Courtney looked around at them all. "Any word of the doctor since then? Has anyone seen her magic flying shoe?

Angel shook her head. "No. She's apparently vanished into thin air."

The chief smirked. "Thin air might be the best place for her. I've never trusted the woman anyway."

Angel asked Courtney, "And you can't remember *anything* about the week you were wandering about? How's that even possible? You must have eaten and drank in all that time and you don't remember it?"

Courtney shrugged. "It angers me too; like part of my life's been stolen from me. I mean, how'd I even escape Florence? We were both in the same jeep."

"It happens sometimes in battle," Chief Oldfield said. "You get hit in the head; it knocks you loopy. Next thing, you're walking around, functioning on instinct; biological autopilot. You revert back to the animal in you, behave like one of our pets would: hide when you sense danger, eat when you're hungry . . . then you find a landmark your subconscious recognizes—maybe even the position of the moon and stars at night—and start journeying home. Though if anyone asked you later, you'd never be able to explain how you got back here." He saw his assistant was frowning at his explanation. "Angel, you look like you don't believe her."

Angel Weiner shook her head. "No, Chief, it's not that. I'm only angry she's lost her memory 'cos now we've no way of knowing if Florence Rigid died in that attack or not."

The others stared at her, realizing she was right.

CHAPTER 44

Finally, on a chilly January afternoon, Courtney was released from hospital.

Radio and Highball took her home, then Highball left she and Radio alone.

Courtney walked through their apartment, picking things up and putting them down again simply to get a feel of having her life back. Everything she touched felt odd, like it wasn't really hers, as though in the four-and-a-half months she'd been away from the apartment, it had erased her from its memory; as if all her belongings had disowned her for her neglect of them.

"You know I never imagined I'd see this place again."

Radio was pulling open the drapes. He laughed. "Oh yeah? I never imagined I'd see *you* again."

She picked up a photograph of the two of them standing by a white horse, then put it down shuddering.

Fixing the drapes with tiebacks, he looked at her. "What's wrong?"

"I doubt I'll ever trust myself to ride a horse again. What happened to Sultan was just horrible."

Radio walked over and took her in his arms. "Try not to think about it."

She wept against his shoulder for a bit, then pulled him toward the bed and looked up at him with teary eyes. "Make love to me, darling. I need to put the past behind me."

"Yes, we both do," Radio agreed.

He pushed her gently down onto the mattress. He pulled off her shoes, then hiked up her skirt and slid down her panties. Then slowly, like he was scared she'd shatter if he went faster, he spread her sexual lips wide and dipped his tongue into the musky pink wetness of her sex. And licked and sucked.

Courtney closed her eyes and groaned and moaned while he ate her. And at first *it was* wonderful, but then . . .

***

That had been the first of their many sexual failures.

Like it wanted to save her from reliving them in detail, Courtney's mind prolapsed out of memory into the present again.

PART 4:
THE EMPRESS'S NEW CLOTHES

CHAPTER 45
Now again: Back Beside Route Zero.

Someone was shaking Courtney hard. Her eyes jerked into focus again. Heart thumping, she sat up. "What? What?"

It was Highball. The redhead's face was serious. "Listen."

Courtney listened. She heard it: A long scream, followed by a woman's pleas—"No! Stop! Please!"—then another bloodcurdling scream.

"I'd imagine we're on the wrong side of the road for that nonsense," Teresa said, leaping to her feet.

Heather and Miki were already on their feet, their eyes cold and hard in the lengthening shadows.

"Yeah, I was thinking that too," Heather said. "Has to be the damn commies. Jeff said they run Misandry now, didn't he?"

Like one escaping a bog, Courtney got her bottom up off the soft grass. Her recollections let her go only reluctantly, clinging to her like weights.

The scream came again, long, loud and pathetic, warbling like birdsong. Now a laughing male voice rose over it, horrible, harsh, and insistent. "Take that, you skanky bitch; I'm gonna rip up your ass so good—"

"What the hell are we all waiting for?" Courtney growled. "Let's go help her!"

"One of us should wait behind," Teresa said grimly. "Just in case our guys return." (Watching her, Courtney almost felt amused: Little Teresa Pollack, all hundred and ten pounds of her, was literally having a fit, bristling with rage like she'd rip someone to death.)

"Best we all go," Heather said, drawing her gun. "We've no idea how many commies there are. Besides, the guys won't be back for at least another hour." Without waiting for a response, she charged out of the door, Miki hot on her heels.

Highball, Teresa, and Courtney ran after them, all with guns in hand.

CHAPTER 46

Cora and Dave were deeply in love. As love between members of the opposite sex wasn't permitted in either Misandry or Misogyny, the pair had to meet secretly.

Cora hated all this secrecy shit. She didn't hate men, period. But living in Misandry one toed the 'men are shits/pigs' line. You didn't, you got punished hard. You kept on being a dissenter, you were offed—killed and mingled with pigswill before your corrupting influence could spread. The Women Council didn't stand for no nonsense. 'Our pleasure is in our own hands, not in any man's!' was the maxim here. Cora had several whip scars from after she'd first been recruited into the ranks. She'd learnt her lesson now. "Toys, not boys!" "Men are the shit of the earth!" "No men means no semen!" "Masturbate to prove your hate!" she quoted like a goodwoman.

(The regime was just as strict in Misogyny, she knew. There, any man caught fraternizing with a woman was branded on the penis with a hot iron by the Men Council. 'Masturbate to prove your hate!' had originally been a Misogyny slogan, but the women had stolen it from them. 'Fuck women—who need a vagina anyway?' was another favorite Misogynist slogan, along with 'Disowned S.O.B.')

But Cora liked men and dick. Enjoyed the caresses, if not being considered the bottom half of the species (which impression she suspected had come about because women generally lay underneath during sex.)

She suspected a lot of the women in Misandry liked men too; they were just terrified of being killed by the Women Council. (The Misandrans weren't lesbians: the same-sex girls had their own town of Sapphia down in southern Innuendo.) So Cora used her toys like a goodwoman, just watching and waiting. She didn't want to leave Misandry, she really enjoyed the sisterhood, but . . . surely a man a month, or even once a week wasn't too much to ask. Each time her sisters castrated another guy all she saw was the waste: *At least we could fuck him first?*

So . . .

Cora was a carpenter; she made furniture. For which she needed wood, which meant she was out in the surrounding forests a lot with her antigrav truck and her chainsaw and axe (and her gun), chopping at trees. She liked the solitude and silence of the forests and generally worked alone.

It was on one of her wood-gathering missions, after she'd crossed to the Misogyny side of Route Zero, that she'd stumbled on Dave. (The people of Misandry and Misogyny considered themselves one city, so she was safe—it was only outsiders that got tortured, raped, castrated, and murdered.)

Dave, a perimeter guard out on patrol, had been fucking a deer, a pretty brown doe with white dots along its back. (He wore the trademark red Misogyny armband with its black 'M.' Cora's pink armband also sported a black 'M.')

A slim man, Dave was holding the animal's rear legs off the forest grass while pumping his penis hard into its sex. His pants were down around his ankles, his rifle propped up against a tree. He was sweating and grunting as his crotch slammed against the animal's rump. The deer was bleating with its tongue out.

Cora had watched for a while, licking her lips and fingering herself. She'd come quickly, but Dave hadn't.

Finally she'd tired of watching him hump the doe. She'd stepped out of hiding.

"Hey, why don't you pick on a female of your own species?"

Startled, he'd turned to her. Seeing the knife in her hand, he'd looked about to bolt. She got a good look at him now: he was youngish, and handsome too, with curly brown hair. Great.

She'd waved the knife at him. "Hey, stud, let the fucking deer go and fuck me instead."

Dave had gulped and nodded. He'd let go of the deer's hindquarters. The animal, its sex a bright red, had limped off into the bushes.

Cora had crossed to Dave, knelt and taken his hard penis into her mouth. It stank and tasted of deer-cunt, but so what? He'd immediately spurted into her mouth. After she'd swallowed the salty liquid, they'd both sunk down to the soft grass.

They'd lain there for a few minutes, properly introducing themselves to each other, then he was erect again. This time she straddled him (God forbid her being beneath any man!).

"Oh God, oh God, oh thank you, God!" she'd gasped as she descended onto him, her womanhood engulfing his manhood like a hungry mouth.

Afterwards, she'd been surprised at how easy it had been. How easy their relationship, their meetings, could be. Dave was almost always in the woods. Like herself, he loved the opposite sex, loved sex with them. (He too had the whipping scars to prove this, had barely escaped penile-branding for openly speaking his mind.) But with the Men Council now threatening to castrate offenders . . . that was how the deer had entered the picture.

"Believe me, I understand," Cora replied his embarrassed confession. "Some of our girls occasionally jerk off the pigs in the sty, just to have something masculine in their hands."

The pair had been lovers since that day.

***

Faking a rape had been Cora's idea. "C'mon, darling, just for fun."

Dave had stalled. "It's dangerous. Someone might hear us."

She stroked his face. "C'mon, don't be a wimp; there's no one else for two miles."

"But why?"

She shrugged. "I'm a woman; lots of us have rape fantasies."

Dave grimaced. "If you want to get raped, come to Misogyny."

"I said *fantasy*, Dave. It's great fun to imagine someone breaking your window, climbing into your bedroom and ravishing you."

"Sounds like the plot of a pirate romance."

"Yeah, that's why they sell so many copies," Cora replied dreamily, already visualizing herself as the distressed damsel being borne off. She looked over at the blown-out windowsill where her axe rested. Dave's rifle and knife sat in a corner on their piled clothes. This house was safe enough—one of the few around still with a roof. They used it regularly now, were currently lying on a blanket they kept here for that purpose. Hell, this bedroom even still had a rotted door.

"It's adult role-play," she insisted. "Let's do it right now."

"Okay," he reluctantly agreed.

She grinned, flicking her black hair with exited fingers. "Okay, I'll lie down and pretend I'm sleeping. Then you climb in the window . . ."

"I'm still worried about someone hearing us."

"I won't scream too loud." She stroked her vagina, then smeared its wetness across his lips. "I promise you it'll be worth it."

He got up to leave.

"Two more things, baby."

"Yeah?"

"Fuck my ass. Anal. Hard, more realistic that way. And also . . . don't stop when I'm yelling . . . remember, don't stop fucking me—I want this done right." She frowned. "You can even hit me to make me keep quiet."

"Hit you?"

"Stop being such a goddam pussy! Yes, hit me! Hard, we're just faking."

Dave winced and slunk away. (He'd watched enough rapes in Misogyny to not want to get involved in one, even a faked one. And he really did love Cora now, didn't want to hurt her for anything. He was planning to ask her to elope with him.)

"Hey, baby," Cora called after him, "remember to do it properly, or I'll be mad at you."

***

It had begun even better than Cora thought it would. Dave had leapt through the window like an enraged pirate; he'd rushed at her like a hungry animal. Grabbed her shoulders, his face flushed with lust, his prick scimitar-stiff in his groin.

"I'm going to ravish you, you damn wench!"

"No!" she'd yelped, as he pushed her down flat on her belly. He'd roughly spread her buttocks and spat between them. Then came the sudden sharp, violent anal entry. Fuck keeping quiet. Yelling her lungs out, she'd orgasmed hard the instant he'd penetrated her ass. Her sex flooded her body with bliss.

"Stop! Stop! Asshole!" she screamed lustily. "Let me go!" She flailed and kicked under him, while he pinned her down and sodomized her brutally. "Fucking stop!"

"Shut up, bitch!" He slapped her hard. "Shut the fuck up!"

She kept yelling. She could hear the fear in Dave's voice, his dread that someone would hear them. *But screw keeping it down,* she exulted. *This is wonderful!* Cora knew there was no one about: Dave was the only one patrolling this part of the woods, and besides they were over on *her* side anyway—none of the other women from Misandry ever came out here.

So she screamed on: "Help me! Someone, please help me! He's going to kill me!" Her ass felt great, packed tight and full of man.

But then:

"Let her go!" a cold female voice said.

"Yes. Right now," another added. "Get your stinking dick out of her!"

The no-nonsense tone of the words pierced through Cora's about-to-orgasm-again ecstasy.

Alarmed, she and Dave rolled over together, he falling off her onto his butt. Together they stared.

Five women now stood just inside the doorway: A slim blonde, a stacked redhead, one skinny Arab-looking girl with bunned black hair and shiny hoop earrings; and two others who both had bright blue hair—one of these two was tall and muscular, the other was petite and busty and looked Asian.

All five women had cold hard faces. Hatred poured from their eyes like visible rays of darkness. Cora was struck silent: were they commies without the headgear?

Then the women rushed over and grabbed Dave, pulling him up roughly from the ground. Four of them held him stiff, while the muscular blue-haired woman produced a knife.

"No!" Cora gasped in horror on realizing the woman's intent. "Stop!"

Too late. The woman quickly sliced Dave's penis and testicles off.

In a streak of bloody drops, the blue-haired woman flung Dave's severed manhood out of a window. The other women dropped him on the ground, where he sat screaming and gripping his bleeding empty crotch.

"Die, you rapist asshole!" the blonde said, spitting on him.

"And do it quietly, wilya, dickspit?" the girl with hoop earrings added. Then she kicked Dave hard in the head. So hard, she knocked him out cold. He fell back to the floor, bleeding out till he stopped moving.

"What the hell did you do that for?" Cora gasped. "He wasn't—"

"Don't worry," the blonde said. "You're safe now. Come with us."

Cora gaped at the blonde then back at Dave's corpse. "Safe? Are you fucking out of your minds!"

The blue-haired woman who'd castrated Dave stepped towards Cora. "We're sorry this happened too. Please try and calm down. You're understandably traumatized but—"

Cora lost it. Utter rage filled her at the thought of what she'd just lost. (These stupid bitches killed my Dave?) And she knew exactly who was to blame for it.

She rolled sideways and grabbed Dave's knife from atop their discarded clothes. Then she lunged at the blue-haired murderess, who'd been kneeling towards Cora, presumably to offer her comfort. Seeing her red outstretched fingers—Dave's blood on her hands— outraged Cora. *You dare offer me comfort after murdering my boyfriend? In this fucking place? Where the hell around here am I supposed to find another man who actually LIKES women?*

Cora knocked the kneeling woman over and clambered on top of her, while the woman, confusion and fright in her eyes now, grabbed her wrists and fought off her stabbing knife.

In a rage of bloodlust, Cora stabbed again and again, somehow not getting through the blue-haired woman's defenses to her face. Then she felt a sudden sharp pain in the back of her neck, then . . .

She felt light, like she was rolling away off the woman; but . . . she also had the strangest of feelings like she'd left her body behind.

And then she hit the grass, bounced, rolled, and found herself lying on her side and looking forward at her own body; her body now headless and jetting blood from her severed neck down over her blue-tressed target; who looked as confused as she, Cora, felt.

And now, like her brains were being vacuumed out of her skull, her thoughts were fast thinning.

One more thing: Before blacking out for good, Cora made out who'd chopped her head off. It was the other blue-haired bitch—the Asian one—and she'd done it with Cora's own wood-axe.

The axe dripped with Cora's blood.

And the bitch even had the nerve to look confused too! *Shit!*

CHAPTER 47

Courtney gaped first at the naked headless body sprawled on top of Heather and squirting blood all over her, then at Miki. *What the . . . ?*

The Japanese girl met her gaze coolly. "I had no other choice; she was going to kill Heather," she said softly. Miki dropped the bloody axe and pushed the headless body off Heather, then helped her to her feet. Heather's head and shoulders were now a wet red.

Miki stripped Heather's top off, wiped her face and shoulders clean with it, then they both got to work wringing the blood out of her hair.

Courtney looked first at Highball, then at Teresa. "What the hell just happened? Please don't let it be what I think we just did."

"I think . . . I think . . ." Highball looked even more confused than Courtney. "They were . . . lovers?"

"A fucked-up misunderstanding, and we're now officially murderesses," Teresa said. She looked from Courtney over to where the dead woman's decapitated head lay by the castrated man's thigh, its eyes staring their way, then sighed loudly. "Whatever else we say, we're not telling the guys anything about this. Matt would never let me live it down. Shee-it, and he told me not to castrate anyone before they got back." Wincing, she pulled a nail file from her jacket pocket and began nervously attacking her fingertips with it.

Courtney nodded, as did both Miki and Heather (who was now staring in horror at the man whose genitals she'd cut off). He lay limp, a broken doll some petulant child had thrown away.

"Shit," Heather finally whispered in shock. "This too just had to happen on my birthday, didn't it?"

"Okay," Highball agreed, "we don't say a word to the guys." She looked down at the dead couple a moment, then she pointed over to their clothes, then back at Heather. "Check if her duds fit you. Just rip off that damned Misandry armband." Her face tightened. "Oops, the guys might recognize these clothes anyway; remember they're currently visiting Misogyny. Even if they don't see any of the townsfolk, Jeff travels this way regularly."

"Doesn't matter," Courtney countered. "We'll say we went for a walk and found these and Heather liked them."

That resolved, Heather quickly dressed in the dead woman's denim jacket.

"And clean hair too," Miki said, producing a bottle of water from beneath the clothes pile. She got to work rinsing the remaining red out of Heather's blue hair.

"We're good as new then," Highball announced once Miki and Heather were through. Her voice was however strained.

Courtney also noticed Highball was now making a point of keeping her back to the two stiffs, as if doing so would make them vanish into thin air. Heather was leaning on Miki; both women had pale faces. Both also avoided looking at the corpses.

Wow, Courtney thought, *we really did it this time.* Now that her outrage had subsided, she was filled with the terrible sense of loss she always experienced after reliving her ordeal in Vaginismus. What had just happened made the feeling worse. She stared past Highball at the bloody mess of the dead man's crotch, his lover's hair too just visible around the edge of Highball's pants. *Shit, man. but why the hell would you two playact a rape out here of all places? Guys, I'm sorry—we really didn't know!*

Realizing that she was about to start crying, she turned around and walked quickly off, back the way they'd come. She turned once, saw the others had begun following, then resumed her solitary tramp.

The communists are making monsters out of us. Slowly but surely, they're turning us into killers like themselves.

And now her tears did come. A flood of them. Tears both for the dead couple back there, and also for her horrible past that had so completely corrupted her future.

CHAPTER 48

By the time the men returned an hour later, the women had sort-of put the afternoon's horrible experience behind them.

Matt, Jeff, and Radio met them lying on their backs, staring nonchalantly at the sky-ceiling. The three men's moods were celebratory; they missed the lipstick thread of melancholy in the welcoming smiles.

"Hey, honey," Matt said, stepping through the doorway. "We survived."

Teresa leapt up and ran to hug him. Highball got up too and leapt on Jeff. Courtney stretched out lazy hands to Radio. Smiling back, he shook his head, sat on a windowsill.

"So, did you guys find us a ride?" Courtney asked from the floor.

Matt grinned. "We sure did, ladies. Someone left their key in the ignition of an AG bus and we stole it."

Teresa looked at him in horror. "You actually entered Misogyny?"

"Just the suburbs," he replied. "We got lucky early—the house was just off a side street."

"The bus has a full gas tank," Jeff added. He scratched his chin. "There's more too."

"What?" Highball asked. (She was frowning, wondering why Jeff looked hairier than usual, and also, why his nose suddenly seemed larger. Then her boyfriend popped a blue pill into his mouth and it all made sense. *Oh, it's those goddamn vitamins of his. Baby, you need a barber, and soon.*)

Matt took over speaking. "Before we took the bus, we had to make sure no one would sound an alarm, so we peeked in the windows."

"What'd you see?" Courtney enquired. Radio was helping her up off the grass. Beside her, Heather and Miki was also getting to their feet.

"Two old guys talking about Dr. Orgasm."

Courtney stiffened. "What did they say?"

Matt frowned. "It's not good news." He raised a hand to forestall her next question. "No, she's not dead; not as far as they said anyway . . . but . . ."

"Her shoeplane's been shot down by the communists," Radio finished for him. "According to those two old guys, it crashed somewhere beside Route Zero; say about five hundred miles farther north, the way we're headed."

Courtney's eyes widened. "Crashed?"

"Yeah," Matt continued. "But we do know Dr. O's still alive. The communists are hunting high and low for her. That's what the two men had been out doing earlier."

"That proves nothing," Teresa said. "She could have crawled off somewhere and died of her wounds."

Heather and Miki nodded agreement.

"Nah," Matt said, "the pilot's ejector seat was gone. She got out while the aircraft was going down. Plus, the commies found her discarded parachute."

Then he grinned at Courtney, who wondered what he found funny. With Dr. Orgasm in danger, she seriously wasn't in a joking frame of mind.

"Just tell her," Jeff said. "Or she might get angry and shoot you."

Courtney looked at them narrowly. "Tell me what?"

Matt gestured at Radio. "Your loving boyfriend here has picked up another broadcast from Dr. O. Oh yeah, she's alive alright."

Courtney and the other women looked at Radio. "Is it true? You've heard from her?"

He nodded. "Very briefly. She said she's at Rabbitfield Air Base, then I lost the signal."

"Where's Rabbitfield?"

Everyone looked at Jeff.

He wrinkled his face. "Not far from where her shoeplane crashed, I think. I'll be certain once we're closer. It's off the main road though."

"So that's it, everyone," Matt concluded. "After a while the two old Misogyny geezers began arguing over a game of checkers, so we took their bus and left." He grinned. "Our sad day just got a happy kick in its ass. Alright, guys, pack up your bags and let's hit the eternal road again."

CHAPTER 49

Travelling north as the night settled over them. Lounging in the AG bus. The bus was long and green, with ten wide rows of seats. Highball sat up front with Jeff, who was driving. The others lay sprawled over the seats. Courtney, Heather, and Matt were asleep. Their other halves were all silent as statues where they sat or lay.

The current plan was simple: Get well away from Misogyny before the two old men sounded the alarm over their stolen vehicle.

***

Jeff (driving the bus with the headlights off) was in a goodish mood.

"The commies are on their way over to Misogyny," he explained to Highball, adjusting the wheel slightly as he spoke. "Those two guys never said why, but . . ." he ate one of his blue tablets, "from what they did say, there's heavy troop movements already well in progress."

Highball shuddered. "Did you guys see any Bees?"

"No, but they're coming, for certain. The commies are planning a major offensive." He frowned. "I think they're looking for us—the convoy I mean."

"Jeff, how can you be so damn sure?"

He shrugged. "Just a feeling I've got. By now the commies must have discovered our exit tunnel. But even with that, they've no way of telling in what direction the convoy headed on leaving Phantasm Station. Best they can do is figure out how much distance we'll have covered since then and set up roadblocks on all Innuendo's major roads at points beyond that limit." He jerked a thumb at the back of the bus. "That's what Radio figures too."

Highball nodded. "They'll be looking for the swallowed-up greenhouses?"

Jeff nodded back. "Yeah. At least until they find the rear half of the one we were in. Then, hopefully, they'll realize what happened and give up the hunt. But still . . ." he pointed ahead at the road, "we're best the hell out of this area before they arrive."

"Yeah. No one's going to be looking for just eight people are they?"

"Not likely; but that's why I'm keeping our speed down to low fifties, just in case they've circled ahead of us and got a roadblock set up already. Any lights up ahead and we head into the woods."

Highball relaxed back in her seat and let Jeff drive.

***

Jeff was trying hard as hell to hide his elation.

The blue pills were working miracles! Yes they were!

Before they'd set off, he'd gone in amongst the trees to urinate and check himself out. He'd been shocked. Erected, his cock was now eight-and-a-half inches long. Oh yeah! Now this was what he'd always wanted! He stood there, pretending to pee, feeling the meaty thick penis in his hand and imagining how it would feel in Highball's tight vagina. He could just see the incredulous look in her eyes when he slid it into her—of course, he'd suggest a blindfold so it would be a complete surprise. But he'd make such sweet love to his baby, give her such incredible orgasms that she'd love him forever and—

He suddenly realized he'd unconsciously plucked a handful of leaves from a tree and was chewing them. What surprised him wasn't how great the leaves tasted, but how natural eating them seemed to him. Like those he'd earlier eaten in the greenhouse, these leaves smelt just like a hot sizzling steak used to.

He'd stood there awhile, musing on that, while the others' voices reached him from the road. Then, figuring it was a side effect of the blue pills and would likely stop once he completed the dosage, he shrugged off any worries. He expected that the pills' other side effects—the increased hairiness everywhere (the hair down his thighs was almost thicker than that on his crotch now), and yes, his nose and ears both felt swollen (but thankfully didn't hurt), and his toenails had turned black and horny (and his feet felt stiff)—would also clear up too then. If only Dr. Brentwood was still available, but . . .

But . . . Okay, chewing leaves in public wouldn't do. His friends would all think he'd gone nuts . . .

So, Jeff took his time, plucking and eating as many delicious leaves as his stomach would hold, until he heard footsteps snapping fallen twigs as they approached him.

He hastily swallowed, spat out green leaf juice, and wiped his mouth clean. He'd just finished zipping away his penis when Highball poked her head around the side of a tree, the evening sun bouncing off her red hair like each was a part of the other.

"Jeff, what's keeping you? Everyone's making jokes about how you're having a baby in here."

He faked a frown. "I thought a dump was coming, but . . . just gas."

"Hey—your tongue's all green!"

He was shocked, but recovered well. "It's a side effect of the damn pills. The doc warned me, but I didn't take him serious. It'll clear up."

Her face squeezed up. "It had better. As it is, you're already way too hairy for my liking."

He pulled her to him, wrapped her in his muscular arms, then kissed her. Gently, with lips closed, so she'd not taste the leaves.

She clung to him, her body soft against his, her head on his chest, clearly wanting more intimacy. Then she pulled reluctantly away and pointed to the road.

"Let's go before the others think we're trying to make a baby."

Jeff laughed. They started back toward the floating bus.

Okay, that was close, Jeff thought as they exited the trees. *I've got to be real careful with this.*

And something else: Later, when Teresa had passed around ham sandwiches to everyone for dinner, Jeff had been unable to eat his— the meat both smelt and tasted horrible to him. He'd passed the meat to Highball and ate just the bread, waving off her perplexed questions with—"Has to be the damn pills." Then he'd grinned. "But, the course ends day after tomorrow, and then I'm back to normal again."

Only, Jeff realized, this new 'normal' wasn't the 'normal' normal that Highball was used to.

So now, as he drove the antigravity bus over the blacktop, Jeff was pleased as punch. His one concern was, he still hadn't decided how big he wanted his penis to be. Ten inches? Eleven? A foot? More than that even? It was very possible: he'd grown over four inches in length (and doubled his organ's girth) in two days and he still had another two days' dosage in the magic bottle.

Jeff grinned. It was such a lovely dilemma to have. All men deserved to have this kind of problem.

Beside him, Highball fell asleep.

CHAPTER 50

Teresa woke up.

This time, after her eyes opened, she made certain that she wasn't dreaming again like that last time on the toilet, but no, she was still seated beside Matt in the darkened bus with everyone else dozing and the Dreamfields streaming past them.

So if we're all asleep, what . . . ?

She realized that what had woken her up was a rhythmic motion on her left, where Matt lounged by the window.

She turned, then stifled a gasp. Right there by her side, her husband had his penis out and was masturbating, his fist rising and falling over his erection.

She peered closer at him. His eyes were shut, and he was gasping silently. His only motion was that of his right arm which had woken her.

For a moment, Teresa was angry that he'd excluded her from his pleasure, then she giggled and decided to share it with him. Jerking him off in the bus had a nice sleazy temptation to it. It wasn't something that Teresa (who was actually quite prudish) would normally do, but for some reason now, likely for the thrill of later remembering she'd once done this, she decided to go for it.

Still, silence was essential here. She reached across to him . . .

Matt's eyes jerked open in fear when her hand fell on his.

"Ssshhh!" she quickly silenced his gasped apology. "I don't want the others to hear us." Then she giggled. "Now relax and let me *handle* this for you." The pun made her giggle louder, then she got to work.

It was even more fun than she'd imagined. His erection was hot and hard in her small fist. She was turned slightly in her seat, so that even if Courtney, who was seated across the aisle, did wake and look their way, she couldn't really tell what was going on. Teresa considered fellating Matt and letting him ejaculate into her mouth (it would save looking for tissues to clean up afterwards), but the sucking sounds might prove rather loud. So she just let her soft fist work on his stiff penis.

Beside her, Matt jerked and fought not to gasp out loud.

"Shit, Teresa, I love you," he whispered. "I'm gonna come!"

But there was something really odd about how he'd said it. His voice was unnaturally low in pitch.

Teresa gaped at Matt in confusion; his face had suddenly become an animal's: it was dark and hairy—he looked like a bear. His eyes were a gleaming red in the dimness.

What the flaming fuck? Alarmed, she moved to pull away from him, but he grinned and stopped her with a massive paw on her arm. (Yes, he *was* a bear now!)

"Keep jerking me off, you shameless little slut," the bear growled, squeezing hard on her arm. "If you don't, or if you dare scream, I'll rip your goddam throat out." It bared its teeth so she could see: they were a long sharp white and dripped saliva onto its shirt.

She glanced quickly around the bus. Everyone was still asleep, and up front in the driver's seat, Jeff was now whistling a show tune.

"Fucking do it!" the bear commanded, grabbing her top, its claws ripping the fabric open and stabbing her breasts, making bright blood dribble down over her cut flesh.

She nodded, and got quickly to work. She was too scared to think straight; utterly confused. *My husband, my husband!* her mind shrieked: *What the hell's happened to my husband?*

She stroked the bear's hairy penis furiously. Despite its threat, she intentionally made a lot of noise so as to alert the others.

Suddenly the bear began grunting really hard. Next it began coming, spurting hot yellow semen over Teresa's hand as she masturbated it through its climax. Finally, its orgasm ended. Its trousers and Teresa's fingers were now coated with its smelly come.

It laughed. Despite her deep terror, she was pissed off now, wondering why no one in this damn bus was waking up like she'd intended.

"And now, you little Metaphor slut," the animal wearing Teresa's husband's clothes announced to her, its softened penis wobbling in its lap, "I'm a communist bear and I'm gonna eat ya!"

It pulled her towards its jaws, and bit down hard into her left shoulder.

Teresa screamed—the bear had completely bitten off her left arm and was wolfing it down. Blood spurted everywhere like it was water and her maimed shoulder an opened fire hydrant. The red jets sprayed the bear's stolen clothes, its head, and the seat and window.

The bear's mouth flashed white and scarlet in the dim light.

"NOooo!" Teresa moaned, her bleeding body wracked with agony. "Don't do this to me! Nooooo . . ."

With a noisy gulp, the bear swallowed her hand whole. She winced as her fingers, their dark burnished fingernails flicking moonlight, vanished into its mouth then slid down its throat.

That done, a ferocious ravenous gleam in its eyes, it grabbed her and began shaking her hard, like it wanted to shake her to bits.

"Nooo . . ." she gibbered plaintively, fighting not to wet herself from the pain. "Don't eat me, please . . ."

Still gibbering, she jerked awake.

Matt was shaking her left shoulder. "Wake up, darling!"

Matt looked very worried and very normal. She was shocked. He had no hairy bear face or paws and no penis exposed in his crotch. She quickly examined her right hand also; no smelly expulsion of animal semen covered it.

Most important of all, her left arm was still attached to her—it hadn't been bitten off.

"You were having a nightmare," Matt said patiently.

It took Teresa a moment to realize that she'd been dreaming. *Hell no, not again? This is utterly ri-cock-ulous!*

A quick glance around the bus showed no one had heard her moaning. She collapsed hard against Matt, sank with relief into his welcoming arms when he hugged her tight.

Soon afterwards, she was asleep again, this time to dreams of colorful meadows where cute bouncy blue bunnies ate Jeep-shaped milk chocolate candy bars.

Around them and the bus, the night proceeded along as before.

CHAPTER 51

Next morning, at about eight a.m., Matt (who'd taken over driving from Jeff at four in the morning) stopped the bus so everyone could get off, pee, and stretch their legs.

He'd parked amidst a meadow—on each side of the road a veritable forest of giant purple flowers and lush grass extended into the distance.

The morning looked supremely glorious.

The only three who didn't alight from the bus were Highball (who was still asleep up front) and Heather and Miki.

"Wait," Heather said, pulling Miki back as she was about getting up. "Make love to me first."

Miki settled back down on the rearmost seat then pointed forward. "She'll hear us."

"Who? Oh, Highball? She won't—we'll keep the noise down; besides, you can hear her snoring from here." Heather leaned forward, kissed her wife softly. "Fuck me, darling, I need to be purged from yesterday. If there's any day I need wiped from the history of the world, it's yesterday—a complete blot on my life. It being my birthday only made it worse."

Miki sighed softly—she definitely understood where her darling was coming from—then she slowly undid Heather's top. Heather was braless beneath. Miki slipped her hands under the coarse denim fabric and cupped the smallish breasts, stroked the soft yielding flesh. She squeezed the breasts, causing Heather to moan sharply, then dipped her lips to her wife's nipples and sucked on them one after the other, while her hands worked to get Heather's pants and undies off. The nipples instantly hardened on her tongue, hot lusty meat begging to be sucked. And Miki really sucked on them.

Heather shrugged her hips out of her pants, Miki pulled the trousers off. The wet-crotched panties followed. Still sucking on her nipples, Miki spread Heather's legs and slowly rubbed her fingers over her wife's blue pubic bush.

Heather moaned louder, leaned back against the seat, gripped its forward edge. She didn't touch Miki, just relaxed into the sensation of her probing fingers, as they first stroked her sexual bud, then split her in the middle, and entered . . . She gasped as Miki's fingers penetrated her body, sliding brazenly into her wet vagina, knowing both that they were wanted there and that they had ownership rights to the dripping hole. Being 'owned' was important to Heather—knowing that she belonged to someone; someone who loved and cherished and nourished her.

And the delicious in-out-in-out motion . . .

The warm mouth shifting from breast to breast . . . the fingers . . . were exactly what she needed this morning. Already yesterday's horrors were fading, washed away by this pleasure only physical love could give one.

Outside, around them, rose the sounds of conversation and laughter. Everyone was upbeat this morning. Radio had reported another conversation with Dr. Orgasm—she was expecting them at Rabbitfield, though apparently Jeff had got the distance wrong: they still had another three hours of driving to go, what with going so slow anyway for fear of driving smack-dab into the commies that one could almost jog alongside the bus.

"Fuck the damn commies!" Heather gasped as Miki dropped her mouth from breasts to vagina and began licking her down there.

Miki looked up from between Heather's thighs. "What, darling?"

Heather pushed her head back down. "Don't stop!" she moaned, "I'm almost coming!"

Miki resumed licking Heather's clitoris, her blue hair floating up and down, left and right as she did so. She enjoyed this. The vagina was wet and stinky with musk, full of womanhood, and she licked everything out, drank the liquids down into herself. The vagina was a mouth against hers, delicious and pure, and she French-kissed it passionately, while stroking the clitoris smoothly and gently with the peculiar diagonal motion she knew Heather loved so much. Her other hand teased Heather's anus. Miki herself was wet, wet, wet now; hot between the legs like she was caressing her own clitoris, not Heather's. She was squirming down there on her knees, grinding her thighs together, wishing she had more hands so she could love herself at the same time.

And now Heather too began wriggling on the back seat. Her vagina felt like a sequence of little explosions were going off inside it. Torrid wet fire pulsed up through her torso, streamed out through her limbs to her fingers and toes, up into her brain till she felt like she couldn't breathe. She trembled, then shook, gasping all the while, desperate to keep her voice down while knowing it was impossible to do so; the feeling was simply too intense to resist. She shut her eyes and seemed to be floating as the pleasure slayed her.

Miki was all over Heather now. She'd stopped the in-out sliding of her fingers and was now just rubbing the shit out of Heather's clitoris while again sucking her breasts. Then, as Heather continued groaning, as her first orgasm expanded into a second, Miki dug her fingers back down into Heather's sex and fingered her hard, causing Heather to both yelp sharply, and her buttocks to lift off the seat.

Miki quickly turned and looked guiltily towards the front of the vehicle. No problem—Highball was still snoring. Outside too, Matt and that utterly gorgeous Radio (Miki found it impossible to lose her crush on Radio) were discussing how far off the main drag Rabbitfield Air Base was. Jeff didn't seem to be with them though.

She returned her full attention to servicing Heather. It always gave Miki great pleasure when Heather was moaning. It was a powerful feeling, knowing you had your lover literally wrapped around your fingers—she twisted her fingers in the dripping vagina, felt it clench tight around her knuckles, was delighted at how Heather's eyes gaped open as fresh pleasure exploded through her body.

Heather's second orgasm seemed to be winding down. Regretting that they didn't have time for a third for her—Miki was sopping wet herself now and needed to climax badly or she knew she'd be bitchy all day—she inserted a third finger into Heather and stabbed her fast with them, pumping out the dregs of the climax.

Heather groaned some more, then went limp. She sat, eyes shut tight, splayed wetly there on the seat, her breasts rising and falling fast, while Miki hoped the others stayed engrossed with the lovely morning outside, and Highball stayed asleep; and that Heather *didn't* fall asleep.

It was a full minute before Heather opened her eyes. She felt purged of all evil; everything was gone. For how long, she didn't know, but 'Oh, my God!' Miki sure was great in bed. Her body felt weak but tuned, ready for the day, ready to take on the world, even.

"Oh, that was incredible!" she gushed to Miki. They kissed, their tongues entwining deep inside their heads, then Heather quickly pushed Miki away. "I can read it in your eyes that you need some too," she whispered. "Quick! You sit down, and I'll get you off before the others come back in."

"Oh yes!" Miki agreed. She pulled off her pants and they quickly switched places.

Heather gasped when Miki flung her legs up and braced her feet firmly on the backs of the seats in front of theirs. "Get your legs down—they'll be seen from outside."

Miki made no attempt to change her position. Instead she giggled. "Who cares if the others work out what's going on? We're married, aren't we?" She draped a hand over her blue pubic plot, V'ed the dripping pussy lips further open. "Love me dear, I need you badly."

"Okay," Heather said. "Your wish is my command." She was about dipping her head into the overflowing pink lake amidst the blue pubic bush when a sleepy voice asked behind them:

"Hey, guys, you two know where Jeff is?"

Highball! Red-faced at being caught about to eat Miki's pie, Heather turned. Highball stood by the side door. She giggled at the expression on the couple's faces. "It's okay; mum's the word." Then her face creased up with worry. "I just can't see Jeff about anywhere. Everyone else is lying around . . . damn, I really gotta pee." She waved a hand at them. "Oh, never mind, I'll go find him. Heaven help him if I catch him masturbating again." She winked sleepily at them. "Go, girls, you two definitely have the right idea."

Her heart pounding, Heather waited till Highball had stepped down off the bus. Then she turned back to Miki and giggled. "You heard what the sexy redhead said, right? We've got the right idea."

"Japanese ears hard of hearing this morning," Miki replied in a lust-slurred voice. She grabbed Heather by the ears, pulled her head down to her crotch. "Sweet Caucasian tongue on clitoris help Asian woman understand English better."

Heather got down hard to work making sweet love to her.

CHAPTER 52

"Hey, guys, I need to take a dump!" Jeff had yelped once they'd disembarked from the bus, then he'd summarily dashed off between the tall purple flowers flanking the road. The others had laid about in the meadow's grass fringe.

Now, concealed amidst the flowers, Jeff was gaping with delight at his penis. *Hell yeah, now THIS is what I'm talking about!* It was utterly unbelievable: erect, his cock had to be at least a foot long now. He gripped it with delight, stroked it, gasped aloud at the electric pleasure that leapt from his scrotum to his anus each time his fist roved over the organ's mushroom head. Oh, yes!

Leaving his penis poking from his pants, he plucked several leaves from the surrounding flower stalks and ate them. *Not as good as tree leaves,* he concluded while swallowing a mouthful, *but for now they'll have to do—there's no trees anywhere in sight. And damn, do I need a razor now, or what?*

His muscular legs were really hairy now. *I look like a chimp down there!* The thick brown hair was coarse too, though it didn't itch, which was good. But . . . Jeff doubted Highball would appreciate him looking like this. *Sure, my babe likes macho men, but this is just way too much hair.*

He plucked one of the humongous flower petals and bit into it. It had a sweet sugary taste. *Yeah, a lot better than the leaves.* Jeff figured he could roll some up and carry them along on the trip—

Through the rows of green stalks, Jeff saw a couple step into view. He froze and watched. It was Matt and Teresa. Matt had a hand on Teresa's breasts; she was busy unzipping his pants while looking furtively around. They disappeared from view again, heading away from Jeff.

Seeing them returned his attention to his penis. He grinned broadly. *Oh, yeah, soon I'll give Highball the ride of her life in bed. She'll come and come and come; so much, she'll think she's died and gone to heaven!*

But . . . am I thick enough yet? I mean some girls do like fisting . . .

He spent a tortuous ten minutes agonizing over the girth of his penis. He just adored the way it stood up hard and straight, a fat pink lovebone, but . . .

No, Jeff finally concluded, while pinching and probing the skin behind the circumcised glans. *It should be a bit thicker, particularly here at the front area...*

And so he got out the pill bottle again. There looked to be about twenty pills left. (Jeff *had* honestly intended to hand the rest of the blue lozenges over to Radio, so he too could grow a MASSIVE penis and give Courtney some good creamy orgasms, but now . . .) Jeff twisted off the bottle top, and shook one out—

"Hey, Jeff, where are you?"

Shit. That was Highball's voice. Jeff quickly shook another pill into his palm, then two more. *I think what I need is a quick burst rather a slow development; force the ol' manhood to widen a bit—*

"Hey, Jeff, baby!"

"I'm coming, babe!" he yelled back.

Then he shrugged a 'Why the hell not?' and spilled two more blue pills into his palm.

He hastily swallowed all six pills. Then he put the bottle away and stuffed his still-swollen penis back into his pants. It wasn't softening fast enough, but his shirt covered it a bit.

He could hear Highball close by now. Best he went to her—if she met him here she'd definitely ask him why he'd ripped off the flower's petal and leaves. She might also notice the tooth marks on the uneaten remnants he'd discarded.

Jeff left there and went to meet Highball. "I'm done, babe. My stomach felt like there was lead in it."

She was still yawning the night out of her mind.

He kissed her. She kissed him back hungrily, squirming deliciously against his manly chest for a moment, then pulling away grinning.

Jeff grabbed at her large firm breasts. She stepped further back, giggling while shaking a finger at him. "No, babe, I can feel you hard in your pants. Don't get me revved up this morning; you know we've no time. Right now I'd like nothing better than to rip your pants off and ride a reverse-cowgirl on you, but Radio says . . ." Then she licked her lips musingly. "Hey, your mouth tastes sweet this morning. Yeah, almost like you've been eating sugar cubes. And your tongue ain't as green either. But, darling, you really do need to shave, your chin's horribly prickly." Then she winced—"Gotta pee, gotta pee, gotta pee!"—dropped her pants and squatted with her back to a flower stalk. Her face clouded with concentration on the task at hand.

Jeff watched Highball urinate with a goofy smile on his face. Intense love for her flooded his heart as it always did. And this time, rather than the apprehension he always felt before their lovemaking (and the disappointment he always felt afterwards), he felt only deep joy now. *Oh yeah! By tomorrow, Highball, I'm gonna give you the sexual experience of your life. Just wait and see if you don't love me forever after that.*

Just to make absolutely certain of that, Jeff got out the pill bottle and ate another two blue lozenges.

CHAPTER 53

Concealed from Jeff, Highball, and the others by the massive purple flowers, Matt and Teresa lay having sex on the soft meadow floor. Their coupling had already startled a bed of worms, which had quickly burrowed out of sight again.

"Fuck!" Teresa gasped as Matt penetrated her deeply with his manhood, so deep it felt like he was nailing her to the ground. Their bodies were naked, hers splayed beneath his. (Their shed clothes and footwear lay heaped at the base of a flower stalk by their feet.) She lay passive and limp, legs spread, knees bent, taking what he gave her. There'd been no foreplay, she was dripping wet after last night's scary dream. (And, oh no, she wasn't telling Matt what she'd dreamt till much later).

She felt content. Her silver hoop earrings floated on the grass by her head like hollow circular boats on a green sea. Now and then, she reached up a hand and stroked Matt's sweaty face. But that was rare; most of the time she was consumed by the pleasure his body was feeding hers.

He thrust into her slow and steady, bracing himself on his elbows while also licking her neck; she moaned louder. Then his mouth dropped from her neck to lick at her left nipple. She felt his teeth clamp on the stainless steel ring filling the nipple's piercing and pull it, stretching out her breast. He let the left breast fall, did the same to the right one. She quivered as his tongue swirled around the darker brown aureolar skin, then slurped sideways over her ribcage, over the face of the spooky graveyard girl tattooed down her side. (She imagined the tattoo suddenly jerking its eyes open in startlement at their shared pleasure.)

He gave a deep thrust then, again nailing her ass to the grass bed. She gasped as her buttocks flattened, his pubic hair spongy against her smoothly waxed vulva. Between her spread thighs, his manhood filled her, pulsing with blood, and now, it felt like it was expanding inside her, or she was contracting around the hard penis, being absorbed into it . . .

It slid in and out of her soaking vagina, jerking their bodies back and forth over the grass. She bit her lower lip to keep from screaming out her enjoyment—the others mustn't hear them. (She was prim like that—it was quite alright that others suspected she was having sex, but why advertise the fact to the world?)

Her eyes fluttered sideways to the bases of the thick flower stalks. A mole cradling a writhing half-eaten earthworm was staring blindly in their direction, the velvety-furred creature confused by their wet thudding of flesh on flesh. Teresa knew she felt much like the worm did now; trapped in a predator's deadly grasp and unable to escape. No! That wasn't so! In her case, she had no desire to escape . . . and . . . she realized that she, not her husband, was the predator here. He was the worm—the hard penis plunging into/retreating from her vagina delicious white meat she was ravenously swallowing, unable to get enough of. She was wet and slippery down there around his flesh, a lower mouth flooded full of sexual saliva to digest him with.

She turned fevered eyes on Matt. "Choke me!" she gasped softly.

He nodded down at her with understanding, and a moment later, she felt his muscular fingers circling her neck and squeezing gently but firmly.

She didn't understand why it worked—that blocking off the airflow to her brain—but it did. Once he wrapped his hand around her neck, her sexual mind filled with anticipation, like a white flame burning inside summoning a host of moths to their deaths. Then, as her air was cut off, the release came—

It happened now as always: Matt choked her, her legs lifted off the floor, her legs kicked at the sky. Her daintily tattooed feet with their glossy black toenails fluttered in the air like butterflies. The lack of air shut off most of her mind, left her body to express its sexual self without conscious control.

And express itself it did. She began coming, a tremendous orgasm that wracked her skinny frame. Her vagina sucked at Matt's penis, clenched tightly around it, threatened to crush it. Her moans loudened. (Now, prude or not, Teresa no longer cared if anyone heard them.) Through slit eyes she saw Matt's expression change, heard him groan as his orgasm was undammed from his testicles to additionally flood her already well-irrigated vagina. She first felt his meat throbbing in her, then the warm jets of semen squirting purposefully forward at her cervix with the intent of fertilizing her field. The squirts of warm come felt like they were washing her clean of the world's dirt.

He grunted, eyes staring wide and white, his body so stiff he looked like he'd break. Simultaneously, his fingers clamped tighter around her neck . . .

Fuck! Her oxygen-starved mind seemed disconnected from the ecstasy she felt. Her vagina had become her entire body, her entire body a sex organ. Her sex felt like a wet sponge being squeezed hard, so hard it dripped honey. Honey that soaked her in pleasure, lifted her . . .

Matt loosened his fingers from her neck. He exhaled long and loud, the tightness wracking his body slackening. Slowly, oxygen revived her brain again; the fog seeped out of her head. She relaxed there beneath him, breathing heavily, feeling like she'd just fallen from outer space and needed to come to terms with herself being human again.

She reveled in the sensation of his hairy crotch pressing on hers, his chest on her breasts, his penis so deep into her vagina that it seemed he'd stabbed her stomach with it.

"Oh, I love you!" Matt gasped, going limp on her.

Holding his softening penis deep inside her with a firm hand on his ass, she kissed him. "I love you too, darling."

He kissed her back, tiredly, but passionately. Teresa expected he'd fall asleep once they were back on the bus. Her body, her sex, her mind, felt fulfilled. (She imagined she still felt his fingers squeezing her neck, filling her brain with pressure that made her pussy explode!) This morning's sex had definitely been worth it. He loved her, she loved him; what more did one ask from the world?

He rolled off her; they lay side-by-side. Teresa, now her body's desire was satisfied, examined her fingernails for cracks (so many so far she felt like shrieking to the heavens for God's mercy), while Matt floated in a thoughtless half-sleep, until they heard Radio's approaching voice calling everyone back to the bus.

CHAPTER 54

Courtney lay staring at the sky. Radio had just left her side to go find the others. It was about time they hit the road again.

Her gaze streamed across the aerial vista. Overhead was pure blue, home to a hundred fluffy white clouds with no touch of Bizarro's brown corruption. The sun beamed down a happy yellow. It was neither too hot nor too cold.

What an utterly lovely view, she enthused. *Simply fantastic.* Watching this sky made the world seem pure.

The scent of the floral meadow beside her was the perfect complement to the view. The combination of vision, smell, and the faintest of insect chirps was almost erotic.

Distracted by the morning, Courtney dropped a hand between her thighs and lazily stroked her sex through the intervening denim.

She winced at the dull spark of warmth that responded from her vagina.

"Meeting Dr. Orgasm would make today the greatest day of my life," she said aloud. Then she smiled sadly, lapsed back into thought. *Only, somehow, I just know it won't happen—she'll likely be dead; or the commies will find her first and murder before she can help me and help the world. Existence has a way of screwing me over when and where it really matters that I get a break.*

CHAPTER 55

"Holy shit! I'm gonna come!"

On hearing that, Heather licked Miki's clitoris faster and harder. The Japanese woman's pale thighs were tense beside her head, her legs bent white poles, the soles of her feet pressed hard against the backs of the forward row of seats. Heather dug her fingers deeper into her wife's dripping sex. Her mouth, nose, and chin dripped wet with saliva and vaginal lubrication.

As each continuing gust of pleasure spurted up through her, Miki's toes first curled in, then splayed out painfully. Her arms roved aimlessly, first down to Heather's shoulders, then back up to grab and squeeze her own breasts; then they flailed sideways to grab at the air; then they smacked the upholstery. The expression on her face was of the utmost pleasure, her mouth gaping open, her slanted eyes squeezed shut. *Oh, fuck—this is just fantastic, whoever knew sex could feel this great in the back of a bus? We must do this more often! Shit! Shit!* The thoughts dissolved in her head till they meant nothing, becoming both less and more than the words they were composed of.

Heather already had three fingers in Miki's vagina. Now she slipped in another, really expanding her. Heather knew this fourth finger felt HUGE—almost painfully so—to Miki (who simply couldn't get her sexual mind around the concept of fisting), so she was careful how she stroked in and out now. Not hard and fast, but with slow delicious stabs, like she was making music—like Miki's sex was a church organ she was playing. She kept her fingers curved upward, so they stroked the G-spot.

Miki gasped and began coming. She immediately dropped her hands to her vagina, pushed Heather's hands away, and began rubbing her clitoris herself.

Heather slipped her mouth down further between her wife's spread-wide buttocks and began tonguing her anus instead, digging the

241

oral muscle deep into the pungent hole, while Miki groaned and squirmed and ground her backside into the seat.

Then suddenly, Miki stopped masturbating, grabbed Heather's hair, and pulled her mouth back up to her vagina again. Then, releasing her grip on Heather's head, she performed a slow erotic dance, bracing herself up on her hands so her body was all off the seat and grinding her pussy against Heather's mouth, tardily and lusciously, creaming Heather's lips with her seeping tangy liquids, while all the while grimacing and yelping like a dog in pain. (Miki *was* doing her best to keep the noise down.)

This went on for a full minute, then Miki collapsed back down onto the seat.

"Wow, that was damn intense," she gasped, her tongue darting amidst her lips like a startled bird.

Heather kept her mouth pressed tight to Miki's clitoris, sucking hard on it till Miki's trembling subsided. Then she climbed back onto the seat herself, pushed Miki down flat on it and lay on top of her, pressing her dripping wet mouth against Miki's, letting Miki share in the sweet and sour taste of her own vagina, making her inhale the distinct pungent odor of her own femininity.

They kissed and kissed. Time froze for both of them—they had no idea for how long.

"I think we'd better put our clothes back on," Miki finally said in a sheepish voice that indicated that she didn't really want to.

Heather nodded sleepily, then stroked Miki's face. "You're right, we're lucky everyone's still lounging. I doubt anyone's actually realized what we've—"

"Hey, girls!" A voice called from the bus's side door. "You done yet?"

Heather and Miki gaped at each other in shock. Then, flinging their hands up to shield their breasts from view, both sat up and stared down the aisle between the seats.

Jeff was peering around the side of the door. Grinning, he waved. "Sorry to bug you two pretty ladies, but if you've refreshed yourselves enough, the rest of us would like to resume this trip."

"Yeah, sure, sure." Both women looked funny; faces red from embarrassment beneath shocking blue hair.

Jeff's head vanished from the door. "Okay, everyone, our sapphic lovers have both come a zillion times each; get your asses back on the bus and let's roll!"

Giggling like mad, Heather and Miki both began scrambling into their clothes again.

CHAPTER 56

The atmosphere as the bus zoomed along the road now was celebratory. Everyone suspected—the feeling was so thick in the air Courtney could virtually smell it—that the end of their trip was on them.

First they needed to reach Dr. Orgasm's crashed shoeplane (which Jeff figured was now only about eighty miles farther along the road), then they'd detour left to Rabbitfield Air Base where the doctor herself awaited them.

Like animals huddling together for warmth, they'd all moved to the front of the bus.

Heather and Miki, both blushing deep red whenever their eyes met one of the others', were busy handing around sandwiches and bottles of water.

Teresa sat snuggled up to Matt, who was snoring against a window. (Courtney wasn't fooled: Teresa's flushed face meant she'd just been fucked. And good and hard too: munching her sandwich, Teresa practically oozed relaxation.)

Jeff was driving again, Highball seated beside him.

Courtney and Radio sat side-by-side holding hands, Radio by the window, listening to the static play inside his head.

Except for her apprehension of what lay ahead of them, Courtney felt almost content.

Highball slid out of her seat and clambered back to join them. She mocked a frown at Heather and Miki. "Sandwiches for the driver and his accomplice too, guys."

Miki said, "We were just coming forward to serve you."

"And, why'd you rat on us?" Heather asked, handing sandwiches to Courtney and Radio. "I thought you weren't going to tell the others you caught us making love."

Highball looked scandalized. "Me? I never said a word to anyone."

Heather smirked. "Tell me the other one, honey."

"Honest, guys. I didn't tell anyone you guys were having sex back there."

Heather frowned in amusement. "So if it wasn't you, then who?"

"Girls, it was obvious," Radio said before biting into his sandwich. "This is an antigravity vehicle—no tires. Which means, it bobs up and down when you're humping."

"Oh." Heather's mouth formed a circle. "You knew all along that we were . . . ?" Beside her Miki gaped too.

"Yup. We just hoped you two wouldn't take all day at it."

Both women's faces reddened again.

Outside the bus, the flanking meadows slowly gave way to thick woodland on their left, and on their right, to a poppy field through which bounded giant brown toads.

Highball grinned and stretched. "Anyway, like I told you, I completely approve of you guys making love. Nothing tops sex for starting the day right. Too bad I was sleepy earlier, I should have thought of that myself." She groaned. "Damn, I can't wait till we hit a town. I need some dick in my . . . oops, I mean I need some Jeff in my . . ." She giggled. "It sounds dirty either way, doesn't it?"

"That's okay," Miki said. "Dick's good for a woman. Nothing to be ashamed of."

"Miki, what do *you* know about dick?" Courtney asked heatedly. While she knew she was being unfair, she was suddenly so not in the mood for Miki's crap. (She knew the blue-haired Japanese girl didn't care for her either, but had no idea it had to do with Miki's longtime crush on her boyfriend.) And then there was the fact that she knew Miki and Heather (and Teresa too) had just had the sort of creamy orgasms that were now denied her. She winced. *Damn, is there anyone who isn't coming in here? Even Highball's making plans to orgasm like she's about buying a Coke from the supermarket.*

Then she smiled evilly. "I thought it was all tongues and fingers with you ladies."

"And strap-ons!" Teresa added with a disarming grin.

Heather (remembering the simmering dislike between her wife and Courtney) rolled her eyes. Miki looked indignant, but still took the proffered bait:

"Think what you like. I like dick—men—as much as you do, maybe even more than you."

Courtney shrugged off the barb. "So, enlighten us. If guys are so great, why are you with another woman then?"

Miki smirked, then bent forward in the aisle between the seats. "Not just me—Heather likes men too."

"But you're not with any," Courtney insisted.

Miki looked to Highball for support.

Highball shrugged back. "You *are* riding the same-sex bus . . ." She giggled. "What the hell is wrong with my mouth this morning? I must be more hard up than I even imagined. You know what? I'm gonna leave you guys to this argument before I really put my foot in it." She collected sandwiches and water from Heather and darted back forward. They heard her growl: "Hey, Jeff, aren't you taking too many of those damn pills? And hurry this vehicle up, we need to find a bed!"

"Yep, she's really hard up," Teresa whispered to Heather. Then she grinned across at Courtney and Miki. "So, who was winning the debate?"

Courtney picked up the thread of her thoughts again. "I was asking Miki to explain how come if she likes men so much, she married a woman?"

"Hey!" Miki growled, anger in her almond-shaped eyes. "Heather and I *have* both dated men in the past, okay?"

Heather laughed. "And we had lots of great creamy sex with them too. And orgasms to die for. Courtney, I really do enjoy having a man deep inside me, enjoy the taste of him on my tongue, love the feel of him filling me with his love milk. So where does that leave your theory?"

Courtney shrugged, suddenly disgusted with herself for baiting the pair. "Yeah, I guess that's shot to bits, now." She waved a conciliatory hand. "Forget I started this."

Miki, however, now stared pointedly at Radio, who'd turned in his seat and was listening with great interest. "It's like this—we love you guys, we just love each other more."

He nodded. "So we can term yours a bisexual marriage?"

"Yes, it is," she replied emphatically. "We still do men occasionally, we just do it as a threesome as a couple—sometimes a friend we both fancy, or a guy we pull in a club . . ." Miki grinned sheepishly. "On special occasions, like for her birthday, we even hire escorts. You should have seen the three guys I booked for yesterday. They all looked like Jeff."

Heather gasped. "Three? I thought you said it was just one."

"Well, I wanted to make it extra-special for you."

Radio made a reflective face. "And neither of you feel threatened by all this?"

"Not at all," Miki replied. "We'd discussed it before tying the knot. So long as we do it together, it's fine."

Heather nodded. "It works for us as two bisexual women anyway. Some of our male friends have similar marriages. And we know quite a few male-female Bi couples too. We find it works better if you're both Bi, rather than you being with someone who's completely straight or gay. In either case it's essentially the same problem: Once you're sexually drawn to both sexes, your partner always either suspects you of cheating on them with the opposite sex, or fears that you'll one day ditch them for a member of the opposite sex. If you're both Bi though, you're unlikely to have that problem."

"As long as you're both straightforward and upfront with each other," Miki added earnestly. "That's what I think is most important."

"Sounds a lot like an open marriage to me," Jeff called from up front. "You hump who you like, I pump who I like."

"Almost, but not exactly," Radio countered. "Although, by letting additional partners into their marriage, they *are* tilling a field for trouble to sprout in later. It's like that well-documented danger of swinging, when what starts as a sequence of casual encounters escalates into an extramarital romantic attraction on one or both spouses' parts."

"I don't think so," Heather contested. "I think our way prevents trouble along the way."

(Courtney kept out of the discussion, as did Miki. Both sat flinging the occasional baleful glance at each other.)

"I suppose in one sense, it does," Radio agreed seriously. "But still, you—"

"How 'bout when only one of you fancies someone?" Teresa asked. "C'mon, that's bound to cause friction."

Laughing, Heather shook her head. "We've worked that out too: The uninterested one comes along to play voyeur; and also to watch that things remain under control. And if the person we want to fuck doesn't like that arrangement, then it's off." She shrugged. "Okay, Radio, I'm not going to pretend that we've a perfect marriage. But then, who does? So we're doing what works for us at the moment. Later, we'll hopefully adjust to whatever challenges we encounter."

Miki spoke up. "I think what's most important is being honest with one another. That way our love will last forever."

"Tell the gang about the fourples," Teresa suggested between sips of water.

Courtney frowned. "Fourple? What's that?"

Heather expounded: "A fourple is a more advanced bisexual marriage grouping. Two men, two women, bound together by marital vows between all four of them." She grinned at the others. "In a fourple all the basic sexual pairings—male-female, male-male, and female-female—are catered for in the same unit, so there's no need to look outside for other partners."

"It's a self-sufficient bisexual family group," Miki added.

"Sounds perfect," Courtney agreed. "So are you and Heather planning to permanently hook up with two guys in a fourple at some point?"

Heather sighed. "We've discussed it. The problem is—fourples are hard to set up right."

"How so?" Radio asked after a glance forward at his red-haired sister, who was stroking Jeff's arm as he drove.

"The thing is, you need four bisexual people, which is very easy to find, who are all equally attracted to one another, which is very difficult to find. Anything less than that and the bonding is weakened. Once any of the members isn't being catered for—either emotionally or sexually—divorce isn't far off."

"It would be real nice though," Miki said, "to meet two Bi guys that we both fancied and who each fancied us."

Radio stared at the bus ceiling a bit. "And each unit's limited to four people?"

Heather shook her head. "Not so. The basic foundational unit has to be four people—two Bi women, two Bi men—but from there you can expand. Queer and transsexual people, and hermaphrodites too, can come in as fifth, sixth, even seventh members, only everyone has to be attracted to the group as a whole, not just to one or two people in it."

"And absolutely no completely straight people involved," Miki added.

"And no completely gay people either," Heather finished.

"Isn't that discriminatory?" Courtney asked. "Bisexual bigotry?"

It was Radio who replied: "No, I don't think so—I think I understand what Heather means: A straight man will only be interested in the fourple's women, a straight woman only in its men. And that skews the group dynamic and puts pressure on the marriage." He stared a question at Heather. "Am I right?"

"Spot on. It's the same deal with completely gay men or women: they're only interested in the members of their own sex."

"Same applies to queers and trannys too," Miki said. "It does take a lot of pressure off the girls, though."

"How's that?"

She giggled. "Well, like . . . most times, guys seem higher-sexed than we ladies anyway; so it's a relief in a way; you know, they can make love to each other if the girls aren't in the mood."

Courtney smirked at that. *Yeah, right, bitch. And are you ever in the mood?* Then she relented again. *Hey, lighten up, me! Stop taking out your own frustrations on the woman!* Beside her, she felt Radiohead abruptly stiffen. She turned to him, saw his eyes glaze over, saw him lift hand to right ear and twist it forward—

". . . Karen, a close friend of ours, is in a fourple," Miki was saying. "She says how great it is, like say, when she's on her period and all tamponed up, to just play voyeur; you know, sit in a chair wanking while watching her wife and two husbands getting all hot and sweaty in bed." Miki visibly tingled. "Oh, watching two men suck each other off or lick each other's anuses or buttfuck themselves is just so arousing."

Courtney winced.

"Where else can you get lovingly double-penetrated every night of the year if you so want?" Heather added. "Just imagine: Hot sweaty guy under you, rubbing his hairy chest against your breasts while you French kiss him deep and hard, and he's penetrating you from the front; while another guy is in you deep from behind, filling your ass, his weight on your back, so you feel like the meat in a hot dog, and he's kissing your neck and back. And they're both sliding in and out of you at once; and if they sync their thrusts perfectly, it feels like you've actually got two vaginas, not one."

Yeah, girl, Courtney admitted to herself. *You really do like dick!*

"Wow!" Teresa gushed in a whisper, to a sideways glance at her asleep husband. "You're getting me hot just telling it."

"So it's great being Bi," Miki said, looking meaningfully at Courtney. "Sure it's complicated—"

"Hey, Jeff!!!" Radio shouted then, completely startling everyone. "Stop the bus! Right now!"

The AG vehicle instantly bumped to a halt.

Courtney twisted to stare worriedly at her boyfriend. "Baby, are you alright?"

Then suddenly, there was no need for any more questions. They all saw it, in the air directly ahead of them.

A massive pink shoe was dropping from the sky down onto the road.

"That's Dr. Orgasm's shoeplane," Highball gasped up front. "She is alive!"

CHAPTER 57

They watched in awe as the HUGE pink shoe landed in the road.

The pink shoeplane was the size of a two-story house. In design, it looked like a woman's peep-toed ankle boot, with a set of glass toes as its cockpit. Along the line of its sole (and ascending the high curve to the base of the eight-foot heel) were emblazoned the fiery words: A WOMAN'S RIGHT TO COME IS NON-NEGOTIABLE. HER ORGASM IS HER HUMAN RIGHT—ONE TO FIGHT AND DIE FOR! I SQUIRT ON THE LADY-HATERS!

It was clearly Dr. Orgasm's famous shoeplane, the one they'd all seen flying overhead so many times before Metaphor fell. But now, now that they'd endured so much and traveled so far to find it, actually being here near the massive pink shoe was overwhelming.

They were confused. The pink shoeplane's surface was scorched in places, and around its heel, a large oval bronze sheet had been welded in place and not yet painted over.

"It's clearly been in a fight," Radio said.

"That thing shouldn't be able to fly," Teresa said nervously.

"I know," Radio replied. "It flies by magic."

"Magic? Is she a witch or a doctor?"

Miki said, "She's a witchdoctor."

Courtney grinned at Miki's statement.

Awake now, Matt was rubbing the cobwebs out of his eyes. "Hey, guys, why'd we sto—!" Then Matt saw the pink shoe blocking off Route Zero. He gaped at it a while, then turned to Radio. "Hey, dude, what's the news? Dr. O's here?"

Brian 'Radio' Lewis nodded.

"Hey, Radio, what do we do now?" Jeff called back at them.

"We wait," Radio replied in a neutral voice. "Put the bus in reverse gear, keep the engine running, but stay put."

Jeff gulped, then nodded and reversed gears. Then his nervousness got the better of him and he got out his bottle of blue pills and swallowed a few.

Angered by her boyfriend's fresh 'vitamin' intake, Highball growled, "Hey, little brother! Can't you even keep us out of danger for one day?"

"Yeah, what's the news, Radio?" Heather asked testily, glancing back at where her shotgun lay across an unoccupied seat. "Is that Dr. O or isn't it? Are we in a fresh pile of crap or aren't we?"

"I don't know," Radio admitted.

Courtney linked her hand in his. "How's that, baby?"

He frowned, then pointed out front at the pink shoeplane. "It's strange: I sensed this aircraft overhead, that's why I asked Jeff to stop, but . . ." he tapped his forehead, "I'm still picking up Dr. Orgasm's broadcast from Rabbitfield Air Base. No way can she be in two places at once."

"So you think this might be the commies flying her plane then?"

"Either that, or this one's a fake. Remember those two old Misogynists claimed she'd been shot down."

"Hey, everyone!" Highball yelped. "The cockpit door's opening!"

Bodies tense, they waited. Behind the shoe's glass big toe, half of a curved pink section was sliding up off the main mass, while its lower half folded down into a ladder.

Then, after a brief pause, a head poked out of the door and a famous female face smiled their way.

"Yesss!" Courtney yelped in delight. "It's her! It's her!!"

Before anyone could stop her, she'd leapt from her seat and was fumbling open the bus's side door. Then she was running, running, running . . . almost extinguished hope rekindling again in her breasts.

CHAPTER 58

Dr. Carol Orgasm smiled at the eight friends.

She was a tall slim brunette, middle-aged but still youthful. Above her smile, though, her eyes were extremely sad.

She'd been injured at some point. Her left forearm was completely bandaged and she winced when it accidentally brushed her side.

Standing between the two vehicles, the green bus and the pink shoe, the eight friends explained who they were and why they'd come.

"So Metaphor really is completely destroyed," Carol Orgasm said in a soft voice after listening attentively. "My warning came in way too late. It's regrettable; I kept getting one Marc Andrews, who for some reason couldn't hear me clearly . . ."

"Andrews was a commie spy," Matt said. "Chief Oldfield shot the jerk, but by then the damage was already done, City Defense was in shambles."

Dr. Orgasm sighed. "All isn't lost, however. Florence Rigid hasn't won yet."

***

Courtney was surprised on meeting the doctor for the first time. Dr. Orgasm seemed a calm, placid woman, not the feminist firebrand who'd inflamed the entire land of Innuendo with her pro-vagina rhetoric. She seemed almost . . . divine . . . goddesslike . . . like she radiated healing. Her presence heated up the morning like an additional sun.

"Can you help me?" Courtney gushed in a desperate rush. "I was captured by the commies and taken to Vaginismus and . . ."

"Now you can't climax in bed anymore," Dr. Orgasm finished for her. Her face turned dark. "Florence Rigid is a total bitch to do that to you."

"But, *can* you help me? The rumored O-pill, is it real?"

Dr. Orgasm laughed, a tinkling sound like happy brook water navigating rocks. "Yes, Courtney, the O-pill is real."

"Does it work? Will I—" Then Courtney was struck by an oddity: "How'd you know my name?"

"Your boyfriend mentioned you. Once, shortly after I fled the city, we had some time to chat at length over the airwaves. I told him the pill was real, and he said he loved you so much and he'd do utterly everything to bring you to me for a cure."

Courtney gasped at Radio. "You did? Why didn't you tell me?"

He grinned. "I didn't want to get your hopes up."

"And yes," Dr. Orgasm continued, "the O-pill works better that you can even—"

"Yaaahhh!" Jeff screamed suddenly. "Nyaaah!"

In shock and horror, the others all turned and gaped at him.

CHAPTER 59

Jeff's body was changing. Like someone was inflating parts of him independent of each other, his body bulged out at several different places at once: his belly, the left side of his face, his crotch . . .

His waist grew suddenly thicker; his belt exploded, his pants and underpants ripped away to shreds.

Everyone, the cool Dr. Orgasm included, gasped at the size of Jeff's revealed penis—a foot-and-a-half-long brown snake dangling from his crotch almost to his knee. Highball covered her mouth in shock, not just at her boyfriend's suddenly monster manhood, but also at how hairy his body now was: he looked like he was wrapped in a dark brown rug.

"Nyaaah! Nyaaah!" Jeff kept grunting. He sounded more perplexed than in pain. And all the while, loud popping and snapping sounds came from his body, like someone was breaking him apart inside.

Everyone leapt back from Jeff and watched nervously from a wide circle away. Even Radio looked completely confused. Dr. Orgasm, however, though her eyes remained compassionate, now had a knowing smirk on her lips.

Jeff kept getting bigger, his torso extending first upward, then when it became too heavy for his legs, falling forward so he was standing on all fours. His remaining clothes and his shoes fell apart like shredded paper. His legs and arms too were lengthening rapidly, and were also growing thicker. Hair squirted out between his buttocks and grew into a long tail. His fingers and toes first shrunk, then turned black and horny.

And his head! His nose expanded and extended forward, as did his jaw. His eyes flowed to the sides of his face, his ears grew out long, his hair slid back along his neck . . .

"He's becoming a horse!" Teresa gasped in horror.

And it was true. With a sudden series of muffled explosions from inside his body, Jeff Bellbrook was gone. In his place now stood a big brown stallion. (Viewed now on the horse, Jeff's previously massive-seeming penis had just the right equine proportions.)

Highball found her voice. "Jeff! What the hell is happening? Say something!"

She started walking toward the stallion.

Courtney grabbed her and pulled her back. "I wouldn't if I were you. I know horses. This one looks wild."

"LET ME GO!!!"

Courtney held on tighter. "Uh uh, girl."

Radio also grabbed hold of his sister. "Hold on, sis."

"Jeff, baby!!!" Highball screamed helplessly. "What the hell have you done to yourself!!!? Fucking talk to me!!!"

In response, the horse neighed loudly, no recognition of her in its eyes. "Nyaaah! Nyaaah!" Then it reared up, kicking its front hooves high into the air. Then it spun around and galloped off the road, into the meadow on their right.

In silence, they all watched the brown stallion pick up speed till it was far away from them, its body a dark streak slicing through the flowers. Then Courtney and her remaining six friends turned to gape at Dr. Orgasm.

"What just happened!?" Highball, tears streaming down her face, demanded of the doctor. "Did you do something to him? Is he allergic to you!?"

"Don't be unreasonable, sis," Radio said.

"Do something, dammit! That's my boyfriend galloping away there!"

"*Used to be* your boyfriend," Dr. Orgasm corrected solemnly and without irony. "I've seen that transformation happen before." She frowned. "He was taking blue *vitamin* pills, right?"

A wet-eyed nod from Highball. The others looked surprised.

Dr. Orgasm continued: "Yes, yes, it had to be that. Had to be Lou Brentwood, my one-time crackpot assistant. Brentwood put some men on a course of penis enlargement pills made from equine serum. Sure, they got bigger, but then . . ." She sighed deeply. "When will you men ever learn that size really doesn't matter? How can it? Guys, the clitoris is OUTSIDE the fucking vagina, and the G-spot two-and-a-half inches inside it, yet you all want ten-inch-long schlongs when all you really need to do is learn to use your fingers and tongue right."

The women (including Highball) all nodded sagely to this. Matt and Radio looked unconvinced.

Dr. Orgasm rolled her eyes at them. "Look, reason this out with me. If penis size was so requisite for a woman's satisfaction in bed, how would the lesbians ever cope?"

"Strap-ons?" Matt ventured.

A firm shake of the head from Dr. Orgasm. "No. You're either reading the wrong literature or watching the wrong movies. Those girls mostly make do with fingers and tongues. And they're happy enough with each other's bodies as they are—no penis . . . too happy even in Florence Rigid's opinion." She sighed again. "Yes, dick *is* vitally important to a woman's happiness, but it's not the be-all and end-all of sex, duh? If you're unsure what to do, watch lesbian porn, goddammit." Then she calmed a bit . . .

"Is there any cure!?" Realizing their discussion had veered off from Jeff, Highball practically shouted the words.

The doctor's placid gaze settled back on her. "None, my dear, I'm sorry. That time, we handed the horses over to a stable for people to ride." Her voice turned wistful. "One was renamed Sultan, I recall . . ."

Courtney blanched. "Sultan? A chestnut Arabian? Wow! That's the horse I was riding the day the commies caught me. You're saying it was once a person too?"

Dr. Orgasm nodded sadly.

Highball now really started weeping. While Courtney held her close, she stared out over the meadow at where the departing horse had dwindled to a mere distant speck.

CHAPTER 60

"What now?" Matt asked Dr. Orgasm. "I'm not comfortable with us all standing out here in the open for so long. The communists . . ."

"The commies are occupied elsewhere," Dr. Orgasm replied, the sun playing off her brown hair so Courtney now saw it was shot through with grey. "Trust me, they won't be bothering us."

"How do you know that?" Radio asked. "And also . . ." he tapped his forehead for emphasis, "if you're here with us, how come I'm still picking up your signal like it's coming from Rabbitfield Air Base?"

"And," Courtney added, joining them (Heather and Miki having now taken over trying to calm Highball), "if your magic shoe was shot down, how's it still flying?"

"Good questions," Dr. Orgasm replied. "I'll answer yours first, Courtney. I had *two* shoeplanes. I let one be shot down as a decoy." She touched her bandaged arm and winced. "I almost didn't make it out before the shoe crashed; the damn ejector controls jammed and . . ." Her eyes turned grim as if she was reliving the experience.

Courtney pointed behind the aging brunette, at the giant pink female footwear now blocking off Route Zero. "This one looks kinda shot up too."

"It's an older shoe from way back when. It's been in tons of scrapes with the communists." She shrugged. "I fixed it but just never got around to repainting it."

Courtney nodded, then lapsed into a grinning silence, holding Radio's hand and staring sheepishly at the woods to their left. She was sure Dr. Orgasm knew her enquiry was just for show. She didn't give a damn about shot-up magic pink flying shoes—she was so overjoyed to hear that the O-pill actually existed and worked, it was all she could do not to scream her excitement to the universe.

She glanced over at Highball. Heather and Miki had now calmed her. Courtney sympathized with Highball—what had just happened to Jeff was just . . . she had no words.

"And *my* question?" Radio asked. "How are you in two places at once?"

Dr. Orgasm brightened up and even chuckled. "I'm obviously not. There's . . ." She checked her watch. "Oops, it's almost time." She glanced around at them, her manner suddenly alert and hurried. "Okay, it's time to leave here; we've an appointment to make." She shook her head at Teresa. "No questions, you'll shortly understand everything." She pointed to their vehicle. "Everyone, get your gear from your bus and come with me into the shoeplane. Hurry, hurry, you'll not want to miss this."

Completely bemused as to what was going on, but infected by Dr. Orgasm's sudden urgency, they rushed off to offload the bus.

CHAPTER 61

Inside, the giant magic shoe looked just like any other aircraft: plastic and metal cabins, connecting stairwells and walkways.

"Come with me," Dr. Orgasm told Courtney after shutting the cockpit door. "The rest of you wait here." She smiled at Radio when he also stepped forward. "You wait too. Don't worry, she'll be just fine. You'll be able to see her later."

She led Courtney up a metal staircase to the upper deck. There she handed her two pink pills and a glass of water.

"Take these," she said.

"Are these . . . O-Pills?" Courtney asked in a shaky voice.

Dr. Orgasm nodded. "Yes. Don't be afraid; they'll fix you. All your suffering's over now."

Courtney swallowed the pills. Once she'd done so, Dr. Orgasm opened a door, revealing a pink bedroom. She pointed to the large bed, winked. "Alright, in you go, girl. You'll have all the privacy you need."

Courtney entered. Dr. Orgasm shut the door behind her and returned downstairs to join the others.

The remaining six—Teresa and Matt, Heather and Miki, Radio and Highball—were seated in a passenger bubble. Highball was silent and looked close to manic. Her face was white, her eyes swollen from weeping, her lips trembled. The others talked in low voices.

The talk silenced once Dr. Orgasm descended into their midst.

She handed Highball a green pill and a cup of water. "This will calm you. Or I can sedate you if you like."

Highball shook her head. "No, no sedatives please; I'm scared to sleep at the moment. I'm certain to have nightmares about Jeff."

Dr. Orgasm nodded. "I understand." A lone tear swelled in her left eye, ran down her cheek. "Believe me, honey, I really do. One of the unfortunate men that that idiot Brentwood fed his equine pills to was my son Paul. He's the one we renamed Sultan when he became a horse."

***

After Highball had taken the medicine, Dr. Orgasm led the six of them forward into her cockpit. She took the pilot's seat, gestured to the co-pilot's chair. Heather (who sort-of understood an aircraft's controls) sat in it. The others stood behind them.

The shoeplane rose silently, without the hum of engines. It flew with little sense of motion.

"Where are we going?" Radio asked as they headed left off the road and over the forest. For a brief moment, the doctor's other, crashed, shoeplane was visible far to their right as a little pink hill beside the endless black line of road, then they'd swept beyond seeing it.

"Rabbitfield Air Base," Dr. Orgasm replied. "Almost the entire communist army are gathered out there right now. Florence Rigid has dispatched her entire military might to capture me."

"Ah," Radio mused to himself. "So that's the troop buildup those old Misogyny guys were talking about."

Teresa, however, gasped. "What the flying fuck? And you're going to fly yourself and us into their trap?"

Dr. Orgasm laughed. "Of course not. I'll stop a mile away so we can watch from a safe distance."

"Watch what?" Matt asked.

"The end of the communist terror," came the bright reply.

"Ah, I think I understand now," Radio said. "It adds up. He touched the brunette doctor gently on her shoulder. "You never were at Rabbitfield, were you? It's been a ruse all this while?"

She laughed louder. "Not exactly. At first *I was* there. I had to set things up right. But once that was done, I got out fast. I left a digital analogue of myself—a computer model—in the airbase to relay my broadcasts. I'd transmit in coded form from here in the shoeplane—if the commies ever intercepted the signal, it'd sound like a talk show— then the program at the airbase would decode it and broadcast it out across Innuendo. Then a week ago, I let them shoot down my regular shoeplane, so they'd think I was hiding in the area. I'd already parked this one outside Rabbitfield so I could escape again."

"What's all this about?" Teresa asked.

"Some kind of trap," Radio replied her. He looked at the doctor. "It's a trap; am I right?"

She swiveled in the pilot's seat to nod at him. The shoeplane had stopped flying now. It hovered low over a group of trees with giant gray wings for leaves.

"You're right. It is a trap. Florence and her communists think they've trapped *me* underground, while really, they've walked straight into my ambush."

Six pairs of eyes focused on her, she continued: "I've been working on this for six months, ever since they tried to kill me in Metaphor. It struck me as the perfect way to take out Florence and her mutant goons once and for all, or, if not completely destroy them, to weaken them so much that the combined allied forces of Innuendo's other cities could easily crush them in a joint military offensive." She snapped her fingers as if at a sudden thought. "Hold on a moment, let me magnify the view."

She turned to a screen, made some adjustments, and the entire windshield altered to a digital monitor.

Now they could see a mass of troops everywhere: a seemingly endless yellow/black Bee tapestry overhead dotted with the metal of communist aircraft; and ranged below those, the oblong glints of troop transports and tanks, and several battle-modded greenhouses. Concealed somewhere in the midst of the attackers sat the airbase's walls and buildings. The monitor was silent, but even so, each of them could hear in their minds the Bees' strident humming. Left-wing insects, right-wing insects, all out to dissolve and petrify one exceptional woman.

"Wow," Teresa gasped. "*That does* look like the entire communist army. Maybe even with Florence Rigid in attendance."

Dr. Orgasm swiveled to face them again. "I wouldn't be surprised if Florence is there right now with her army. She's so obsessed with murdering me . . . Oh, screw the frigid bitch, where was I?"

"What's the nature of the ambush?" Radio prompted. "A bomb? A mini-nuke"

She shook her head. "Yes and no. I do have several bombs set up around Rabbitfield, but they're just to take out a few of the troops and vehicles, enough so Florence thinks my trap didn't work. And also to camouflage what I've actually done."

"Which is?" Highball asked in a doped voice.

"Infecting them all with a biological agent. A modified plague virus; one that's only deadly to the commies and their oversized bug pets.

It'll release into the air at the same moment as the bombs go off. They'll all be dead in a week max—rapist bastards and Bees alike—before they've even worked out what's killing them."

"Wow!" Teresa gasped.

Miki and Heather gaped at the doctor in awe. "That's fantastic," Miki said. "Will it really work?"

"Yes it will," Dr. Orgasm replied with a hint of anger that the other woman dared doubt her genius. She spun back to face the cockpit instrument panel, then pulled a small red cellphone from her pocket. She pressed four keys in sequence, then tapped 'ENTER/SEND.'

"And there she blows," she said enthusiastically, as onscreen, fire erupted from the ground to grasp the sky in incandescent orange fingers. "Good riddance to bad-pussy rubbish. The female orgasm is free again, hopefully forever this time."

***

They watched the flames rage a mile off, the airborne magic carpet of Bees burning fiercely. Aircraft exploded down out of the sky, ground transports were blown skyward. All was fire and brimstone, like judgment day had arrived early for the communist army.

Gazing thoughtfully at the burning army, Radio said, "Doc, I thought you said you planned to take out just *a few* of Florence's troops? You're having way more success than that."

Dr. Orgasm nodded. "I think my bombs are setting off some abandoned air force stockpiles. Better for us."

Occasionally building walls appeared amidst the inferno, but this was for only the briefest of intervals, orange fire and black clouds of smoke almost instantly filling in those viewing ports in the burning air. (And, all watching knew this fire was merely symbolic, that communism's real doom—the unstoppable undetectable deadly virus—was already mingling with the smoke, infecting all the enemy.)

"Hopefully Florence goes down with her army today," Dr. Orgasm said. "Though it doesn't really matter—a week from now, she'll have no forces left anyway. We'll mop her up like spilt coffee. We'll have to watch the borders to prevent her fleeing Innuendo if we want to put her on trial though. But knowing Florence, she'll likely try to pull a Hitler martyr number—some bullet-to-the-brain bullshit."

"Why does it take a week?" Matt asked.

"Just to play it safe. It's a slow-acting virus so the communists don't catch on that they're infected till it's way to late to do anything about it. The bug lays dormant in their bodies for six days, then multiplies rapidly on the seventh—they'll be dropping like turkeys in a shoot."

"I get it," Radio said. "The long incubation is also so the infection can be spread to all the commies left at home, right?"

"Yes, it's spread by touch, sex, breathing . . ." She grinned. "So long as you're either Bee or commie—you're fucked. And this one final time, the come-filled bitches and bastards don't get to come. Or come back. And that is definitely a good thing for the human race." She punched the air with a fist and yelled, the tendons in her neck standing out stiffly: "FEMALE ORGASM FOREVER!!!"

"FEMALE ORGASM FOREVER!!!" her six companions thundered back, also punching the air.

"Yeah," Dr. Orgasm said, more calmly now. "A woman's got a right to come and come REAL good."

They regarded the onscreen devastation: The dreaded Bees like glowing airborne coals. Burning yellow bodies like living matchsticks. Fiery red flames that seemed blood dripping from the combined communist aorta. It was an utterly great feeling watching the evil empire crumble.

"I wonder how Courtney's doing now," Teresa mused after a while, fingers stroking her hoop earrings.

Dr. Orgasm turned and winked at Radio. "I think she's ripe for you to go check on now. It's the third door on the left upstairs. Give her one for me too."

Looking sheepishly unlike himself, Radio hurried off.

CHAPTER 62

Courtney Taylor lay in bed, trapped by pleasure, a victim of the delicious sensory overload she'd almost forgotten existed.

It had begun simply, deceptive as a sucker punch:

After swallowing the O-pills and entering the pink bedroom, she'd stripped naked and lain in bed. Flat on her back, the white ceiling panels segmenting her vision, she'd at first felt nothing. She didn't dare touch herself: despite Dr. Orgasm's assurance that all was well now, she was still terrified of disappointment.

But like a mugger, erotic feeling stealthily crept up on her. And possessed her. Courtney felt her body—her sex—growing warmer and warmer, wetter and yet wetter, till finally her vagina was a boiling cauldron of sensation from which the rest of her—gaseous torso and ethereal arms and legs and head—billowed as steam.

This is the most aroused I've ever been in my life! she managed to think. *I'm so horny I could be a bull!*

The sensation, a delicious vaginal swirling that sucked the rest of her in like a whirlpool, continued. Her breasts seemed to expand on her chest; her nipples were burning flares at their tips like Fourth-of-July fireworks.

Still, she'd not touched her sex. She just lay there with her arms either side of her, her palms flat on the smooth bedspread while her body slow-burnt in her excruciating vaginal flame.

She writhed with her fear of herself, terrified of her own desires, scared that despite what her swollen clitoris and leaking vagina promised, she'd once more be disappointed. Her legs bent and stretched, her toes drawing lines in the sheets.

Then, just when it felt like her brain would burst if she delayed any more, she dipped her fingers into herself.

She came instantly. That one touch was all it took.

BOOM!!!

Courtney had had fantastic orgasms before, but she'd never felt anything like this. It felt . . . it felt like her limbs—her arms and legs, her entire body—were endlessly melting and flowing to her core, pumping into her crotch and being squirted out into the universe.

"Oh, my God! Oh, my God!" She was aware of herself groaning loudly, but not of what she was saying. The sensation of her orgasm was all-conquering. If she'd previously felt melted to liquid, now her vaginal heat vaporized her completely; she became gas seeking to escape her skin as her fingers, now seeming to possess minds of their own, penetrated and caressed her.

It felt like every orgasm she'd missed since her captivity in Vaginismus was ganging up on her at once, all intent on having their share of her flesh. Like she was a million explosive vaginas all being sexed at once. Like . . . like . . .

The first orgasm became the second, then the third, then the twentieth.

And she just lay there, touching herself, calling the pleasure out from her core, her fingers playing her like a guitar, filling the air with sweet sexual music.

Courtney writhed and groaned and moaned. Eyes rolled up in her head, seeing nothing because she'd become the female everything.

Every part of her body felt orgasmic. She stroked her thighs, she came; touched her breasts, she came; once she merely parted her legs too wide and the stretching of her labia wrenched a juddering climax from her.

Tears of joy streamed down her cheeks. There was no doubt in her mind now: *Oh, holy shit! I'm cured! I'm fucking cured!*

Was it a permanent cure? It didn't matter: the O-pill existed, and it worked magic! She imagined hundreds of millions of women, all empowered to have orgasm on demand; a billion women no longer the slaves of prejudice or genital mutilation or their own poor sexual self-image or . . .

The door opened.

She gasped out of her reverie. Radio stood in the entrance staring at her in surprise. She couldn't blame him: her body still jerked about like she was spastic. The pleasure kept overloading her; once she'd climaxed, it drained off, then filled her up again like she was a bottle. Her orgasms exploded out of her lungs in gusts of breath, streamed from her fingers and toes, tingled her ears; felt like they were cooking her brain . . . almost popped her eyes . . . hot tears flooded, drenched her boiling cheeks.

Radio saw she was crying and rushed over to the bed. "Courtney, are you okay, baby?"

She managed a grin through her tears, then weakly stretched her arms out to him. "Fucking-A I am, darling," she gasped in ecstasy. "It works, it works! I feel utterly rapturous! Hurry up—get your clothes off and make love to me! Fuck me! Hurry up! Hurry up!"

She watched as he stripped off, was delighted to see that his penis was hard with desire for her. Stiff and throbbing. The fat purple head, the balls swinging.

Her vagina twitched with wet anticipation as he climbed onto the bed, clear pre-come already dripping from his cock's head-slit.

He knelt over her; she spread her legs wide to admit him to her inner sanctum.

He poised his crotch over hers, groaned, "I love you, baby," and thrust his meat missile deep into her slippery sexual silo.

The moment his penis entered her vagina, another set of explosions wracked her body. These new orgasms were of a different sort from when she'd pleasured herself—now she was freed from involvement in her own satisfaction: the O-pill had done half the work, Radio's cock could do the rest.

She lay limp on the bed as these fresh climaxes consumed her—as her raging flesh both tortured and exalted her—eyes tightly shut, her rapidly rising and falling breasts her only sign of life. Her body moved with her lover's, but she was somewhere outside of them both. As his manhood tilled her sex, sliding sweetly in and out, Courtney felt she was splitting off from herself.

Fresh tears of joy squirted from her shut eyelids. As the O-pill and her lover's penis flooded her with yet more orgasms, Courtney Taylor imagined she was going mad from sheer pleasure.

"Oh, God bless you, Dr. Orgasm!" she groaned softly. "God bless you!"

The End.

ABOUT THE AUTHOR

Wol-vriey is Nigerian, and quite tall.

He currently resides in a state of uneasy stalemate with his threatening-to-thin-beyond-redemption hair, and believes there actually are things that go bump in the night.

Wol-vriey recycles the ridiculous into reasonable reality for the reader.

His WEIRRRD philosophy?

WEIRRRD = Warp/Write Everything into Realistic Ridiculous Readable Distorted Dream Dimension Descriptions.

Wol-vriey blogs at:

http://oddityfarm.wordpress.com

WOL-VRIEY
BIZARRO AND TRANSGRESSIVE FICTION

BOSTON POSH (BUD MALONE #1)

In 2028 AD, the USA is a nation ravaged by hungry dragons and dinosaurs. In Boston, Massachusetts, private eye Bud Malone is hired to rescue a kidnapped heiress. But nothing is as it seems.

Malone works to unravel a tangled web involving Boston Chinatown, a 200-year-old woman with a 9-year-old body, white robots, a human-liver-eating psychopath, a golem, a porcelain dragon, and a snake goddess with a crush on him. There's also a woman obsessed with chicken sex. Then Malone meets Posh Lane, a gorgeous call girl who's desperate to quit her pimp.

Romantic sparks ignite between Posh and Malone, but Posh's past suddenly catches up with her in a BIG way. To save Posh, Malone agrees to run a quest for Earth's new rulers, the Forks. But, Malone has no idea that agreeing to the Fork's odd request will send him on the weirdest trip he's ever been on in his life.

BOSTON CORPSE (BUD MALONE #2)

MAGIC CAN BE MURDER! - Drag queen Lucy Tang is back in Boston, and is hell-bent on settling her vindetta against casino owner Sookie Ling. And suddenly, Bud Malone, PI, has the case of his life to resolve.

When Boston's robot police force are baffled by a mind transfer case, they come to Malone for help. The one person who can likely help Malone out here is the witch Soledad Bathory. But Soledad seems to know a lot more than she's telling him. It's a case not made easier when Malone meets Soledad's beautiful cousin, Josephine 'Slave' Bailey. Slave has her own plans for Malone, most of which involve teaching him BDSM and making him her new Master.

Oh, and Rick Rogers owes Sookie Ling a whole lot of money, a gambling debt that's going to be literally Hell to pay!

BOSTON CORPSE - Not your average detective novel!

Burning Bulb
PUBLISHING

WOL-VRIEY
BIZARRO AND TRANSGRESSIVE FICTION

VAGINA MUNDI

Rachel Risk is a professional thief with super-strong hair that can stretch like tentacles to manipulate objects. Ashley Status has both a digitally augmented brain, and 'muscle-purses' in her arms and legs in which she stores inflatable objects—cars, guns, rocket launchers, etc.

When Raye is framed as the fall girl in a jewel robbery, the pair flee Chicago's vengeful robot gangsters and take refuge in the Hotel Bizarre, where the gorgeous 'vagina singer,' Femina, is performing for a week.

But the Hotel Bizarre is even stranger than its name suggests, and very soon Raye and Ash are involved in an deadly adventure, a struggle for survival the likes of which they'd never imagined possible—with loads of deviant sex, drugs, music, and violence at every turn. And just what is the old woman in the skin desert really doing with all those cats glued to her walls?

VAGINA MUNDI—a Bizarro Hymn in praise of WOMAN!

VEGAN VAMPIRE VAGINAS

The biggest bank heist in US history. And Tom Palmer can't remember pulling it off. And no, this isn't your standard case of amnesia. After a one-night-stand gone horribly wrong, Boston salesman Tom Palmer wakes up with a vagina implanted in his left hand. Then his day gets worse.

Tom is transported across space-time to a nightmare version of Boston, one where the Bizarro virus has transformed half the population into cannibals. Worst of all, Tom discovers that in this new Boston, he's the infamous gangster Pussypalm, wanted for robbing the Federal Reserve Bank of Boston a year ago. He also learns that the vagina in his hand is prophetic, i.e. it talks . . . after sex.

With 130 people left dead during his bank heist and six billion dollars missing, Tom knows he's living on borrowed time. It is in his best interests not to remember anything. Because once he does . . .

Burning Bulb
PUBLISHING

WOL-VRIEY
BIZARRO AND TRANSGRESSIVE FICTION

VEGAN ZOMBIE APOCALYPSE

In the post-apocalypse worlderness, zombies rule the earth. They're allergic to meat, and brains literally make them explode. Zombies now eat blood potatoes, parasitic tubers grown in the flesh of humancows corralled in maximum security farms. Two fugitives meet in the ancient ruins of Texas. The first is Soil 15-f, a womancow who's escaped her farm a week before she's due to be killed and her blood potato crop harvested. The second fugitive is Able Kane, former head necros food technician, now sentenced to death for heresy. But Soil is no ordinary humancow.

Unknown to herself, she's the vegan zombie agricultural revolution, and the zombies desperately want her back. And the necros equally desperately want Able Kane dead. He's fled with a forbidden discovery which will reshape the world for the worse if used. And Able is just hardheaded/misguided enough to use it.

MELANIE NEMESIS CATCHPOLE

In Springfield, Massachusetts, Melanie Catchpole is hired to fetch back a magic teddy bear worth millions of dollars from a warehouse across town. Problem is, the warehouse is down in Springfield's O-Zone-that totally weird sector of the city where Bizarro fell to Earth. The 'O' is a fairytale land, a place where dreams and nightmares literally live and breathe.

Worse still, the gingers—mutant cannibals—prowl the O. The gingers have already eaten everyone else Melanie's employers sent to get back the magic teddy bear.

Accompanied by the handsome but ruthless Doug Fisher (who she finds sexy but doesn't dare entrust her heart to), Melanie enters the O-Zone. Melanie and Doug are instantly caught up in an adventure they'd never have believed credible even if written as fiction . . . and Melanie's used to experiencing the very weird as the norm.

And now, additionally, there's a mystery to unravel: What does the dark, freezing-cold being called The Fixer want with Mary, the barkeep's daughter?

Burning Bulb
PUBLISHING

WOL-VRIEY
BIZARRO AND TRANSGRESSIVE FICTION

BIG TROUBLE IN LITTLE ASS

From Bizarro master storyteller Wol-vriey comes a truly weird western tale that will leave you awe-struck and on the edge of your seat...

In the town named Little Ass, tight-assed prostitute Rosa overhears a gunslinger's plans to assassinate rancher Edison Bennett. Once the badass Bennett learns of the plot, he ensures there'll be hell to pay for any attempt on his life!

Yes, it's going to take all of gunslinger Jude's shooting prowess, his eclectic collection of strange firearms, a trusty horse that requires an owners' manual, and the help of the lovely and invigorating Nell (who's EXTREMELY odd when the going gets weird), to survive the Bizarro hell that Edison Bennett unleashes in order to hold onto the land that he'd stolen from Madam Zizi.

BIZARRO 101 (A BASIC PRIMER)

Welcome to the strange place:

A collection of 37 flash fiction stories designed to introduce one to the Bizarro/New Weird Genre.

Weird, dreamy, nightmarish, absurd, sad, surreal, humorous . . . this collection of tales is all this and more.

***

"This primer is the very essence of any and all styles and types of Bizarro writing. Wol-vriey collects, distills, and bottles up these 37 tiny stories for your sensory enjoyment. This is an absolute must-read for anyone new to the genre, because it demonstrates the scope of what Bizarro is, and what it can be."
— Teresa Pollack, Bizarro commentator and blogger

Burning Bulb
PUBLISHING

OTHER GREAT TITLES FROM

Burning Bulb

PUBLISHING

WWW.BURNINGBULBPUBLISHING.COM

BELLY TIMBER

From the writers of Darkened Hills, Detour to Armageddon and Night of the Living Dead comes a novel unlike any other...

In the 1800's, ordinary people learned the secret of the Kala and undertook extraordinary measures to rid the earth of this evil. This is their story.

For John McCormick, life on the Indiana frontier held nothing but promise. His settlement along the White River would soon become the crossroads of America. Friends and family from back in Ohio and other points east were all making plans to see what all the fuss was about in the newly-formed city of Indianapolis. Yes, things were good. John had his general store and his friend George Pogue had his blacksmith business. Claims were being staked and relations with the native Indians were amicable. The town was growing and nothing could be better... or so he thought.

In Ohio, an evil was brewing. The Lecky Family, a group of ruthless Mongolian nomads, had made their way to America and were practicing their cannibalistic religion of Kala with reckless abandon. No one was safe, not even John McCormick's family.

Burning Bulb
PUBLISHING

EVERYTHING HERE IS A NIGHTMARE
Collected Works Vol 1.

"Pyles makes it look easy. His characters come instantly alive with the cocksure verve and swagger of rock stars."
> *- Daniel Knauf, creator of HBO's "Carnivale,"*
> *Executive Producer/Writer, ABC's "The Blacklist."*

The critically acclaimed author of Demons, Dolls and Milkshakes returns with fifteen tales of horror and suspense with Everything Here is a Nightmare.

From zombies in the old west, to a young boy tempted by the Devil. From vampires with romantic longing, to an abandoned lighthouse haunted by vengeful spirits. From a serial killer getting unholy justice, to a haunted English race car, Nelson W Pyles invites you to explore a landscape of fear, suspense and horror.

Take his hand and hold on tight. Remember that whatever you find here, whatever you see, no matter what you might think it could be... know this: Everything Here is a Nightmare.

Burning Bulb
PUBLISHING

ANTHOLOGIES
BIZARRO AND TRANSGRESSIVE FICTION

THE BIG BOOK OF BIZARRO SPECIAL KINDLE EDITIONS

OTHER AWESOME COLLECTIONS

 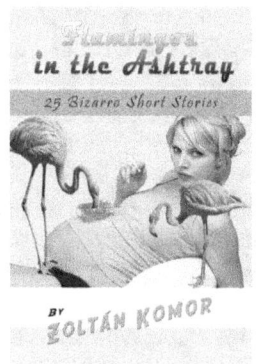 

Burning Bulb
PUBLISHING

ANTHOLOGIES
BIZARRO AND TRANSGRESSIVE FICTION

THE BIG BOOK OF BIZARRO

The Big Book of Bizarro brings together the peculiar prose of an international cast of the most grotesquely-gonzo, genre-grinding modern writers who ever put pen to paper (or mouse to pad), including:

NIGHT OF THE LIVING DEAD horror writers John Russo & George Kosana; HUSTLER MAGAZINE erotica contributors Eva Hore, Andrée Lachapelle, & J. Troy Seate and established Bizarro genre authors D. Harlan Wilson, William Pauley III, Wol-vriey, Laird Long, Richard Godwin and so many more!

From Alien abductions to Zombie sex, The Big Book of Bizarro contains OVER FIFTY STORIES of the most outrélandish transgressive fiction that you'll ever lay your capricious and curious hands upon!

WESTWARD HOES

Nine outlaw writers rode into town from obscurity to pen nine tantalizing tales of horror and fantasy, and leaving once they branded their own personal marks on the weird western genre and became living legends of the American Frontier experience.

Like drunken Indian scouts, the writers fervidly tracked down and captured the Western genre, tore off its fashionable veneer and ravished its exposed essence.

So belly up to the bar with your favorite soiled dove and enjoy perusing these thrilling tales of Old West debauchery, danger and desire; compiled by the publisher of The Big Book of Bizarro and featuring the bizarro novella *Big Trouble in Little Ass* by Wol-vriey.

Burning Bulb
PUBLISHING

GARY LEE VINCENT'S
DARKENED
THE WEST VIRGINIA VAMPIRE SERIES

DARKENED HILLS

When evil descends on a small West Virginia town, who will survive?

Jonathan did not start out his life to become a rambler, it justworked out that way. William was a troubled youth with something to hide. Both were from Melas, a small town tucked away in the West Virginia hills... a town where disappearances are happening more and more frequently.

After the suicide of a wanted serial killer, the townsfolk thought the nightmare was over. But when a centuries-old vampire is discovered they find out the hard way it's just getting started. Dark secrets can only stay hidden for so long and when the devil comes to collect, there will be hell to pay. Can Jonathan and William find a way to stop the vampire before it's too late? Find out in *Darkened Hills!*

DARKENED HOLLOWS

In the heart-stopping sequel to the award-winning *Darkened Hills*, Jonathan and William must return to West Virginia to face possible criminal charges stemming from their last visit to the damned town of Melas, where both had narrowly escaped the clutches of a vampire seethe.

And as livestock start mysteriously getting murdered with all of their blood drained, worried farmers are searching for answers - leaving the local Sheriff and his deputy racing against time to learn the cause before a more violent crime is committed.

Burning Bulb
PUBLISHING

WWW. DARKENEDHILLS.COM

GARY LEE VINCENT'S
DARKENED
THE WEST VIRGINIA VAMPIRE SERIES

DARKENED WATERS

When the world goes to hell, the chosen must arise!

As Talman Cane orchestrates a flood of epic proportions in this third installment of the *Darkened* series the towns of Melas and Tarklin are caught completely off guard by the deluge. Hell-bent on finishing what they started, the evil brothers return to the lunatic asylum to take care of the witnesses and add to the ever-growing army of the undead.

Aided by Lucifer himself and the insane vampire demon Legion, the stage is set to channel all of the forces of hell to come forth. In an all-out race to survive, Jonathan, William, and Amanda soon discover they are up against impossible odds as Lucifer opens the Gateway to Hell, ushering in the zombie apocalypse and the End Times.

Find out who will survive this cosmic battle of the ages in *Darkened Waters*!

DARKENED SOULS

Melas and the Madison House are about to be rebuilt.
True evil is about to be reborne!

Young ex-priest and vampire-killer William is drawn back to the West Virginian town that almost killed him, where his vampire arch-enemy Victor Rothenstein still stalks the earth.

The town of Melas lies destroyed after the battle of the End of Days. But why is wealthy Jackie Nixon so eager to rebuild it using the bone dust of murdered souls?

Terrible evil has visited before, but the Gateway to Hell is about to be reopened in a horrific climax. And this time – it's personal.

WWW.DARKENEDHILLS.COM

Burning Bulb
PUBLISHING

DAVID J. FAIRHEAD

"David Fairhead writes compelling stories that offer very human characters and very inhuman monsters. There is no subtlety in Fairhead's imagination - he is simply dying to scare the hell out of you." - Nelson W Pyles author of DEMONS, DOLLS AND MILKSHAKES

THE FALL

Hopelessness... How do you protect your loved ones when Hell itself opens its insidious mouth?

Horror... Nightmarish Creatures invade your world and there is nowhere to hide.

Blood... How long can you hold out before they come for you?

Pain... Where do you run to avoid being eaten alive by monsters with a voracious appetite for your flesh?

Screams... While you selfishly run for your own life.

Questions... Who is to blame? Where did they come from? How many people survived...and how does the human race find the means to fight back?

THE FALL OF TOMORROW is man's last tale of desperation told by those that are striving to salvage some hope against a ravenous bastion of evil beasts bent on ruling our world.

DWELLING IN THE DARK

From David J. Fairhead, author of the FALL OF TOMORROW, comes DWELLING IN THE DARK- A soulful anthology of creeping terror to keep you up in the small hours with horror set in the past, present and future. Overlapping bits of puzzle fitting each other, before and after The Fall of Tomorrow.

A place where three children facing a monstrous foe can only pray that their bloody summer would just come to an end. Go back to the 1960's- THE COMMUNE where overindulging hippies use a mage's diary to control the end of the world, only to see first-hand that their drug induced visions have horrific ramifications. Where a young boy's visit to a haunted house becomes a lesson in RESIDUAL morality. The story, DEEPER- plunges two brothers into a sinkhole only to find they were being hunted by an insidious creature from its depths. Visit the old west as hero Dekker Collins battles evil gunslingers in DEMONEYE.

And so much more...!

Burning Bulb
PUBLISHING

WWW.*FAIRLY DARK PRODUCTIONS*.COM

ZAKARY MCGAHA
BIZARRO AND TRANSGRESSIVE FICTION

SEA OF MEDIUM-TO-HIGH PITCHED NOISES

The zombie apocalypse is changing; the world is coming to an odd demise; and a serial killer tries to change his ways and redeem himself before it all goes away. Now, Crabby has entered the world he left behind; the world of the undead. And things are changing. Everything will come to an end. In this new wave of the apocalypse, everything changes every five minutes. And death would be an absolute luxury. Psychological torment meets physical bloodletting in Sea of Medium-to-High Pitched Noises.

PARK MASTERS

Bad breakups, Bigfoot costumes, ghost bears, and more. Park Masters is a wacky, intelligent, quirky comedy about the power relationships have on people, good or bad. Also, it's just plain fun!

Burning Bulb
PUBLISHING

WEST VIRGINIA-THEMED HUMORROROTICA
BY RICH BOTTLES JR.

HELLHOLE WEST VIRGINIA

From the heights of Mothman's perch high atop the Silver Bridge in Point Pleasant to the depths of Hellhole Cavern in Pendleton County, evil lurks within the shadows as the sun sets upon the haunted hills and hollows of West Virginia.

Bizarro author Rich Bottles Jr. blows the coffin lid off horror genre clichés with this tour de force cast of Eco-friendly vampires, beach-yearning zombies and sex-starved she-devils.

LUMBERJACKED

If you are easily offended or do not possess a truly depraved sense of humor, this story may not be the light summer reading fare you desire. As for the four feisty female freshmen stranded on top of West Virginia's third highest mountain, they have no choice but to experience the sick, twisted debauchery and perverted mayhem described deep inside the tight unbroken bindings of this horrific missive.

Lumberjacked takes the reader to a nightmarish world where character development and aesthetic integrity are prematurely cut short by the swinging axes of maniacal lumberjacks, who are hell bent on death and destruction in the remote forests of Appalachia. And at the climax, when paranoia crosses over to the paranormal, Lumberjacked makes Deliverance look like a family raft trip down the Lower Gauley.

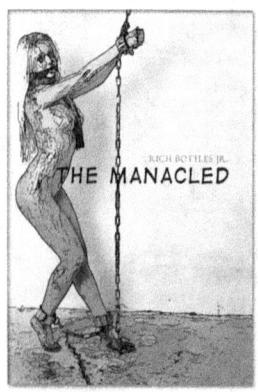

THE MANACLED

What happens when twin brothers lease out the former West Virginia State Penitentiary with the false purpose of filming a documentary on supernatural phenomena, but their true intention is to make a pornographic movie?

Chaos ensues as the disturbed spirits of murdered convicts, along with the reanimated dead from the neighboring Indian Burial Mound, take their vengeance on the unwary and undressed trespassers.

Zombies, ghosts, mobsters and porn collide in this bizarro tale from horror author Rich Bottles Jr.

Burning Bulb
PUBLISHING

RISE OF THE DEAD - a collection of seventeen tales of unspeakable zombie terror. Featuring a foreword and short story by John A. Russo!

www.TheJohnRusso.com

THE BOOBY HATCH

With NIGHT OF THE LIVING DEAD, John Russo helped blaze a path in the horror genre that has never been equalled. In this hillarious erotic novel, he blazes a path through the wild, zany Sex Revolution of the 1970s.

Sweet, innocent Cherry Jankowski works for Joyful Novelties, where she tests sex toys ranging from the ridiculous to the sublime. But she can't find love or peace of mind and her efforts are hampered by a Peeping Tom, an exhibitionist, a cross-dressing boyfriend, a quack psychiatrist, and even her own product-testing partner, Marcello Fettucini, who can't get it up anymore and is scared of losing his job!

www.TheJohnRusso.com

Burning Bulb
PUBLISHING

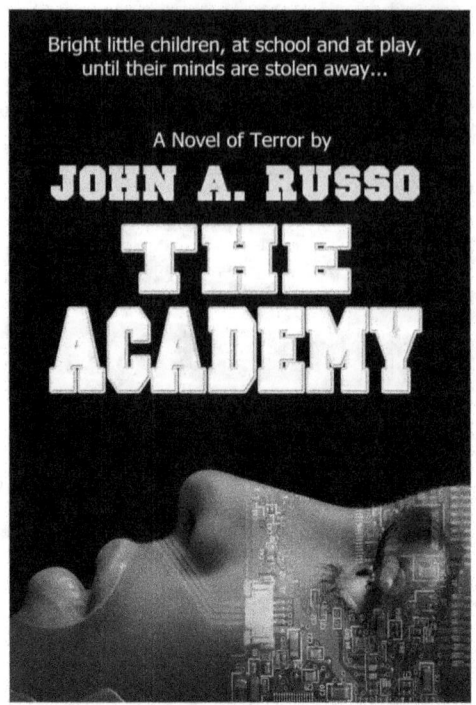

Bright little children, at school and at play,
until their minds are stolen away...

A Novel of Terror by

JOHN A. RUSSO

THE ACADEMY

THE ACADEMY

The Academy. It's every parent's dream, turning their little
darlings into geniuses, superachievers, perfect little
children.

And if there's a problem, the Academy fixes that too. It's a
simple operation. Just a little device. Then a teeny pink scar
on a tender little skull . . .

One boy knows the secret. Now he wants his mind back.
But it's much, much too late. Too late for anything but the
ugly feelings. The bad feelings. The messy sexy feelings. The
knife-cold hatred, the murderous rage, for total, screaming,
blood-drenching revenge . . .

www.TheJohnRusso.com

Burning Bulb
PUBLISHING

THE AWAKENING

For two hundred years, he has rested. Now he rises. Now he will be satisfied. Nothing can stop him. No one can resist him.

Benjamin Latham is young and handsome, his eighteenth-century mind wakened to a bizarre twentieth-century world. And there is the need deep within . . . an animal need, frightening, murderous, unholy . . . a vital need that must be fed.

And with his need comes a power over men and women to do his bidding, to quiet his dark craving . . .

Until the murders begin. And the inquiries. All suggesting the same hideous truth.

Now Benjamin must find a sanctuary: a lover, a partner, a friend. Someone who can share his darkness. Someone he can lead to . . . The Awakening.

www.TheJohnRusso.com

Burning Bulb
PUBLISHING

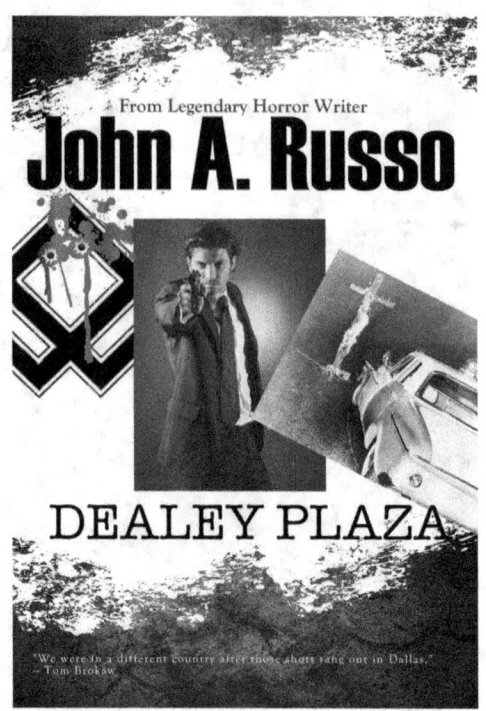

DEALEY PLAZA

From legendary horror and suspense writer JOHN RUSSO comes a harrowing tale where no one is safe!

Dealey Plaza is one of the most notorious places in America, and when youthful conspiracy buffs go there in 1964 to stage their own reenactment of the Kennedy Assassination, four of them are brutally murdered ~ the first victims of a hate-filled legacy that continues for four more decades.

The survivors of that long-ago Dallas trip, each of them now icons of the American way of life, are about to be honored ~ or killed.

Who will live and who will die? Will it be country-western star Lori McCoy? Her loving husband? Her scheming ex-husband? Or the case-hardened FBI agent and longtime friend who risks his life trying to protect them?

www.DealeyPlazaBook.com

Burning Bulb
PUBLISHING

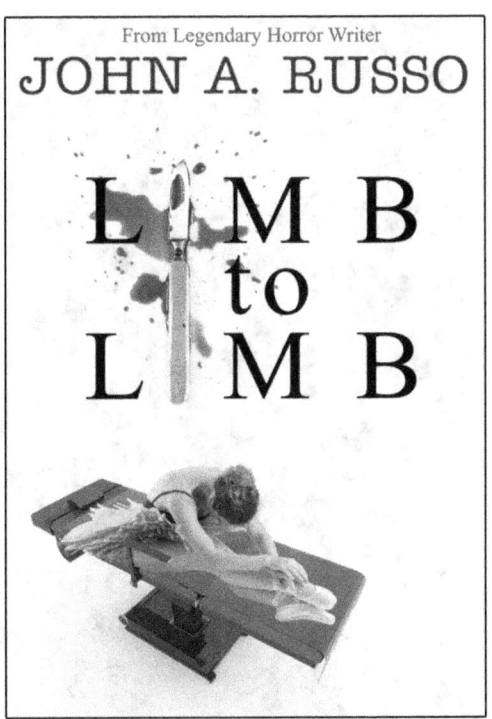

From Legendary Horror Writer
JOHN A. RUSSO
LIMB to LIMB

LIMB TO LIMB

SUCH A PRETTY GIRL . . .
Tiffany Blake was a beautiful long-limbed dancer with a glorious future and
the backing of a rich benefactor. Then a monstrous accident severed her leg
at the hip.

SUCH A COLD, CRUEL KNIFE . . .
And now her fellow dancers are disappearing without a trace. One by one
they fall victim to a dark and deadly pattern of evil – caught by the bloody,
brutal logic that would have them pay with their lovely bodies for the cruel
fate of another . . .victims of the sadistic madman whose flashing knife will
make them writhe a gruesome new dance.

www.TheJohnRusso.com

Burning Bulb
PUBLISHING

"A sense of infectious fun, straight from the author's pen."
– Nightmare Library

From Legendary Horror Writer
JOHN A. RUSSO

LIVING THINGS

"Russo carries his talent for the horrific neatly over into the novel form."
– West Coast Review of Books

LIVING THINGS

Beneath the shimmering Miami sun sprawls one of the Mafia's biggest empires, a glittering world of lavish beachfront mansions, neon-painted nightclubs, beautiful women, expensive cars—and absolute control over the state's billion-dollar drug trade. But, one by one, its ganglords and henchmen are falling prey to a new rival. His powers are fueled by monstrous ancient rituals; his hellish undead legions slaughter mobsters and innocent citizens alike, his unholy lust for power is virtually unstoppable.

Now a burned-out ex-detective and a brilliant anthropologist must enter a gruesome, nightmare world to fight this master of malevolence and illusion. Their time is short, their weapons few, and they face an ultimate, terrifying choice - annihilation or the loss of their souls to the eternal torment of those who never die. . .

www.TheJohnRusso.com

Burning Bulb
PUBLISHING

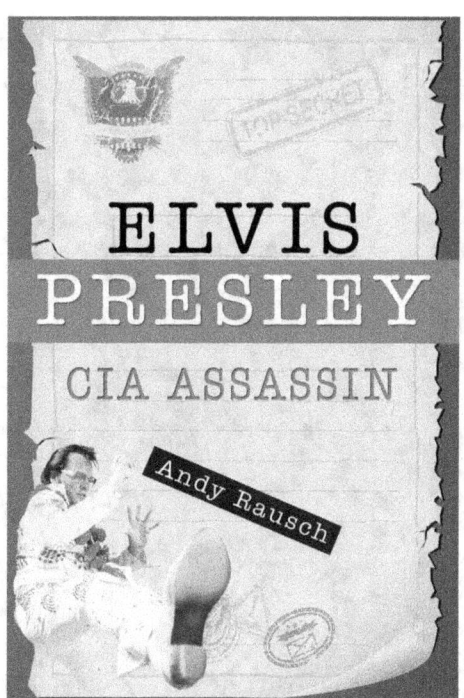

ELVIS PRESLEY, CIA ASSASSIN BY ANDY RAUSCH

"I can guarantee you. Read this book and you'll never look at Elvis the same way again!"
~ Douglas Brode, author of ELVIS CINEMA AND POPULAR CULTURE

SOON TO BE A MAJOR MOTION PICTURE

In 1970, singer Elvis Presley secretly met with President Richard Nixon. This new comedic novel imagines that Presley became a Central Intelligence Agency operative, eventually moving up through the ranks to become a skilled assassin.

Presented in an oral history fashion, the book tells us about Presley's secret transformation by the people who knew him best.

Did he fake his death in 1977? Was Presley involved with the Watergate scandal? The Iran hostage crisis? Communicating with aliens?

Read this book to find out the answers to these and many more questions.

Burning Bulb
PUBLISHING

MAD WORLD BY ANDY RAUSCH

"*Mad World* is dark, twisted, no-holds-barred fun."
—Jason Starr, author of *Bust*, *Slide*, and *The Max*

EVERYONE'S PLAYING AN ANGLE IN THE CITY OF ANGELS

Mad World tells the stories of a black hitman who doubles as a university professor, a Catholic priest who longs to be a gangster, a would-be author from Kansas, a gay phone sex operator who claims he's straight, a group of rich twentysomethings playing a deadly game of life and death, a vicious Mafia boss, and a sleazy Hollywood movie director. As each of their stories intersect, the body count piles up and the action comes nonstop in this tense, white-knuckle thriller by first-time author Andy Rausch.

"A wild ride. If you like it gangster, *Mad World* delivers."
—Daniel Birch, author of *Get Some*

Burning Bulb
PUBLISHING

BLOODLETTING: A TALE OF REVENGE BY ANDY RAUSCH

"Relentless… Addictive… The kind of nightmare you don't want
to wake up from."
—Heywood Gould, screenwriter of *Rolling Thunder*

He was just an average Joe. But when he finds his family held at
gunpoint by merciless thugs, he's told he must murder a Mafia
chieftain if he ever wishes to see his loved ones again.

Against all odds, Joe keeps his end of the bargain, but the criminals
don't. Now at his wits end, Joe is pushed beyond his breaking point
and forced to exact bloody revenge against those who've done him
and his family wrong in this powerful and violent novella by author
Andy Rausch (*Mad World*).

"Andy Rausch has a tight noir style that combines gritty, realistic drama
with a cinematic flair that makes for a powerful, compelling (somewhat
Stephen Kingesque), authentically visual reading experience."
—Stephen Spignesi, author of *Dialogues*

Burning Bulb
PUBLISHING

THE TAILSMAN

From the creators of *The Big Book of Bizarro* and *Westward Hoes* comes a new comic unlike anything you have ever seen!

He's hot on the trail, looking for some *tail...*

Sly Franko was a man of the West, a forger of the wild frontier. Like the Country Western song that would be written years after he died, the words, "Faster horses, younger women, and more money," seemed to be the anthem of this horn dog cowboy.

Franko would ride into town on a blazing saddle, find the closest saloon to wet the whistle, belly up to a good card game, and find him a hot-loving hussy to get his cowpoke on with.

However, Sly might have met his match when a visit to bathroom leads to terror and death. Can Sly and his poker buddies solve the mystery before more of the townsfolk are murdered? Find out in this exciting premier issue of *The Tailsman!*

WWW.BURNINGBULBCOMICS.COM

THE HAGS OF BLACK COUNTY

by Michelle Bowser

Ruled by a committee of Hags, and fueled by toothless rivalries, Black County lurks just far enough out of the way to be completely unnoticed by the rest of civilization. Its inhabitants have been mentally warped for generations and the land itself seems to have the power to drive anyone unlucky enough to visit into ridiculous hillbilly madness. When a construction Company needs to bury a pipeline through its ludicrous hills and valleys, a twisted charm goes to work and every aspect of already bizarre Black County life takes a gory turn for the hysterical. Take a preposterous trip along with its citizens, both native and new, through escapades such as the Hag parade, the grand opening of Madame Skunk's House of Ill Repute, the demolition derby riot and the rabid, zombie clown apocalypse.

THE ABANDONED SOUL

by Daniel Sellers

After spending most of his 20s in a drug and alcohol fueled daze, a young man finally hits rock bottom. Having used up his friends and their good graces, he ends up squatting in an abandoned house. Forcibly sobering he begins to realize that he is not alone in this abandoned house. Left with one last friend and a mountain of regrets, he must decide if this presence is a guilty conscience, or a malicious hunter.

WE WISH YOU A HAPPY KILLDAY

by Jason Heroux

"We Wish You a Happy Killday" is the story of an international b eloved holiday called "Killday" where one day a year everyone over the age of fifteen is permitted to register for a license allowing them to kill one other person. But this year Chad Ovenstock doesn't feel like killing anyone. His friends and family urge him to participate in the festivities, but he can't seem to get into the holiday spirit. On the day before Killday Chad comes in contact with Ambrose, an old friend who suffered a nervous breakdown and is now part of The One Ant Army, a mysterious cult dedicated to making the future disappear. When the holiday finally arrives Chad refuses to participate and tries to survive on his own, surrounded by constant gunfire, countless corpses, and the nagging suspicion that Ambrose may have secretly brainwashed him into becoming a member of The One Ant Army cult.

Burning Bulb
PUBLISHING